A Handful of Destiny

Tony Nash

D1744193

1

Other works by Tony Nash
Murder on Tiptoes
Bled And Breakfast
The John Hunter thrillers:
Carve Up
Single to Infinity
The Most Unkindest Cut
The Iago Factor
Blockbuster
Bloodlines
Beyond Another Curtain
Historical sagas:
A Handful of Destiny
A Handful of Salt
A Handful of Courage
Other books:
The Devil Deals Death
The Makepeace Manifesto
The World's Worst Joke Book
Panic
The Last Laugh
The Sinister Side of the Moon
Hell and High Water
Hardrada's Hoard (with Richard Downing)
And The Harry Page Thrillers:
Tripled Exposure
Unseemly Exposure

Apart from the details concerning the First Fleet this is a work of pure fiction, and any similarity between any character in it and any real person, living or dead, is purely coincidental and unintentional. Where actual places, buildings and locations are named, they are used fictionally.

AUTHOR'S NOTES OF LIBERTIES TAKEN: 1. Although Captain Phillip, later to be Admiral and First Governor of New South Wales, was interviewed by the other officials mentioned at the Admiralty, Earl Sandwich is unlikely to have been present in person, having by that time retired from that body, although he undoubtedly had a hand in the scheme. 2. The English Leicester breed of sheep was not introduced into Australia until 1826. 3. The name 'Australia' is used by characters in this book, but was not in general use until 1820, though it was referred to in general terms two hundred years before. 4. Semaphore was not invented until 1792.

The following excerpt is taken directly from the English Manorial Rolls: page 111 of the Court Book:

"It is presented by the homage of the court that Jonathon Worroth late of Hainford in Norfolk and since of Island of Barbados in Americas, but whom the City of Norwich esquire & copyhold of Manor of above said...come before Thomas Eland the Younger of City of Norwich, deputy steward of the aforesaid Manor lawfully authorise by virture of deputation under hand and seal of the above named guardian, Harwood chief steward of aforesaid Manor & House Courts – To house and hoof of James Nash of Newton St Faiths in the aforesaid county, Norfolk gentleman and of his heirs and afsigies forever and absulutly and without any manner of cowham whatsoever. Now to this court comes aforesaid James Nash in his proper person and humbly prays the favour of the Lord and Lady of this Manor to be admitted honest to all and every the House Menorials and premises to him. (that is to say) To fourteen closes on pieces of low."

PROLOGUE

11th June 1701

The faint pearly glow on the horizon between the two massive, ancient oaks on either side of the distant gates brought a smile to James Nash's face as he thought of the distant ancestor who had planted those trees so that future generations could watch the sun rise between them. The day would begin fine, though the mackerel sky the previous evening forebode of rain and wind before nightfall. As always, James began to whistle cheerfully as he completed his toilet, buttoned his jacket and opened the bedroom door, relishing the thought of breakfast.

His whistling ceased suddenly when he entered the dining room and he swore under his breath; the breakfast table was still set for one.

Rachel Weemes, cook to the family since long before he was born, urged, 'Quickly, Emma, the tray.' She had judged to the second when to fry the eggs as she heard his movements in the bedroom above and then his whistling. He liked his eggs set, but only just, and piping hot.

The serving wench, the youngest member of the staff at fourteen years of age, a cloth over her fingers to avoid burning them, removed the plate of ham and eggs from the side of the stove where Rachel had placed it, slid it onto a tray and tripped quickly towards the dining room door from the kitchen, the tray carefully balanced in one hand as she thrust open the door with the other.

Rachel smiled, remembering her own early days as a young maid in that household.

Their master's regularity was one of the many things that his servants appreciated about James. His every action was predictable, unlike those of his twin brother, John, younger by ten minutes and poles apart in his looks, habits and behaviour.

James, broad shouldered, muscular and almost six feet in height, with sandy coloured, unruly hair and friendly hazel eyes in an attractive, angular face, was staid, sober, hard working and courteous, even when speaking to the lowest housemaid, and totally honest. John, with the rounded dark Gallic looks of his ancestors, was a bone-idle, drunken, foul-mouthed, cheating libertine from whom no woman was safe.

James knew well his brother's faults, but still loved and indulged him, allowing him to lead his life as he wished, not doing a hand's turn on the farm and spending much of their income in the inns and brothels of Norwich, often remaining away from the farm for two or three days at a time, only returning when he ran out of money and needed more from his brother.

James' bottom had barely touched the seat of the chair when his breakfast was placed in front of him, and he smiled at the serving wench as he reached for the loaf and the bread knife.

'Thank you, Emma. My brother has not returned?'

Emma shook her dark brown locks vigorously, 'No, sir. Not yet.' Thank goodness, she thought. The way John ogled her, stripping her with his eyes, left her in no doubt as to the outcome if she were ever to be alone with him, and she feared her own weakness.

James held back a deep sigh, not wanting Emma to know his feelings. This time John had been gone for six days; longer than ever before, and James was becoming worried. The iniquitous drinking and gambling dens that his brother frequented in the city were the preferred hunting grounds of many vicious criminals, not to speak of the footpads that abounded in the countryside, and James had a deep foreboding that something was badly amiss.

It was Friday, payday for the farm workers and the busiest day of the week for him, a day when he could not take time to go gallivanting off in search of his recalcitrant brother, who was probably merely lying drunk in some bawdy wench's bed, and he decided he must leave it until Monday. If John had not returned by then, he would go into the city and try to find him, though where to start would be a distinct problem; he had no knowledge of the low places John frequented. For now there was much work to be done.

Finishing the last small piece of crust, he rose and strolled from the dining room to his study to make up the wage packets for his men.

The battered old iron cash box was kept in the mahogany roll-top bureau, and James turned the key, which was always left in the lock, and with his hands gently helped the roll drop into its recess.

As he pulled the box towards him he was filled with sudden alarm. The weight of golden guineas and other coins it contained always made it difficult to move. Now it slid easily over the polished wooden surface as if it contained nothing but feathers.

He quickly turned the lock and lifted the lid. The box was empty; not a single penny piece left of the two hundred-odd guineas it had contained.

James felt a sudden sharp pain in his heart, and a relentless pounding began in his head. Disaster was staring him in the face. The savings he had laboured so hard to build up over the years; the money needed to keep the estate running efficiently; every bit of it gone!

A lesser man would have sent for the constable and accused his staff, but James knew immediately who had taken the money: his own brother.

It was no wonder John had not come home. He was afraid to do so, for this time he would have realised that he had gone too far. He must, James thought, have run up a huge gambling debt and had to pay it off for fear of physical reprisals.

It was a massive blow, but even as James tried to come to terms with the dire effects the loss would have on his life he felt no anger but only sorrow for his brother, whose gambling habit James had always believed to be some kind of uncontrollable disease, like his womanising and drinking.

He collected his thoughts; the first and most urgent problem was the men's wages, and he had to do something quickly.

He rose, opened the window of the study and looked out. One of his workers was striding across the yard, a broom in one hand and a bucket in the other.

James shouted, 'Adam, stop what you are doing and saddle my horse, please. Quick as you can.'

He sighed deeply. He hated to go cap in hand to men with whom he did business and who respected him, but there was no alternative.

By the time he had changed his outer clothing to something more befitting a man in his position calling on business colleagues and added his Sunday best silk cravat, his horse was saddled, and he thanked his man, Adam Grey, before mounting the roan and immediately urging it into a gallop.

Matthew Sullivan, another of the workers, ran out of the barn as James rode off and asked, 'Where's the master orf tew in such a rush? Hen't never sin him a-gallopin' out o' the yard afore. Is th'other one in trouble agin? He hen't come hoom yit.'

Adam shook his head, 'Don't reckon thass th'other one this time, Matt. He's a-headin' fer Buxton, not Norridge, and blass' my heart alive, bor, he do look hully worried.'

They stood watching the horseman, until Peter Green, the tee-man, came out of the barn, wondering where his erstwhile helper had got to.

He bellowed, 'What the blurry hell are yew tew up to, standin' around an' scratchin' yore arses?' he shouted, 'That in't a blurry Sunday! Get on wi' it!'

The two men scurried back to work.

Colin Blake, the butcher in Buxton to whom James sold many of their animals, was behind the counter of his shop, serving the housekeeper of one of the local landed gentry.

He smiled at James as he entered the shop and greeted him with, 'Morning, James. Be with you soon as I've finished satisfying Maggie's deepest desires.' He gave the woman, a plain looking, lifelong spinster in her mid-50s, an openly lascivious grin, and she blushed to the roots of her hennaed hair, trying to hide her pleased smile.

James waited impatiently until she had finished her order and left the shop, with Colin's loud assurance that her purchases would be delivered within the half-hour ringing round her ears.

He turned to the farmer, 'Now then, James, to what do I owe the pleasure?'

James felt uncomfortable but asked, 'It's unusual, I know, Colin, not yet being the end of the month, but could you possibly pay me for the animals we delivered to you last week?'

The butcher frowned, 'How do you mean, James?'

'As I said; could you possibly pay me now, instead of at the end of the month?'

Blake's frown deepened, 'But I've paid you for them already. Your brother John came in several days ago and asked for the cash.'

His words hit James like red-hot balls from a musket, and for several moments he was unable to speak.

When he found his voice again, it sounded strange and forced, 'Oh, I am sorry. I completely forgot. Of course he did.' He turned away quickly to hide his dismay.

Watching the farmer's back disappear through the open door, the butcher's puzzlement increased. James' surprise and hurt had been obvious, and there was something dreadfully wrong if one brother did not know what the other had done. He had been uneasy paying John for the first time, when he had always previously dealt with James, but had seen no reason not to. Now he wished he had not. There was deep trouble afoot!

James next rode to the shop of the greengrocer, Jim Marshall, at the other end of the street.

There he asked a different question, 'Has my brother been in for the payment for goods we delivered last week?'

Marshall nodded, 'And he asked for an advance on next month's deliveries as well, which I naturally refused. What is going on, James? Are you bankrupt?'

'No! No, of course not.'

'Well, it is a most strange way to do business, if you ask me. If I had not always dealt with you and found you fair and honest, I would be changing my supplier, I can tell you. There are plenty out there besides you wanting to sell fruit and vegetables. And,' he added, 'your brother was not at all pleasant at the time.' He did not want to tell James how John had reeked of booze and sworn at him, using unbelievably foul language that had seared the devout Methodist's ears.

James grovelled for the first time in his life, 'I can only apologize, Jim, and assure you that it will never happen again. I will ensure that you deal only with me in the future, and I thank you for your continued support.'

Marshall was only partially mollified, 'Well, all right, James, but mind we do get back to straightforward trading.'

James nodded, unable to speak, the lump in his throat like a large, sharp flintstone.

What on earth had John been about?

Back on horseback, James headed for the only other place to which they sent produce: Rainforde Manor.

There he always dealt with Lord Edward Rainforde's general factotum, Robin Clarke, and he found the lean, rangy man outside in the yard, watching one of the grooms schooling a young grey stallion.

He turned as James cantered up, came to a halt and slid down from his mount.

'James, what a pleasant surprise. Have you come for a particular reason, or is this a social visit?'

James had gone over what he would say a dozen times as he rode there and began, 'I need help, Robin. My brother has done something very foolish and has left me with an urgent problem. I have no ready cash to pay my workers, and I wondered if you could possibly pay me for part of the produce we have delivered to you recently.'

Robin immediately realised what had occurred and would have liked to let James down lightly and do as he asked by diverting some funds, but his position, although one of some authority, left him with no alternative but to tell the farmer the truth, 'Your brother John came calling at the end of last week and virtually demanded payment up to date. He was drunk and highly abusive. Though angered, I paid him what you were owed and considered telling Lord Rainforde we would no longer be dealing with you for our extra requirements but thought better of it and gave him the benefit of the doubt, seeing that he was in his cups.'

James sighed deeply, 'I can't thank you enough for that, Robin. My brother has his problems, as you probably know. Is there any way you can possible help me?'

Robin liked the farmer but had his own master to think about. He considered for several moments and then suggested, 'There might be a way. Lord Rainforde was talking the other day about having our own small flock of sheep. Could you deliver a dozen lambs this afternoon? If so, I could pay you for them now.'

James nodded vigorously, 'Of course, Robin. Thank you, my friend. Thank you.'

It would keep the farm afloat until the end of the following month, when the next payments from his customers were due.

'I am glad I could help you, James,' Robin's voice became deadly serious, 'but please ensure that your brother never comes here again. He will not be welcome, though you are at any time.'

'Of course, Robin, and thank you again.'

'Come into the house, and I will pay you the money.'

As he rode off, with the most immediate problem solved, James' mind was on his brother's whereabouts. There was one man who might know.

Arthur Ingleby, a fop and a moneyed wastrel, was the youngest son of Sir Edward Ingleby, a local landowner. When he was not in Norwich debauching with John, he was at the local inn, the Queen's Arms in Hainford. James headed there and found the young man outside, drinking with two friends and ogling the pretty serving wench.

Ingleby watched James pull his horse to a halt and jump down from the saddle. As the farmer began to approach, he said something to the other two men with him that caused great hilarity. He then turned and shouted, 'James, old boy, come, sit down and partake of an ale with us!'

James halted by the bench where the men were seated. They were still giggling.

'Thank you for the offer, but I have not the time to stay. Do you know where I might find my brother?'

All three burst out laughing again, and James, his face darkening with anger, had to wait until Ingleby could control himself enough to speak.

'Why!' he exclaimed, 'I wager somewhere on the high seas to the west of Ireland by now, if the ship has not sunk.'

James frowned, not understanding.

'You mean…?'

The increasingly inane laughter of the three men confirmed his worst suspicions: his brother had gone off to the new land of America.

He turned away, and as he strode back to his horse, the hilarious laughter behind him sounded like the baying of the hounds of hell.

Thinking furiously he considered the future. His brother's constant debauchery, which had been such a huge drain on their income, would thankfully no longer be an issue, and provided the weather produced no major disasters, it would be possible for the estate to recover. It would entail a period of strict austerity, but within a year, God willing, the finances should be back on an even keel.

He would have to explain the problem not only to Elizabeth Easterby, to whom he was betrothed, but also to her father, Sir Basil, and might have to request that the wedding, intended for the following March, be postponed for a few months. He was not looking forward to that task.

By the time he reached home, he was feeling somewhat relieved and realised with more than a little guilt that deep down he had for many years wished that his brother was not there to be a financial drag on the estate.

Three weeks later, what remained of that guilt feeling was swept away forever, when it was brought home to him just how black hearted John had been.

As James was leaving the house to oversee the cleaning of the piggeries, a gig he did not recognise, driven by a portly man dressed in black, a complete stranger, pulled up by the front steps.

The visitor jumped down from the step of the gig and demanded loudly, 'Are you John Nash?'

James disliked the man's uncouth manner but answered, 'No, I am his brother, James.'

'Where is he?'

'Not here.' James was damned if he was going to give the man any more information.

'I can bloody well see that, Nash! Shit! He was to have made a payment to my master in Norwich this morning and did not turn up. I have had to drive all the bloody way out to this godforsaken place, and now you say he is not here.' He sighed heavily, 'Have you a beer?'

James did not like the man's stance but could understand his annoyance and needed to know just how much trouble he was in.

He pushed open the door and shouted, 'Emma! A flagon of ale, please.'

He waited until the beverage was brought and the man had taken a deep draught, before asking, 'What was the payment for that my brother should have made today?'

The visitor looked amazed, 'You mean you do not know?'

'No, sir, I do not know.'

'Shit on a broomstick! You poor bastard! It should have been the first payment on a loan, and the contract spells out that if one payment is not made your land and buildings are forfeit. So where is he?'

James reeled back as if from a physical blow, his heart pounding fiercely at the crushing news.

'I think you had better come inside, sir' he suggested when he had recovered his breath, 'and tell me your name.'

'The same as yours: James - James Stewart, bailiff.'

James led the man into the parlour and bade him sit down.

'Please tell me the exact details of the contract you mentioned, Mr Stewart.'

'In a nutshell, your brother took a one-year loan of seven thousand guineas at five percent interest per month from my master, the money lender, Monsieur Guillaume Regisse, recently arrived from France; payments to be made regularly on this date each month, and the money repaid in toto within the twelvemonth, the estate to be forfeit, as I said, if any payment is missed, or the terms of the contract not adhered to in any detail.'

James was thunderstruck at the enormity of the sum involved and John's diabolical duplicity in deliberately taking out the loan, having no intention whatsoever of paying back a penny of it and knowing full well the position it would leave his brother in.

At the end of each year, the clear profit made by the estate averaged some three hundred guineas. It would take something like twenty-five years to repay even the principal of the loan, and the money lender's ruinous interest rate made any thought of repayment unthinkable. James was ruined!

He gulped, his mouth and throat dry, desperately trying to think of something that might offer a way out.

There was but one straw that he could clutch.

He begged, 'Please, could you give me two days to try to find a solution to this problem, of which, as you must realise, I had not the slightest notion until you spoke of it?'

Stewart shook his head, 'You know not what you ask, Nash. This Froggie is not one full of the milk of human kindness. Though I can clearly see your problem and to some extent sympathise, it will carry no weight with him; none at all. He is, like all money lenders, without a heart, and he employs other men far more dangerous than yours truly to obtain his pound and a half of flesh.'

James sat in silence, his face grey, his world dissolving around him.

Stewart considered for a moment; the man before him was distraught, and he could read between the lines: the brother had scarpered and left him to sort out the debt. He seemed a decent fellow.

Stewart was not a cruel man, unlike most of those in his profession, and made a decision that he hoped he could justify. He would say that no one had been at home when he called and ride out the tongue lashing he would receive. He relented.

'One day, Nash. That's all I can give you. Tomorrow at this time.'

'If I was to repay the whole sum tomorrow, plus the five percent interest for one month, would that satisfy your master?'

Stewart was dumbfounded; had the man been playing him for a fool and had the money all the time?

'Do you think you can?'

James shrugged, 'I have but one hope, that I can borrow that sum.'

Stewart shook his head, 'It would not do. Monsieur Regisse is a devious and clever bastard and eager for land in this county. There is an early payment clause included in the contract, requiring a lump sum of twelve thousand pounds to be paid, plus any accrued interest.'

With total disaster staring him in the face James blurted, 'I will try! Bring the contract with you when you return.'

Stewart rose from his chair. 'I wish you luck.' You will need it, you poor bastard, he was thinking.

James watched the man mount his gig and drive out of the yard and then went to dress in his best attire. He had two visits to make and was not looking forward to either.

Easterby Manor lay to the north and Rainforde Hall to the west, and it was towards Rainforde Hall that he first directed his horse, wanting to know his fate before informing Elizabeth's father of his new state as a pauper.

Even to ask to see Lord Rainforde without an appointment was an imposition, and one he would never have dreamt of making in the normal way of things, but he had no alternative.

Edward Rainforde was vexed at being disturbed from the book he was reading peacefully in his library but came downstairs to speak to James, his anger dissipating as he saw the man's downcast manner and the way he was wringing his hands.

Rainforde was a kindly man who invariably had the best interests of the lesser landowners around his estate at heart. James was one of the better farmers, one he had always admired, and he now looked desperate.

Rainforde suggested, 'You had best come into the study and tell me about it.'

He listened carefully as James described the problem, leaving nothing out.

The amount of money mentioned was a vast sum, even for him, but he could provide it. How to deal with the matter was something that needed thought, however.

Though the sum was far more than the land and buildings were worth, he could give the money as the purchase price for the smaller estate that James owned and allow the man to continue farming, but as one of his tenants. It was an attractive option but would entail a massive change for the man before him. From gentleman farmer to tenant farmer was a terrible drop in class. Rainforde felt he could not do that to the man. There was the other far worse alternative: to refuse to help. That would destroy James completely and bring an evil sounding rogue, and what was worse a French one, to live close by, to work God knew what devilment in the locality, something that he could not allow to happen. Rainforde wished he could horsewhip James' brother for what he had done. There was a third choice, and he thought long and hard before deciding to offer it.

'Would you be prepared to take on a loan from me for the full sum, to be repaid over a long term with an interest rate of two percent per annum? The details will have to be worked out, but I suggest that the repayment be made by you and your descendants in goods, sending the entire produce of your estate to me and my descendants in payment, retaining enough for your own personal use, of course. My factotum will value the items as they arrive and will at each year's end deduct the amount accrued, less the interest, from the total sum borrowed. You will naturally wish to ensure that your male descendants remain gentlemen, I am sure, despite your reduced circumstances, and to that effect part of the contract will state that my family shall undertake their schooling between the ages of six and eighteen entirely at our expense.'

James closed his eyes, envisaging the years passing. He would not see the final sum paid in his own lifetime, but at least the estate would still be farmed by him and those who followed him, and with the schooling provided, he need have no fear for the future of the family. In fact the schooling alone was worth the sum of the interest at least. In effect Rainforde was giving him an interest-free loan. It was a wonderful offer.

He opened his eyes.

Lord Rainforde was regarding him with compassion, his head cocked to one side.

With tears in his eyes, James rose to his feet, his hand outstretched.

'My Lord, words cannot describe my feelings. I came into your home a man destroyed, and now you have made me whole again.'

Rainforde felt a lump in his own throat.

'I am sure I can depend on you, James. My men will bring the money to you tomorrow and await the arrival of this bailiff. They will then follow him and ensure that the payment is made to the lender and the loan documents recovered. I will have an attorney draw up the contract that we shall share, and you can sign it then.'

James was astonished; Rainforde was trusting him with an enormous sum.

'But…'

'No buts, James. I know you for an honourable man and I trust you implicitly. One must hold the faith that our descendants will be men such as ourselves. Now go and do what you have to do.'

Two hours later, James rode away from Easterby Hall a dejected man, no longer betrothed to a distraught Elizabeth, who was sobbing pitifully as she watched from an upstairs window the man she loved with all her heart disappearing from her life forever, a man who would now have to find a local farmer's daughter to provide him with an heir. Despite her tearful pleas, Sir Basil had been adamant: he was not about to allow a pauper to become his son-in-law.

It was a bitter blow, but as his resolve hardened, James set his roan into a wild gallop and made a firm vow that he would work every hour God sent to right the wrong his brother had done to the family. The estate would survive.

BOOK ONE – THOMAS 1760-1836

CHAPTER ONE
13th May 1786

The tears Thomas had fought against for so long finally flowed unchecked as the lid of the cheap pine coffin disappeared below the top of the open grave, and he cursed himself for being a weak, emotional fool. With great strength of character in every other respect, his emotions were something he had never been able to control. A sick animal, the sight of a glorious sunset, or the song of a high-flying lark could reach deep into his breast and wrench at his heartstrings. It was just one aspect of his being that he hid from his contemporaries, along with the highly refined speech he had learned from his tutors and so much preferred to the thick Norfolk dialect that he spoke in his everyday dealings with his peers and at home; virtually another language. Even his wife of seven years, Martha, was unaware of that linguistic ability, though she was fully aware of his sensitivity. Other things he had hidden from her: in his own mind he was a man wearing two hats; that of the bucolic farmer, who loved every moment of that life; the feel of the plough handles jerking under his hands as he breathed the faint, vinegary, damp smell of his old horse pulling it; the sight of a straight furrow or any animal playing or seeking its pray; a bird singing or building its nest; the smell of new mown hay, of cider fermenting, of the blooms of the rambler roses that grew outside the front door and of brimstone during a thunderstorm; the vagaries of the weather and the effect it had on the shape of the landscape; in fact, every facet of nature and every inch of his land. The other hat had below it a born intellectual, whose churning thoughts brought a constant turmoil to his brain throughout every waking hour, urging him to improve everything around him and to spread his wings. In truth, the only time he was ever truly at peace was during the winter hours that he spent in Lord Rainforde's library, a book open in front of him, learning, always learning.

To Martha, he was the staid, hardworking farmer and she loved him dearly. She remained quiet, knowing what he was feeling and that it made him so much more human, and so different from his hard, unbending father, whose corpse occupied that coffin. She was not sorry that he was dead, but for Thomas the injustice was unbearable, and for good reason: had his father held on to life for just a few more months, the coffin would have been of good solid English oak with brass handles; the security and wealth he had laboured for throughout his life finally assured.

As did all those around him, Thomas Nash shivered uncontrollably in the bitterly cold, gale force north-easterly wind, each gust slamming over the spindly top of the two hundred year old yew tree near the western wall of the churchyard like a timid diver on a high cliff, repeatedly urged forward, only to lose courage at the last moment and jump back again. The wings of that wind carried the barks of an anxious dog in the nearby village, accompanied by unnatural tympani as the ancient lych gate banged loudly against its post with each gust. Bulky dark grey, black-edged clouds that in his mind resembled an armada of angry, full-sailed galleons bustling their way to the destruction of battle filled the sky above him; precursors of the heavy rain that would fall before dark.

Thomas realised that he was holding his breath and exhaled slowly and silently, as if fearful of destroying the solemnity of the moment. He had to resist the urge to take Martha's hand, knowing that, like tears, it would be seen as a lack of manliness by the small group of tenant farmers and labourers who looked up to him as an educated leader, though save for his father's fine leather boots and buskins, which he now wore, his outward appearance was no different to the other mourners: grey pantaloons, off-white cotton shirt, brown homespun jacket and short stovepipe hat.

Twenty-four year old Martha, just half an inch shorter than her husband at five feet nine, with a similar stocky build and the same brown hair and eyes, stood beside him squeezing the hand of their five year old son, James, her eyes dry. In her view, the bitter old man they were burying had not been a patch on her husband, of whom she was inordinately proud. She saw him as standing head and shoulders above those around him. He had changed all their lives so much for the better in just a few short years, introducing into that part of Norfolk the four-crop rotation system, so superior to the ages-old three-crop system; shorthorn cattle in place of the old longhorns, giving double the meat and milk yield; the Leicester sheep, with its longer, easier to weave wool, to replace the older Norfolk breed, and most importantly the growing of the Scottish variety of turnip, their staple vegetable, which did not rot in the fields like the Norfolk variety and kept its shape in boiling water instead of turning to mush. He was both a thinker and a doer and, more privately, a considerate lover; so different in his approach to lovemaking than so many men of that age, with their animal-like lust and their distorted view of womanhood.

The members of the congregation wore the only clothes they possessed, all of the poorest quality, worn daily throughout every season, repeatedly darned and repaired and replaced only when the garment literally fell off the body. All those present were cold to their bones in the bleak, open graveyard, its more ancient stones leaning at all kinds of irregular angles, like rotting teeth in great danger of falling out.

The impecunious parson, Josiah Fitch, shook with them, his clothing thinner even than that of his parishioners. He knew there would be no other payment but a basket of vegetables for his trouble that day, as so often in this parish, and had kept the proceedings to the bare minimum. There had been no service in the church with hymns and oratory, only that at the graveside, and he had shortened that too and now gabbled the last of it, the words running into one another. 'For as much as it has pleased Almighty God to take out of this world the soul of Joshua Nash, we therefore commit his body to the ground, earth to earth, ashes to ashes, dust to dust, looking for that blessed hope when the Lord Himself shall descend from Heaven with a shout, with the voice of the Archangel, and with the trump of God, and the dead in Christ shall rise first. Then we which are alive and remain shall be caught up together with them in the clouds to meet the Lord in the air, and so shall we ever be with the Lord. Amen.'

Not waiting to hear the echoed repetitions of the last word from the assembly, and without a word of farewell or acknowledgement, he turned away, pulling his threadbare cassock about him, and doubled back towards the doubtful shelter of the cold hovel he was pleased to call the presbytery, where no fire was ever lit before the first of November or after the last day of March.

Led by Thomas, the men came forward one by one to cast the required handful of earth down onto the top of the coffin. As the last handful landed, the two gravediggers began frantically shovelling and infilling with their long, pole-handled spades, desperate to get out of the wind.

With rapidly muttered farewells, the members of the congregation hurried away, leaving Thomas, Martha and James the last to leave the churchyard.

Turning to move off, Martha shivered more violently and asked, 'Who is that, Thomas?'

A lone horseman sat astride a pitch-black stallion on the ridge that was topped by Wilton's Spinney three hundred yards to the north, the leafy branches of its trees fluttering madly in the wind, like a series of random, unreadable semaphore messages sent by a drunken signaller.

The horseman appeared to be watching them.

Thomas was puzzled, 'I know not, Martha. I have no recollection of such a horse, or of its rider. He is a stranger to the district.'

'He means trouble for us, Thomas. I know it.'

She prayed that her husband was not aware of the bolt of fear she had felt on seeing the horseman, as tangible as a heated dagger in her breast.

Thomas took her pronouncement seriously; he knew that she had inherited her mother's second sight, something they hid assiduously from others, the mere suspicion of such powers being enough to be branded a witch, with the hideous consequences that would surely follow. Even so, for his life he could not imagine how an unknown stranger could possibly impinge upon their lives.

He hastened to allay her fears, 'There is no need to worry, Martha. Look now, he is leaving.'

The horseman was spurring his mount down the ridge, and as they watched he disappeared behind it.

Their old bay horse, Blaze, now sixteen years old, his coat greying with age, waited patiently for them in the shafts of the farm cart on the track beyond the badly maintained lych-gate, which Thomas latched behind them to stop its infernal racket.

Dark thoughts of the horseman disappeared when they saw their Springer spaniel, Rascal, sitting upright on the driver's bench, looking for all the world like some ancient coachman waiting patiently for an errant master to leave the ball in order to begin the journey home.

James giggled helplessly. He loved the dog with a boy's simple passion for his pet.

Thomas helped first Martha and then his son up into the cart before climbing onto the front bench and taking up the reins. It was force of habit, but totally unnecessary. Without a word or a tapping of the reins the old horse set off at his usual sedate pace, knowing the way home as well as his master.

Thomas sighed, 'If only father could have lived until Michaelmas.'

Martha knew the basic facts of the business but not the detail; financial matters were never discussed with women, but now that Joshua was gone she believed Thomas might tell her. She asked, 'May I know more, Thomas?'

With no need to control their progress, he turned, surprised, 'What will you know?'

'The history, and why your family almost lost the land.'

Thomas hesitated. His father would have forbidden it; it was men's talk and not for women, but with Joshua's disapproval now no longer a factor he could see no reason why Martha should not be told. After all, the matter was all but settled.

'Very well.' He took a deep breath and began, 'The men of our family were not always farmers, but important soldiers. They fought in the armies of the kings of England, from the time that our French ancestor, Arnaud, came to these shores as a senior aide to William The Conqueror, but when Charles the First came to the throne, the head of the family at that time, Robin Nash, became disillusioned with the tyrannical absolute monarch and his outlandish religious views and joined the army of Oliver Cromwell, the Protector of England. Robin fought with great valour at the battles of Marston Moor and Naseby and again at Preston, where he was so badly wounded that he could no longer continue soldiering. Cromwell was sufficiently pleased with Robin's devoted service that he gave him our land in perpetuity.'

'Perpeter, father?' Little James piped up.

'It means forever, James, providing the family pays its dues and stays out of bankruptcy.'

Martha said, 'But that happened, did it not?'

'Not quite, but almost, due to a rogue in the family. His name was John, a name so dishonoured that no male child has carried it since. The younger of two brothers who farmed this land, he went off to America, having stolen every penny from the house and far worse, taken a large loan on the land. That loan was taken up by the then Lord Rainforde and we have been paying it off ever since. It has taken us eighty-five years to pay off the debt and interest, and father made the last but one payment at Michaelmas last year, leaving just fifteen guineas still to pay. This Michaelmas, after that sum is deducted from the total value of produce supplied during the year, we shall have almost the full payment for a year's crops, and our lives will change. Though I am legally entitled to be called a gentleman, I do not wish to live that life. It will be enough that we can afford to wear clothing without darns and patches and eat the best of the produce of the farm instead of the leavings.'

'It worries me that every part of our produce goes to the Manor and nowhere else. Supposing something happens to Lord Rainforde. He is an old man.'

'He is but forty-five, Martha, three years younger than father was, and has he not had the vigour to impregnate his young wife? Not for him the hardships that reduce a man's lifespan. He has not had to leave his bed every day of the year at five of the clock or earlier or spend the night delivering lambs.'

'And what of the harvest; shall it be good this year?'

'For our sins, though we know not of them, the good Lord often visits us with storms and lashing rain as the cereals come fit, but we shall pray for His understanding and hope that He hears us.'

They were now passing through their own fields, and Blaze's steady clip-clop missed a beat as the old horse expertly avoided the rush of an hysterical mother moorhen, disturbed from her dyke by a stalking fox, clucking madly to bustle along her newly hatched chicks; five tiny black balls of wool moving as if on casters in her wake, the shaping of the group changing from second to second, like that of frantic tadpoles in a pond.

In the field to the right, two hares stood up on their hind legs, shadow boxing in pursuit of male dominance, and nearer to the hedge a hen harrier hovered, the only movement the silent flutter of its wingtip feathers, waiting patiently for the vole it had spied entering a clump of grass to exit on the other side.

Thomas surveyed his kingdom, his breast so crushed with the love of this land, these acres, that breathing became difficult.

That summer was country-kind, with long days of unbroken sunshine as the grain ripened, and for once the reapers, including the itinerant gypsies who habitually arrived with their gaily-painted caravans in time for the work, had a dry harvest under cloudless skies, making them even more thankful for the jars of home-brewed ale that were provided as part of their wages.

Though neither Thomas nor Martha recognized it as such at the time, the beginning of their troubles came as the last cartload of wheat straw was leaving the field at the end of the harvest and Thomas stood looking along the dead straight rows of stubble, renewed proof of his master ploughmanship, into an evening sun that seemed to him to have melted the sky and set afire the entire horizon.

He saw Martha rush through the gateway, pulling her skirts tight to her to aid her speed. She came up to him out of breath.

Worried at her expression, he asked, 'What ails you, wife?'

Shaking her head as if she still did not believe it, Martha blurted, 'Lady Mary is dead.'

With her vast experience of birthing animals, Martha was in great demand as a midwife and aided the doctor with all births at the important houses in the area.

Lord Rainforde's young wife of twenty-seven summers had been perfectly well until she began labour, but after the baby was born, seemingly without difficulty, an internal bleed had started which the doctor was unable to stop, and the young mother had expired from loss of blood. The baby, a boy, was stillborn, as were so many others.

It was a sad blow, but not one that immediately affected the Nash family. Death being a regular event it was soon put behind them.

With the harvest in and delivered to Lord Rainforde's barns, less the requisite percentage kept for brewing and the making of bread and pottage, Thomas was able to enjoy the best time of the farmer's year. The weather was pleasant, work was less intense, fruit was harvested and preserved, and meat was salted down and stored in barrels for the winter, each day bringing Michaelmas, on the thirtieth of September, nearer.

CHAPTER TWO

Lord Henry Rainforde stood looking disconsolately out over the immaculately kept formal gardens which had been Lady Mary's pride and joy and where she had spent so many happy hours directing the team of gardeners who tended the serried ranks of roses and perennials, the interspersing, weed-free lawns an exact one inch high and as smooth as the baize on the billiard table in the games room. Beyond the gardens the waters of the moat shone like burnished silver, its edges blurred with flowering lily pads, a source of great pleasure to him in the past, but now of not the slightest interest.

He had as yet received no answer from the many letters he had sent to every important house in the county seeking a willing or, if necessary, unwilling replacement recipient for his seed. An heir was his most urgent requirement, and he had made it clear that she could have the face of a horse, be deaf, dumb and blind, grossly fat or painfully thin, mild or moody, provided she was fecund. He had offered an obscene sum in payment in the hope that one of his missives would reach a father desperate for funds.

It was inconceivable that the bastard, as he always thought of his dead brother Charles' only offspring, born out of wedlock from a gypsy wench, should inherit the estate.

He had seen the boy only once, at Charles' interment in the family vault. The bastard had been of some seventeen summers at the time and had come uninvited, angering Lord Rainforde not only by his mere presence but far more by the obviously intended appearance of ownership as the bastard gazed at his surroundings.

He could not, he must not, inherit.

Rainforde had taken pains to obtain regular reports of the bastard's doings, all of which spoke of a life of gambling, whoring and unethical dealings; in particular card manipulating, viciousness and murder. He had killed one man who, he claimed, had been attempting to rob him, and was involved in the death of two others, whose purses were not found upon their bodies. In all an obviously bad lot.

He turned at a knock on the door of his study and observed that Josiah Smith, his major domo, appeared disturbed.

'My pardon, your Lordship, a visitor: Silas Rainforde.'

Rainforde was shocked; the bastard had had the temerity to visit uninvited!

'Where is he?'

'In the library, my Lord.'

Rainforde tried to collect his thoughts as he descended the ornate circular staircase, stepping on marble brought at great expense by his ancestors from the famous quarries of Carrara in Italy.

His ire increased on entering the library. The bastard, now a man of twenty-six, nearing six feet tall and with the slim figure of a young wench, almost pitch black hair and the swarthy complexion of his mother's tribe, had helped himself from the decanter of vintage brandy and stood with one hand resting insolently on the antique credenza and the other lifting the crystal tumbler to his lips, which curled with disdain as he offered, 'God's teeth, Uncle! You astound me with your negligence. How remiss of you to lose both your brat and your milch-cow at one fell stroke. What will you do now, an old man with so little time left?'

Rainforde tried to control the tremble in his voice as he replied, 'You are not welcome in this house. You come uninvited and expect me to receive you as a guest?'

Silas laughed aloud, 'Guest, Uncle? No, indeed not. As your rightful heir, of course. We need to discuss arrangements for the transfer of the estate.'

Rainforde's breathing became harsh with anger as he gritted out, 'Not as long as I have breath in my body.'

'Which may well not be for much longer, Uncle.' Silas drew a finger across his throat. The meaning was obvious.

'You have the gall to threaten me, *boy*?' The epithet was intentionally derogatory.

Silas Rainforde ignored it, smiling with his lips but not with his eyes, 'That is exactly what I was doing, Uncle. How clever of you to notice.'

Rainforde lost what little patience he had had, 'Get out! Get out! Do not ever come here again!'

Silas laughed nonchalantly, 'Oh, but I shall, Uncle, very soon, and when I do you will be in no fit state to welcome me.'

He drained the last contents of the glass and threw the vastly expensive crystal vessel into the stone fireplace, where it burst into smithereens, before sauntering casually from the room, leaving behind a man whose heart rate and blood pressure had both increased to dangerous levels.

As Rainforde tottered back unsteadily to his study, his mind whirling with black thoughts, he was unaware that Silas had not left the property but had walked round to the servants' quarters, where he spoke with a wench he had been surreptitiously grooming and bedding for some weeks, promising her that she would soon be the Lady of the Manor with a life of unending luxury if she merely did his simple bidding. The poor girl, believing herself to be in love and ignorant of the ways of the world and men such as Silas, could not know that her own life would be forfeit as soon as she had carried out his wishes.

A few words of instruction and a small vial of liquid were passed to her before the bastard left the property, grinning viciously.

Lord Henry Rainforde died a most painful death five days later.

CHAPTER THREE

Thomas learnt of the demise of his benefactor and mentor the day after the death and hurried to the Manor to present his compliments to the new Lord Rainforde, worried that the agreement between the two families might not be understood by the new incumbent.

On entering the grounds, he came across the late Lord Rainforde's factotum, Charles Gray, a man of some fifty years who had been head of the estate staff for more than half that time leaving the Manor grounds carrying a portmanteau containing his few worldly possessions. Across his forehead was an angry red weal from a blow with a riding crop, wielded without reason as he was ordered loudly to leave the estate when attempting to remonstrate with Silas after one of the serving wenches had come to him with a story of vicious rape in the night.

Thomas, unknowing, greeted him with a smile, 'Whither away in such haste, Charles?'

Gray surprised him with the vehemence of his reply, which sent Thomas' heart down into his father's boots, 'That creature is the very devil; an ogre; a foul beast! He has not a vestige of decency or honesty! I wish you well, for you will need all of that and more if you wish to do business with him.'

'You are leaving?'

'Aye! Sacked without reference after a lifetime of service to the family.'

'What of Josiah Smith?'

'You may well ask. I received one blow, he has had many and will be shown the door very soon no doubt. Poor man, he is near the end of his useful life and can only end up in the poor house, where I may also well find myself. The wenches walk in terror, particularly those who are virgins. Silas Rainforde is a vicious predator, totally without conscience.'

Thomas took his leave of the unfortunate man and with his hopes in tatters continued along the half-mile tree-lined drive to the Manor.

A wench with red-rimmed eyes met him at the door and took him to the library, where he was announced and entered, for his hand to be taken by a smiling Silas, who strode across the room to greet him and astonished Thomas by appearing to accept him as an equal.

'Thomas Nash, yes. I have heard much about you and your innovations. You have wondrously improved the lot of the farmers hereabouts, I hear. Well done, indeed. We shall indubitably be very good neighbours.'

Thomas was impressed with Rainforde's knowledge of his doings, 'My condolences on your loss, My Lord.'

'Yes, a sad event, and my Uncle appeared to be in such rude health. I feel that the loss of his young wife was the cause of his sudden demise. He was truly endeared of her. Now, what did you wish to discuss with me?'

Thomas explained the importance of the coming Michaelmas and the ramifications of the return of the deed and the yearly payment, Silas Rainforde nodding the while.

Thomas did not see the avaricious look, quickly concealed, that crossed Rainforde's face when he related the details of the land deed he hoped to regain. It was news to the usurper, but news he intended to make good use of. Land equated to wealth, and there was no way he was going to allow it to go out of his hands if he could help it.

When Thomas finished speaking, Rainforde assured him, 'That seems straightforward enough, Thomas. I shall need to confer with Smith, of course, who will have all the details and documents, but I am sure there will be no difficulty.'

Thomas' fears were dispelled. He could not understand how this man before him, apparently the very soul of decency, saturnine in appearance though he might be, could in any way be the devil described by Charles Gray. He had no option but to accept him at face value and was heartened once more as he took his leave by Rainforde's final words, 'You must leave it to me, Thomas, and all will be well. Go with God.'

Despite Silas Rainforde's assurances, however, Thomas was on tenterhooks during the final weeks leading up to

Michaelmas. So much hung in the balance. The animals were out to grass and needed little attention, and the other tasks were pleasant, mainly the chopping of wood for the winter fires, the salting down of meat, and the repair of fences. What he was not aware of was Martha's quiet introspection.

Two weeks before Michaelmas, at just after two in the morning, they were awakened by a fearful banging on their door.

Thomas rose and on opening the door had a fainting female body fall into his arms.

He lifted her and took her through to the bedroom, where Martha had lit a lamp, and as he sat her down on the bed saw that the nightdress the woman wore was torn and bloodied. He vaguely recognised her as having been the personal maid to Lady Mary Rainforde before her demise. The woman's nose had been broken, and with his male lack of appreciation of the situation he assumed that the blood came from that organ. Martha had taken one look and knew otherwise.

Thomas told her, 'She is called Elizabeth Fryer, from the Manor.'

Martha told him to go to the kitchen and heat water, which he was to bring back with a clean cloth.

She laid the woman, who had fainted away, on the bed and lifted the skirt of her nightdress. What she saw appalled her.

The insides of the woman's legs were black and blue and covered with blood, which was still oozing from her vagina. Five large tears in the skin around it told their tale, and when Martha gently inserted her fingers she could see that the damage extended to the walls, which were torn as far as she could see into it. Had the woman been mounted by a stallion the damage could hardly have been worse.

She heard Thomas returning with the water and pulled the nightdress down. Elizabeth was still comatose.

Martha knew Thomas had never seen the intimate parts of any other woman and did not intend that he should now. She told him, 'Leave the bowl on the night stand, Thomas, and then go into the other room. I have work to do.'

Elizabeth regained consciousness some fifteen minutes later and immediately began sobbing. Martha took her in her arms and gradually eased the story from her.

Silas Rainforde had subjected Elizabeth Fryer to practices that appalled Martha and made her fear mightily for the future of her own family. If the man was so evil then God help them.

Against her best intentions, she told Thomas the truth of the matter, and he was adamant: no matter the consequences, Rainforde must be held to account. He would hear nothing to the contrary and set off at seven of the clock to fetch the constable from Buxton.

They arrived back a little after ten, and the constable took Elizabeth Fryer's statement, after which he and Thomas departed for the Manor to face Rainforde.

A different wench opened the door to them, a very much younger one, who looked to Thomas as scared as a rabbit faced with an adder.

Rainforde appeared in the library doorway, a glass in his hand, swaying slightly, and demanded, 'What is it?' His gaze shifted, 'And what the hell are you doing here, Nash?'

The constable had been fearful as soon as he heard Thomas tell the story. Now he was quaking in his boots at the thought of accusing a noble lord.

'I have just interviewed an Elizabeth Fryer, my lord, who has made certain allegations concerning rape.'

Rainforde laughed loudly, 'Oh, that! Good job you came, constable. Come with me.' He strode past them and out into the yard, where he led them across to the stables.

Inside, he showed them the body of one of the stable boys, no more than thirteen years old, dead on the straw with a hole in the centre of his forehead, his breeches open and covered in blood near the crotch, and his bloody deflated member lying outside in view.

'One of the wenches came to me last evening. She had heard screams coming from the stables. I took a pistol and came running, hearing the continuing screams myself. As I entered I saw this wretch' He kicked the lad's foot 'making the two-backed beast with the woman, who was attempting to get out of his clutches and screaming to wake the dead. I kicked him and shouted to him to stop, but he would not, so I shot him.'

Thomas could not help himself, 'He was on top of her, my Lord?'

Rainforde snorted, 'Of course he was, you bloody fool. You think she would scream if she was helping herself to his goods?'

'Then why is he shot in the forehead and not in the back of the head, my Lord?'

Rainforde looked unsure for just a fraction of a second before avowing loudly, 'He turned his head to look at me.'

Before Thomas could ask where the lad had been kicked, thinking he could look for the bruise to disprove Rainforde's story, the constable seized on a way out of his dilemma, 'I can see that you have done the county a great service, my Lord: the removal from society of a rapist who would no doubt have raped again on the one side, and a saving of costs, since there is no need to try him for his crime. Do you wish me to dispose of the body?'

Rainforde smirked, 'That will not be necessary. He will be thrown on the dung heap, where ordure such as he belongs.'

'Thank you, my Lord. Thank you.' The constable's low bows and obsequiousness made Thomas feel physically sick.

With double entendre, Rainforde glowered at Thomas and growled, 'I shall not forget your part in this business either, Nash.'

CHAPTER FOUR

On the morning of Michaelmas Day, the thirtieth of September, Thomas rose early and went to put Blaze into the shafts of the cart for the trip to the Manor. His head was aching. The night had not been kind to him, sleep eluding him for most of the hours of darkness, his mind in turmoil. The pre-dawn lightening of the sky had come as a relief. A thick mist met him as he exited the house to cross the yard, the weak early morning sun merely a faint halo in the eastern sky above the barn. When he pushed open the gate into the paddock, his boots becoming wet with the autumn dew, he saw that the old horse lay on his side in the corner, his breathing heavy and slow, his eyes closed.

With dread overcoming him, Thomas approached his old friend and knelt down beside his head, ignoring the cold moisture soaking the thin material of his breeches at the knees. He stroked the horse's brow and called his name, and the eye flickered half open and seemed to recognise him. Blaze made an effort to lift his head but was unable to move it one inch from the ground. The attempt was too much, and the eye closed again as he took one last gasping breath, exhaled in a flutter as his heart stopped.

Thomas stood up and looked around him. The mist was beginning to lift, and he could see the far paddock fence and the ghostly outlines of the barn and house. All appeared normal and yet he had a sudden intense feeling that nothing would ever be the same again.

On leaden feet, he trudged back to the Hall and into the kitchen, where Martha was preparing their son's breakfast.

She turned, hearing slow footsteps whose unsteady beat seemed to her to carry an infinite sadness.

'Blaze is dead.' Thomas told her bluntly.

He expected sorrow, but not the open terror that showed in her eyes and expression. He felt a sudden jolt of fear himself without knowing why.

He said simply, 'I must go on foot.' and turned away to begin the four-mile trek to the Manor.

The sun quickly burnt off the last of the mist, revealing just one small, unusually shaped cloud in an otherwise azure blue sky, a cloud whose shape changed rapidly from an innocent, small, soft white fluffy ball with playful, extending fingers to a soaring, swirling, dark grey mass, whose ragged top raged forward unchecked, as if driven by a demented demon whose desperate desire was to capture and enslave the entire heavens, and Thomas was no more than halfway to the Manor when a single bolt of fork lightning almost blinded him as it struck a three-hundred-year-old oak at the corner of the nearest field, less than two hundred yards from where he stood stunned, followed by a deafening clap of thunder immediately overhead. The heavens opened, soaking him to the skin in seconds.

The rain ended as quickly as it had begun, and the cloud moved on, leaving behind a clear blue sky.

When he reached the end of the long drive that led down to the Manor, his soaked clothing steaming from the heat of his exertions and the now warm sun, he saw a closed black carriage standing by the front door with two horses hitched to it and a black uniformed coachman dozing on the box. It seemed that he was not the only visitor to Silas Rainforde on that morning.

At the door of the Manor, he was let in by another of the serving wenches. She had the red cheeks of someone who has wept recently and copiously.

He announced his business and was directed to the library, where he was surprised to see Silas Rainforde in the company of two other men. From their dress, they were evidently not of the gentry, but appeared to be some kind of official. All three had their backs to him. Rainforde, his right hand in the pocket of his elegant royal blue morning coat, murmured something to the two men, and all three turned as one.

Silas Rainforde was a much different individual from the last time Thomas had been at the Manor. His first words, spoken with venom, were, 'You are late, Nash, and you are wetting my carpet.'

'My horse died and…'

'My Lord!' The words came as a shout.

Thomas was puzzled, 'I do not understand...'

'My Lord! That is how you are to address me. I do not give a tinker's cuss for your horse, Nash, or for you either, if it comes to that matter. Now state your business!'

'I am come to retrieve our deed of land, my Lord, which as you know has been held by your family until our debt was finally paid. That has been done during this year. Also, to collect the payment for the remainder of the produce delivered to the Manor during the twelvemonth since last Michaelmas.'

'You have not cleared the debt, and you have already been paid for all produce delivered. Smith paid you each time a delivery was made.'

Thomas was astonished and appalled, 'That is not so, my...'

Rainforde screamed and lifted his fist, 'You say I lie, dog? I have killed men for less.'

Thomas stuttered, 'No, I did not mean to infer that, my Lord, of course. There must be some discrepancy in the records. I have been paid not one penny during the past year.'

'Then you are saying that the man Smith has falsified the records?'

Thomas shrugged his shoulders in desperation, 'If they show that I have been paid then that must be so, since I have not.'

'My Lord! My Lord! What are you, a cretin?'

Thomas had not noticed that the other two men had during the altercation moved round behind him, and they now took him firmly in their grip, each holding an arm.

Rainforde glared at him belligerently, but with a satisfied sneer on his lips, 'You are attempting to obtain pecuniary advantage from a lord of the land by false pretences. These gentlemen have inspected the deed of land, the agreement showing the details of the loan, and the ledger showing the deliveries and payments made this year. They have seen that you lie through your teeth. As Lord of this Manor, I have full legal right to try you, find you guilty and hang you, here, today, but I will have no man say I used my high position to destroy a man with whom this family has for many years had dealings. You will be taken to Norwich jail and will come before the next Assizes and a jury of your peers.' He indicated the door with a flick of his head and ordered, 'Remove him from my sight.'

Thomas was hustled out of the room, across the hall and out of the front door to the waiting carriage, his head reeling with the suddenness of his arrest and the enormity of the injustice inflicted upon him with such unexpected vindictiveness.

The elder of the two men who had arrested him banged his cudgel on the side panel and shouted, 'Wake up, Dozey!' He then pulled open the door of the carriage and nodded his indication that Thomas should step in. Both men took their hands from his arms.

There were seats fore and aft, and Thomas elected to sit facing forward, his face portraying clearly his utter bewilderment at what still seemed at that moment to be a living nightmare from which he might perhaps emerge. The two men entered and sat opposite him, their expressions betraying nothing of their own feelings.

The carriage pulled away with a jolt.

Once out of sight of the Manor, the elder of the two men spoke, 'I am Stephen Blake, and this is Jacob Masters. My apologies for your rough treatment, but you must understand that we had to be seen to do our duty as officers of the law. You have fallen foul of a most vindictive character in Lord Rainforde. Whether your tale or his is the correct one I cannot comment upon, but I have my own opinion. You are lucky in that he did not insist upon his Manorial rights. He could quite legally have done away with you as he said. At least you are still alive.'

'The Assizes he mentioned; when are they and what will happen?'

'The next are on the fifteenth of November. The crime with which you are charged is not a hanging offence, but you will be sentenced to either seven or fourteen years, perchance with hard labour, unless you can afford an attorney.'

Thomas shook his head, 'That I cannot, unless you give me time to take some animals to market.'

'You jest, Nash. We would also spend time incarcerated were we to allow that. Those animals are yours no longer I fear, but Rainforde's.'

Thomas sighed sadly, 'I could but ask.'

He expected the coach to head for Norwich but noticed that they were headed the other way.

'What is our destination?'

'Why, Norwich jail, of course.'

'Then why are we heading this way?'

Blake realised that Thomas did not know what was required in cases of this nature, 'We must take your wife also. She is deemed by law to be equally guilty with you.'

It was an issue Thomas had not for one moment considered, and it struck him like a hammer blow to the head.

His greatest surprised came when they reached the Hall, and he saw Martha standing outside, waiting for them with a sack of belongings beside her. He suddenly realised that even though he had been blissfully ignorant of what Fate had in store for them Martha had not. He was puzzled by one thing: where was his son?

CHAPTER FIVE

When Thomas had set off for the Manor, he left behind him a woman who could not remove from her mind the omen of the dead horse. At the door, she watched until Thomas was out of sight and then immediately began making preparations, calling to James that he must collect every piece of his clothing and bring it to her.

She took the pan containing the boy's intended breakfast from the fire and instead smeared goose grease on a slice of bread before starting to collect small items and putting them in a sack.

When the boy came to her, carrying what little spare clothing he possessed, she added it to the contents of the sack.

Kneeling down, she looked into his eyes and told him, 'I must take you far away, James. Bad men will come looking for you, and they must not find you. You must be very brave and be a good soldier for your aunt Jane, and one day your father and I will come to find you.'

'Can I take Rascal with me?'

At the sound of his name, the old spaniel lying by the fire lifted his head and gave a wag of his tail.

Martha heaved a sigh, 'No, my son, you cannot. He would give you away, though it would not be with intent. Come now, take this and eat quickly. We must be on our way.'

Her unmarried sister Elizabeth lived three miles away in their father's house on the outskirts of Buxton, and she was surprised to see Martha and the boy approaching her down the road as she hung out the washing.

The two sisters embraced, and Martha asked her sister urgently, 'Can you go now and take the boy to Jane? His life depends upon it. They will come looking for him with intent to kill and must not find him. If you are asked, you must insist that you have not seen him.'

Elizabeth had a hundred questions but could plainly hear the urgency in Martha's voice and see the pain in her expression. She asked just one question, 'You and Thomas?'

Martha shook her head with infinite sadness, 'Alas, we are lost.'

Her sister's hand went to her mouth in horror. 'But why?'

'For no good reason. We live in bad times, Elizabeth, where the law takes no account of truth.'

'I will go now.'

Martha bent down and kissed her son, 'Be good for your new mother, James.'

The little boy regarded his mother solemnly and told her, 'I will, mother.'

Martha embraced Elizabeth once more, turned and strode off, never once looking back, her hot tears running uncontrolled down her cheeks.

When she reached the Hall she first took up the sharpest of the kitchen knives and then called to Rascal. The dog came to her, his tail wagging. She took him out into the paddock and across to the body of Blaze. Rascal sniffed at his old friend, his eyes as he looked up to Martha betraying his sure knowledge that the smell emanating from the body differed from that which he was used to. Martha bent, laid the knife on the grass and stroked the old dog with her right hand, lifting his head with her left. Then, picking up the blade again, and with the experience gained in the killing of hundreds of pigs, sheep and cattle over the years, she sliced across his throat with one lightning fast movement, holding the head high so that the blood would flow out quickly, shortening his pain.

It was over in a few instants, and she let the body down so that the two old friends were together in death.

It was time to make her own preparations.

CHAPTER SIX

As the carriage came to a halt, Martha stepped forward and pushed the sack in, then climbed in herself, not waiting to be invited.

As if they were going for a day's outing she sat down next to Thomas and took his hand.

The carriage did not move and Blake asked, 'Where is the boy?'

Martha's gaze was completely innocent, 'Boy? What boy?'

'Your son.'

'We have no son.'

Blake looked quizzically at his companion and the younger man shrugged and lifted his eyebrows expressively.

'Must we return to the Manor to report that there is no child?'

Masters shook his head, 'I do not believe that was part of our remit, Stephen, and Lord Rainforde does not pay our stipend.'

His companion nodded thoughtfully, 'That is true.' He pushed open the door and shouted up to the driver, 'Guildhall, Dozey.'

As the carriage moved off Martha opened the sack and pulled out chunks of bread and cheese, which she passed to Thomas and the other two men, entreating Thomas, 'Eat while you can, husband. Your next meal may well not be as wholesome.'

She had never before visited Norwich, though Thomas had done so many times. Looking at the city from a distance she had the impression of the lower jaw of an ogre whose teeth were in disarray and with some missing; buildings of all shapes and sizes, some new and of straight lines; others that were leaning and in disrepair, with gaps between where fire or fatigue had caused the collapse of an edifice. As they neared the outskirts they met more traffic. Carriages of many kinds were in evidence: whiskeys, landaulets, gigs, chariots, barouches, phaetons and a tiny curricle, driven at speed with panache by a young gentleman, the tasselled ends of his white silk cravat flying in the wind, but by far the most intriguing was a Royal Mail stagecoach in bright red livery, a recent innovation to replace the running boys who previously carried the mail and so often lost it to robbers, causing many people sending money notes to tear them and send each half by separate posts. Despite their dire circumstances, she was entranced with the size of the buildings and the scores of people walking along the sides of the cobbled streets in all manner of unusual clothing from the urbane to the outlandish. She saw her first black man, walking behind his master. Most of the pedestrians wore clogs, but some sported tall, intricately-patterned leather boots, and there were toffs, lording it in their fine attire as they strolled along twirling silver-topped ebony canes, regularly accosted by obviously loose women, who lifted their skirts to display their wares with no regard for the passing public. Driving along the Earlham Road Martha saw a ragamuffin being chased by a tall, gaunt gentleman, wig askew, shouting 'Stop, thief', while the other pedestrians moved out of the way, making not the slightest effort to stop the urchin and laughing with pleasure at the spectacle.

It was an education that was brought to a sudden end by their arrival at the Guildhall, situated grandly on the hill next to the sprawl of Norwich market, its dozens of stalls selling everything one could imagine. Across behind it, Martha could see the Theatre Royal, built but twenty years since by Thomas Ivory, and she had a momentary sense of loss that she would now never see one of the many plays produced there. In particular she would have liked to see Monsieur Beaumarchais' recent play, 'The Barber of Seville', of which she had read so much in the Norwich Mercury, copies of which were passed to her from the Manor after they had been read and discarded.

They had arrived five minutes before the departure of the regular post-chaise to Ipswich, loading no more than fifty yards from the Guildhall at the Haymarket. Luggage was being fastened to the roof rails, while passengers struggled to seat themselves between the boxes and cases. Others wealthier travellers were being handed into the interior by one of the grooms. As at any public event, no matter how mundane, passers-by stood and gaped at their only entertainment of the day. Relatives of those embarking on the journey hung precariously from the rickety, overhanging balconies of nearby buildings, shouting exhortations and goodbyes, unheard in the general clamour. A seaman, now a landsman, with a wooden peg-leg and still wearing his now tatty seaman's short jacket, lounged indolently on their side of the gathering. Martha looked on with disbelief as a ragged urchin dashed through the milling throng and swerved suddenly at full speed into the legs of a gentleman who had stopped to watch the proceedings. Immediately, a young man close by stepped forward, ostensibly to stop him from falling, and Martha saw a hand streak out and steal something from the gentleman's pocket as that worthy fought, with the aid of his supposed helper, to regain his balance. The young man moved off rapidly to join his young accomplice waiting at the corner. Both were laughing with glee.

In all, it was a scene of organised bedlam.

Their two jailors allowed them to descend of their own volition from the coach. It was to be their last free action for many long months.

Once on the street, they were taken into the Guildhall, where a lugubrious, aged official, dressed entirely in black, complete with high hat, sat at a well worn, ink stained oak desk and wrote their names in his book before they were taken below to the cells.

There were four, only one of which held prisoners - two women, one of not yet twenty years, the other nearer forty, both of whom were regarding the newcomers with scarcely concealed interest.

'The accommodation is not of the best, I fear.' Blake was apologetic as he opened the door of a tiny cell, no more than seven feet in length and three feet six inches wide, bare but for a wafer-thin palliasse on the stone floor, filthy and stinking of stale sweat, urine and semen, and a malodorous, slatted wooden bucket for night soil, caked with hard, dried excrement.

Thomas held his hand out to Blake, 'Thank you for your kind consideration.'

The agent nodded, taking his hand, 'I wish you well, though I fear for you.'

'You are a good man in an evil world.'

Blake nodded, 'That last is true at least, as you have recently discovered to your detriment.'

The official from the desk upstairs, having accompanied the party down to the cells, locked the door, and the two agents departed.

Thomas took Martha in his arms and whispered, 'Be brave, my love.'

Though well intentioned, it broke loose the tears that had been suppressed for so long, and sobs shook her whole body while he held her close.

From across the corridor, a squawk came from the older woman, 'Aw, look at that there mawther, Lizzie. She's upset, poor dear. Never bin in clink afore, have you, ducks? You'll get used to it and you'll make do if you know what's good for you.'

Thomas glared at them over Martha's shoulder and was astonished when the younger of the two stuck her tongue out at him, lifted her skirts and pushed her stomach forward, displaying herself crudely to him. She wore no undergarments, and he realised that they were women of the street.

He turned disdainfully from the woman and whispered to Martha, 'Come, sit.'

He told her all that had happened at Rainforde Manor.

She listened in silence until he had finished his story and then asked, 'And what is to become of us?'

'Prison for seven or fourteen years, Blake believes.'

'Shall we be transported to America?'

'No, my love. Since the recent American Revolutionary War ended, the new United States has refused to take any more prisoners. We shall be kept here in Norwich.'

'But I have seen us over water.'

Thomas felt a sudden frisson of fear, 'And shall we survive?'

'I believe we shall, and the family will one day regain the land you so love, though there will be desperation, disease and death along the way.'

'And James? Where is he?'

'Methinks it best you know not, Thomas, though he is safe, at least for now. Silas Rainforde will do all he can to find him, for he is fearful that his acquisition will not be secure until our family is destroyed utterly. I would gladly die, and so would you I know, my love, before betraying him, but you may be tortured for knowledge of his whereabouts, and I have heard there are ways a torturer uses that a man cannot resist.'

He could see the sense in her reasoned argument and nodded acceptance.

They conversed quietly for the rest of the afternoon, the only disturbances to their whispered talk the sound of the women opposite urinating noisily in their bucket from time to time.

The only light came from two small, heavily grilled windows high in the walls at street level, and dusk was falling before they received a visit from above; a bloated figure of a man, clothed all in black like the first jailer they had seen, with a face that brought vividly to mind a raven: a hooked nose, a vicious snarl on downcast lips, and a badly pockmarked face with only one eye, the other a socket with a flap of purple-mottled skin covering it. The man's most striking feature was a hump back as pronounced as that of Richard the Third in pictures that Thomas had seen. Strangely, among the other odours of decay that he carried with him, there was a distinct smell of freshly roasted flesh.

In his grubby left hand he held a bag and in the other a water jug and a metal pint flagon.

He came to Thomas and Martha first, placed the flagon and jug on the floor, shoved his rankly filthy hand into the bag and came out with two thin slices of grey bread, which he passed through the bars without speaking. He then lifted the jug and filled the flagon, which followed the bread.

Thomas handed the flagon to Martha. She drank its contents and passed it back for a refill.

To their surprise, the jailer turned away from them to serve the women.

Thomas called, 'Could I have some water, please?'

The figure turned and grunted sardonically, 'I heard the 'please', but not the 'sir'.'

Thomas swallowed to hide his ire, 'Could I please have some water, sir.'

What was meant as a grin, but which came across as a smirk, preceded the pronouncement, 'Only one ration per cell.'

He continued over to the women. Thomas watched angrily.

The jailer pushed bread through the bars, two slices for each of the women, and the older one of the two asked, 'Did you bring our chicken?'

He cackled, 'Are you ready to skin my pullet?'

The younger woman came to the bars in front of him and went down onto her knees. Thomas was astonished to see the jailer fumbling at the closure of his breeches and even more astonished to see his engorged member come into view.

Thomas turned away quickly and pulled Martha around, so that she was facing the far wall.

Behind them, they heard grunts and groans of pleasure as the woman did the jailer's bidding, and a final, long 'Aaaah'.

They heard the older woman's voice asking, 'Our chicken?'

The smell of roast flesh became much stronger as the hunchback drew a packet from his clothing and passed it through the bars.

Thomas turned his head to observe the women tearing the flesh from roast chicken thighs, making his mouth water. Most annoying was their obvious pleasure in taunting him. He turned away again as the jailer departed and clambered awkwardly up the stairs.

Night fell, and the dungeon became almost Stygian in its darkness.

Martha and he both used the bucket, trying to do so as quietly as possible, before lying down to sleep.

He lay down with Martha and tried vainly for several hours to fall asleep, his efforts punctuated by loud farts from the older

46

woman opposite, farts that filled the air around him with a noxious smell redolent of tainted, rotten flesh.

He came wide awake suddenly hearing the call, 'Two of the clock and all's well.' as the night watch passed on the street above.

He realised Martha was also awake and in the faint ambient light struggling in from the tiny, filthy windows could see she was looking deep into his eyes.

She whispered in his ear, 'Come to me, Thomas.'

He whispered back, 'The women?'

'Are fast asleep. They are to take you from me, and this will be the last time we lie together for many moons, if, indeed, every again. For what we have to suffer ahead of us I wish to be with child - your child. Please, Thomas, we can be very quiet.'

She fumbled with her lower clothing and her urgency transferred itself to him.

As he entered her she uttered a sigh that encompassed her whole being, and when his seed poured into her she clutched him so fiercely that he feared she would break his neck.

He stayed inside her until dawn's first dusty rays began their daily invasion of that iniquitous place, only then parting and adjusting his clothing and hers while she slept on, a smile of deep contentment on her beloved face. He lay quietly, not wanting to wake her, disturbed in his quiet contemplation by the movement of one of the women to the bucket and the loud, squelching splatter of soft faeces leaving her body.

The act brought home to him, as nothing else could possibly have done, the depth of degradation to which he had fallen. His life to that point had been hard, and shit was something with which he was well acquainted, collecting and distributing it on his fields, but to be subjected to this closeness to the depositing of body waste by a female stranger in full view was something he would have wished never to experience.

He sat up, facing determinedly away from the other cell, and tried not to think of their future.

Martha awoke soon afterwards, and they sat arm in arm on the uncomfortable floor, with no knowledge of how the day would unfold.

At just after seven of the clock, they heard footsteps descending the stairs and expected to see the ghoulish jailer from the evening before, but this time a dark haired young man of some twenty summers came bounding across to them, a big open smile on his face, followed closely by a grinning, blue-eyed, fair-headed urchin of about seven, his outward attributes betraying a long distant Viking ancestor who, while raiding, had left his seed in the county. Behind him appeared another well-dressed man of about thirty summers, wearing a wig.

The first young man greeted them with, 'Good morning to you. I am Jasper. Break your fast now,' He passed in chunks of the same, low quality bread as the night before, but double the thickness and then poured a flagon of water and handed it in. Thomas was not to be caught out again so easily and asked, 'May we have two cups, please, sir?'

The young man laughed, 'Your request tells me that you have fallen foul of Cutter. Of course, you may have two cups of water and more if you wish. Of bread, I can give you no more, but water is free from the pump. And there is no need to call me sir. I am told that your station in life, though now in doubt, far exceeds my own, so the epithet, if used, should go the other way.' He leaned closer, jerked his head towards the women opposite and spoke in a whisper to Thomas, 'Did he…?'

Thomas nodded.

The lad grimaced and shook his head in disgust. 'He is an animal.'

Martha insisted that Thomas drink first, just in case, but the lad was true to his word and refilled the flagon three more times.

He then introduced his youthful companion, ruffling the boy's hair as he said, 'This is Fartbox. He will take your night soil out to the street. If you give him a farthing and thus double his day's pay he may also wash it for you.'

Thomas sighed, 'Alas, I have no money.'

48

He was astonished when Martha's hand came in sight holding a coin of that denomination; a coin that was snatched with the speed of an adder strike by the urchin's fist.

He turned and lifted his eyebrows enquiringly, and she said, 'I brought the contents of the box. It was no use left there.' The box, which resided on the mantelpiece, contained the only coins they possessed.

'How much do we have?'

'One shilling and nine pence three farthings, now reduced by one farthing to a half penny.'

Jasper unlocked the door and Fartbox crossed to the bucket, heaved it up and bore it out of the cell. Jasper removed the one from the women's cell and the urchin picked that up also. Jumping up the stairs two at a time he happily allowed the contents to slop over the sides of the buckets, taking no account as it spread onto his slippers and the stone treads, adding to the already foul-smelling atmosphere in the dungeon. Outside, he took the bucket to the gutter and poured the waste onto the encrusted, stinking mass of drying faeces and piss already there. No heavy rain had fallen for three months, and the mess would remain there until it fell again. It was the same story across the whole of the city, and, indeed, of every city in England, and citizens walked through it daily, accepting it as part of the rich pageant of their lives. He then danced over to the communal pump below the Guildhall, waited his turn while women filled jugs, then filled one of the buckets with water and used his bitten-down nails to scrub at the hardened faeces around the top and his hands to wash the softer mess at the bottom, until the bucket was at least somewhat less abhorrent. The women's bucket he left in its filthy, stinking state, making no effort to clean it.

Below, Jasper handed the women their breakfast, and Thomas was relieved to see that last night's performance was not repeated, nor attempted by the women as they were fed with bread alone.

The third visitor introduced himself, 'I am James Pomeroy, attorney. I am told you are a gentleman and thus will, no doubt, have need of my services.'

Thomas sighed, 'Alas, that will not be possible. As you have no doubt heard we have no money.'

'Ah. I see, but you do have a fine pair of boots and buskins to match. Where you are bound they will not remain in your possession for many minutes, and your life could well be forfeit while they are forcibly removed. If you give them to me I promise to provide you with what services I can, ensure that while you are incarcerated here you are well fed, with meat, eggs and fish as well as bread, and send you clogs to replace the boots.'

Fartbox returned with the pails, which were put back into the cells, and Jasper handed him his breakfast slice of bread, which he grabbed with the hand he had used to clean the bucket and began to eat with gusto. He and Jasper listened while Thomas outlined their problem.

Pomeroy's frown deepened as the tale unfolded. When Thomas ended it, the attorney offered, 'I fear that your sentence is a foregone conclusion. There is nothing I can do to stop it, but I can, just possibly, restrict it to seven years, at least for your wife. The fact that Rainforde spared your life when he could, under present English law, so easily have taken it and with the full force of that law behind him, will lie heavily on the judges. I understand his cunning actions. Should any query into the case be made, he would wish to appear completely blameless in the matter, and he will know in any case that the outcome will not differ. As an acknowledged gentleman, you will have the benefit of a jury of your peers, but that will be of little moment, since bribery is ever a factor with them, as it is, I fear I must admit, with the judges, and they will listen to direction from him. A noble lord has brought you to court, and his word will be accepted without question above yours. Your only tiny hope is this man Smith. His entries in the ledger are those that are in dispute. Though Rainforde would deny that they were forgeries, it might perchance help your case if we could have him as a witness. You say he was dismissed. Have you any idea where he might be found?'

'He is old and frail. I believe he would have taken himself in the direction of Norwich but would have tried for sustenance and shelter at the Hellesdon poorhouse.'

'In that case I shall try that establishment first.'

Thomas sighed again and unlaced his boots and buskins, hoping that his father would understand and forgive him.

Two hours later Jasper again bounded down the stairs and came up to the bars of their cell carrying a pair of clogs, which he passed to Thomas. He then produced two hard-boiled eggs from his pocket and gave them to Martha with a flourish.

'You have serious enemies.' He told Thomas, 'Money has changed hands to have you transferred to the Castle today.'

'And Martha?'

'She stays. You go. They are on their way here now.'

They heard the door above open and heavy footfalls on the stairs. Thomas slipped the clogs on, turned quickly and kissed his wife as two burly men came into view. The larger of the two issued the order to Jasper, 'Open up!'

Thomas did not wait to be grabbed but walked out of the cell voluntarily.

One of the men preceded and one followed him as he climbed the stairs. At the top, his hands were manacled, and he was pushed outside and marched towards the forbidding stone walls of the gaunt looking square Castle a quarter mile away, no less forbidding with the bright sunshine turning the grey of the stone to ochre.

Climbing the mound, he felt the full weight of his new state. The building had the strength to withstand a lengthy siege by an army and would guard his body with cold, inhumane vehemence.

The huge double doors, of centuries-old oak studded with blackened ironwork, opened to the knock of one of his jailers, and Thomas was bundled inside and down a long corridor, which echoed with the sound of metal being struck with a hammer. There hung in the air a smell with which he was at that time unfamiliar, but which he would later feel would never leave him: the smell of incarceration, the convict smell, like no other on earth; a base odour of decay like that of a tomb containing a long dead corpse, vying with a confused melange of putrid body excrescences.

The sound increased until they reached a room to the right. Inside it, there stood a giant of a man, naked to the waist, below which he wore a thick leather apron. With his massive right hand he was wielding a four-pound hammer, smashing it down onto the end of a red-hot glowing rod, held by a clamp in his other hand.

On the bench behind him lay the results of his labours: half a dozen sets of leg shackles; short bars on which ran two metal rings.

He stopped pounding and pointed to a low stool by the bench. The two warders indicated to Thomas that he should sit.

The blacksmith pushed over an even lower stool and lifted Thomas' feet up onto it. He slid one large metal ring over each leg, shoved a bar through the smaller rings on the sides of the larger ones until it came up against its heavily burred-over end stop. Then, with a pair of long pincers, he brought over a glowing curved piece of metal, one end of which he inserted in the small ring at the other end of the bar before using a second set of pincers to curl the ends till they met. He brought over a pail of water, dipped his cupped hands into it and threw the liquid onto his work, causing a small cloud of steam to rise and Thomas to issue a silent thanks for the end to the pain of burning on the skin of his leg. Twice more the blacksmith applied the water before feeling the metal to make sure it had cooled sufficiently.

Shackled now, Thomas was pushed and cajoled along the corridor again. Another sound became audible, at first an indistinguishable hum, like thousands of angry bees disturbed at their nest, but with each step it grew louder, until he could recognise it as a babble of human speech, and as they descended a long set of stone stairs at the end of the corridor he could distinguish individual voices.

As they came into view the noise stopped dead, as if switched off by a superior being, and over fifty pairs of eyes assessed the newcomers.

Thomas saw two aged jailors seated on a bench and watched as one of them rose to his feet with difficulty to unlock the cage.

The two men with Thomas took one arm each and with malice aforethought lifted him a foot in the air and threw him bodily onto the stone floor, taking skin off both arms and hands as he tried to save himself.

As he rolled his eyes caught a gesture from one of his erstwhile warders, a flick of the head towards Thomas, with his eyes directed to a big, bearded hulk of a man who had the look of a gypsy about him, wearing better clothing than most in the cage.

Thomas saw the man give a nod of understanding, and a shiver ran through him. He had been marked out, and now he knew the reason for his transfer to the Castle. It did not require a mental genius to see the hand of Rainforde behind it, and the obvious intent.

He crawled to the back of the cage and almost fell into a foul-smelling hole with wet faeces adhering to its top and sides; the Castle's alternative to a bucket. He shuffled away from it and sat down close to the wall.

The mumbling began again around him, but no one approached him or attempted to speak. Few even looked. He took stock of his cellmates; more than fifty men and half a dozen boys, the latter ranging in age from about six to eleven. He felt more alone than at any time in his life in the midst of all those bodies.

The weak light came from open bowman slits high up in the walls, and as the afternoon faded towards nightfall bread was brought in by four warders and passed through the bars. Thomas tried to work his way through the crush for his portion, keeping an eye out for the gypsy, but by the time he reached the front there was no food left. He managed to obtain two handfuls of water, however, poured from a pewter jug into his cupped hands.

He resumed his place and as night fell was determined to stay awake, knowing an attack was imminent and hoping to be able to fend it off. As the hours passed, to the sounds of heavy farting and snoring were added the heartrending cries of children; screams and sobbing, punctuated by the grunts and groans of male bodies exerting themselves and carrying out God knew what inhuman acts on their unwilling victims.

In the early hours, however, he dozed but came awake in a flash, to find hands like hams around his neck, forcing the life from him. He tried to fight, pounding with his fists at his assailant, but in vain. Life was slipping from him and lights were flashing across his eyes when suddenly the hands went from his neck, and he felt the body holding his down become a dead weight. He rolled to remove it, gasping for air in his ruptured throat, gradually regaining full consciousness and awareness, knowing that the slimy liquid on his hands was that of the dead man's blood. He rubbed them hard on the clothing of the body, with which he found himself isolated. In the pitch darkness of the dungeon, he was aware than there were no live bodies close to him. All had moved away, afraid to be associated with the deed.

He stayed awake for the rest of the night and as the first vestiges of grey appeared through the slits he used what vision he had to crawl behind the crowd, even though he had to pass close to the noxious latrine.

Not long passed before the same four men as before came down the steps. This time one of them shouted, 'Bring out your dead.'

The body of a boy of about ten, his throat slit and with blood soaked clothes, was pulled forward, along with that of an old, white-haired, rake-thin man. They were hauled unceremoniously out of the cage, the door of which was almost closed again when an anonymous shout rose from the back of the throng, 'There's another.'

One of the jailers came into the cage and walked around until he came upon the body. When he did so he drew back in surprise and blurted, 'S'wive me! T'is Black Jack!'

After jabbing his toe into the body to make sure it was dead he shouted, 'Charles, I need a hand.'

His fellow jailor joined him and between them they dragged the heavy body out of the cage.

Every one of the jailors stood looking down in wonder at the corpse and at the large, bloody stab wound in its back.

When the bodies had been cleared, breakfast was brought. This time, Thomas was determined to be at the front for his share but found that he had no necessity to shove his way through. As he approached, the crowd in front parted like magic for him, much as his Bible described the parting of the Red Sea for Moses.

He was served first and received a double handful of pottage and two slices of bread.

Afterwards, he found that several of the men nodded to him, though none spoke, and he realised that he was seen as their benefactor, having relieved them of a hated sore in their sides. It was clear that he not been the only recipient of the gypsy's attentions.

Life became a well organised round, in essence little different to his life outside, which had involved working, eating, sleeping, defecating, urinating and, when lack of fatigue allowed, fornicating. Now only the first and last were absent from his daily round, though some of his fellow prisoners would not accept the loss of the last. Not one of them had attempted a conversation with him, for which to some extent he was grateful.

On his twentieth day in the Castle, he saw Pomeroy descending the stairs and went over to the bars to speak to him, surprised when the jailor opened the gate to allow him out to converse with the attorney by the bottom of the stairs.

'Martha is well.' Pomeroy told him. 'She asked me to tell you that she is well fed and as comfortable as possible. She particularly asked me to give you a certain message, which was "All is well". I trust you understand the meaning?'

Thomas nodded, 'I do.' Martha had missed her menses and was with child. His heart bounded.

'I also carry bad news, however. The man Smith did go to the poorhouse in Hellesdon and had been there for a day when he was called outside to see a visitor. Since he had not returned within the hour, a serving wench was sent outside to look for him. She found him stabbed to death on the path near the door. His assailant had disappeared and was no doubt well on the way to London or the coast, his pockets lined with gold. We have, therefore, no way of refuting Rainforde's allegations. I am sorry.'

Thomas sighed, 'You have done your best, for which I thank you.'

Pomeroy nodded, 'I tried. I shall, of course, be there at your trial and will make the best defence I can for you, although the outcome is in no doubt.' He shook hands and left, and Thomas was let back into the cage.

On the morning of the fifteenth of November, his name and that of eleven others were called out, and they assembled in front of the cage. Stumbling and falling in their unwonted shackles, they were herded up the stairs and along the draughty corridor leading to the main doors. Outside, four warders waited to escort them to the Guildhall, looking as miserable as the prisoners in a cold, steady, misty drizzle.

The convicts shuffled their way down the hill towards Castle Meadow, recently planted along the bottom of the mound with cherry trees, now long past flowering and looking as droopy and miserable as the men, with raindrops streaming from their late autumn leaves.

Thomas was surprised to see a crowd waiting on the roadside below, but the jailers knew what was to come and were dreading it, having endured it many times before.

News of an Assize always brought hundreds to the centre of the city. Entertainment for the poor was restricted to public hangings, miscreants in the stocks and this: the gauntlet run by convicts on their way to trial. For days, ammunition had been set aside in readiness, and the moment the little convoy reached the road it began.

Rotting vegetables and fruit of all sorts and scores of rotten eggs began to pelt the convicts and the jailers, along with lumps of shit picked up from the gutters and hurled by urchins, while filthy abuse was screamed at them from all sides.

Their torment was unending, as they descended the steps at Davey Place, shuffled through the Back of the Inns and continued on to the Market Place, where the crowd and the amount of ammunition hurled increased.

Thomas' hair, face and clothes, like those of the other convicts and their escorts, ran with a stinking mixture of egg, faeces and rotting vegetable matter, the smell of hydrogen sulphide strong in his nostrils.

Entering the Guildhall was a blessed relief from the bombardment but brought no betterment in their condition.

They were herded into a room large enough for four bodies to stand comfortably. The twelve of them were crushed together like pigs in a pen at the market, their stinking bodies in such close proximity to one another that there was little room to move an arm and scarce enough to breathe. The man nearest to a door other than that through which they had arrived, tried it, but found it locked.

Above them, they could hear the sound of dozens of feet moving and stamping and loud conversation, interspersed with peels of laughter. Thomas knew enough of what happened at Assizes to realise that there waited for them above a crowd as rowdy and eager for entertainment as their erstwhile attackers. There was to be little of any legal niceties attached to the proceedings.

Someone near him farted loudly; a long, blattering fart that seemed to go on for almost a minute, and men swore as the foul smell rose in air already tainted with the ordure clinging to their persons and clothes.

The noise above abated suddenly, and it was obvious that the judges had arrived at their benches.

The door to the court was unlocked and pulled open by a jailor who indicated with a slight flick of his head that they were to follow him, and one by one they negotiated the steep stairs with difficulty, restricted as they were by the leg irons.

Above, they found themselves in a cage no larger than that below, with a view of the court through a trellised partition.

The whole courtroom was crowded; the public galleries with citizens from all levels of society, but that on the left predominantly full of affluent men and women, the latter flaunting themselves with huge, feather embellished hats while the men attempted to outdo one another in long frock-coats with buttons of silver and flamboyant waistcoats of scarlet, royal blue, purple, pink and the latest fashion, light grey. At the very front of that gallery was a figure of hate: Silas Rainforde, dressed to the nines, with a cherry red waistcoat beneath a stylish grey topcoat, white pantaloons and an elegant stovepipe hat worn at a jaunty angle. He stood silently, expectantly.

To the right, another gallery held what appeared to Thomas to be a mixture of riff-raff, their clothing no better than his everyday apparel. All appeared eager for the fray. In front of that gallery sat the twelve members of the jury, not one of whom, to Thomas' eyes, had the slightest appearance of a gentleman. Rather did they appear to be merchants of one kind and another, one quite obviously a butcher, still wearing his bloody apron.

Directly in front of them, on the opposite side of the hall, sat the five judges, with the senior judge in the centre.

There was a general low hum of conversation.

A bailiff banged his staff on the oaken floor and bellowed, 'This Court of Assizes for the City of Norwich now in session. Judge Harold Arthurton.'

He consulted a scroll and shouted, 'Helena Gray.'

From another box to the right of the male victims, sealed off from their gaze by a wooden wall, came a scraggy, lanky female of some thirty years of age, filthy blond hair falling over her unlovely face and wearing what could only be described as rags, her arm held firmly by a warder.

She was taken to the box used by the accused and the warder remained by her side. The woman glared belligerently at her surroundings and at the judges.

The bailiff read out the charge, 'that the said Helena Gray has carried out the act of prostitution with a citizen of this City and received monetary reward for said act.'

One of the junior judges asked, 'Helena Gray, how do you plead, guilty or not guilty?'

She had been before the bench enough times to know that to plead guilty gave the best chance of a reduced sentence. She answered, 'Guilty.'

The senior judge then spoke, 'You will be subjected to an inspection for disease. If found, you will be imprisoned until healed. If you are found to be free of infection you will be imprisoned for one month.'

In the galleries loud conversation started, and Thomas heard several mentions of 'pox'. Feet were banged on the floor.

The bailiff hit the floor with his staff again and shouted, 'Silence!'

The woman was removed, and the next name was called. This time, Thomas saw that it was the younger woman from the cell opposite to that which he had shared with Martha when imprisoned below in the Guildhall, and a warm feeling spread through his breast at the thought that his beloved wife could be just feet away from him at that moment.

The woman in the dock tossed her unkempt, shoulder length hair as she cockily regarded her judges and betters. Again the charge was read out, and a plea of 'guilty' was made, with the same recommendation from the judge.

As she was about to be led away, she cheekily lifted her skirts to show the judges her delights and shouted, 'Come and see me any time, dearies.'

This time the uproar and hilarity in the galleries was louder and full of ribald shouts to the woman. The bailiff had to wait for several minutes before order could be restored.

The older prostitute was sentenced next but went quietly, to the obvious dismay of the crowd.

The bailiff shouted, 'Henry Stock', and a tall, cadaverous individual to the right of Thomas began to move.

The warder who had accompanied the convicts into the box took the man's arm and led him down to face the court.

The charge was read out, 'That you did, on the sixteenth of August, remove and steal a grey palfrey from Alwyn's Meadow, Cringleford, the property of Jacob Keen.'

The man had had the misfortune to steal the horse from a citizen who could afford to have him arrested and taken to court. The law was such that legal action in cases of attack against the person or property was solely in the remit of the person so injured, and the expense of taking the offender to law was entirely met by the plaintiff. Thousands of offenders escaped an appearance in court for that reason alone, and many thieves depended on it for their continued freedom.

'What say you, Jacob Keen?'

A rotund, middle-aged man, prematurely bald and with a glass left eye, stood up in the gallery behind the jurors and stated, 'I had left my horse in the meadow after returning from the inn at ten of the evening and closed the gate. The next morning I found the meadow empty. There had been a heavy dew, and I followed the trail of footsteps and hoof marks for two miles to a field rented by Henry Stock, where I saw him feeding the animal. I returned to town and called the constable, who came and arrested Stock.'

The judge asked, 'How do you plead, guilty or not guilty.'

Knowing the prescribed punishment Stock was shaking with fear as he gulped and gasped out, 'I found the horse in my field and was feeding him because he looked hungry.'

'Are you trying to maintain that you are not guilty?'

Stock nodded, 'Yes, your Honour. Not guilty.'

The judge emitted a loud, disbelieving 'Hmphh!' and looked down at the jury, 'What say you, gentlemen?'

A whispered conversation between the men in the jury box lasted less than twenty seconds before the foreman stood up with their verdict, 'Guilty.'

The judge nodded at their collected wisdom and told Stock, 'You have been found guilty by a jury of your peers of the crime of horse stealing, which is a capital offence. You will be taken from here and hanged at Norwich Castle tomorrow morning at dawn.'

Stock collapsed onto the floor and was dragged from there to the cells by two ushers.

One after another of the offenders were brought before the court, charged and sentenced. Only two were found 'Not guilty'. Thomas had just two fellow convicts remaining in the box with him when his name was called, and he was led down to face the court.

As he descended the steps he first noticed a bewigged Pomeroy sitting at a table to the left with five other attorneys, then caught the movement of the senior judge's head as he turned to look up at the public gallery. Thomas followed his gaze and knew his fate was sealed when he saw Silas Rainforde nod meaningfully to the judge.

The latter gazed on Thomas with undisguised disgust.

'You come before us described as a gentleman, Thomas Nash, but you have not the slightest vestige of that appellation about your person, Sirrah. Gentlemen are not prone to the wearing of clogs, or the application of ordure as part of their daily apparel. To me, and I am sure to the rest of the court, you have the appearance of common riff-raff.' The entire courtroom broke out into hilarious laughter, with many shouted curses addressed to Thomas, and the judge gazed around him, nodding at what he perceived as merriment at his clever remarks. He waited until it died somewhat before ordering, 'Read the charge, bailiff.'

The official did as requested, 'That you knowingly and with malice aforethought made efforts to obtain pecuniary advantage of Lord Silas Rainforde by false pretences; to whit, by demanding payment for goods and services having already received such payment in full.'

With a derogatory sneer towards where the advocates sat, the judge continued, 'It seems that you have legal representation, of some sort at least.' He looked down his nose disdainfully in the direction of the defence attorney's position. 'Attorney Pomeroy, do you wish to make a statement on behalf of this criminal?' The use of the word by a judge in relation to an as yet unconvicted defendant was common, and one not at that time to be questioned by an attorney.

'I do, my Lord. The items in question were entered into a ledger by one Josiah Smith, the factotum of the former Lord Rainforde, Lord Silas Rainforde's deceased uncle, and it seems there is some discrepancy in the matter of whether payment was made on delivery of the items, which is, as Your Honour knows, not common practice in large households, payment normally being made only once a year, at Michaelmas. My client insists that not only were no payments made to him during the year, but also that the deed of ownership of his land, which was to have been returned to him on this anniversary on payment of a final fifteen guineas, has been withheld.'

The judge glared down on Pomeroy with open contempt, 'At the request of the plaintiff I have personally inspected both the entries in the ledger of which you speak and the original agreement between the parties' ancestors pertaining to the large loan magnanimously made by the Rainforde family to their impecunious neighbours, and have found both to be completely in order. I have seen nothing to persuade me that any amount has ever been paid to reduce the total amount of that loan and have been advised that nothing but the yearly interest has been paid each year. It follows, therefore, that the land in question continues to belong in its entirety to the givers of that loan.'

Pommeroy tried again, 'It seems, your Honour, that the Nash family has always trusted the successive Lords Rainforde, who alone have kept the records of payments made over the eighty-five years of the loan's existence.'

'Then more fool them if it were true, which I am assured it is not. This man Smith you refer to, I take it you have him here as a witness to explain his entries in the ledger?' The judge looked up at Rainforde, grinning knowingly.

'Unfortunately, your Honour, upon looking for Smith, I found that he, while at the poor house in Hellesdon, was murdered by person or persons unknown.'

The judge adjusted the ruffles of his sleeves, indicating clearly how unimportant he considered the matter, 'How remiss of him when we need him as a witness. So you have no others?'

'No, your Honour.'

'I see no hint of honesty in the claims of your so-called client, nor in the man himself. He has to me the face and appearance of an unmitigated scoundrel, who should be punished to the full extent of the law. In my considered opinion t'is pity the offence is not a hanging one. What is his plea?'

'Not guilty, my Lord.'

'Members of the jury, how find you?'

The senior juryman immediately stood without consulting his colleagues.

'Guilty as charged, my Lord.'

The judge nodded with satisfaction and pronounced, 'Thomas Nash, you have been found guilty by a jury of your peers. You are sentenced to fourteen years' transportation. Take him down.'

As Thomas was led back below he heard Martha's name called and tried frantically to stay on the last step to obtain a glance at her beloved face, but was shoved roughly from behind into the holding room, where the two remaining convicts waited their turn.

He asked the warder, 'Could you open the door just a trifle, please, sir. It is my wife being tried.'

The warder, a man who had heard every tearful story imaginable during his eleven years' service at the court and was in no way a humanitarian, had a mind to refuse, but something in Thomas' expression told him that what he was hearing was the truth, and he considered for a moment what his feelings would be were he in the same position as this man before him. He opened the door a fraction and beckoned Thomas forward.

With his ear to the crack he could hear the judge's comments and Pomeroy's attempts at amelioration. Surprisingly, there was little in the way of merriment from the gallery and quiet after the sentence was passed, 'Seven years transportation.'

Thomas was surprised to remain in the waiting room, but a few minutes later he understood why.

Pomeroy came in to see him, looking grim.

'Rainforde had the judge and jury in his pocket. He had them bought and paid for. You had no chance. Fourteen years was the maximum he could give, but at least he did not include hard labour, although that is what it will no doubt turn out to be. Here, I brought you some food.'

Thomas thanked him and took the offering: slices of roast chicken wrapped in fresh bread; the best meal he had had since leaving home.

He wolfed the food while Pomeroy watched, and when the last morsel had disappeared he told the advocate, 'You did your best, and I am thankful for your efforts, but tell me, how can we be transported? I understood that transportation ended after the American Revolutionary War.'

'It did. Apparently there are moves afoot for convicts to be taken to New Holland instead.'

'New Holland? But is that not…'

'At the far end of the world, yes, beyond Asia; a journey of many months.'

'And shall Martha travel with me?'

Pomeroy shook his head, 'I have no way of knowing, Thomas, but see, I must be leaving; I have another client to attend to. I wish you well.' He held out his hand, his countenance showing his concern and fears for Thomas' future.

As he watched the man depart, the deepest sense of loss he had ever felt in a life strewn with disastrous losses came over Thomas; not of freedom, although that was a part, but of the loss of free will. He had always been his own man, doing his own thing his way, rightly or wrongly, making his own mistakes and having his own successes. It seemed he would never have that choice again.

CHAPTER SEVEN

Captain Arthur Phillip, later to become Admiral and First Governor of New South Wales, descended from the carriage with not the slightest idea why had had been summoned to the Admiralty.

Joining the Navy as a boy, he had, by the end of the Seven Year's war, reached the rank of lieutenant. After a spell as a landsman, he joined the Portuguese Navy with the rank of Captain and passed an eventful three years, during which his ship was almost lost in a storm, only saved by the convicts he was carrying, and later, in a sea action, he captured a large Spanish galleon, of which he was made Captain.

Stories of his exploits became legend, and in 1778 he returned to service as a lieutenant with the British Navy, later promoted to Captain and given a command.

Aware of Phillip's knowledge of the South American coastline, Thomas Townshend, later to become Lord Sydney, had asked his advice for a raid across the Atlantic. Phillip obliged with a daring plan, in which he expected to see more action, but was disappointed in that expectation when the war ended. Sydney, however, had remembered the officer's usefulness, and though Phillip was unaware of it, it was the reason for the summons he was now answering.

Since it was no longer possible to transport convicts to America, some other destination had to be found. The coast of Africa was considered, but rejected due to the warlike reception found whenever parties were landed there. Lord Sydney, now Secretary of State for the Home Office, in consultation with Lord Sandwich, whose name would forever be remembered as the originator of that particular item of food, Sir Joseph Banks and other notable persons had decided upon New Holland as the destination.

Phillip was directed to the office of the Admiral of the Fleet, where he was astonished to find awaiting him an elite group of senior officials, comprising John Montague, the Fourth Earl of Sandwich and long time First Lord of the Admiralty, Lord

Sydney, Philip Stephens, Secretary of the Admiralty, Sir Gilbert Elliot, Treasurer of the Navy, and the President of the Royal Society, Joseph Banks.

Phillip had heard vague rumours of a fleet to the Antipodes but was astonished when told that he had been selected to organise and be in charge of the entire project.

A talented multi-linguist, he had a brain that could compartmentalise with ease, and though he recognised it as the massive task it was, he was sure he could achieve the required aims.

Lord Sydney told him, 'You will be Commodore of a fleet of twelve ships: the flagship, *'Sirius'*, whose second captain will be Captain John Hunter, with whom I know you have served. The second naval vessel is the *'Supply'* under the command of Lieutenant Lidgbird Ball. There are seven convict transports, *'Lady Penrhyn'*, *'Prince of Wales'*, *'Friendship'*, *'Jayne Doe'*, *'Scarborough'*, *'Alexander'* and *'Charlotte'* and there will also be three supply transports. We are deciding at this moment on their selection.

Most of the ships are already in Portsmouth or on their way there. Once on land you will become the First Governor of New South Wales, and exercise full legal rights, with the power of life and death over the King's subjects there, both convict and free man.

Lord Sandwich has told us of your exploits and of the devilishly clever ideas you have come up with. The most important point I can make is that our trust in you is so complete that from this moment you have absolute freedom in organising and carrying out this project. These documents contain all that you need to know as to what has so far been arranged. What are your thoughts?'

Phillip could immediately see the potential pitfalls and dangers in the scheme, not least of which was the shepherding of so many ships on a journey of almost fifteen thousand miles, many with civilian crews not under Royal Naval discipline, but he was not only a successful seaman but also a man of learning, and he had complete faith in his own abilities. Above all, this was a once-in-a-lifetime chance of a great leap in his career and an interesting one to boot.

He drew himself to his full height, 'I shall do my very best, my Lord.'

The men around him nodded with pleasure.

There would be many, many times in the days and months ahead when he would look back on that moment and bitterly regret his eager acceptance.

CHAPTER EIGHT

After being returned to the Castle, under attack from the mob again, as on the way to the Guildhall, life returned to what passed for normal in the dungeon.

Thomas found that he was still accorded the same rite of passage when going for food and made way for if he approached the latrine hole for that most difficult of bodily functions with both legs shackled together.

Men and boys died; sometimes one, sometimes more, always at night and rarely naturally. Petty squabbles broke out, but never once concerning him. One day followed another, and it seemed the status quo would never end, until a day he reckoned to be the second of May seventeen eighty-seven, when his name and the names of seven others, six men and a nine year-old boy, were called out by the jailors before breakfast.

They made their way to the door of the cage and were let out, to make the same difficult ascent of the stairs, and the journey down the long corridor.

This time, they found an open farm wagon with two aged carthorses spanned, waiting just beyond the door. Four warders they had not seen before stood by its side, rubbing their hands and smacking their arms around their bodies, trying to keep warm; three middle-aged men and one much younger, in his mid twenties.

A late frost covered the roofs and grass, and though the breeze was light it came from the northeast; a 'lazy' wind that seemed to drive straight through the body, instead of around it. Within seconds, the convicts were shaking with cold, their ragged, thin clothing no protection at all.

They were bundled on board and found that the cart was fitted with planks on either side, forming benches on which to sit; an unexpected luxury, and they squeezed close to one another in an effort to obtain warmth.

The warders climbed up, two to sit on the benches with them, the others on the front bank, with one of them holding the reins.

The horses were told to 'Gee up!' and set off at a pace slower even than that of a man walking.

They descended the Mound and Timber Hill, passing the hostelry called the Blue Bell, before turning right to drive along Castle Meadow and then down via Tombland and past the Cathedral to the ancient, stone Bishops Bridge, with its forbidding guard tower, built at the site of the old Lollards Pit where religious heretics had been burned at the stake during the fifteenth and sixteenth centuries. Once over the bridge they turned right along Riverside Road, following the course of the river, where dozens of coastal trading ships were moored along both banks, and then turned left onto Thorpe Road. Thomas knew almost for certain then where they were headed. From the position of the morning sun he reckoned they were heading due east, and the only possible destinations were the market town of Acle, where there was no prison and precious little of anything else of note, and the town of Great Yarmouth, given the designation 'Great' by King John in 1207; the port at the head of the River Yare, close to where the Roman fort of Gariannonum had stood so many centuries before.

If Yarmouth was to be their destination it could mean but one thing: they were to take ship there.

It was an important port, where much shipbuilding went on, but Thomas doubted that a journey to the far ends of the earth would begin there. Whatever, there was nothing he could do about it, and what would be would be. Acceptance had become a way of life.

The old horses plodded their way along beside the river at Thorpe, still heading east.

The convicts and their jailers were so numb with cold in the open cart that not a word was spoken, not even by the warders, each man's mind almost as frozen as his body.

The sun climbed higher in the sky, and though no discernable heat came from it by the time that they drove up the slope out of Thorpe it had melted the frost on the grass.

Almost five hours after they left the Castle, having stopped only once for the men to relieve themselves, the driver reined in close to an inn, with a sign above the door *'The Kings Head'* in the straggling street that was at that time Acle; just the inn, a score or so of hovels and the Saxon church of St Edmunds. The sky had cleared of high cirrus, the breeze had dropped, and the sun was finally giving sufficient warmth for the travellers to feel their limbs again.

The three older warders jumped down and entered the inn, from which came sounds of laughter and merriment. One, the warder Thomas had marked as the warder he would least like to fall foul of, a man with a sly, vicious look about him, came out from the inn with a brimming tankard of ale and a warm meat pie, which he passed up to the younger man who was still in his earlier position on the driving seat.

The man turned, about to go back into the inn, when Thomas was amazed to hear one of the convicts, a man he had never heard speak before, ask, 'Are we to have food?'

It was more than brave of the man, since such temerity was easily enough to occasion a severe beating, and Thomas and the other convicts looked at the man with new interest. Thin as a beanpole and with a long, angular, sick-looking face, he was a man of some sixty summers and spoke with an educated voice, with no trace of the strong Norfolk accent.

The warder he had addressed regarded him angrily and with a sneer said, 'I suppose Your Honour has the wherewithal to pay for it?'

The man seemed to draw himself up with self-possession and amazed all of them by declaring, 'I have half a crown.'

The looks on the faces of the convicts would have made a fine picture. In the parlous state they were in, half a crown was akin to a king's ransom. Surely this old man was lying or had lost leave of his senses?

The sly look on the warder's face had deepened, 'Give it to me. I will bring you food.'

The younger warder surprised Thomas by his tone of authority when he gave his older colleague a withering look and gritted, 'And we all know that that will be the last anyone ever sees of it, Jacob, do we not?' He turned and addressed the old man, 'If you have such a coin pass it to me. I will buy food for you.'

The older warder's face suffused with blood and he clenched his fists, his vicious anger obvious, but equally obvious was his inferior standing with the young man, who blithely ordered, 'You can stay on watch.'

The old man fumbled with his clothing, feeling along the lower edge of his short jacket until he found the stiff edge of the coin he had sewn into the garment months before. He lifted the material to his mouth and chewed at it until eventually the stitching gave way and he was able to extract the coin; a bright, glinting, solid silver half crown.

He passed it to the man on his right, and it was then passed hand to hand, each man gazing at it lovingly while he held it, until it lay safe in the young man's palm.

He jumped down from the cart and ran into the inn, deliberately catching the older warder's shoulder with his own as he passed and almost spinning him around.

Minutes later he emerged again carrying a large tray, heavy with steaming pies, which he passed up to the convicts, their eyes huge with anticipation, then went back into the inn, to return laden with a large pitcher of ale and several pint flagons.

From a group of bedraggled, disillusioned, downtrodden dregs of men, who had never exchanged a word one with another, the group became animated, excited, communicating individuals.

The unwonted ale quickly went to their heads, and with their stomachs filling they suddenly felt that life might just perchance still be worth living. It was something of a miracle and not to be lessened by the glares they were receiving from the warder left watching them.

The younger man came out again, finishing a pie he held in his hand, and he jerked his head to indicate to the older man that he could go to finish his meal.

He climbed back up onto the cart and asked, 'How did you come by the coin?'

The old man swallowed the piece of meat he was chewing and said, 'I had much, much more, but had not the time to recover it when the constable came to arrest me.'

Thomas asked, 'What was your crime?'

A look of deep sadness came over the old man's face, 'My dear sir, I committed no crime; not once during my entire life. I was the major domo for the same gentleman for over forty years, and always had the reading of the books in his library. We had become more like companions in our old age; friends even. He suffered a severe stroke and though he seemed to recover, his brain had been affected more than we in the household knew. One evening, I was reading a book in my room when a constable burst in and arrested me for stealing it. My master had called him when he found the book missing from its shelf. When we went below, my master, who appeared fully compos mentis, said he knew me not; I was a thief broke in to despoil his house. Despite my entreaties, I was taken from the house and incarcerated.'

It was a tale told in many variations every day of the year, all over the country. Though highway robbers, smugglers, thieves, pickpockets and card sharps abounded, they for the most part ran free while innocent men were so often flogged, imprisoned and hanged.

One by one they gave their stories.

Only two of the men admitted to being guilty; the man next to Thomas on his left, who had been arrested for misdealing at cards, and another opposite, who had bludgeoned his wife's lover, though he had stopped short of killing him. The boy, who told them his name was Peter, had the most poignant story of all. His master, a farmer, had sent him to drive a pig to market.

Unbeknown to the boy, after he had left the farm his master had imbibed a great deal of ale and had fallen from his seat on the farm wagon and beneath the wheels, dying from his wounds where he lay.

At the edge of the town, a constable had become suspicious seeing a boy in charge of a pig and had arrested him for stealing it. The boy told his story, and when the constable and two others went to check its veracity they found the farmer dead. It was assumed that the boy knew of the death and had subsequently stolen the pig, intending to pocket the proceeds of the sale for himself. He stayed locked up.

The constable, not one to look a gift pig in the mouth, sold it to a farmer at the market and kept the payment, knowing that if he handed it to his superior it would only end up in that individual's pocket.

At court, his testimony had ensured Peter's sentence. The boy stopped speaking suddenly, looking embarrassed. He did not want to tell them of the painful indignities he had suffered in the prison.

Before any questions could be asked, the other warders returned to the cart, and they set off again, an almost convivial party in the now warm sun.

The remaining seven miles took them along the rutted road that led across the marshes, dead straight but for one slight kink half a mile from Acle.

Thomas had never been to that part of the county before, although he knew the history of the area and the work that the Dutchmen had done to drain and reclaim the land from the sea by the formation of dykes, as they had done in their own homeland.

The dykes, he saw, were perfectly straight lines, crisscrossed at intervals by others, the water in them under the bright sun like molten gold poured into moulds, the only disturbance to their surface caused by the abundance of ducks, water rats, voles and moorhens going about their daily business. The cattle, put out to graze on the lush grass for the summer, were in the main like his own newer shorthorns, sleek and well-fed, with just a couple of dozen of the older longhorns, which some recalcitrant, stick-in-the-mud farmers refused to part with. At one point, he saw a fox, its belly close to the ground, stalking a pair of mallard ducks that were feeding on the bank of a dyke, and there were swans everywhere, lording their way with regal disdain among the cattle.

Almost as soon as they left Acle, it was possible to see the spires and taller buildings of the port, at first a distant mirage floating on grey-green feet, the architecture becoming ever more distinct the nearer they approached.

The horses were extremely weary, and it was after four in the afternoon when they finally reached the bridge over the river at the head of Breydon Waters, the swirling ebb tide carrying so much mud that the waters resembled the churning of the slurry Thomas poured into the pit on the farm. With the town of Yarmouth in front of them on the other side of the Yare, the driver turned right, to follow the road running alongside the river towards Gorleston, the edges formed of baulks of heavy timber, to which craft of all shapes and sizes were moored.

The mouth of the river was almost half a mile from the Haven Bridge, and their progress was slowed by other road traffic and huge carts standing at rest, being loaded or unloaded from the larger ships they were now passing.

At last they stopped alongside a two-masted brig with the name *'Pride of Hull'* painted on its bow. Tied up immediately in front of it was an armed naval cutter, the *'Fly'*.

The convicts were unloaded and herded on board, to be met by the master of the vessel, Abel Soames, and his first mate, John Mason. The other two members of the crew stood to one side, watching.

They were seafaring men, hard men, used to the harsh life of the open ocean and had carried convicts before, but for all their faults they were human and felt inordinately sorry for the poor specimens of manhood that stood assembled on their deck.

The young warder, who Thomas now realised was in charge of the party, asked Soames for a signature on a paper, accepting the handover of the convicts, and the two men went to the wheelhouse for the master to make his mark, after which Thomas and his fellow prisoners watched the warders remount the cart and trundle off towards the town and their accommodation for the night.

Soames regarded his passengers. They would be no trouble, he knew, shackled as they were, and they looked a sorry lot. He had that afternoon for a shilling bought a bucketful of herrings from a drifter that had come in with a full catch and made a quick decision.

'Sit down for a while. Do you fancy a fine silver darling for your tea?' He lifted one of the fish to show them.

He saw gaunt faces unused to kindness suddenly smile and he nodded to the youngest member of the crew. The lad fetched a brazier to the deck and lit it, then started cutting off the heads of the herring and pulling the guts from them, throwing the heads and offal overboard. As he threw the first handful there was not a gull in sight. When he threw the last there were more than a hundred screeching, plunging white bodies swooping for the thrown delicacies, coming, as they always did when food was in the offing, seemingly from nowhere and creating amusement in the watchers as one caught a piece in midair, only to have half a dozen others snatch at it immediately, often ending with huge splashes as they crashed into the water in a jumbled heap, feathers flying, still fighting and tearing at the offering. The seaman placed a wire mesh over the fire and the herrings on top of it, turning them as they cooked until the skin had blackened and the interiors, containing the delicious milts and roe, had softened.

As they cooked, he served first of all Soames and Mason, then his fellow crew member and himself, and then the convicts, who fell upon the repast as if it were the nectar of the gods, the first time any of them had ever tasted that most delicious of fish, the humble and yet so magnificent herring, cooked to perfection in the best way possible – almost straight from the water.

After months of nothing but bread, pottage and water the two repasts they had eaten during the day made them feel like men again, and when they were herded below into the hold they went gladly, their prison shackles almost forgotten.

Sleep came easily to Thomas that night, and he slept soundly until footsteps above and the sounds of activity woke him.

The hold was almost pitch black, save for two tiny slivers of light coming through the warped timbers of the hatch cover above; not enough to see around him, though he could hear the heavy breathing of the others.

Preparations for departure were underway, he felt sure.

An hour later, the hatch cover was removed and a container of pottage was lowered to them, with a sack containing pewter dishes and a dip.

They broke their fast and sent back up the empty container and dishes in the sack, then the two buckets of night soil, hearing again the cries of the gulls as it was tipped overboard.

Above, Soames and his small crew made ready to leave on the ebbing tide. Aboard the naval cutter, the '*Fly*', similar preparations were afoot, since the abiding tasks of that vessel were the protection of British shipping against the depredations of the privateers in the lanes off Yarmouth and the apprehension of smugglers, who were becoming ever more impudent in the locality.

At seven twenty-five, both vessels cast off and made for the roiling waves of the bar at the harbour mouth, where below deck all but Thomas and one other of the convicts first threw up their breakfasts.

Though for a few minutes it had been in the balance, particularly with the offensive smell of the spew from the other men, the feeling of impending sickness gradually left him, and Thomas wondered at his own seeming immunity from this indignation, but he gradually realised that the motion of the vessel that was causing the discomfort and sickness was similar to that of riding on horseback and the body's sway when following the plough.

It was to be the last time he suffered from the feeling of mal de mer, unlike most of his companions, some of whom would suffer greatly and even succumb to it.

The two ships set course south, at a distance of some four hundred yards from the shore, avoiding the dangers of Scroby Sands, the graveyard of many a brave ship and so close by to the east.

Beyond the sands, Soames, using the spyglass, espied two other ships, a three-masted brigantine and a faster, two-masted sloop, bearing in towards them, but as he watched they suddenly veered off, having seen the *'Fly'* come about to see what business they had, and their hulls quickly disappeared over the horizon. Privateering was about the easy acquisition of money and booty, not about being killed or injured whilst acquiring it.

Their progress south was unhampered, the vessels running easily and with full sail before a north-easterly breeze coming from almost directly behind them, and off Southwold the *'Fly'*, having reached the southernmost point of its patrol area, came about, closed for a shouted farewell and turned back towards its home harbour.

For most of the next ten miles, they were alone on a sun-drenched sea in plain sight of the sandy dunes of the Suffolk coast, near enough to see the tough blades of the mirram grass on their tops.

Off Aldeburgh, with no harbour to run to, the sails of the two privateers Soames had seen off Yarmouth appeared again out to sea, closing fast.

The *'Pride'* was no thoroughbred and was already under full sail. Soames put her on the most direct heading to take advantage of the following wind, but to no avail. Within two miles, a shot from a six-pounder was put across his bows. He had no choice but to come up into the wind and await boarding.

The smaller of the two privateers came alongside, and the *'Pride'* was boarded by four Frenchmen, whose leader demanded, 'Your cargo?'

'Convicts - prisoniers, mon sewer.'

The privateer captain looked down his long nose. He had enough knowledge of English to realize the insult but ignored it. He was annoyed at the loss of time and effort with no profit.

'Vous avez du liqueur? Genievre?'

'No, mon sewer. No gin, no cognac, just hommes.'

'Montrez-les moi. Show me.'

The hatch cover was removed, and the Frenchman looked down at the upraised faces below.

He asked a question of his mate, and the man nodded.

'Le garcon, the boy. We take him.'

Soames shouted down, 'Do ye want to become a pirate, boy?'

The boy Peter looked around at his fellow prisoners, all of whom were nodding with approval.

The old man who had provided their lunch on the previous day told him, 'Whatever may befall you on that ship, Peter, no matter how bad it is, will be better than dying on the journey to New Holland.'

The boy had already suffered humiliation and repeated rape in prison and had been so fearful of the coming journey that he decided in an instant to take the chance offered. He nodded to the men above, and a rope was lowered for him to clamber up.

The last they saw of him was his wave from the hatch.

The French captain made a scant search of the master's cabin but came away empty handed, and he and his crew returned to their ship and cast off, heading back with the three-master northwards, looking for more prey.

They were boarded twice more, once off the Essex coast by another Frenchman, who, like his countryman, was disgusted by their cargo's lack of value, and again in clear view of Dover Castle by a Spaniard, who was so incensed that he discharged his pistol into the deck and wrecked the captain's cabin before leaving.

At last, after having covered the one hundred and seventy-four sea miles from their starting port, they entered Portsmouth Harbour through the narrow, fifty yard wide entrance, Soames fighting the wheel continuously, trying to maintain way against the fluky five-knot current for which the harbour is infamous, at four seventeen in the afternoon of the eleventh of May 1787, just as an angry sun was setting redly in the west, making the sky above the horizon and the sea appear a molten oneness, thirty-seven hours and twenty-two minutes after leaving Yarmouth bar.

Once inside, Soames brought the vessel up into wind and waited for direction to a berth. After a wait of only a few minutes, the pilot cutter came alongside and led him into one on the Gunwharf Quay, close downwind from two huge prison hulks, the cloying, unmistakable stink of long incarcerated human prisoners pervading the air.

His crew made the vessel shipshape for the night and fed and watered the convicts. Soames was then approached by the two youngest men of his crew for permission to go ashore. They had heard wondrous tales of the joys of Portsmouth and wanted to head off for a night of debauchery in Point, a district renowned for its scores of whorehouses, gambling dens and inns. Soames pointed out the dangers of thieves and whores and in particular the likelihood of catching the French pox, with its disastrous, life-affecting after-effects, which he described in lurid detail, but could see that his words were falling on deaf ears. He could only hope the two would fall foul of the dozens of pickpockets who worked the streets around the port before losing their virginity to some filthy diseased whore.

Below decks, there was a feeling of relief among the prisoners that they had overcome the trials of their first sea journey and a faint optimism that they could withstand the next much longer sojourn on board another vessel.

The change that conversation had made was remarkable, and they felt, if not friendship, at least companionship one for another. Soames had sent down candles in order that they should not be in the dark.

Thomas found that the big-boned, affable man with the shock of untidy, sandy hair calling himself Roger Clarke, the one who had admitted to misdealing cards, seemed to be keeping close to him, and he had the distinct feeling that Roger wished to impart some information, though what that might be he had no idea.

After they had eaten, Clarke moved even closer to him and murmured very quietly, so that no one else could hear, 'You have no doubt wondered who saved you from Black Jack.'

Thomas pulled back in wonder, 'You?'

'I had my reasons. You did me a big favour in diverting his attention from me. I was to be next on his list.'

Thomas felt at a loss for words, but eventually stammered, 'My sincere thanks.'

'Accepted. We may need each other's help again before this is over.'

'You will have mine whenever it is necessary.'

'That is good to know.'

~~~oOo~~~

Not a quarter of a mile from where the *'Pride of Hull'* rode at anchor, Silas Rainforde sat in the corner of the bar of a less than salubrious inn frequented by the marines who were to accompany the Fleet as guards and later to form the garrison of the new territory.

He had travelled by post-chaise from Norwich to London, where he had stayed the night at the main hostelry in that city, *'The Swan with Two Necks'*; an intriguing establishment, which maintained almost four hundred horses for the carriages, all kept below ground, the cost of land in the metropolis being so expensive. From there he had boarded the fast four-horse chaise to Portsmouth, of a type where the two young postillions, mere boys, rode aback the two leading horses, taking their lives in their hands with every yard travelled.

He had arrived at Portsmouth the night before and was seeking a particular type of man.

Enquiries of the early drinkers had elucidated the information that there were two men he should look out for: a vicious sergeant by the name of Bullock, feared by all Rainforde spoke to, and a one-eyed lieutenant of marines called Arthur Sloane, who, he was told, was a sadistic, seasoned killer and seemed to enjoy it, having killed many men; three of them in duels.

Bullock came in first, a huge man of six feet three with a barrel chest and a head scraped clean of hair, overhanging eyebrows almost concealing his vicious looking little pig-like eyes, a disaster of a nose that had been broken several times and not reset once, and a narrow-lipped, badly scarred mouth that wore a perpetual sneer. Rainforde watched as Bullock quickly drank himself into a near stupor, challenging everyone around him to arm wrestling and winning every time against those foolish enough to take him on. The man was clearly an animal, not to be trusted near alcohol. He would certainly be useful in a brawl or for a murder in a back alley, but was not the one for Rainforde's nefarious work.

The lieutenant came in shortly after nine and sat down alone at the bar without greeting anyone.

Rainforde took stock of him: a full head of dark brown hair with a slight wave, one eye covered with a black patch, several sabre slashes on his cheeks and forehead, some of the scars red and angry, the little finger missing on his left hand, a disinterested look on his heavily tanned, rugged face.

The innkeeper knew the officer's requirements and placed a glass and a full bottle in front of him on the bar without being asked. Sloane filled the glass, held it to the light, sniffed the contents and savoured the smell before downing it in one gulp.

Rainforde watched for over an hour while the level of liquid in the bottle gradually lowered until only a quarter remained. Sloane appeared unaffected by the liquor.

One of the half dozen whores roaming from table to table decided to try her luck with the officer and going up to him slid her hand over his thigh and fondled his crotch.

He reacted viciously, lifting his hand to strike as she cowered from him, his face a picture of violent emotion, before filling the glass again and swallowing another drink as the woman slunk away.

Rainforde decided that the lieutenant had just the mixture of qualities he sought and he slowly moved across the room to take up position on a stool to the right of his quarry.

Sloane took no notice of the newcomer, feigning total ignorance of his presence, which annoyed Rainforde for a while until he considered that the action was one that even increased the man's potential value.

He cleared his throat before offering, 'Could I replace the bottle, lieutenant?'

Sloane half turned, regarding his new neighbour with annoyance.

'I know you not, sir, and am not in the way of accepting favours from those not of my acquaintance.' He sounded completely sober.

Rainforde could see he would need to handle matters with kid gloves, 'I do beg your pardon, lieutenant. I am Lord Besthorpe, of Besthorpe Manor in the County of Lincolnshire. I shall leave you alone if you so desire. It is, however, a fact that you have been recommended to me as a man who could carry out a paid commission, should he decide to do so.'

Sloane's expression did not give away in the slightest the surprise and avarice that he felt. Money, always a problem, had become deucedly tight of late, and an injection of cash would be more than welcome.

He asked coldly, 'Am I to understand that you believe the recommendation of others should in any way influence my decision?'

Rainforde was alarmed that he might be losing control of the conversation, 'No, sir. Not at all. I mentioned it merely to point out that my approach was not fortuitous.'

Sloane knew he had his fish landed and gutted and gritted out, 'State your business.'

'You are to accompany the Fleet on the voyage to New Holland, are you not?'

'I am.'

'Could I ask in what capacity?'

'I am third in command of the detachment of marines.'

Excellent, thought Rainforde, he will have access to all the prisoners.

'I am told that you hold life cheaply.'

'Some lives, perhaps.'

'What of convicts?'

Sloane's answer was carefully non-committal, 'They deserve their just rewards.'

It was exactly what Rainforde wanted to hear.

'It is precisely that which I wish to discuss with you, lieutenant. There is one such travelling in this batch who inveigled his way into my young sister's confidence and had his way with her against her will. She was a committed virgin, intending to take holy orders, and felt so sullied after he did the filthy deed that she took her own life. He was sentenced merely to transportation and not death, but my family's honour has been besmirched, and our good name destroyed. I want him dead, at any price.'

Sloane smirked, annoying Rainforde, 'And how much is 'any price', if I might make so bold?'

Rainforde tapped his coat pocket, 'One hundred golden guineas, lieutenant.'

Sloane's expression showed not the slightest sign of the mixed emotions he was experiencing. He had long since learned the value of keeping his feelings hidden and his one good eye hooded, both in the fighting of duels and during games of chance. One hundred guineas was more than his pay for a whole year and would clear his debts and leave a goodly sum over, placing his life on a much more agreeable footing. The man this Besthorpe wanted killed was a convict, and a fair number of those would no doubt die on the voyage in any case. The man might die without his interference, and if he did not there would be opportunities at their destination. Even if he decided to let the man live Besthorpe would never know of it, being at the other end of the earth. It was a win situation whichever way one looked at it.

'The man's name?'

'Thomas Nash.'

'The money?'

Rainforde slipped his hand inside his coat and brought out the leather pouch, concealed in his palm as he slid it across the counter.

It disappeared in a flash into Sloane's pocket before he held out his right hand.

Rainforde took it in his grip, hoping he had made the right choice, but still unsure if his wishes would be carried out. He determined to check and if necessary to use a second agent. Nash must die. There could be no possibility of a comeback.

Without another word Sloane slid off the stool and made his way to the door, his gait as steady as that of a teetotaller.

CHAPTER NINE

Thomas lay awake before dawn and saw the first dusty rays of an early bright sun seeping through the cracks in the hatch cover. He rose and used the bucket before regaining his seat on the floor.

He had more than enough time to reflect and was hoping that somehow Martha had reached Portsmouth also and would be making the voyage, though it was too much to hope she would be included among those on his own ship.

He was not to know that she had been in the town beyond the harbour for over a week, having also been transported by sea with eleven other women. They were now guests at the Bridewell in Gosport, which replaced the original prison that had recently collapsed.

He was also in ignorance of the fact that the officer Phillip had placed in charge of the distribution of prisoners among the various ships had noted the fact that Thomas and Martha Nash were husband and wife and being a humanitarian had decided that they should travel on the same ship, so that should the ship founder both would be lost, leaving neither to grieve. The '*Jane Doe*' had been nominated as one of the transports for men prisoners only, but he added Martha's name to the list and, so that she should have a companion, a fourteen year-old girl by the name of Elizabeth Crean. The prisoners' accommodation on board would not be suitable for them, but he had decreed that they should be kept in the forward chain locker, unshackled.

When the hatch cover was removed above the prisoners on the '*Pride*', a rope ladder was dropped for their ascent, made almost impossible by the leg irons, but with the pulling power of four men each one was hoisted to the deck while standing on the lowest rung of the ladder and holding on to the side ropes.

They were given a breakfast of fried egg on bread, with water to wash it down, and then led onto the wharf and along to where the rest of the thousand or so prisoners were mustering.

They were kept standing for over an hour while checks were made, and many fainted from hunger and weakness. They were left where they fell on the ground.

A sergeant of marines began the roll call, and as a man answered he was taken to a designated spot where all who would travel on the same ship were to be gathered.

One transport, the '*Lady Penrhyn*', was to be for female prisoners only, and two others, the '*Scarborough*' and the '*Alexander*', would carry only men. The rest would carry both, although the majority on the '*Charlotte*', '*Jayne Doe*' and '*Friendship*' were to be men and on the '*Prince of Wales*' women.

Three other ships, transports for food and other necessities, had joined the Fleet and been loaded with provisions and some sheep, cattle and swine, to which later on in the voyage would be added other animals. These were the '*Borrowdale*', '*Fishburne*' and '*Golden Grove*'.

Over thirty other men had been called to the muster station for the *Jayne Doe*, including Roger Clarke, before Thomas was called.

He shuffled forward to take his position and suddenly felt he was being watched. He swung his gaze to the left and noticed a marine in officer's uniform watching him intently, though he could not perceive any ill intent. He had never set eyes on the man before and could not think why he might be interested. He was not aware that in the jeering crowd of town citizens that had been kept back behind barriers there was another watching him, and that one's eyes held a great deal of malice.

The men were herded onto the ships before the women were brought out and sorted into groups. Thomas had no sight of his beloved Martha before they sailed, and his heart was heavy at the lack of knowledge.

Below decks, he found himself cramped in a hold not much larger than the main room of his home, fitted out with rows of wooden benches. Sackcloth-covered palliasses, generally referred to as 'ticks', were provided for every man. Though the hold smelt musty, it had been hosed down after the removal of the last cargo and was at least clean, and to have a bench to sit on instead of the floor was a welcome improvement. Total darkness was relieved by the light of two weak oil lamps, suspended on chains from the ceiling outside the end bars. If any of the prisoners considered that they lacked in space they would have been relieved to view the rest of the ship's accommodation. The seamen, in particular, had so little room that the off-coming watch had to take the place of those who had just left their hammocks, which were strung together so close as to be touching. Every inch of spare space was crammed with extra provisions and equipment. Only the captain and Sloane had their own tiny, private quarters; a few square feet apart from the rest of the crew with a small raised area for a bunk. They could by no stretch of the imagination be called cabins, but did, at least, have doors.

Overhead, Thomas could hear a continual scurrying of feet, like dozens of rats in a ceiling space racing for food, as the crew carried out their urgent duties.

When a heavily pregnant Martha and the girl came on board, they were led down to the forward chain locker, where they were given a lit candle and locked in.

A hot evening meal of unusually succulent meat and vegetable stew, provided on pewter platters, raised the spirits and hopes of the convicts and gave them the totally wrong impression that the future might not be as black as they had thought. As a result, their sleep on the floor beside the benches that night was less troubled than in recent days.

When the *Jayne Doe'*, a two-masted 'brigantine of three hundred and forty-eight tons, square-rigged on the foremast and fore-and-aft-rigged on the mainmast, made ready to sail the next morning, she carried seventy-four male and two female prisoners, lieutenant Sloane, a sergeant, two corporals, one drummer, five privates of marines, a so-called surgeon's mate - a man with six months' lean experience of aiding in a hospital ward and a crew of twenty-eight. In total, the ships carried more than eight hundred prisoners, almost two hundred of them women, and seven hundred or so crewmembers, marines and their wives and officials, beginning the arduous journey to what for most of them would be their new home on the far side of the globe.

Well before the first faint silver snake of dawn slithered up from the depths of the sea to lie along the eastern horizon, the ships of the First Fleet became hives of activity, as last-minute preparations were made for departure, and shortly after eight of the clock on the thirteenth of May 1787, the '*Sirius'* slipped from the dock to head for the entrance to Portsmouth harbour, accompanied by the naval frigate '*Hyena'*, escorting them as protection until they finally departed from home waters. The other ships, fully rigged, followed them out into the broad expanse of the English Channel, making a brave sight under a clear sky, with the sun already warming those working on the deck and in the rigging, tightening halliards and checking cleats. A light breeze from almost due west, two points abaft their beam, drove the vessels easily through the calm green water on their journey south to the Canaries, giving each ship's master a sense of security that could, they knew well from past experience, be as false as the alluring look in the eyes of a keen-eyed port wench seeking to strip them of their money.

On the deck of the '*Jayne Doe',* Sloane stood beside the master and asked, 'How long will this last, do you think?'

'The glass is steady; a week, perchance a little longer.'

'But it is a false beginning, is it not?'

The master snorted, 'I have never yet crossed the Atlantic Ocean without getting my feet wet. You will need to be a good sailor before this little jaunt is over, lieutenant.' He bellowed down to his First Mate, 'Mister Brace, bring up the prisoners.'

Sloane was surprised, 'You will allow them on deck?'

The captain surprised him even more, 'Many of those poor bastards are innocent, though we shall never know which. The law of England has much to answer for, but even if they are the dregs of the earth and as guilty as hell they deserve to see the sun when we can allow it with impunity. It will be many months before they stand under it again on dry land, and some of them will never do so. There will be deaths on the voyage. It is inevitable.'

Sloane watched them shuffle out into the sunlight, not believing their luck, smiles on some faces; many, particularly those who had come from the living death of the prison hulks, squinting from so long with no exposure to such brightness.

He watched the prisoner called Thomas Nash cross to the starboard gunwale with that strange wobbling motion occasioned by the leg restraints and tried to gauge what kind of man he was observing.

Twenty-one years in charge of all types of men, from some who were the salt of the earth and as honest as a man could wish for to others he would not dare turn his back on for fear of a bayonet in the ribs, gave him an instinctive feel for a man's integrity.

Nash, to his eyes, did not have the look of a rapist, but looks could deceive as he well knew. He had been surprised that one of the two female passengers, the attractive, heavily pregnant one, had the same surname, and could well be the spouse of the man he was watching.

There was a simple way to find out.

He cast off a simple salute to the captain and descended the ladder from the upper deck, then crossed to the starboard side, stepping between the legs of the convicts seated on the planking.

He stopped by Thomas, who was gazing across at the majestic line of other ships, and sat down beside him on the gunwale.

The moment Thomas became aware of the officer he tried to stand, but Sloane told him, 'Stay seated.'

Thomas was perturbed; to be singled out by a marine was bad enough, for it to be an officer and even worse the one who had been watching him ashore had to mean serious trouble.

He asked, 'Have I somehow incurred your wrath, Lieutenant?'

Sloane was faintly amused, 'I think not. At least, not yet. Your name is Thomas Nash, is it not?'

'It is, sir.'

'And what, pray, is your trade?'

'I am a farmer, sir.'

'And does your wife rejoice in the name of Martha?'

'I think not that she has at this time the least reason for rejoicing, sir, but she is certainly called by that name.'

'She travels with us.' Sloane watched the sudden, beatific smile crease Nash's entire face and knew instantly that this man loved his wife.

'Oh, sir, thank you. I had no idea…'

'She looks well and is heavy with child.'

Thomas was overwhelmed, his breathing heavy and uncontrolled, and his heart overflowing with pleasure, but a worry that had been twisting his guts, as if attacked by a massive, uncontrolled intestinal worm forced itself to the surface. He flicked his gaze about the deck, to include the dozen or so seamen going about their duties, 'Will she be safe?'

'Why should she not be?'

'Now we are but shortly out from land. Men, when they have been without female companionship for weeks or months, become raging animals on heat. I am so afeared she will be attacked.'

Sloane was on the point of saying that her pregnancy would put off any rapist, but he had witnessed before and after battles so many women in her condition being raped and far worse and in many cases put to violent death by soldiers who, under normal conditions, were ordinary, caring human beings, and some he had been happy to call comrades.

He made an instant decision that would, though he was unaware of it at the time, affect the whole of the rest of his life.

He told the convict, 'I shall take pains to ensure her safety.'

Thomas' face showed the tumultuous relief he was feeling inside. For some reason, this officer instilled in him a confidence that few men had achieved before.

Sloane watched, knowing now that the man calling himself Besthorpe had lied, but why? He had to find out.

'What crime did you commit?'

'I committed no crime, sir. My Lord Rainforde had always been my beneficent mentor and holder of the deed to my land, which my ancestors down to my father have been buying back by yearly payments, the last of which was made last year. Lord Rainforde died suddenly and unexpectedly, shortly after the demise of his young wife, and his heir not only refused all knowledge of the payments, but accused me of false pretences. And so you see me here, stripped of my land, my possessions and my freedom, through no fault of my own.'

There was one last question to ask, 'Did you know the sister of Lord Besthorpe?'

He could see clearly from the instant frown that creased Nash's forehead that the man had never heard the name, 'I know neither that Lord nor any of his family, sir. The name is one I have never heard.'

Sloane had dealt with many shysters, cardsharps, liars and other devious characters during his lifetime and knew immediately that his first impression of the man who had given him the bag of coins was correct; he was an outright villain. Thomas Nash was the victim of a scoundrel out for all he could grab, and the farmer's land had been there for the taking. Rainforde wanted Nash dead, so that there could in the future be no possibility of a claim against his holding. Reading between the lines, he was most likely also responsible for the death of the previous Lord Rainforde and possibly of his wife.

Sloane considered for a moment his course of action. Should Nash be told? Of course he should.

'The name of this heir?'

'Silas Rainforde. I have heard tell that he is the bastard son of the previous Lord Rainforde's younger brother by a gipsy woman. He has no right to the title.'

Sloane pursed his lips before saying, 'You have a bad enemy in that man, Nash. He has paid me well to kill you and your wife.'

Thomas was suddenly hugely afraid, and his eyes gave away that fear.

Sloane gripped his arm, 'Hold up, man. I am not about to do his bidding. I took his money since it was there for the taking, judging him to be a rogue, trying to buy the services of another. He told me a tale about the rape of his innocent sister by you, and I took the telling of it with a large pinch of salt at the time. Had I believed it, your life would not be worth a brass farthing, and you would now be out there drowning in that green water, but you must be on your guard; I may well not be the only one he has attempted to bribe.'

Thomas' heartbeat had begun to slow and his equanimity to return. He took a gulp of air and managed to say a heartfelt, 'Thank you, sir. Thank you.'

Sloane nodded silently. He rose and made his way back to the upper deck where he rejoined the ship's master, leaving Thomas with a whole new set of black thoughts.

One day followed another, with steady westerlies taking the Fleet happily on its way. On most ships, the convicts were allowed on deck for the greater part of the day to enjoy the unbroken sunshine, though on those of mixed sex it was the males in the forenoons and the females after lunch.

The food was good and fresh, and minds were lulled into a sense of well-being.

Martha, seven months on in her pregnancy, and the young girl, Elizabeth, had become fast friends. The girl was a simpleton with a mental age of eight but she was a happy soul, content with the simplest things, and Martha played easily understood games with her that she remembered from her own childhood.

The baby gave hard kicks from time to time, and Elizabeth loved to feel Martha's stomach, giggling loudly when she felt one.

To that point, they had been well fed and left unmolested, but it was not to last.

All the ships of the Fleet were in good order, though the 'Friendship' was taking in water and had to be continually pumped. On the 'Scarborough', a planned mutiny by convicts was foiled and the supposed ringleaders flogged, but for the most part the convicts were enjoying the nearest thing to a holiday that they had ever experienced in their lives and were not about to cause waves. Were it not for the leg irons and the less than five-star victuals provided, they might well have been paying passengers en route to their future lives.

Fresh meat and vegetables had long run out by the time the Fleet arrived at the open port of Santa Cruz de Santiago de Tenerife, in the Canary Islands, where the ships stayed for a week, taking on fresh meat and fish and attempting to buy vegetables, which were poor and in short supply. Fruit, which Phillip so urgently needed to ward off scurvy, was out of season. After buying what was available and topping up their water tanks, he moved the Fleet on to the Island of Mayo, a Cape Verde island, and made another abortive sortie for food before heading across the ocean.

The next destination was to be Rio de Janeiro, on the other side of the Atlantic, and with favourable currents and the prevailing trade winds Phillip hoped to make the four thousand mile crossing without serious trouble and in good time, expecting to make more than one hundred and twenty sea miles per day with the help of those winds and currents.

At first, after leaving Santa Cruz, the convicts were again allowed on deck during the forenoon on the 'Jayne Doe' and also on some of the other ships, a very necessary arrangement as they reached the tropics and endured temperatures of well over a hundred degrees in light winds that failed completely for a week. They were left in the doldrums, and tempers ran high.

Among the seamen on the '*Jayne Doe*', there had been mutterings for days concerning their need for women, and one, Caleb Crann, was intent on fomenting trouble.

A rat-faced, raw-skinned thirty-one year old, with the lean body of a whippet and the libido of a jack rabbit in the Spring, he had harboured lecherous thoughts about Elizabeth Crean from the first moment he had set eyes on her and had relieved himself of his seed more than once on deck behind a hatch cover while feasting his eyes on her, not giving a damn about the other seamen nearby watching his performance with grins on their unlovely faces.

He knew that should he take her alone he would be flogged. It was something he had experienced once and was not in a hurry to enjoy again. For days he had been muttering to his crewmates and now had more than twenty of them prepared to act with him, enough, he believed, to dissuade the master or the few marines from interfering.

The bosun held the key to the chain locker but at each mealtime passed it to Simon Gray, the cook's mate, for delivery of food to the women.

Crann had his chosen men loiter in the area close to the chain locker, and that evening when Gray carried the tray downstairs they pounced, grabbing the key from him, the tray and food ground underfoot.

Crann told Gray to lose himself, and he ran for shelter.

Elizabeth was dragged, screaming, from the locker. Her clothing was ripped off her, leaving her completely naked, and she was thrown down onto the floor and held there. Martha had stood and tried to fight off the men, but Crann smashed his fist into her face, knocking her back onto the sackcloth bundle that was their bed, unconscious.

One by one, Crann first, the men viciously raped the girl, her screams cut off by each one holding his hand over her mouth.

On a ship of that size, just one hundred and eight feet from stem to stern, every sound was transmitted to every man on board, and in the convicts' hold there was everything from anger to desire as they listened to what they knew was ravishment, though they had not set eyes on the girl.

Thomas was frantic, knowing it was not Martha screaming, but imagining what might also be happening to her.

In his cabin, the master heard too. For just a few moments, he was inclined to intervene but realised that any intervention on his part could easily lead to a mutiny. After all, the girl was a convicted prisoner. What could she expect? He went back to his charts.

Sloane took a very different approach. With his pistol drawn he raced across the deck and took the stairs to the forward hold two at a time. As his feet touched the bottom he saw just ten feet away the last man enter the girl, the others all standing around her, their eyes closely following the action, their attention so focussed that none of them had seen or been aware of his arrival on the scene.

He bellowed, 'Get off! Now!'

The seaman on top of Elizabeth stopped his vile motions and turned his head. Seeing the pistol levelled at him he withdrew with alacrity and scrabbled away on all fours, his erection dwindling fast.

Sloane was immediately faced with twenty belligerent men, muttering oaths and ready for anything. He knew he was in one of the most dangerous situations of his life and could well be overwhelmed and killed if he made the slightest wrong move.

He had studied every manual on combat available at that time and knew that advantage was everything.

Crann had been obvious to him as the ringleader from the start, and he aimed the pistol steadily at that seaman's forehead.

'You die first,' He told him, his voice like ice, 'in exactly ten seconds, if you are still here. One...two...'

Crann, like most of his ilk, was a down and out coward and knew the man facing him meant exactly what he said.

Muttering curses he turned on his heel and ran for the stairwell, followed by the rest of the mob.

Sloane crossed to where the girl lay. She had fainted, and he hoisted her up.

He eased her back into the locker, noticing that Martha was unconscious and had a developing black eye. He laid Elizabeth down onto the sacking next to Martha as the girl began coming to, her hands and arms twitching, and he covered her as best he could with her torn clothing.

Martha, too, was regaining consciousness, and as she realised someone was in front of her she opened her mouth to scream.

He urged, 'Hush! I have come to help you. Can you look after the girl? She has been badly used.'

Martha's eyes focussed on his face. She drew back in horror. In the weak light from the guttering candle he could have been the very devil with his eye patch and scars, but he was smiling grimly, and her tense muscles began to relax until she suddenly thought of the baby. Sloane saw her instant terror as she placed her right hand on her stomach.

'Are you all right?' He asked.

She shook her head, 'I know not, sir, but...'

A sudden kick made her face relax into a weak smile, 'I do believe so.' She sighed.

Elizabeth had curled into a ball and was sobbing piteously.

Martha urged, 'Leave us, sir. I will see to her.'

'You have lost your victuals. I shall see to a replacement.'

'Please, no, sir. Leave us be, but do please lock the door.'

It was the first time Sloane had spoken to Martha, but he was as impressed with her as he had been with Thomas, and was determined to keep to his promise to protect her if at all possible.

He left, locked the hatch, and went back to the deck, where he handed the key to the bosun, telling him, 'You need to keep this in your possession, bosun. That chain locker holds something more precious than gold to your men.'

The rapes on the '*Jayne Doe*' were not isolated to that ship. On all the ships carrying female prisoners rape and promiscuity between the men, including marines, and the women prisoners was general, and in only a very few cases was punishment meted out.

CHAPTER TEN

Three days passed with no let up from the debilitating heat. The sun, a huge golden orb, beat down from a permanently cloudless sky without the trace of a breeze to relieve the sweating men and women, badly burning the skin of many whose bodies had once been brown with exposure, but were now vulnerably pink. Only the vermin seemed to thrive: cockroaches, lice, fleas and other bugs made the life of everyone on board a living hell, and the rats seemed to outnumber the human beings, everywhere openly looking for sustenance, seemingly aware that they would not be hunted by their erstwhile killers, too lethargic now to take up a weapon.

Flagged orders from the Commodore instructed all ships to pump out the bilges, which had become almost unbearable with their stink, at least once every day, but some captains ignored the order, and several convicts died as a result.

Elizabeth had uttered not a word since the rapes, though Martha had held her in her arms and cleaned her, urging her to speak.

On the fourth day after the attack, she and Martha were again allowed on deck. By the merest chance, as they came out of the hatch into the sunlight the girl came face to face with a leering Crann, whose gaze went straight to her breasts and then to her groin.

She saw the lewd expression on his face and screamed. She rushed past him to the gunwale just four paces away and threw herself over it before anyone could stop her. Martha and a dozen seamen rushed to the edge and looked down. The ship was scarcely moving, and the girl's head was visible for a few moments before it slipped below the surface.

Two seamen did not hesitate; they climbed onto the gunwale and dived, as the watching master shouted orders for a longboat to be lowered.

Martha saw the two men enter the water and begin diving for the girl, whose body was now a dozen feet down in the clear blue water. Four times she saw them dive before one came up holding Elizabeth's body, which he held while he trod water waiting for the boat, already in the water and heading for him and his fellow seaman, now joining him to help hold the girl's body up.

Elizabeth was pulled into the boat, and Martha saw men leaning over her, one lifting her and leaning her forward to try to force the water out of her lungs.

They worked for several minutes before one stood and turned to look up at the expectant faces. He shook his head and Martha uttered a disbelieving cry.

Sloane had been on the upper deck with the master and saw everything. It served to strengthen his decision.

'The other woman; I'll take her for my own.'

With a lifetime at sea behind him, the ship's master understood men and the workings of their minds well, but the lieutenant's statement puzzled him for a moment before understanding dawned. She was to be protected.

He knew perfectly well that she would be a target for the rampant seamen, either before or immediately after she gave birth, and that it would involve him personally in doling out severe punishment to men he might well have to rely on in dangerous situations before this journey was over. If she were with Sloane the men would not dare to approach her. It was a perfect solution to a difficult problem.

'You will have her in your cabin?'

'I shall.'

The master, never normally one quick to show emotion or give credit, slapped Sloane on the shoulder and told him, 'You are a good man, lieutenant.'

At twenty-three minutes past nine, at that point when the tropic night falls like a lead-weighted black curtain, Caleb Crann finished splicing the topsail sheet, which had frayed against a spar, and began clambering down the rigging. As he looked down, the deck was clear but for one lone figure, seemingly looking out towards the other ships.

Crann reached the bottom step and jumped to the deck. As he twisted round a stiletto slid between two of his ribs into his heart and his body was tipped over the gunwale in one fluid motion. The helmsman, from his higher position, and lulled by the motion of the ship into a state almost akin to somnolence, neither saw Crann's demise not heard the splash as his already dead body hit the water.

The following morning before breakfast, Sloane accompanied the bosun down to the chain locker.

Through the small grilled opening at the top of the door, he could see that Martha, sitting uncomfortably on the sacking, had been weeping. Elizabeth's death had hit her hard.

After the bosun unlocked and opened the door he turned away and left the lieutenant alone with the woman.

Sloane told her, 'Do not be afraid. I will not hurt you.'

She surprised him, 'I know that well, lieutenant. Our destinies are linked.'

He frowned, suddenly unsure, and then shrugged. She must mean that they were both bound for New Holland.

'Yes, of course. I wish to offer you my protection, if you will allow it. I shall make no demands of any kind from you, now or at any time in the future; of that I can assure you. I wish only for your safety, and if you stay in this place I cannot ensure it. I have a mind that you should use my quarters. When your time comes, the baby can be born there in somewhat better conditions than these.' He waved his hand around the stinking, uncomfortable locker.

She looked enquiringly at him, 'Shall it be now, sir?'

'Of course. Let me help you up.'

Martha's belly was hugely distended. Her time was rapidly approaching she knew and she welcomed the thought that she would not be alone for the birth, though whether this gallant officer would have the guts to watch it was a question for the future.

'I should tell you, sir, that I have lice and fleas in great abundance.'

He laughed out loud, 'And think you I have not? There is not a man aboard who is not infested with the creatures.'

'I have had little experience of them before, except on the animals.'

'But I have. On some campaigns, they were almost as bad as they are now.'

His quarters, she found, were just as cramped as the chain locker, but there was, at least, a raised platform with a thick palliasse on it, and he insisted that she should use it.

'But where will you sleep, sir?'

'I shall not want for space. There is plenty of deck.'

More days were spent in the doldrums. Water was becoming short on every vessel, restricting the amount that could be drunk, and the situation generally was becoming dire, until, at ten to midnight on the night of the seventeenth of July, men asleep were suddenly thrown sideways as the ships heeled to a cooling gust of wind that was the first sign of the steady blow that would take them to their destination.

At almost the same moment, Martha felt the first huge contraction and at a quarter past three, with the ships surging forward with full sail on a following wind, she gave birth easily to a healthy baby boy of seven and a half pounds.

Sloane, sleeping just beyond the cabin, heard the baby's cries and knocked on the door.

Martha had tied off the umbilical cord with the piece of string she had ready and cut it and had laid the baby by her side but was still waiting for the placenta. She called, 'Just a few minutes, please.'

The placenta came away quickly less than two minutes later, and she wrapped it in the piece of cloth she had asked Sloane for and had already wiped the baby with, then covered it and herself with the rough blanket, after lifting the baby to lie close by her head.

She called, 'Come in now.'

Sloane entered with some trepidation, childbirth and babies being unknown foreign territories to him, but he could see she and the infant were well and he took an inordinate pride in what he felt was partly his achievement. Had she still been down below in the chain locker she might well have died.

'His father will be proud.' He said.

'Shall you tell him?'

He smiled broadly, 'When the infant can be moved, I shall show him.'

'You know little about babies I see.'

'How so?'

'They are much stronger than you think. Were Thomas outside at this moment you could take the infant to show him.'

His smile widened, 'I have much to learn in that regard, Martha…I may call you Martha?'

'I am a convict, lieutenant. You may call me what you will, but may I tell you now that I shall remember your kindness to my dying day and shall repay it a thousand fold. My husband too will be deeply in your debt.'

'We shall not talk of debt. There lies before each of us a difficult life, where nothing can be taken for granted. If you are willing I have a mind to ask for you to be assigned to me as my housekeeper once we are established at the settlement. Would you accept such an arrangement? I repeat, I shall ask for nothing of you bar the duties of the household, and if at any time I am in a position to obtain your husband's services also, I shall arrange for you to be together.'

Tears filled her eyes, 'You are a good man, sir. One of the best I have ever met.'

A small cry came from the baby, 'You see, he agrees with me.'

Sloane shook his head, 'A good man I most certainly am not, though you are the second to assert it on this voyage. I have killed many men.'

'But none that did not fully deserve it.'

He nodded thoughtfully, 'That is true.' Then he moved away from the difficult subject, 'Is there anything you have need of?'

'No. Thank you.'

'Then I shall leave you to sleep.'

The moment he left, Martha eased aside the material from her breast and drew the infant to her. The baby suckled greedily and she felt a small frisson of happiness for the first time since last Michaelmas day.

CHAPTER ELEVEN

On the wind there came a series of tropical storms with spectacular sheet and fork lightning and lashing, monsoon-like rain, and the convicts were unable to come on deck, their lives becoming even more miserable.

Many of Thomas' fellow prisoners who had previously seemed to have got their sea legs after weeks of sickness began to suffer from mal de mer again, though he had never succumbed. The hold, like many another on the other ships, stank worse than ever before, its floor running with yellow decaying spew. The palliasses were sodden and useless, and the rags they were wearing were, for the most part, falling off them, the material rotten. On top of everything else, their lives had reached a new low point.

On the third of August at just after eleven in the morning the lookout on the 'Sirius' shouted, 'Land-ho!', the excited cry repeated soon afterwards on all the other vessels.

At a distance of ten miles the outline of Cape Frio, on the southeast coast of Brazil, appeared like a line of faintly inscribed, indecipherable script on a parchment that ranged in colour from bright blue at the top to a misty grey below, its crazed, illegible lettering gradually re-forming into cliffs, forests and inlets as the distance diminished.

Two days later, on the fifth of August, the vessels arrived at Rio de Janeiro, and Phillip set about the huge task of bringing his charges back to some kind of order.

He sent his master surgeon, John White, a Sussex man who had travelled on the 'Charlotte', to each of the ships in turn to inspect the condition of the convicts.

He found that the state of their clothing, especially that of the women, was such that it must of necessity be destroyed, rotting and infested with lice as it was.

Every bit of it was burnt, and replacement clothing made from rough sacking. Many of the women complained that it itched more than the lice, and it was certainly not the height of fashion, though for the moment it did smell considerably sweeter.

Every ship was scoured clean, and though the convicts were kept below decks their holds were hosed down, and they had ample fresh water and meat, vegetables and fruit. Damage to sails and rigging was made good.

When every bit of necessary work had been carried out the longboats of the ships carried seamen ashore to visit the bars and prostitutes of the port; a necessary evil, which would hopefully see them on an even keel until the next port of call.

Phillip bought huge quantities of food, relayed by bumboats during every hour of daylight, replenishing the larders on the ships.

They stayed a scant month and sailed again on the fourth of September for the relatively easy run to the Cape of Good Hope, a distance of three thousand seven hundred and sixty-five miles, but all of it utilizing the extra power of the prevailing westerly winds.

One thing which caused merriment among the seamen was the screaming of the convicts on some ships as they left harbour. The Rio officials gave them a parting twenty-one gun salute, and those below decks and out of sight believed they were under attack and would be sunk while still locked up below.

Once they were two days out the convicts on most ships, including those on the '*Jayne Doe*', were allowed on deck again for the first time in almost six weeks.

Their eyes, used only to the diffused light that filtered from the overhead hatches and the weak oil lamp glow, had to be shielded with their hands as they tried to reaccustom themselves to that of the burning sunlight.

Thomas went to his usual spot and had not been there ten minutes when Sloane approached and murmured, 'Come with me.'

Thomas shuffled behind him back across the planking and up the eight steps to the quarterdeck, where the helmsman stood at the wheel.

He knocked at the door of what passed for his cabin, and Thomas' heart bounded when he heard Martha's voice call, 'Come in.' He urged to take her in his arms.

Sloane held the door open so that Thomas could look in but restrained him with his hand from stepping over the raised sill. 'I am sorry.' He said, 'You may see your son, but you may not enter.'

Martha came to the door with the child, standing so close that they could touch. She brushed his arm, holding the infant close to his face.

The boy had grown quickly and now, at six weeks of age, weighed more than nine pounds. Thomas ate in his appearance, his emotions so mixed that his expression changed from moment to moment: love, happiness, worry for the future, pleasure and longing, all mixed in a kaleidoscopic jumble of thoughts.

He touched the boy's face and then Martha's, while Sloane looked on, pleased for them but with a tinge of jealousy that he had never in his life felt the way that Thomas did now, regretting the opportunities that he had rejected during his career.

Martha asked, 'What shall we call him?'

Thomas had been thinking much about that very subject. 'Joshua?'

It would be fitting, naming him after his grandfather, and Martha had also considered it, but a name had come to her in her sleep and been in her brain when she woke. She had the fixed idea that it had been planted there by some supreme being and now told Thomas, 'His first country is to be New Holland, which I have heard is likely to be called Australia. I believe we should call him Austin.'

'But there is no such name.'

'There will be now.'

He mulled it over for a few moments and liked the sound of it: Austin Nash. It had a certain ring to it.

'All right. Why not?'

Sloane saw two seamen climbing the ladder to the upper deck and urged, 'I have to hurry you. This cannot happen again.'

Martha leant forward and kissed Thomas on the lips, a fleeting kiss, but one that would sustain him for many, many months.

He pulled back and Sloane pushed the door closed.

'You realise that fraternising, even with your own wife, is expressly forbidden, and could cause a great deal of resentment among the crew and the prisoners?'

Thomas knew Sloane had taken a one-off risk and could not repeat it.

'I know it, of course. Once again, lieutenant, I am deeply in your debt. It is impossible for me to thank you enough for protecting Martha and my son. Even if I do not see the end of this journey I would die happy, knowing that she is safe. Thank you from the bottom of my heart.' He turned and shuffled away from the door behind which lay everything he held dear.

CHAPTER TWELVE

The crossing to the Cape of Good Hope on the tip of Southern Africa took five weeks, almost all of it under good weather and excellent sailing conditions with no serious storms.

The convicts still enjoyed the use of the deck on most days, and below decks the hold smelt a great deal less noxious than on the voyage to Rio.

Thomas looked enviously at the little cabin door every time he was allowed on deck but never caught sight of Martha again.

She was allowed out every day in the early morning and again in the evening, and Sloane had from somewhere wangled a stool for her to sit on and nurse the baby.

Despite himself he was beginning to develop a proprietary feeling towards both Martha and the child, though not prepared to admit it, even to himself. Had he done so he would, perhaps, have realised that he was falling in love for the first time in his life.

The Fleet arrived at the Cape in good order on Saturday the thirteenth of October in the year of our Lord 1787, their last landfall until the final one, three months and many stormy seas away.

Here were loaded the many animals needed to set up the new colony, along with their necessary fodder: pigs, goats, cattle, horses, geese, chickens, ducks, pigeons, doves and dogs, with males of each species included. As much fresh food as they could carry came on board, and the cooks made much of it, feeding up all and sundry, including the convicts, knowing full well that it was the last chance to replenish the energy of weakened, worn-out bodies before the inevitable dire fasting and hardships to come.

Though he had suffered with hunger and the heat along with the rest of his fellow convicts, Thomas felt remarkably well. He had not had to endure the torment of raging diarrhoea that had so debilitated most of those incarcerated with him and had never been sick, despite the smell of it all around him.

If he thought about it at all it was to believe that his well being was to do with the knowledge that Martha and the child were near him and being well looked after.

Roger Clarke too was in good condition, and the hot meat stews with good fresh bread were putting new life in them.

As with any group of human beings thrown together in an eclectic mix of downright crooks and basically honest citizens small cliques had formed, some with mal intent, discussing intended future criminal activity, others with like-minded, simpler souls, talking only of their health and the day-to-day state of their surroundings.

Thomas and Roger conversed only with each other and found that they had similar ideas on many subjects. Even at that early stage in their friendship Thomas had formed in his mind the ghost of an idea so vast and unbelievably impossible that it was not at that point for disclosure, depending as it did on so many variables, but if things worked out the way he hoped Roger could well turn out to be the living deus ex machina he needed most in the world.

One month to the day later they heard the shouted commands and running feet of the seamen on the deck above and realised that the ship was once more preparing to sail.

'How long this time to port?' Roger shrugged his shoulders enigmatically, not expecting an answer. 'And how many of these poor buggers will make it?'

Surprisingly, all of them on the '*Jayne Doe*', although a total of forty-six of the voyagers, including four women, three children, marines and seamen, as well as convicts would not arrive at their final destination, to be seen by many interested parties as nothing short of a miracle considering the length of the voyage, the unaccustomed ships and captains, the vagaries of the oceans and weather and the dreadful state of many of the convicts, some of whom had come on board having been incarcerated and rotting away in the notorious prison hulks for anything up to three years before being placed in the holds of the First Fleet vessels.

Though the convicts below could not know it the beginning of this last part of the journey was fraught with difficulties, the ships attempting to sail into strong headwinds, which delayed them from losing sight of the Cape for almost a week, but finally progress was made, and the ships began the crossing of the Indian Ocean.

Nine days out they ran into a patch of pleasant sunny weather with light winds, and the convicts on the '*Jayne Doe*' and three of the other vessels were allowed on deck once again.

Thomas and Roger shielded their eyes from the glare as they shuffled onto the deck, Thomas fervently hoping for a sight of Martha and his son.

He saw Sloane conversing with the captain, close by the helmsman, and caught the lieutenant's eye long enough to see him nod almost imperceptibly. Thomas' huge grin in reply brought the semblance of a smile to Sloane's face while he continued speaking.

The two convicts sat together on the gunwale, watching the other ships.

'Do you not think it incredible, Roger, that so many tiny man-made coffins could, with the help of a few pieces of canvas, have travelled so many leagues over huge oceans and still be together?'

'Methinks 'tis a farmer speaking, Thomas. They are made of good stout English oak remember. However, I agree with you, though before we arrived at Yarmouth the nearest thing to a ship I had sailed in was a punt along the river in Cambridge.'

'I have heard tell that it is a fine city.'

'The buildings are some of the finest in the world and most impressive.'

'What did you there?'

'Some of my finest work.' He winked and made a pretend deal with the cards.

'Well paid, I trust?'

'Enough so that I had to leave in a great rush and not publicly.'

Thomas laughed and found it incongruous that he could do so. The nod from Sloane had changed the shape of his entire world on that glorious morning, sailing on the surface of an incredibly blue, peaceful ocean.

Roger nodded, 'You are in fine spirits this day.'

'Aye, my friend, I am, and may it long continue.'

CHAPTER THIRTEEN

They did well to enjoy that day, for it was the last on which they were allowed sight of the sea, although they were to know all of her ugly moods.

The glass fell rapidly, and sails were shortened on all the ships, making them ready for the blow.

When it came, even though they were prepared, conditions on board the ships deteriorated swiftly.

For seventeen days and nights, ferocious storms in the Roaring Forties had the decks of all the vessels under water throughout the twenty-four hours of each day, and the salt water, which reached every nook and cranny, made the lives of the convicts infinitely worse than before. On the few occasions that the salt dried, it itched worse than the lice, but for the most part they were soaking wet, cold and miserable. Food was almost impossible to prepare, and what was offered was cold and soaked with sea water.

One particularly bad morning when the '*Jayne Doe*' was standing on its head one moment and on its stern the next, and the convicts were being thrown from one end of the cage to the other, bodies tumbling over bodies, hitting the bars at the one end and the wall at the other, Roger managed to grit out, 'Are we to die, Thomas?'

His friend, his back being slammed repeatedly against the bars, stuttered, 'Nnnot if Mmartha is rrright, and ssshe always is.'

'That is…' Whatever word Roger was about to utter was driven from his lungs by the arrival on his chest of one of the other convicts, his body flying through the air almost as fast as a horse could run.

When he had thrown off his unintentional attacker both of them suddenly saw the humour in the ridiculous situation and started laughing in a moment of lull between waves.

Within seconds every man in the cage, though still being thrown about and hurt, was howling with laughter, tears running from his eyes, caught by the sheer hysteria emanating from Thomas and Roger. Forever afterwards many would look back on that moment as both the high and the low point of the voyage.

The ship's log noted, "Extremely heavy seas, continually bursting over the vessel, with strong gales reaching near hurricane force. The situation for everyone on board is dire."

Although it was midsummer in the southern latitudes, the temperature was no higher than a winter's day in England and was the lowest they had so far met on the voyage. Attempts to celebrate Christmas were set to naught by huge seas. Night after night, captains stayed awake, believing that their ships would founder before daylight.

Many of the older seafarers muttered that the seas were the worst they had ever encountered. Phillip was sure that he would lose some of the ships. Suffering even worse than the men were the animals, soaked with brine and thrown about with abandon, their fodder inedible.

The weeks passed with little let up, until on the fourth of January 1788 they sighted Van Diemen's Land, later to be renamed Tasmania, off to the northwest. For two days, the weather relented marginally, the skies heavily overcast and with moderate winds that continually changed direction, making sailing difficult but easier than before, and the desperately fatigued crews began to believe that the worst might be over when the most violent squall of the entire voyage, a squall of truly hurricane strength, hit the ships without warning. Bolt after bolt of lightning shattered the heavens, with deafening thunder and sheets of rain accompanying them. Seamen worked frantically in desperate, life-threatening situations to lower sail and loosen sheets. Despite their valiant efforts, every ship in the Fleet was damaged. Some lost topsails and main yards; two had been in danger of being dismasted. Many were the heartfelt prayers offered up to a God who seemed not only to have deserted them but who was intent on destroying them with his forces.

To the men subjected to it, the squall seemed to go on forever, but it in fact lasted less than two hours, its short duration saving several of the vessels, which could easily have foundered had the travail continued much longer.

It was the start of a most difficult run up to Botany Bay, with strong headwinds all the way, and a cross sea current that caused every helmsman to end each watch with aching arms from continually fighting the wheel, but despite the problems, the fleet at last reached its destination. The first ship, the '*Supply*', arrived on January 17th 1788.

The seamen were intrigued to see a small crowd of virtually naked men with black skin on the shoreline, some holding spears, watching their arrival without apparent fear.

The new Governor of New South Wales immediately went ashore with his Chief Surveyor and John White, the Chief Surgeon, along with a small party of seamen and marines, to inspect the site given such a good description by James Cook.

They found the soil almost infertile and the water supply poor and of bad quality.

Phillip stayed only two days and on the third set off to look for a better site. He found one, Port Jackson, later to become Sydney Harbour, only eight miles to the north, described by John White as "*the finest haven on earth*".

Just inland Phillip found a sheltered cove with plenty of fresh water and named it Sydney Cove, after the then Home Secretary.

He immediately decided that the penal settlement should be set up there and sailed back to bring the rest of the fleet to the spot.

Once again, the weather resisted them, with violent headwinds and awkward seas almost wrecking them on the rocky shore. For two days, in great danger, they fought wind and tide, trying to leave Botany Bay, finally achieving their aim and arriving on the afternoon of the twenty-sixth of January in Port Jackson, but every ship had even more damage to sails, spars and rigging.

Below deck on the '*Jayne Doe*', the convicts had been told by one of the seamen that they had finally arrived at their destination, and many men, who before the voyage had never uttered a prayer, thanked their God for their salvation.

They were not to know that their troubles were far from over.

CHAPTER FOURTEEN

The animals that had been carried were in a parlous state, particularly the cattle, whose fodder had been destroyed by the salt water.

One of Phillip's first orders was for a party to fetch fresh fodder for them from on shore. After a few feeds to give them enough strength for the transfer the animals themselves would be sent ashore to browse.

Shortly thereafter he called a council of war, comprising all the senior officials and the marine officers, and once they were seated in the large cabin on the *Supply* he began, 'The problems of the oceans are now behind us, gentlemen, and thank the Good Lord that He has brought us safely to our new home. Different and even greater problems now confront us. As some of you may know I have some farming experience, having farmed at Lyndhurst in Hampshire for eleven years, but little of that was hands-on experience; all of the actual work was carried out by my tenant farmers and labourers, although I made a study of animal husbandry and crop rotation. What little knowledge I have may be of some advisory help, but my other duties will not allow time to involve myself in the task of farming per se. We are in dire need of experienced farm workers, and I require you all to question the convicts on your vessels to ascertain whether there are any such. The next fleet will bring free men, wanting to find land and farm it, but although I made great efforts to have free men accompany this fleet, my requests were turned down.' He smiled and made what was for him a rare joke, 'The authorities in England have much to answer for in this respect, for not having convicted more farmers.'

Sloane was making slight gestures with his hand and caught Phillip's eye.

'Lieutenant?'

'There is at least one farmer among the convicts, sir, on the '*Jayne Doe*'; a man called Thomas Nash. His wife travelled on the same ship. I know something of this man and believe he may have been falsely accused and convicted. His sentence was fourteen years.'

He found every head in the room turned towards him, viewing him much in the way they would if he had farted loudly in mixed company.

He reddened but continued, 'I have spoken with him on two occasions and I was impressed. My long knowledge of men leads me to believe he is honest and intelligent and a hard worker.'

Phillip pondered the situation for a moment. What he was considering was highly unusual, but these were far from normal circumstances.

He ordered, 'Bring him to me later this forenoon. I would like to judge for myself. If he is indeed a farmer and knows his trade we must use him and anyone else with similar skills. Now to other matters: I have decided that the male convicts should be taken ashore as soon as possible to begin the task of clearing land and preparing timber for building. That is one of our first necessities. Once the convicts and their warders are housed and the layout of the settlement has been decided, the prefabricated shell of the first Government House can be transported to land and erected. It will be important to have at least the façade of authority in place. The female prisoners shall stay on board until we have made separate provision for them, for reasons I am sure I do not need to delineate. Now as to victuals: of the two years' supply of provisions we loaded before leaving England we now have less than a quarter that has not been ruined during the voyage. We must ration what we have, unless we can find enough additional foodstuffs naturally occurring in this new country. I have watched the aboriginal people through the glass and they appear well fed. Ergo, there must be food available. Finding it will be one of your first priorities if we are not to starve before the Second Fleet arrives. So, gentlemen, let battle commence.'

Thomas, Roger and their fellow prisoners were taken up to the deck, where a blacksmith removed their shackles. Among the seamen around them there seemed to be almost an air of carnival, not a man among them who was not rejoicing at having survived the worst experience of their lives.

Looking down at his ankles, at last free of the iron menaces, Roger asked, 'Will we ever lose these scabs and scars?'

Thomas shook his head, 'I fear never. Perchance we shall one day wear them as badges of honour.'

He saw Lieutenant Sloane approaching and managed a smile of greeting.

The marine said, 'Come with me, Nash.'

He led him to the foredeck, where two seamen waited with brushes and buckets.

Sloane ordered, 'Strip.'

The rags almost fell from his body, and he stood stark naked, being watched by all the convicts assembled and feeling like a prize hog being prepared for slaughter.

Sloane nodded, and the two men set to work, throwing first of all a bucket of water over the convict and then handing him a bar of soap.

To be able to clean himself for the first time in so many months was an unexpected delight, and Thomas set to work with a will.

When he had soaped himself all over, the two men energetically worked over him with their rough scrub brushes, almost tearing the skin from his body, then more buckets of water were thrown to wash off the scum and lather.

A third man who had been standing to one side brought over a rough towel and handed it to Thomas.

When he was dry the same man who had held the towel handed him a longitudinally red-striped new shirt, followed by a new pair of breeches, a short blue coat and leather moccasins.

The lieutenant was looking on, grinning, and when the convict was dressed jerked his head for Thomas to follow him.

Thomas was puzzled but followed to the side of the ship, where he found, on looking down, that a longboat had been lowered. A rope ladder hung from the gunwale.

Sloane went first, followed by Thomas, who was itching to ask what lay afoot but had learnt over the last months to keep his own counsel.

Sloane leant towards him and murmured 'All is well with your family.'

He straightened up and looked towards one of the other ships as the six seamen began plying the oars.

Thomas noticed that they were headed for the largest of the Fleet vessels, the '*Supply*'.

With the current against them and a two-foot swell the rowers had their work cut out for them but managed the trip in just under the quarter hour.

Once again a rope ladder hung down the side of the ship.

They clambered up it, Thomas hugely thankful for legs free of the clanking, unwieldy shackles.

At the top, as he scrambled over the side, Sloane told him, 'You are to see Captain Phillip, the Governor of New South Wales.'

A sergeant-at-arms led them to the main cabin and knocked on the door.

They heard a shout of 'Enter' and went in.

Phillip stood in front of his desk and began sizing up his visitor.

He was convict-pale, as was only to be expected, but had the look of a son of the soil. Though obviously overwhelmed at being brought into Phillip's presence he was not as cowed as the Governor had expected and seemed to carry a natural pride in himself.

'The lieutenant tells me you are a farmer, Nash. Does that mean that you worked for a tenant farmer as a labourer, or actually owned land?'

Though his pride had been badly dented Thomas drew himself up and told the Governor firmly, 'My family has farmed at Danfield Hall, in Norfolk, for almost two hundred years, sir. We were given the land in perpetuity by Oliver Cromwell, as reward for my ancestor's bravery in battle.'

Phillip was an old hand at not showing his feelings but could not help being impressed. He had not heard of the place, but a farm with a hall was not something to be sneezed at, and if Cromwell had given land to a soldier the man must have earned it the hard way. Cromwell was not renowned for his open-handedness.

'How many acres?'

'Five hundred, sir.'

Phillip was not about to get into a discussion as to the whys and wherefores of Nash's demise. If Sloane was of the opinion that the man might be innocent it could well be so, but it had little to do with the present situation. An honest man, of course, would be preferable to a rogue, and somehow Phillip did not think the man in front of him fell into that category.

'Do you read and write?'

'I do, sir, and reckon. I have some Latin also.'

Now Phillip was impressed. An unusual character, this farmer.

'What rotation system did you use?'

'The four-year method, sir.'

So, Phillip thought, he was up-to-date in that respect.

'Did you have cattle?'

'A herd of over thirty, sir.'

'Longhorn or shorthorn?'

'Shorthorn, sir. I introduced them to the county.'

'Sheep?'

'Leicesters.'

'Swine?'

'Four dozen.'

'What crops?'

'Wheat, barley, oats, clover, turnips and other vegetables.'

'What can we grow here?'

Thomas shrugged, 'Possibly everything we grew in England, but with no knowledge of the likely weather I cannot predict the results. After a year or two…'

'A luxury we do not have, unfortunately. I must tell you truthfully, Nash, though I ask you not to repeat it, we are in very real danger of dying of hunger here if we cannot feed ourselves. Much of what we brought with us has been ruined, including, I must point out, most of the seeds we carried with us for planting. Only approximately one fifth of those seeds remain of use, which

119

will make your task much harder.' He continued to size Thomas up. Finally, he made the decision, 'I have a mind to place you in charge of the first farm. You may use any of the convict labour you need. Lieutenant Sloane will oversee your work and that of the men. Now, what will be your first priority?'

'Timber clearance and hutted accommodation for the men. They will not work well if they are wet and cold, though at present the last does not seem likely. Then the breaking up of the earth and the planting of seed, depending on the season. It now seems like summer, and if we plant now and the winter is as it is in England we could lose the entire crop.'

Phillip was impressed. The man was not attempting to bluff him with big ideas of his farming ability but thought instead immediately of his labourers' comfort. It was a great pity he was not a free man; Phillip knew he needed such men as this if his plans were to come to fruition.

'True enough. This is the equivalent of our July, and we have no idea what winter here will be like. I agree with you that we must wait until the Spring to plant cereals, but vegetables could well be grown. Lieutenant Sloane will see to your requirements and will bring your reports back to me.' He considered for another few moments before adding, 'I cannot immediately make you a free man, Nash. Rightly or wrongly you were legally convicted by a court and sentenced, but it is within my powers to reduce your sentence to seven years, and if you make a success of this I shall reward you in that way. Good day, gentlemen.'

Once outside Thomas asked, 'Can I take one of my fellow convicts with me? He saved my life once, and I owe him the chance to make good?'

'His name?'

'Roger Clarke.'

'That is acceptable, and any of the others on the '*Jayne Doe*' that you think suitable as convict supervisors. You will be in overall charge of operations, since you alone have the knowledge of what is required, but each supervisor will have a team of twelve workers, and the supervisors will report any slacking or criminal activity to you. You will then pass those reports on to me for action.'

Back on board the convicts were lined up for him, and he chose seven of the most likely by looking at their physique, age, and apparent health, leaving out those he had seen as inherent troublemakers during the voyage.

When Thomas told Roger of their relative good fortune his friend was ecstatic, and coined an expression that he was to use so often and be heard by so many that it would become part of the new nation's basic vocabulary, 'You beauty!'

It did not take long for them to moderate their appreciation. The trip to shore in a heavy sea, followed by weeks of back-breaking, urgent work under skies that one minute drenched them with stinging, torrential rain and the next burnt them under a blazing sun while they toiled in temperatures well over a hundred degrees Fahrenheit, with humidity over ninety percent, seemed to be like a never-ending bad dream. In the early mornings and the evenings, they were plagued by hundreds of marauding flies and mosquitoes that seemed intent on sucking the last drop of blood from them, the raw bites leaving them wanting to scratch their skins off during the days and making them toss and turn in their sleep. Poisonous spiders and snakes caused several casualties, three of them fatal. They had little time to appreciate the delights of the very different flora and fauna. What astonished Thomas most was the abundance of colourful parrots, cockatiels and parakeets, more numerous than the ubiquitous sparrow back home.

The keeping of discipline was paramount, and Phillip issued a list of punishments prescribed for those breaking certain laws.

Stealing an animal which was to be used for food or breeding would carry the death penalty, along with murder. Stealing of any other food, in no matter how small a quantity, would get a man fifty lashes. Rape, depending upon the severity, would be punished with anything from fifty lashes to death. A full list of other crimes was given, with their related punishments.

The settlement was a going concern.

For the first fortnight they slept under lean-to canvas, but Thomas insisted they build huts.

Not only his workers, but all the teams attempting to use timber for building were finding the same problems: the tools they had brought out with them were not up to the job of cutting the hardwoods - the Forest Red Gum, the Red Bloodwood, the Cabbage Tree Palm and the She Oak, many of them breaking and the rest quickly becoming blunt and useless for the job. One officer reported that the tools were of a quality worse than those cheaply made for the African trade. Phillip was incensed but could do little except send a report back to England on the returning ships, asking for good quality tools to be sent as soon as possible. Soon, only the 'Sirius' and the 'Supply' were left anchored in the Cove, the former to founder the following year off Norfolk Island. It was mainly the Red Gum tree that was initially used for building, but they soon discovered that its wood split and warped very quickly, and buildings built with it fell down. It was reported, tongue in cheek, that it was very good for burning.

Thomas was finding that, human nature being what it was, some convicts worked well, and others liked to slack, some surreptitiously and some openly. The latter seemed to have a kind of jungle telegraph that warned them when Sloane was on his way for his regular inspections and would leap up and pretend to be working frantically while under his eye. The worst offenders were two men called Chatto Barnes and Willy Crabb, who blatantly refused to work, and would sit down all day watching the others labour. Charles Black, the convict supervisor of that group, had reported them to Thomas more than a dozen times, and Thomas had warned them as often.

The first time he did so, they had reluctantly taken up their tools and made a token effort until he was out of sight, but the second time Chatto stood up to him.

'You can piss off, Nash. I'm not taking orders from you. You're no better than me. You're just a bloody convict like the rest of us.'

Thomas tried to keep his temper. The damned man was right, of course. He had no authority except that delegated, and that stood for nothing. It was not possible for him to report a fellow convict to Sloane, much as he would wish to do so.

Keeping his voice even, he said, 'You can think what you like, Barnes, but we are all in this together, and if we do not grow food both you and I and all these other men will die of starvation. Why don't you do your bit to help?'

It was in some strange way, Thomas felt, like giving orders to a brother. Looking at his fellow convict was almost like looking into a mirror, except for Chatto's lips, which were the petulant, over-large lips of a sadist and pervert. Chatto was the same height and build, with a shock of the same shade of brown hair as Thomas, brown eyes and a similar shaped face, aside from the Nash nose. A murderer, who loved to torture and rape women before he murdered them, he had killed six times. On the seventh attempt, he was caught before he could kill the woman and had been charged merely with battery and sentenced to seven years.

He sneered, 'As I said, piss off.'

Sloane was no man's fool. He had years of experience with barrack-room lawyers and slackers in the marines and had realised from the off that maintaining discipline would be almost impossible for Thomas and was not restricting his observations to the daily visits. He had a ladder built and tied to one of the trees, just beyond the area being cleared, and climbed it two or three times a day with a spy glass to take a measure of exactly what was going on. He had seen several men slacking and had particularly noted Barnes and Crabb sitting and lying down all day, making not the slightest effort to work.

He watched as Thomas spoke to them and noted their belligerent attitude, and he saw them sit down again when Thomas walked away.

He collected four of his men and marched them into the work area and straight towards Barnes' and Crabb's work party, where the two miscreants were working furiously, having leapt to their feet and grabbed their tools when they saw the marines approaching.

123

Sloane brought his men to a halt and they stood watching the sweat breaking out on the brows of the two men for the first time in a good many days.

He enjoyed watching them toil for a long ten minutes before he drawled, 'You two like work, do you?'

Barnes looked up with a subservient look on his face, making a show of rubbing the sweat from his brow with the back of his hand, 'That we do, sir. That we do.'

Sloane glared at him with his one good eye, 'But only while you know I am observing you, it seems. For your information, I have been watching you through my spyglass for some time, and you two seem to have had a good long rest, which I can tell you will be your last for many a day. You will be closely watched from now on, twenty-four hours a day, for you will be employed on the chain gang for the entire remainder of your sentence. There you will not sit around, I can assure you. It is even possible that those weak, unused muscles will develop.' He looked around at the other members of the party, 'And that goes for anyone else I catch slacking!'

He turned to his marines and ordered, 'Take them!'

The chain gang had been instituted by Phillip from the very start, to control the worst criminals who could not be trusted. Those thus employed were used for building roads, breaking rock and other hard labour tasks. The men on the chain gang were permanently leg-shackled and often chained together. It was the worst punishment possible, short of a sentence of death.

The two men were watched by every work crew as they were marched away. From that moment on Thomas and his supervisors were free of any further problem with slackers. None wanted to follow in Barnes' and Chatto's footsteps.

The natives who lived nearby had approached to within a few hundred yards every day, squatting on their haunches to observe the quaint efforts of these newcomers to make huts. Thomas observed them. They seemed happy and contented with their lot, well nourished and apparently with plenty of time on their hands.

One evening when work had finished and Thomas and Roger, who shared a lean-to, had finished their poor repast, Thomas said, 'I am going to try to talk to the natives.'

Roger laughed, 'And how in hell are you going to do that?'

Thomas shrugged, 'Sign language to begin with. They must have a spoken language of some sort.'

He stood up and walked slowly towards the group of eight males, who rose from their squats as he approached, two of them lifting their spears in warning. They were naked apart from strings of carved pearl shells covering the penis, and their faces were painted with charcoal and ochre; an orange clay pigment. He held both hands up with the palms towards them and they lowered the tips of their weapons.

When he got to within five yards of the group he stopped and with a broad smile on his face nodded several times in greeting, receiving strange looks in reply as they leaned their heads forward, wary and trying to gauge his intent.

He moved two paces nearer, and the spear tips came up again.

He pointed to his chest and said, 'Thom-as', making the two syllables distinct.

One of the men, who might have been the oldest, though it was difficult to tell, moved forward half a yard, pointed his finger at Thomas' chest and repeated, 'Thom-as'.

Thomas nodded and pointed at the old man.

He saw a grin develop, and the man looked at his fellow tribesmen. Suddenly, Thomas realised there were grins all round.

He heard what must be the name, 'Apari.'

He repeated it, 'Apari', and the grins widened. It would be many months before he found out that the word meant 'father'.

Another of the men, next to Apari, pointed to his own chest and said, 'Curriquinquin'.

Thomas tried it without success, and it was repeated three times before he managed to copy it. The man looked pleased, pointed to his chest again and then flapped his arms like a bird.

Thomas got the message, pointed to the sky, flapped his own arms and said clearly, 'Bird.' He was almost correct. As he found out much later it meant 'Butcher bird.'

One after another they gave their names, 'Warra', with the man pointing to the sea. It sounded so like 'water' that Thomas decided, correctly, that it was the translation.

'Banjora' pretended to be climbing a tree using paws, and Thomas guessed 'koala'. 'Tuart' pointed to a tree, 'Makuwata' lifted his spear with one hand and pointed to it with the other, then back at his chest and repeated his name. That one was obvious. 'Mandu' pointed to the sky and moved his hand across the heavens. He had to be either the sun or the moon, and 'Thala' crouched down, put one hand behind the other and made wiggling motions, leaving behind a trail in the sand that could only be that resembling a centipede.

Thomas was hugely encouraged by their understanding.

The old man entered into the spirit of the thing and lifted the shell decoration covering his penis. He tapped one of the shells and said, 'Gal-gal', then moved his hand along the line of shells and enunciated 'Riji'.

Thomas repeated the words to nods of approval, and then the old man pulled the covering aside and lifted his penis. He shook it vigorously, repeating three times, 'Gool-gah, gool-gah, gool-gah.' Then he cupped his testicles, 'Boom-be-rah'.

Banjora joined in, describing with his hands the shape of a woman and uttering the word, 'Din', before dropping one hand and making groping signs with his fingers where the pudenda would be, laughing hilariously, as Thomas heard from all sides 'Dun-gah, dun-gah'. The meaning was obvious, but whether the word was the equivalent of the crude English name for the orifice or a more refined one there was no way of knowing. From their actions, Thomas could plainly see that the interest of his new friends in that particular part of the female anatomy was no less keen than that of his fellow Englishmen. Mandu was not to be outdone and formed a woman's breasts with his hands, repeating 'Nup-pun' three times.

Thomas wanted to learn a few more words before leaving them, preferably some not referring to the female anatomy, which were of such little worth in his present situation, so lifted his hand to his right eye and with finger and thumb pointed away from the eye he opened them, to indicate looking.

The younger native called Mandu caught on first, saying 'Naa…naa'.

They all nodded and joined in a repeat. Thomas was pleased. The words were building up, and he found it easy to remember them, realising as he had when learning Latin that his brain found the task of assimilating a new language relatively easy.

Mandu pointed to Thomas' skin and said, 'Bur-rah', then pointed to his own and said, 'But-ton.' Thomas, with only his Latin learning to go on, used the same kind of mental clicks as he had with that language: word association, 'white barrow, black button'. It was easy.

He did not want to overload his brain with too many new words at one time, however. This meeting could easily be repeated. He used his fingers to show the act of walking, and was rewarded with the word, 'Yen', and he leant his head to one side and closed his eyes, which brought a laugh from the natives and several renditions of 'Nangah, nangah'.

He held up his hand in farewell and received a chorus of 'Ek-u-bas'.

He repeated, 'Ek-u-ba' and was rewarded with smiles all round. He had found a way of communicating with the natives, the first Englishman in the colony to do so. He was not to know that Governor Phillip had received direct instructions from King George III to *"obtain intercourse with the natives and gain their affection by friendship and kindness."* As a loyal subject, Phillip intended to do just that, but the natives were generally staying away. Almost desperate to do the King's bidding, he sent out marines to capture some. Three were brought back and treated with kindness. One, Arabanoo, enjoyed the company of the Englishmen, but died the next year of smallpox. Another, Wolarawarre Bennelong, became almost one with the colonists, wearing the same clothes and learning both their manners and the language.

Having supervised the beginning of a new phase of tree felling with Lieutenant Sloane, Thomas and Roger attempted to make their own hut, their efforts watched by his new friends with hilarity. Thomas had deliberately chosen for the position of their dwelling an area at the far western end of the area selected for the colony, in order to be near the natives, since he, alone among the new inhabitants at that time, felt sure that they held the answer to survival in this new land, imagining that they were, like him, farmers, and wanted to learn from them. He and Roger had chosen a post of the Cabbage Palm as the central upright for their hut, with the walls made of wattle, criss-crossed with twigs and plastered with clay, and had roofed the rough dwelling with reeds, collected from the shore.

It looked relatively substantial and rainproof, and he and Roger were quite proud of their small achievement, but it caused much merriment and head shaking among his new friends, and for a time he did not understand why.

While trying to converse with them on the evening the hut was finished, Apari pointed to the hut and said, 'Gun-ya birree-wel goo-ran.'

Thomas was unable to get the gist of what Apari was trying to say, then the old man made motions with his hands to indicate the shape of the hut and said, 'Gun-ya'. Thomas nodded, showing he understood that the old man meant 'house' or 'hut'. Then Apari shook his head several times and repeated, 'Birree-wel goo-ran'.

Thomas suddenly understood. In Apari's eyes, the hut was no good. He shrugged his shoulders. Time would tell.

Three days after the hut was completed a sudden storm blew up, and the lashing rain washed out every bit of clay from the rushes and wattle, the water coming straight through as if there were no roof and soaking the two of them inside. Thomas determined to do better next time. The same thing had happened with every hut that had been built, including those for the officers and officials, but since building experience was so sadly lacking the re-roofing was carried out in the same manner.

The following evening, after greeting the aborigines, Thomas started the conversation by first of all pointing to himself and then at the group, saying 'Naa gun-ya', which he hoped they would understand as, 'I want to see your huts.'

Mandu immediately understood and gabbled something unintelligible to the others. They looked at each other and then seemed to agree.

Apari gestured with his hand for Thomas to follow.

About three hundred yards away, they came to a hollow and there Thomas saw how the aborigines constructed their shelters. They were rude affairs, made of posts set at an angle of roughly forty-five degrees from the ground, criss-crossed with smaller branches, open on both sides and one end, but interestingly covered with nothing but sheets of bark from the eucalyptus trees. Thomas was impressed. They certainly did nothing to keep the wind out if it came from the wrong direction, but were obviously completely rainproof, and that was what mattered most. Though he was unaware of it, the design of the shelter he was looking at had been developed over thousands of years, and the natives utilised the bark of the Red Bloodwood, the Eucalyptus Corymbosa, to cover their rude shelters, knowing that rain could not penetrate it. Their canoes were made of the same material.

He had several days earlier learnt the word for 'Thank you' and used it now, 'Mur-rum-boo'.

Apari leant into one of the dwellings and brought out a roast lizard, which had been grilled on a spit of wood. He held it out to Thomas, obviously with the intention that he should eat it.

Thomas had eaten many strange things in his life and back in England liked nothing better than a pig's stomach, the 'jot', and the intestines, the 'chitterlings', in his mind the most succulent and best tasting parts of a pig, but a lizard? Trying to keep his expression from showing his uneasy inner feelings, he smiled and took the delicacy.

The first bite took him by surprise. It was delicious; somewhere between a chicken breast and a pork chop. He grinned, nodding, and began to tuck in to the rest.

Suddenly wondering if he should have shared it with them, he held out what was left, but was reassured by universal head shaking and smiles.

He finished it off and rubbed his stomach to show his appreciation. The grins showed their pleasure. Thomas was more than impressed by these people; their speech, their attitude, their interdependence upon one another, and above all their ability to live happily in what was to a great extent a hostile environment.

The next evening after work he and Roger collected a large quantity of the eucalyptus bark and re-roofed their hut, to the amusement of the nearest convicts, whose amusement would quickly turn to envy with the next downpour.

The days of heavy toil repeated themselves endlessly, a great sameness, only relieved by the tremendous changes in the weather, from steaming hot, cloudless days to monsoon conditions.

One particularly hot evening at the end of the day's work when the temperature still hovered close to ninety degrees Fahrenheit, Thomas, pouring with perspiration, decided to use the sea to cool down. Though none had been seen, apocryphal tales of sharks close in to the beach had kept all the convicts out of the water, despite the obvious benefits.

With trepidation, he cast his glance all around over the smooth surface of the sea looking for telltale fins, removed the rags he was wearing and then took two steps into the water, until it was up to his knees on the sharply shelving beach. It was blissful, and he sat down, scooping water up with his hands and casting it over his head.

He looked around again at the surface and still seeing nothing untoward slid on his backside until the water came up to his neck. The feeling, after so long with no full immersion of his body, was almost miraculous. He felt renewed and ready for anything.

It was seventeen years since he had last swum, in the moat in front of Rainforde Manor, and he wondered if he would remember how.

No shark could be seen, and he had the sudden thought that in his present situation he had so little to lose that it would be worth taking a chance.

He pushed his body forward and tried a couple of strokes, delighted that it seemed so easy in the salt water. He felt weightless and suddenly without worry, with a sense of freedom that he had not had since the day of his arrest.

He swam for more than a quarter of an hour before climbing back up the beach, finding himself the centre of amazement among the other convicts. Once in the water and swimming he had forgotten his fear of sharks. From that moment he swam every day, morning and evening, lengthening the time spent in the water and the distance swum, blissfully unaware that there were indeed large numbers of great white, tiger and bull sharks in the local waters, mainly during the summer months, and that he was incredibly lucky he did not fall foul of them.

Despite his addiction to the water, none of the other convicts would chance it, and Roger decreed, 'You are mad, Thomas; bloody mad. You will not get me in there.'

With great difficulty, some land was cleared and seeds planted. With the failure of the tools, the size of the tree roots and the great difficulty removing them, it was often necessary to leave them in the ground and plant the seeds around the stumps. The surgeon, John White, observed at one stage that he could not believe the fact that twelve men had worked for five days to remove one stump. The work was hard but no harder than it had been in England, and they became inured to the new life, which for Thomas was little different from that of his past where work was concerned: dawn to dusk sweat and toil. His thoughts when not concentrating on the work had been almost exclusively of Martha, and at the beginning he had hoped for a sight of her from time to time, but she was at the far end of the settlement, out of bounds to the convicts, and his work kept him away from that area. Sloane visited occasionally and when he did always brought good news concerning Martha and Austin, but those visits became less regular as he was given other duties. The Governor's prefabricated dwelling was brought ashore and erected, and efforts were made to complete it, although lime had not yet been found in the new country, and what little they had brought with them was dwindling fast. Food became much scarcer, and not only the convicts but also the marines and officials were suffering on tight rations. Thomas, however, was learning all the time from Apari and his band which of the native flora it was safe and good to eat and which to leave well alone. One thing in particular that Thomas ate regularly and Roger would not was warrigal greens, which grew in abundance. Many of the convicts had tried them and had bad stomach upsets afterwards. Thomas had watched the aborigines prepare them the first time he tried them. They placed the greens in boiling water for around a minute, then tipped that water out and washed them before putting them in fresh boiling water for several more minutes. With no science to help them they had, over the millennia, realised that the leaves contained something noxious, in actual fact oxalates, as does spinach, which needed to be removed before eating. The greens grew like weeds, readily available, and would one day become a favourite 'bush tucker'.

Thomas found them refreshing, though very different from a Norfolk cabbage, and ate them daily. Roger refused to try anything but the food issued and was losing weight, despite Thomas' efforts to have him try the local additions to the diet.

One evening, Thomas was presented with a handful of witchetty grubs, which the natives dug up from the roots of acacia bushes and loved eating.

They showed him how to eat them, and with great trepidation he put one in his mouth and chewed. Astonishingly, he found them, like the lizard, very tasty, although the texture was rather strange in his mouth and difficult to get used to.

Other delicacies he was given were raw oysters, for which he quickly acquired a taste, some berries that looked somewhat like large blackcurrants that the natives called 'muntry', a green fruit shaped like a finger and tasting of lime, and a tree fungus, later called a beefsteak fungus, having the taste of beef but needing minutes of hard chewing, no matter how long it was cooked. He tried snake, emu, and koala, and one day found his friends in fine form, having just hunted and killed a kangaroo, whose meat he found unusual but highly palatable. Roger agreed to try that, since it looked similar to beefsteak, and he enjoyed it, but would still not give in on the vegetables.

On one occasion, while Thomas was talking to his new friends, another group of aborigines approached, holding their spears belligerently and jabbering incessantly.

His hosts stood to their own weapons, and a confrontation seemed inevitable, but eventually the other aborigines drifted off again, muttering among themselves.

Apari conveyed to him with sign language and a few words that he knew, that the other group were, in fact, the locals, and that his group did not normally live there but further to the north. He said something else that Thomas did not understand, but which gave him the impression from the hand waving accompanying the description, that their group had fallen out with others of their tribe and had left their home area. Apari indicated first his own group and said, 'Kat-tang' and then the group that was leaving, describing them with the word 'Eora'. It was only years later that it became known that all these people were, in fact, the Cadigal, seven tribes living in that area, using the same language group, but with individual languages. When he said they were Eora, he was actually saying, 'people from this place'.

One interesting adjunct to Thomas' language learning was that Banjora's knowledge of English improved rapidly, until he was able to convey many simple ideas that he kept trying to use on Roger, much to the latter's annoyance.

The work continued apace, and life progressed peacefully enough for six more weeks until two thatchers, collecting reeds down by the water's edge of the Cove, were killed by natives; the first inter-nation deaths, which were to escalate dramatically in later years.

The marines and the newly formed New South Wales Corps were given orders to round up all natives in the area and carry out sample punishments, and Apari and his band, the only unfortunates close to hand, were rounded up and brought into the settlement.

Thomas sent word to Sloane that they were peaceful and had had nothing to do with the incident, but it had been decided that an example had to be set. Apari and Banjora were lashed to a frame and given one hundred lashes each, leaving their backs flayed open and raw. The punishment would have killed an Englishman. The other aborigines were made to witness the flogging, appalled at the severity of the punishment, and were then driven off. The marine officer who had ordered the action had not the slightest idea that the various tribes of aborigines hardly mixed and spoke over two hundred different languages. He was far from alone in his ignorance.

Once the marines giving the punishments had left, Thomas and Roger cut the two men from the frames, carried them into their hut and laid them on their own beds. Both of the aborigines were in a bad way and close from death. Thomas had a jar of grease, which they used for cooking. For two days, four times a day, he smoothed the grease into the wounds on their backs, easing the pain and aiding the healing. He and Roger fed and watered them as they would small children, sharing what little food was supplied, and gradually they began to recover. On the third day, Mandu appeared at the door with a large leaf containing a mixture of some pulped green vegetable matter, which he worked into the raw backs of his fellow aborigines, after making signs to Thomas about what he wanted to do. It appeared to ease their pain, and Thomas ceased using the grease.

He had another problem: Roger himself was beginning to worry him. He was lethargic, not wanting to work, and complained daily of malaise.

By the end of the fourth day after the whipping the two aborigines were sitting up and though still in great pain were out of danger. The rest of the little band had returned to the vicinity but remained some quarter of a mile away. Thomas had tried to approach them on three occasions, to tell them that Apari and

Banjora were all right, but each time they melted away almost by magic, seeming to disappear into the earth.

On the fifth day, Banjora said, 'Thom-as, we go. Thank you.'

Thomas nodded.

He watched them hobble away, and when they were only twenty paces from the hut saw the rest of the group running towards them. Suddenly, the two men were swallowed up by the others as they moved away, almost as one body.

Thomas returned to the hut to find Roger looking even glummer than usual and feeling inside his mouth. He asked, 'What is it?'

Roger pulled his lip down, 'Look'.

His gums looked spongy and were bleeding.

'And this too.' He pointed to his legs where dozens of large spots had formed.

Thomas had seen others in the settlement with similar symptoms and knew Roger was suffering from scurvy, which was spreading rapidly among both the convicts and the marines, slowing the work.

He wondered why he had not been affected and could only put it down to the oddments of aboriginal diet he had been samplings.

That night after dark, Thomas heard a scrabbling noise outside and imagined one of the kangaroos they had seen far off had come into camp.

Something slithered in by the entrance, and Thomas jumped up, prepared to defend himself.

A whispered voice said, 'Thom-as', and he realised it was Mandu, the youngest of the aborigines.

Thomas lit the candle and saw that Mandu was carrying something wrapped in a huge leaf.

He held it out and passed it to Thomas, uttering what sounded like, 'Roo-ga'. He nodded downwards at the sleeping form of the convict.

Thomas opened the leaf and found nine of the green finger fruits that tasted of lime. He realised the natives knew they had properties that would cure the scurvy.

Before he could thank Mandu, the little aborigine had disappeared again out through the entrance.

Thomas woke Roger and insisted he eat two of the fruits, telling him they would begin his cure. This time they were not refused, and when Thomas prepared warrigal greens to go with his rations the next day, Roger accepted and ate those too.

While he was eating the last of the fruits, Thomas broke the one unwritten law all convicts obeyed, save those who liked to boast and lie.

He asked, 'Tell me of yourself.'

Weak as he was and friend that he was, Roger reacted much in the way Thomas had expected.

'That is my business.' He insisted, and his face suffused with sudden anger.

Thomas lifted his hands in supplication, 'Yes, of course, it is. I apologise.'

Roger's anger dissipated on an instant and he sighed, 'Oh, why in hell should I not tell you? I may die within days; we may never leave here alive. I know of your past; much of it anyway. At least you are an innocent man. I am not.'

Wearily and with long pauses, he told his tale:

'I come not from Norfolk originally, though I have lived there a good many years. My father inherited four hostelries in Boston, Lincolnshire, and I enjoyed a good education and a happy childhood. He drank heavily, that I knew, but what I did not know was that he was also a gambler and a womaniser. He became deeper and deeper in debt and lost one inn after another, until we found ourselves on the road, escaping from his debtors. My mother was ill, and he would not pause in our flight for her to rest. I was fifteen.

One night, he stopped the carriage at the edge of a village and went to an inn. We had not eaten since the previous day, and he angered me by spending money on ale. I left my mother and went to forage for food. When I returned the carriage was gone, but my mother's body lay in the road. He had strangled her.

It took me six days to find him, though he had not gone far. He was lying dead drunk beside the carriage, which was standing on the side of the road. Five minutes later he was dead. I had pushed his own dagger into his black heart. In his pockets, I found more than thirty guineas. If I was unsure before, that convinced me of his evil. We could have eaten for months with that money or stopped for mother to recover. I had no sorrow at my deed, nor have I now, but from that moment on I was a murderer.

The nearest town was King's Lynn, and I stayed there for two weeks. One day in the market square, a travelling circus had set up, and I watched the different antics, since I had little else to do. One of the tricksters was a card sharp, and I watched him carefully. After a while, I could see how he was manipulating the cards, and when the crowd dissipated I approached him and asked if he would teach me the trick, since I had seen how he did it. He was upset that I had noticed but showed me one or two moves, which I learnt very quickly. The upshot was that he took me on as a helper. We fleeced the public in every town, and I travelled with the circus for five years, by which time I was much the better with the cards. He was arrested one day when we were in Aylsham, and I left the circus and began to play in gambling houses. Norwich seemed to offer more opportunity, and I settled there at the age of twenty-two. I cheated and lied every day until I was arrested and thrown into the Castle. So there you have it: murderer, liar, thief, cheat. A pretty story, you must admit. And you would have me for your friend?'

'You never married?'

'In my occupation, a wife would have been a most unnecessary distraction. Women of ill repute have had much to thank me for over the years.'

Thomas regarded him thoughtfully, 'You are not a bad man, Roger.'

His friend grinned sardonically, 'You may be the only man on earth to believe so, Thomas.'

Within three days, the spots began to disappear, and Roger declared that he felt better. 'You were right; those bloody blacks do know a thing or two.'

Floods washed out some of the vegetable seeds they had sown; others wilted in the burning dry heat spells, despite valiant efforts to keep them watered. By the time it came to plant the cereal crops, they had little to show for their determined efforts.

Thomas felt that he had failed the Governor.

One steaming hot day, when the sweat ran heavy down every brow, and the very air through which the tools moved seemed almost to have taken on a plastic, resistant substance, Thomas saw Sloane coming towards him.

He greeted him, 'Lieutenant. You are somewhat of a stranger.'

Sloane agreed, 'I have so many other duties now, and the 'Rum Corps' is taking over the policing of the convicts.'

'You have come because of the poor harvest?'

'No, I spoke to the Governor yesterday, concerning that very matter. He is acutely aware of the problems. He has observed closely the setbacks you have endured, and has asked me to ensure that you do not blame yourself.'

Thomas sighed with relief, 'That is good to know.' He was itching for news of Martha and Austin.

Sloane had saved his good news, 'If you will come with me, it may be possible for you to see your wife and son.'

A happier man never walked a mile, and though Sloane said not another word while they progressed through the work area, observed as they were by other jeering convicts, and needing to preserve the appearance of warder and prisoner, Thomas' heart was overflowing, and the urgent need to grin and jump for joy was hard indeed to suppress.

They reached a piece of ground that had been flattened and prepared for housing, with the beginning of a road under construction before them. The Governor's house at the far end, the only two-storey structure in Australia at that date, was coming on apace and was taking on the appearance of a dwelling; five other structures were partially built.

Sloane's was the last in the row and was merely an oblong some twenty feet in length and fifteen wide, built with several uncut round uprights, with smaller branches horizontally laid between them, covered with wattle and daub and roofed with clay-packed rushes. There was no door, and the window openings had no glass.

Looking carefully around him and observing no onlookers Sloane said, 'Remain here.'

He walked into the building and came out a few moments later carrying an infant, which he brought over to Thomas.

He said, 'I cannot let you take him, Thomas, it would appear unseemly to any watcher, but you may touch him if you will.'

Thomas' eyes were full of happy tears. The boy was bonny and well nourished. He had the dark brown eyes of the Nash family and a shock of curly brown hair. Thomas found himself being scrutinised as an unfamiliar face, but the child was happy, he could see. He ran his work roughened hand over his son's forehead and was rewarded with a giggle.

Sloane then surprised him greatly. He looked around once more and then urged, 'Martha awaits you in the back room. You have fifteen minutes.'

He turned and carried the child towards the trees.

Thomas rushed inside and through to the back room, into the waiting arms of his beloved wife.

They kissed and hugged and hugged and kissed, the kisses becoming uncontrollably passionate, until Martha pushed him away slightly and whispered, 'Quickly, Thomas, quickly.'

She lifted her skirts and lay down swiftly on the palliasse, opening her legs to him.

It was over in less than a minute; more than a year of urgent, frustrated desire encapsulated in a mad moment of time, a madness that engulfed their two bodies as one, before they both lay panting frantically, trying to recover their breath, as Thomas' seed still spurted insistently into her belly. Without warning he was overtaken by another madness: what began as a giggle in his throat became, in seconds, a guffaw, followed by another, turning into hysterical laughter, so infectious that he found Martha overcome too, and howling with laughter beside him.

When the laughter subsided slightly he asked, 'Another Austin?'

She nodded, 'You will have another son, and he will be called Thomas.' She became suddenly sober, 'I fear for you, Thomas. You will suffer greatly, and I cannot see you on the far side of that suffering. The mists are too thick.'

'But I am well, look at me, healthy and fit.'

He could see the pain in her eyes, and though she made no reply he knew she had seen a future that bode ill for him.

She began to get up, 'Come, Arthur has been kind acceding to my request, but we have such little time, and I would not want to make misuse of his good offices.'

Thomas did not want to but had to ask, 'Has he...?'

She smiled, 'No, Thomas, he has not. Nor made the slightest remark or gesture. He is the very best of men; a true gentleman.'

They held each other tightly and kissed frenziedly until she pushed him away again and told him, 'Go now, and keep me in your thoughts, as I shall keep you in mine.'

She turned and disappeared into the back room. He noticed that the front room, furnished simply with a rough-hewn table, two stools and a chest, also had a palliasse on the floor. Martha and the lieutenant had separate sleeping compartments. It reassured him, and he thought of the months of heartache and impotent desperation he had endured, attempting vainly to repress thoughts of her lying with a new lover.

Outside, Sloane was repeatedly holding the child over his head and pretending to drop him, catching him at waist level each time, causing howls of laughter and giggles. Thomas wished with all his heart that he could do the same, but was more than thankful for what he had been allowed. Sloane had taken a great chance in allowing him this meeting.

He walked quickly to the pair and said, 'One day I shall shake your hand, Lieutenant, when I am allowed that privilege. You are a good man.'

Sloane grinned, 'Have you a mind, then, to ruin my bad reputation, Thomas?'

'That I would never do. I am sure you know that.'

'I do. Now you must get back to your work.'

His heart bursting, Thomas told him, 'I can never thank you enough.'

Amazingly he detected moisture at the corners of Sloane's eyes as the lieutenant urged, 'Go, man. Now, before someone demands to know what you are doing in this area.' He quickly turned his back.

Weeks turned into months. Thomas and Roger remained in good health, thanks to the finger limes, the warrigal greens and the other occasional additions to their diet provided by the natives, who seemed to be making extra efforts to provide them with food.

The rest of the convicts and many of the marines, however, were in a dire state, the scurvy having debilitated them terribly. Rations had been cut to the bone, and there seemed no let up in sight. Rats, crows, the ubiquitous cockatoos, lorikeets and other birds were killed, though in insufficient quantities to help matters greatly, their stringy flesh providing little nourishment and difficult for men with bleeding gums to tear from the bones. Worse, they were of no help whatsoever in fighting the scurvy. Thomas found his work force reduced, though he had managed to sow the cereals in mid-August.

Dwellings erected using the Red Gum wood continued to fall down. By July, apart from those who had made huts like Thomas, all the convicts and all the marines were still under canvas. The large hospital building collapsed and had to be restarted.

Thomas' greatest worry, however, was the lack of rain. The cereal seeds had sprouted and reached two inches in height when the last rain fell, succeeded by weeks and then months of terrible drought, with unbearably high temperatures and days of searing strong winds, removing what little moisture the leaves held. It was impossible to water such a large area, though some efforts were made in one corner of the field, with little visible gain. The plants withered and died. For the colony, almost starving, it was an unmitigated disaster.

For most of the settlement food became desperately scarce, and though Thomas and Roger tried to spread the word about the native flora most of their words fell on deaf ears. Even Governor Phillip was losing weight fast.

It became more and more necessary to eke out what food was left, and Phillip decided to set up another penal colony on Norfolk Island, ostensibly for the more hardened criminals. To this effect, he sent the '*Supply*' with two dozen convicts to prepare the site. They found the soil a great improvement on that of Garden Cove and were easily able to catch green turtles for food. The timber, too, at first appeared to be of better quality and easier to work.

Thomas continued his friendship with the aborigines, who gradually came into the settlement, along with three other groups that Apari pejoratively referred to as 'Bulboh Eora', the first word of which Thomas initially fancied to mean 'bastard' or an equally rude word, afterwards realising that the first imagined meaning was impossible, since they had no such thing as a bastard in their society. On questioning Banjora, however, he found out that the word 'bulboh' meant 'kangaroo rat', which apparently was the lowest form of life the aborigines could imagine.

Word of the sight of sail on the morning of the third of June 1790 spread like wildfire, and hopes were raised of relief from the famine.

They were to be dashed when the truth became known.

The '*Lady Juliana*' had sailed from England alone for the voyage to the colony, carrying two hundred and twenty-one female convicts, almost every one of them a prostitute, and later accounts showed that it became a travelling brothel, with every man on board conjugating with the women. Even in the ports that they visited men were welcomed aboard to taste the doubtful delights of the long unwashed women, provided they paid for the privilege. The ship, which had taken three hundred and six days to reach its destination, the longest run by any convict ship, had used up every ounce of its victuals, and the arrival was seen as a disaster. Phillip was horrified at the addition of two hundred plus virtually useless drains on his almost exhausted supplies. A ship load of that many highly promiscuous women was a gift he could well have done without.

The ship did, however, bring news that another fleet was coming, and its vessels began arriving later in the same month, the first of them, the *'Justinian'*, the Fleet store ship, bringing some unused supplies and welcome amounts of seeds and animals, all urgently needed by the settlement.

The mild euphoria resulting from the arrival of the store ship was diabolically destroyed with the arrival of the other three ships, transporting the convicts.

Though the voyage for convicts travelling with the First Fleet could in no way be likened to a stroll in the park, they had, at least, been subject in some respects to a benevolent overall control in the form of the Royal Navy, with their health of some concern, and rude medical care had been provided on each ship, but the one thousand and twenty-five convicts travelling with the Second Fleet had no such benefit. They were carried by private contractors, whose ships' masters, like their owners, were greedy men, and hence were subject to the demands of profit margins.

The Admiralty had put the transportation business out to tender, and what it received for its money was literally hell on water. The convicts were held in shackles throughout, kept below decks for the entire duration of the trip, given the most meagre of rations and on one particular ship deliberately starved to death. As they died they were thrown overboard, after their shackles, worth money, of course, had been removed. More than a quarter of the total number of prisoners on the voyage died en route, an incredible figure, and almost all the rest were seriously ill with pneumonia, scurvy and other serious ailments, as well as being riddled with lice. Rats fed on the flesh of men too sick to ward them off, and on the dead until they were removed.

On arrival, men who were too ill to walk were thrown overboard to drown willy-nilly, and of the five hundred survivors who did reach land a quarter died within a month.

A humanist, Phillip was enraged; apart from the supplies off the '*Justinian*', which barely saved the colony from total starvation and extinction, the Second Fleet had weakened still further the settlement and his plans.

When just part of the truth reached England anger raged, but little was done, save for a court case brought against one ship's master and his First Mate for one murder, but even then the two evil men were whitewashed and released, to carry out more such voyages.

Unknown to Thomas, one of the new arrivals was to bring personal disaster to him.

William Blakely, a sergeant in the New South Wales Corps, newly formed to replace the marines, who considered guarding convicts below them and not a genuine use of their military abilities, was Rainforde's man, bought and paid for with another hundred guineas, though in truth he would have happily carried out the commission free of charge.

A lifelong bully and vindictive sadist, viciously abused in his youth by a psychopathic, drunken father, he had spent his whole life inflicting pain and suffering on those around him, and found the army, and now the Corps, the perfect vehicle for his dastardly desires. The Corps, christened the 'Rum Corps' by the locals and the marines, because of the way it cornered the market in that liquor, were all malcontents - officers on reduced pay and soldiers whose regiments wanted rid of them, or who had been released from prison sentences to join the Corps. They formed the ideal vehicle for harsh convict control and ethnic cleansing. The officer who would be in command, Major Grose, would arrive two years later and single-handedly destroy the infant legal system in the colony by instituting military rule in its place, changing many of Phillip's humanitarian designs.

Rainforde had been directed to Blakely by several soldiers who had fallen foul of that NCO. Within minutes, watching Blakely's sadistically gleeful expression as he described his requirements, Rainforde knew he had found the perfect agent for his nefarious plans. If Sloane had failed him, this man would not.

He even gave Blakely his real name and asked him to make sure Thomas Nash knew who was responsible for his death.

Blakely had travelled on the '*Neptune*', the ship on which there had been the most deaths; a perfect henchman for its captain.

Thomas was unaware that he had mere days of relative peace remaining.

CHAPTER FIFTEEN

After the drought, Phillip realised that the soil in Sydney Cove was just too poor for serious farming and sent out forays looking for better quality land. One of his emissaries travelled up the partially tidal Parramatta River and found, where the salt water became fresh, the ideal spot for a settlement, with rich loam ideal for growing and an abundance of local fruits and animals: kangaroos, wallabies, koalas and emus, by that time hunted virtually to extinction around the first landing site. Phillip initially named the site Rose Hill, later changing it to Parramatta, and decided to make the main settlement there.

Thomas and Roger returned to their hut from work one evening to find an anxious Banjora waiting for them.

He rushed up to Thomas and said, 'Thala bad. Makuwata bad. You come?'

He turned and began to run back to where the natives had built their new lean-tos.

The two aborigines were lying under one of the shelters and Thomas had only to look once to know what was wrong.

Their bodies were covered from head to foot with raised small blisters, some over a quarter of an inch in diameter, ranging from almost flat red dots to pustules full of fluid, some turning yellow. The two men were plainly lethargic. They had contracted smallpox, and in his mind he automatically connected it with the arrival of the new ships.

He shook his head sadly, 'Bad bad.' Repetition of a word, he had learnt, underlined the meaning.

Banjora asked, 'Die?'

Thomas nodded, 'Die.'

Banjora's face showed his mental exertions as he searched his vocabulary for a suitable expression. Finally, he asked, 'What do?'

Thomas knew that none of the qualified surgeons or surgeons' helpers would treat a native and he had scant knowledge. He did know that those with smallpox were always thirsty. It was little enough, but he made drinking motions and used the aborigine word 'Wida' twice, to signify 'often'.

He was terrified, not only for his native friends, but also for himself, Martha and Austin.

He was not to know that these two victims were the first in an epidemic that would wipe out not only four of the little group, but over half of the aboriginal population of New South Wales in a very short space of time, and later spread to the indigenous population of the entire continent with the same percentage of fatalities. The white men had brought the fatal scourge, even before they took it into their heads to commit genocide.

While working the next day, Thomas saw a huge, bull-headed man in a strange uniform with sergeant's stripes walking through the encampment, striking convicts without reason, then asking questions. His round face looked like a ruddy moon, with no eyebrows and a scalp that had been scraped clean of hair. His small, almost black eyes were those of a psychopath. Two other evil-looking soldiers, one thin as a rake and scalp a copy of the sergeant's, the other almost six feet tall and well built, with a flourishing moustache and heavy eyebrows, followed him.

Thomas noticed that the answers he was receiving gave the man pause to look his way and then stride toward him.

Coming so close that his nose was almost touching Thomas' own he growled. 'Are you Nash?'

Thomas replied, 'Yes, Sergeant.'

'Lick my boots!'

'I beg your pardon, Sergeant?'

'I told you to lick my boots, you ignorant bastard!'

Thomas was puzzled, 'But...'

He was struck a violent blow on the head with the soldier's pay stick, which almost rendered him unconscious.

As he reeled, another blow fell, which brought him to his knees.

The sergeant grinned and grunted, 'Now, that's better! Get licking!'

Thomas knew he was in serious trouble. The man had sought him out deliberately and obviously intended him serious harm. The other two soldiers had come up close to him also. Sloane's warning came back to him: these were Rainforde's men.

He knelt and made licking motions with his head, not touching the boots with his tongue. He could see and smell that they had been deliberately covered with stinking human faeces.

As he did so, he felt hot water on the back of his head and neck and knew that he was being pissed on, and not by just one man.

He noticed Roger looking on, appalled.

The sergeant roared, 'You pigshit son of a whoring bitch! If you won't do what you're told we'll soon find a way to teach you some manners! Get up!'

Thomas rose with difficulty and his arms were grabbed by the other two soldiers. He was frog-marched over to the punishment frame and tied to it, after which his shirt was ripped off him.

Blakely grinned, 'Insubordination! That's got to be thirty lashes. We'll have ten each so we keep fresh, boys. Me first.'

Thomas noticed now that one of the other two men had a cat-o'-nine-tails stuck in his belt and saw it being passed to the sergeant.

Thomas had witnessed many dozens of punishments meted out during their stay in that place; even a wrongly interpreted look could entail a beating, and some of the marines treated it as a sport, but neither he nor Roger had been whipped, and it was the major reason they kept apart from the others, for by doing so they avoided petty squabbles.

Blakely set to, twisting his huge, beefy shoulders before each stroke to obtain maximum power.

The first stroke felt to Thomas as if someone had set fire to his back, a burning streak that went from the top of one shoulder to the other. The next fell just one inch lower, and the next a similar distance down, every lash directed with expertise to cause the most agony.

It was Blakely's favourite sport, and he was a past master at it, knowing how to inflict the maximum pain with each stroke. He was laughing madly at the fact that he had even been paid to do it. What this poor bastard in front of him had done he didn't care. Up to this point in his inglorious career, he had whipped eighteen men to death. He was going to make sure this one died too, right enough, but it was going to be a long drawn out death and as painful as he could possibly make it, breaking open the skin every time it began to heal.

After ten strokes, he handed the lash to the larger of the other men, a brute with the same sadistic bent.

He had not the mastery of Blakely, but what he lacked in finesse he made up for with strength, and the strokes cut through the skin just as deeply as had those delivered by the sergeant.

He gave up the weapon with regret, and the lashes continued.

By the time the last stroke fell Thomas was near fainting with the pain, but he clearly heard Blakely's whispered words in his ear, 'With compliments from Lord Rainforde'.

The three men swaggered away, laughing loudly.

Roger had watched from a safe distance but came as quickly as he could once the three soldiers were out of sight, joined by Banjora, who had remained hidden while the punishment was meted out.

Roger cut the bonds and eased Thomas' body to the ground, on his stomach.

'Do I use the grease, Thomas?'

'No, Roger. Salt.'

'Salt? But the pain!'

Thomas knew well what the pain would be like, but it was the fastest way to heal bleeding flesh, and the most hygienic. He had learnt that trick from William Greaves, the butcher in Buxton, when he saw the man cut deeply into his hand while butchering a hindquarter of beef. Greaves had grabbed a handful of salt and crushed it into the wound. His face had screwed up with the pain and Thomas had almost felt it too. What had impressed him was the man's hand a week later, healed, and the wound closed. When Thomas had used grease on the aborigines instead of salt it was because he did not want them to think he was punishing them further.

When Roger applied the salt it felt like hot vitriol, and Thomas fainted away for some minutes.

Banjoro disappeared but came back half an hour later with the same mixture of pounded vegetation Mandu had applied to the two aborigines who had been thrashed. He smoothed it into the cuts, and Thomas felt the pain easing. The plants contained natural anaesthetic properties.

Blakely did not return for fifteen days, and on Thomas' back the scars were healing well.

He and Roger had discussed the dire implications of Blakely's words.

'Rainforde will have asked him to kill me and probably Martha and Austin too.'

'And Sloane?'

'Perchance. Rainforde would be furious that Sloane had not carried out the actions he had been paid for, although his death would be more difficult for a subordinate to arrange. We must try to get word to him to beware.'

'A dagger some dark night.'

Thomas nodded, 'All too easy. I fear for Martha.'

Roger saw the more present danger, 'You should fear for yourself. He will not stop with what he has done so far.'

Thomas sighed, 'That I know only too well, but what can I do?'

'Escape?'

His words caused a wry laugh, 'Where to, Roger?'

'Could you not go with your native friends?'

'Possibly, but they would come after me with dogs, as they did the other two, and would kill me and the natives too.'

He was referring to the only two convicts who had made a run for it, six months before. They were both young shirt lifters and were being mercilessly bullied, beaten and raped by the other convicts. Had they been strong men they might have been luckier, but they had no knowledge of living off the land and had been almost at death's door when found. The marines had killed them out of hand and dragged their bodies back to the settlement, where they were suspended from a tree as examples for all the rest to see.

Thomas knew he stood more of a chance of staying alive in the bush, but with no knowledge of the area would be on a hiding to nothing.

The wonderful properties of the vegetable material provided by Banjora had somehow speeded up the healing of the epidermis, and his wounds had reached the scab stage a week earlier than normal.

While the sores were open he did not swim, fearing the scent of raw wounds would attract the predators, but now he did begin again, not venturing far out, ready to leave the water the moment he saw a triangular fin, and the salt water aided the healing process.

His heart fell when over a fortnight after his beating he saw the hated sergeant and his two bully boys heading their way again.

He stood rigid, expecting to be hit, but they walked past him as if he had not been there.

Blakely dipped his head to go through the entrance to their hut and was inside for half a minute before he came out holding a loaf of bread in his right hand. Bread was like gold dust in the encampment, a delicacy neither Thomas nor Roger had tasted for many months.

Now Blakely did speak to Thomas, 'I reckoned you as a thief as well as a filthy son of a bitch. Where did you get this?'

Thomas dared not show anger, but had to resist, 'I have never seen it before, Sergeant. It is not mine.'

'Your queen's then?' He leered at Roger and made copulating motions with his torso.

Roger looked scared to death.

'Not his either.' He desperately wanted to say, 'You have planted it', but knew it would only serve to make matters far worse.

Blakely sneered, 'I reckon that is a hanging offence, wouldn't you say, Charles?'

The thin soldier nodded, 'Definitely, Sergeant Blakely.'

Blakely pretended to consider before grunting, 'I dunno. 'E looks pretty sorry for stealing it. I reckon fifty of the best should do this time.'

Thomas felt himself grabbed by both arms and dragged over to the frame again, where his wrists and legs were lashed tightly.

This time, by the time the last stroke fell, he was unconscious.

Blakely was annoyed, 'It's no bleeding good if he can't feel it. He takes all the fun out of it.'

He turned and shouted to Roger, who had stood watching, feeling every stroke that fell on Thomas on his own back, 'You! Come 'ere!'

Roger came at the run.

'You tell your mucker 'ere when 'e does come round that 'e's on the list for the next transport to the penal colony on Norfolk Island. That's the place for 'ardened criminals like 'im, wot we can't trust in an open prison like this.' With a grin full of malicious meaning he added, 'That's if 'e makes it there, a-course!'

He turned and swung the cat twice again, as hard as he could, for emphasis.

Roger was pleased Thomas could not feel the strokes.

The healing process began again, with Banjora helping by producing more of the poultice.

Roger agonised over the state of the man he had come to know as a good friend in a desperate situation. He had killed for Thomas, and he knew that gift would be reciprocated in a moment if needed. He felt he had to do something to aid him.

After midnight one night, he eased himself out from his bed covering and crawled out of the hut.

The officers' area was segregated from the penal colony and guarded by marines who would shoot him on sight, but he had to take the chance.

Staying close to the new edge of the forest, he eased his way along, moving painfully slowly, as if stalking a wary deer.

When he reached the compound, he stood completely still for over half an hour, watching the movements of the sentries. There seemed to be just two, and they patrolled the beat from one end of the rude street to the other, crossing in the middle. At the far ends, they went round to the backs of the buildings and he imagined they must be doing the same thing there, for it was a matter of ten minutes before they appeared again at the front.

After Roger had watched them three times, the moment they disappeared round to the back for the fourth time he ran quickly across to the hut Thomas had described after his visit to Martha.

There was no door, but he stopped at the entrance, before tiptoeing in.

He almost died when a stern voice gritted, 'One step more and I shoot.'

His heart hammering so loudly he was fearful the sentries would hear it, he whispered, 'Lieutenant Sloane, please. I am the friend of Thomas Nash.'

Sloane's voice clearly showed his anger, 'What do you want.'

'Thomas is in great trouble. Perchance you also.'

A low chuckle of disbelief came through the darkness, 'Me? What foolishness is this?'

Roger told him about Blakely and his cohorts, and the unfair punishments meted out to Thomas.

When he had finished, a different and much more understanding voice pronounced, 'There is nothing I can do about the punishments, even if my duties had not changed. I no longer have anything to do with camp discipline. That is now the purlieu of the New South Wales Guards, of which this sergeant you mention is a member. As you know they can do exactly as they like short of murder, and even that could easily be covered up. I also cannot stop the movement of Thomas to Norfolk Island, but I do thank you for taking such a risk in coming to warn me, and I shall be doubly on my guard from now on and keeping a watchful eye on Sergeant Blakely. Now go, and be careful you are not seen.'

Roger stopped in the doorway until the guards moved once more to the back of the buildings, then ran for his life back to shelter of the forest.

In Sloane's hut, Martha had come to the doorway of her room. He could not see them, but he knew the tears were coursing down her cheeks.

Sloane crossed to her and took her arm. 'There is nothing I can do, Martha. You know my situation now that we have been replaced. Soon I will be told to prepare for embarkation back to England. I have not told you this, but I have already decided to resign my commission and make my life here as a farmer at Rose Hill rather than go back. There is nothing for me back home; in fact it has not been home to me for many years while I was away soldiering. This country has great potential, and there will be very few of us, with plenty of land for the asking. It will be easier for you and the children also.'

'You mean you would keep me with you, Arthur?'

'Yes, I would.'

She kissed him quickly on the cheek. 'You are a good man.'

He gave a quick laugh, almost overcome with emotion after the kiss from a woman whom he already loved passionately. 'Both you and your husband have entirely the wrong idea about me.'

She shook her head vehemently, 'I think not, Arthur.'

CHAPTER SIXTEEN

Roger made it back safely without being challenged and crept back into the hut.

Thomas' voice came through the darkness.

'That was a long shit, Roger. I hope you didn't get any on your feet.'

'No, Thomas. I did not.'

'Did you see Martha?'

So he had guessed. It did not surprise Roger.

'No.'

'He cannot help, can he?'

'No, but at least he is warned.'

'It seems I shall soon be parting from you, my friend.'

'Blakely will kill you.'

'That does seem most likely. Martha foresaw pain and suffering for me, and could not see beyond it. Rainforde will have his way after all, but at least he has not destroyed my family, and I know Sloane will do his very best to stop him hurting Austin or Martha.'

Though usually staying away from the other convicts, except for work, Roger began tapping the settlement grape vine for information about the '*Supply*' and its trips to Norfolk Island.

The nearest idea he could get was that the ship was expected back from such a visit in three days' time, and usually stayed at Sydney Cove for a week to ten days before leaving for the Island again.

He feared Thomas might have to suffer another beating before then, but as days passed without sight of Blakely, his spirits and those of Thomas rose just a trifle.

The '*Supply*' returned from the Island and lay at anchor in the bay, with little activity around it.

The scars were almost healed again when Blakely's two bullyboys arrived one morning.

The taller one growled at Thomas, 'Come on, quickly, or you'll be on the frame again. You are going for another nice little sea voyage, this time with extra benefits!' Both of them laughed knowingly, and the thin one said, 'Benefits courtesy of Sergeant Blakely and Lord Rainforde.'

Thomas knew that he should be scared, but instead felt nothing but resignation. He had, without realising it, been a fatalist all his life. Farming had made that happen.

Walking through the colony he was prodded painfully and regularly by both men with the sticks they carried, and saw many faces portraying all kinds of emotions, from jeering looks by convicts who just loved to see others suffer to those who realised that if he, as one of the convict supervisors, could be taken to the much harsher penal colony on Norfolk Island, their own semi-freedom was also at risk.

Thomas had heard snippets of gossip about the Island, none of which gave him comfort.

First of all it was a thousand miles from Port Jackson; a thousand miles from Martha and Austin; a thousand miles he knew for certain he would never travel on a return journey. The Superintendent of the new penal colony was D'Arcy Wentworth, a character who sounded less than salubrious, having been a trainee surgeon, charged in England with highway robbery, though not convicted. Punishment on the Island was said to be the harshest of any English prison anywhere. Thomas decided he would rather die than go there, but was doubtful he would have any chance with these jailers.

At the quay a jolly boat with four rowers waited, with Blakely on board, already three parts drunk on rum and clutching a large bottle in his hand.

'Thash goo'!' He greeted them, 'You got the bastard! Sling 'im down there an' sit on 'im. 'Ave a swig.' He passed the bottle and one after another the other two downed a good swallow apiece.

'No, 'ave some more. I got another one 'ere, see?' He bent down and pulled another bottle from under the seat. He peered short-sightedly at Thomas, 'None for you, you poor, stupid bastard. Your bloody noble Lord Rainforde wouldn't like it, would 'e? You got to feel all the suff'rin'.'

Lying partially beneath the thwarts, with the weight of the warder's legs on him, Thomas could not move, but his brain was active enough. He made a promise to himself that if it was the last thing on earth that he did, God willing, he would have his revenge on Rainforde.

As soon as the thought had crossed his mind he could not help smiling grimly. Who was he trying to fool? Just look at him: pinned down, with three thugs just itching to see him on his way to the Pearly Gates. Rainforde would, without the slightest doubt, live out his long life enjoying his ill-gotten gains, with no interference from Thomas Nash.

Some quarter of an hour later the jolly boat bumped against the side of the '*Supply*' and Thomas was made to climb the rope ladder to the deck first.

Blakely yelled as he climbed, 'You up there! Grab 'im when 'e gets there!'

Thomas' arms were taken by two seamen as he went over the gunwale, but not roughly, and they led him to a hatch cover where they sat him down.

Preparations were well under way for setting sail, and the master had been waiting only for the jolly boat to arrive before hoisting the anchor.

Blakely sat himself down on one of the other hatch covers, his bottle in his hand, while his two henchmen sat either side of Thomas.

There were four other prisoners in a group near the stern, and more than a dozen seamen on deck, rushing hither and thither to the commands raining down on them from the master on the upper deck.

As the sails filled with the strong northerly breeze, the ship suddenly heeled sharply, and Thomas and his two guards were almost thrown forwards off the hatch cover.

With sudden clarity, Thomas realised that this was his moment. The guards were using both hands, trying to regain their balance and stay on their seats, too busy to try to hold on to their prisoner. Thomas used the forward momentum instead to gain his feet and make a rush for the gunwale, where he jumped without hesitation into the sea.

He went deep, holding his breath as long as he could, while the ship moved past him, picking up speed.

Finally, he had to come up for air. The '*Supply*' was two ship's lengths away from him, but on the stern he could see there were five men, including his erstwhile jailors, holding guns trained on the surface behind the ship.

He heard the shots and saw the strike of the balls in the water close to his head, suddenly feeling a sharp pain below his left shoulder, as one passed through the fleshy part of his upper arm.

He dived again, swimming directly away from the ship, which was turning slowly to come into wind, knowing that the blood flowing from him would bring every shark from miles around.

On deck, Blakely was incensed, 'You stupid bastards! Why couldn't you 'old 'im! S'all you had to do!'

His man Charles foolishly said, 'He'll drown anyway, or the sharks'll get him.'

Blakely slammed his fist into the man's face. 'When I want your advice I'll ask for it.'

His other man said, 'I am sure I hit him.'

Blakely said, 'Well, I din't see 'im 'it, an' you can't see 'im now, so 'e's still swimmin'. We need some fresh meat to throw in, to attract the sharks.'

Charles indicated the other convicts with his head and Blakely got the message. Every man on deck had his eyes on the water and it would be easy.

Blakely drew a dagger but hid it in his palm. He crossed quickly to where the four convicts stood, pulled the rearmost towards him and with one movement slit his throat and threw him overboard.

He shouted, 'My God! Look at that brave bastard! 'E's dived in to save 'im.'

It happened so quickly that even the other three convicts in the little group, who had been looking the other way with everyone else, could never be sure afterwards exactly what had happened.

The water around the body, which was at that moment still floating, turned bright red with the arterial blood gushing from the jugular, and already two triangular fins were homing in on it from two hundred yards away.

Thomas had covered a quarter of the distance back to the shore, heading for a grove of trees well away from the settlement. A strong flood tide was aiding him, and he felt sure he could make it until he saw three fins cutting through the water directly towards him.

He stopped swimming and floated.

They were still headed straight for him.

Three huge bodies passed within inches of him, one of them bumping him hard as it passed.

Two of the sharks carried straight on, but the one that had hit him turned and came back, its head moving from side to side, attempting to locate the source of the weak smell of blood.

His wound had leaked a lot to begin with, but the cool salt water had almost stopped the flow.

The shark circled him three times, then came straight in, slowly, its huge mouth open, showing the rows of vicious-looking teeth. It seemed to be trying to smell him. When it was only inches away Thomas punched its nose as hard as he could with his right fist.

The water boiled, and he was thrown violently around, with his body almost out of the water at one point, and it was then that he was seen by Blakely, who took a desperate shot, the distance far beyond the capability of the weapon.

The shark decided it did not like the inanimate object that suddenly came to life and inflicted punishment, and it was also being urged by its senses to join in the feeding frenzy with its two companions and the other sharks. The source of blood was much stronger there. It sped off.

The shore was now only two hundred yards off, and Thomas made an extra effort.

On board '*Supply*', Blakely had insisted the master drop anchor again, so that he could go after the escaping convict.

The master refused, but with the ship held into wind dropped the jolly boat from its davits and allowed Blakely and his two men to take it, not allowing them any of his seamen, who would be needed on the crossing, as rowers.

Blakely had never rowed in his life, and nor had either of his men. He was not about to participate in something he felt below his dignity, and the other two, ill assorted by both size and weight for the task of rowing, made a pig's ear of the business of directing the craft. An overhead diagram of their progress as they attempted to row to shore would have resembled the insane scribbling made by a centipede with no legs on one side. They lost count of the crabs they caught, falling in between the thwarts time after time and losing two of the four oars overboard. The rum had not been a good idea.

Blakely, sitting on the rear thwart scanning the shore, saw Thomas drag himself out of the water and into a belt of Red Gum trees, immediately disappearing out of his sight. He swore roundly and tried to urge his men to greater efforts, ''E's bloody alive and out of the water. If you two bastards don't stop pissing about and get us there I'll 'ave you both flogged within an inch of your lives when we get back. Bloody pull!'

They renewed their efforts, and it seemed that they might finally reach the shore, but as they were nearing it the tide turned, and within minutes they found themselves being driven out to sea and along the coast to the south faster than they could row.

Their panic was palpable, and through his rum-fogged brain Blakely realised that the other two idiots' efforts could well see them arriving at Norfolk Island before the '*Supply*'. The thought of being marooned at sea in a tiny boat with no food or water was as urgent as a rocket up his arse.

He staggered up from the rear seat and growled at the thinner of the two men, whose efforts had caused most of the problems, 'Get out of the bloody way, Amos.'

He took over the oar and with the two strongest men rowing, they finally made some progress towards the shore but were still continually being driven southward.

They finally made landfall nine and a half miles south of the colony, at a point where the trees came right down to the water's edge at high tide.

Burning with frustrated anger, Blakely was desperate to get after his quarry.

'Tie the boat to that tree, Charles, and get a bloody move on. 'E's got a good 'ead start, but I'm gonna bloody catch 'im!'

CHAPTER SEVENTEEN

Thomas lay panting in the cover of the trees, recovering from the long swim. He inspected the wound. It looked clean, and he knew the salt water would have helped with the process. The ball had gone through the flesh of his upper arm, just missing the bone. It was painful but bearable. He had watched the boat with the three men in it disappearing down the coast and knew he had gained some time. He reckoned he was roughly a mile from the northern edge of the colony, but did not know if the Governor had ordered outlying patrols. He determined to act as if they did exist.

He knew Blakely would be coming after him with a vengeance, possibly with dogs. Staying near the river would be his best chance. He could always take to the water again if necessary. Neither Blakely nor his men would be swimmers; that he was sure of, and if necessary he would rather drown than give Rainforde's agent the pleasure of killing him.

One thought that suddenly came to him brought an unexpected euphoria: the realisation that he was free; no longer a convict. It might well not be for long, but he could die a free man; die by his own choice, rather than at the whim of a sadistic psychopath. He would make it as difficult as he could for Blakely, and if it finally came to a life or death decision he would have the final say. They would not take him alive!

He pulled himself to his feet and set off through the huge trees, using the sun to guide him west and keeping the water in sight on his right.

Another thought came to him: was the stretch of water a river or a tidal bay? He could see the opposite shore a couple of miles away. Convict rumour had spoken of a river called the Parramatta, but whether the water here was part of that river he had no idea.

Blakely had seen him leave the water, of that he was sure, and would start his search at that point. No matter, the important thing was to put as much distance as he could between him and his pursuers. At least, apart from the flesh wound, he was as fit as any man in the colony. He strode off as fast as he could move.

After what he judged to be an hour, he moved back down to the water and entered it, going in just a yard till it reached halfway up his calf, then turned westwards again.

It slowed him down, dragging his legs against the pull of the water, but would throw his followers off, at least for a while.

It was a procedure he was to follow for the rest of the day, an hour on land and an hour in the water. Each time he left the water he found a dry branch and tried to erase his footprints. After three hours of steady progress, he could see that it was indeed a river whose course he was following. Each time he came to a side stream, he took in as much water as he could drink, having tried the water in the main body and found it salty.

He was just leaving the water again at what he judged to be somewhere near three o'clock in the afternoon when five aborigine men stepped out of the tree line ahead of him, spears raised.

He held up his open hands, palms towards them, as he had done the first time with Apari and his band, and after a short discussion between them the men lowered the tips of the spears and came forward.

He greeted them, 'Ko-je ig-go.'

Their faces showed surprise, but they repeated the greeting. Thomas, in his ignorance, believed it meant 'Hello'. In effect it did, but a more accurate translation was, 'Come to me'.

He tried to explain that he was on his way west, but the words he was hearing in reply made little sense to him. Strangely, the language this group spoke seemed different to that of his aborigine friends.

He moved his hand to cover the whole band and asked, 'Eora?'

They all nodded, indicating that they were people of that place, and the elder added, 'Daruk – walari.'

They were words he had not heard before, and he realised that at even this short distance from the colony he was in fact hearing another language and that these natives were of a different tribe, either the Daruk or the Walari.

Thomas pointed to his breast and told them his name, which they repeated, then he pointed at the old man's chest.

'Yen-da-ra' He was told and thought it might be something to do with walking, with that prefix.

The elder poked his spear towards Thomas' shoulder and asked something unintelligible though obvious.

Thomas raised his arms as if holding a rifle and said, 'Bang.' It provoked a minute-long highly animated conversation between the men, who kept sneaking glances at Thomas while they did so.

He realised they understood that his own people had injured him and also that he was trying to avoid being tracked by staying in the water.

The elder waved his hand for Thomas to follow, and the band moved off, all except the youngest, who broke off a leafy branch and erased Thomas' footsteps from the water's edge up to where they had stood.

Thomas was unsure. They were obviously friendly towards him, but he could not afford to lose much time. One thing would help, however: with his footprints mixed with theirs for a time it might confuse his pursuers.

He walked between them and ensured that he twisted his feet with each step to distort the prints.

Less than half a mile from the shore they came upon their little encampment, where he was invited to sit.

There were three aborigine women there, the first he had ever seen, all of them old and stark naked, their withered dugs hanging down to waist level, their pubic hair as grey as that on their heads. Both their bodies and their faces were painted with the charcoal and ochre, the decoration different to that of the men. He wondered if there were younger women nearby, hiding or being hidden from him.

They all squatted in the manner he had become used to, and the elder of the tribe spoke to one of the women. She delved under one of the shelters and brought out a large leaf on which there were two baked lizards. She held out the leaf to Thomas, who took one, and then to the elder, who took the other.

The old man pointed to the lizard and said, 'Mug-kun', a word Thomas knew. He repeated it, making the old man smile, then set to with the lizard. It tasted good and made him realise that he had eaten nothing since the previous evening.

A second woman brought two raw fish. Thomas was unsure, having rarely eaten fish, and never uncooked, but the old man picked one up and began tugging flesh from it with his teeth. Thomas followed suit, surprised that he did not gag at the first mouthful, which tasted like something he might have found on the floor of his cow byre, but he persevered and gradually managed to eat it all apart from the head and bones. He knew it would help to maintain his strength and was beginning to realise that man could eat practically anything.

The old woman came back, chewing madly. When she reached him she grabbed his left arm roughly, spat the stuff from her mouth and initially appalled him with her obvious intention of pushing it into the bullet hole. He pulled back, almost tugging her over, then remembered how good Banjora's ministrations had been.

He stopped pulling and allowed her to carry out her intention.

At first it felt as if another bullet, red hot this time, was passing through his arm as the vegetable matter was pushed in, and he gasped, but within a couple of minutes it felt easier and he nodded his thanks.

Another of the women brought a handful of muntries, which were delicious and highly refreshing. Thomas realised he would have to make an effort to find food as often as he could along his way. If he did not keep his strength up he would soon lose out to better fed pursuers.

The moment he had finished chewing, the elder stood up again, issued instructions Thomas could not follow and indicated Thomas should follow him.

The small band arranged themselves so that the elder and Thomas went ahead, and the others followed, eradicating their footsteps. One of the men, however, joined the women, who headed off south, and Thomas realised they were laying a false trail.

Without a word from Thomas indicating which way he wanted to go, the elder headed due west, selecting a path that for much of the way went over rocky outcrops where no footprints would be left.

Every few hundred yards, one or other of the party would go off and come back with some delicacy from the bushes and trees, passing much of the booty to Thomas.

They stayed with him until the water of the Parramatta, off to the right, had turned from a sheet of molten gold, reflecting the dying rays of the sun, to a dark grey, ambiguous mass.

The forest ended suddenly, and in front of them stretched half a mile of rock. The old man stopped, touched Thomas' chest with his forefinger and pointed ahead.

Thomas realised that this was the end of their company, and he said a heartfelt, 'Mor-rum-boh', causing the aborigines to laugh gleefully like little children.

What they had done for him might not save him but it would certainly baffle his followers for some time, and give him a better chance of evading them.

All in all his efforts since he dived off the ship had resulted in at least six or seven miles covered through difficult country. It was nowhere near enough but it was a good start.

He had to show them just how much he appreciated their help and took the elder's right arm in his left hand and placed his right hand in the man's right hand. He squeezed the hand and then shook it.

A look of pure amazement came onto the elder's face, but he quickly realised that the gesture was in friendship and shook back, while the others looked on with questioning looks until the elder smiled, and then they all broke out in renewed guffaws of laughter.

Thomas tried a goodbye, 'Ek-u-bah'

The elder repeated, 'Ek-u-bah' and turned away.

Thomas watched them until they reached the edge of the forest, where they seemed to just melt away.

He knew it would be impossible to continue all night; he would have to sleep, to refresh himself for a full day tomorrow. In any case, progress would be dangerous in the dark, and a broken leg would mean the end of all his hopes. Equally, he doubted even Blakely would be stupid enough to hunt in the dark.

Night was falling fast and he looked around until he found a patch of thick grass to lie on, ignoring from old habit the swarming hordes of mosquitoes that had been plaguing him since dusk.

He was asleep almost as soon as his head touched the ground, and despite his dire situation his sleep was untroubled for the first time in three years.

When he woke to the singing of scores of birds, doing their best to outdo one another in the dawn chorus, he was unsure for a moment where he was but quickly remembered.

It was still dark, and he could not see the Parramatta, but off to his right the hilly horizon was just visible with a line of indistinct grey, like a line drawn weakly on a blackboard with a worn-out piece of chalk by a small child with no control over its direction.

The line quickly strengthened, and by the time Thomas had relieved himself it was light enough to move on.

He re-entered forest, this time smaller trees, mainly cabbage palms, but beneath them there was undergrowth, which made progress difficult.

After two hours of struggle, he came to a wide track that had clearly been hacked out recently by humans, to make the transport of goods easier, and realised that it must lead to the new settlement at Rose Hill. He was dismayed by the thought that Blakely could easily overtake him if he used the track but quickly reassured himself that the sergeant would try to follow his quarry's tracks, not knowing in which direction he was travelling.

He stayed fifty yards to the right of the track and an hour later, from the vantage point of a small hill, he was able to watch the activity of those engaged in clearing the site.

He considered by-passing it by going inland a mile or so but knew that would take up almost a day and give his pursuers a tremendous time advantage. He would lose all the lead he had gained.

The only other alternative was the river, and he was quick to make the decision.

Keeping well clear of the workers, he crept down to the water, entered it and began to swim, surprised at how well his shoulder was holding up.

He headed towards what seemed to be a gap between the distant trees, imagining that a small river must flow through them to enter this larger mass of water, and was proved correct when he found himself struggling against the current of water pouring from it.

Instead of fighting it he swam to the shore on one side.

Before crawling up into the woods he lay in the water and cast his glance all around, pleased that he had done so when he saw a small boat being rowed out from the bank near the new settlement. Someone had decided to fish.

He waited until the rower had his back to him and then quickly rose out of the water and ran into the trees, turning immediately to see if he had been noticed.

The boat was still making its slow progress in the same direction as before.

Once again Thomas decided to spend part of the time in the water, to throw off those hunting him, but soon discovered that it was not the good idea he imagined.

He had travelled a few hundred yards, wading knee deep under trees whose hanging branches were trailing in the water, when the surface erupted just ten yards away from him. A huge crocodile more than twelve feet long was hurtling towards him, its gaping jaws open wide.

Shock, amazement, horror, fright, all had to wait while automatic reaction took over.

Instinctively and without thought, he grabbed the hanging branch that was brushing his body and hauled himself bodily upwards.

The crash of water and the slamming shut of the mouth of the beast below him lent wings to his efforts, and he pulled himself up the dangling branch with hands and feet, listening with horror to the cracking sounds in the wood above him.

Below, the croc was thrashing the water, looking for the meal that had mysteriously disappeared, while Thomas hung on for dear life, his body shaking the creaking branch, atavistic fear making him more terrified than he had ever been in his life.

Rumours had spread among the convicts about the scale-covered saurian predators, but his imagination had never been able to conjure up a vision of a creature so utterly horrific; one that had surely come straight from the depths of Hell.

He could hear the branch breaking, its fibres splitting with the unequal weight, and looked around him desperately.

Another branch hung two feet away from the one he was clinging to, and he weighed up the difficulty of letting go of his present one and grabbing for the other.

He had no time to make that decision; the branch snapped.

He fell with a thump onto the back of the creature, whose tail began slashing from side to side. Thomas knew instinctively that one swipe of that armoured tail would kill him instantly.

The crocodile was beached and trying to turn, its feet churning up the mud from the bottom of the river, turning the water thick brown. The branch had fallen near its mouth and was ripped to matchwood by the beast, infuriated by the weight on its back.

A primeval instinct made Thomas get to his feet on the creature's back and run along it to the neck, where he made an enormous leap for the bank, landing in six inches of water, expecting his leg to be seized at any second.

The croc began scrabbling even harder with its legs, trying to move forward enough to catch its breakfast, but Thomas was out of the water and running madly away from the horror.

Terrified that it would follow him, he ran over a hundred yards before daring to look back.

Seeing the leviathan still on the bank, he stopped, trying to recover.

His heart had never pounded harder, and he could hear its beats, like a distant drummer urgently trying to work up a rabble. His breath came in red-hot gulps that seemed not to help at all.

He sank to the floor, pulling up his knees to his chin, trying desperately to regain his equanimity.

He sat there in a stunned state for over half an hour, aware of the distant presence of the croc, now sunning itself on the bank of the river, breakfast for the moment forgotten.

At last he pulled himself to his feet, feeling exhausted from the latent fear, but he knew he must press on, and on, and on...

CHAPTER EIGHTEEN

It was nearing dark when the three men reached the edge of the colony. The other two would have happily crawled into bed and called it a day, not caring a hoot about the escaped prisoner, but Blakely's blazing anger had only increased with each blistering mile through difficult woodland.

He had had an idea and questioned several of the convicts who had finished their work for the day and were eating their scant rations, ready to go into their huts and tents to escape the attentions of the dusk-loving mosquitoes.

'Is there one 'o these abos who speaks English?'

He was directed to look for Banjora and found him squatting near Roger, listening to some story or other.

Blakely strode up and said, 'You, come with me.'

Banjora shook his head.

Blakely pulled the pistol from his belt, pulled back the flint and held the muzzle an inch from Banjora's head. 'No?'

Banjora knew instinctively that the white man would pull the trigger if he refused. He had no idea what the sergeant wanted, but with the aborigine's typical acceptance of what could not be changed he got to his feet.

They moved off quickly, and Blakely led the way to the soldiers' quarters at the far end of the settlement. He knew pursuit would have to wait till morning. They had lost so much time already that a few hours more would make little difference. It was pitch dark before they reached their hut, the only relief from the darkness the pinpoints of candle light from tents and huts where the occupants were prepared to put up with the hordes of flying horrors the lights attracted. An ignorant visitor might have been persuaded that they were the pretty lights of resting fireflies. Blakely had no intention of losing his acquisition and tied Banjora tightly to a post for the night.

He rose at first light and kicked his two cohorts awake. They breakfasted at speed, but gave Banjora nothing, not even water.

Blakely led the way to the point where he had seen Thomas leave the water, and showed Banjora the tracks.

The aborigine then knew what was wanted of him and stoically accepted the task, imagining that as soon as it was over he could return to his little group, now reduced to three after the deaths resulting from the smallpox. Only he, Mandu and Curriquinquin still lived. He could see from the footprint that the man he was to track was a white man, but had no idea that it was Thomas.

They made rapid progress, and Blakely was pleased enough that he let Banjora divert a trifle off course occasionally for a drink and to pick fruit, which he ate while continuing the hunt.

By mid-afternoon, they had reached the point where Thomas had joined forces with the little band of aborigines, and for a while Banjora was puzzled. Blakely could clearly see that there were many footprints and realised that Thomas had found allies.

Banjora trailed them to the deserted campsite, which the wise elder had moved from as soon as they returned from leaving Thomas, knowing it would be found by his pursuers and that remedial action might be taken against them for helping him.

Blakely's anger had not diminished one wit, and he regularly launched a kick at Banjora for not working faster.

The aborigine found the multiple trail to the south and followed it for half a mile before deciding that the white man had not travelled that route.

He told Blakely, 'Not man.'

The sergeant was incensed anew, 'You ignorant bloody blackface!' He hit Banjora a mighty blow on the nose with his fist and kicked him twice. 'Find the bloody trail!'

They returned to the deserted camp, and the aborigine quickly discovered where the trail had been eradicated. From there it was easy to follow until they reached the rocks, where there was no soil and no vegetation to hold tell-tale signs of human passage.

Banjora indicated that the trail was lost and received another kick for his trouble.

Blakely pondered the situation. Had Nash continued due west, the direction he seemed to be heading before this or had he used the rocks as a means of throwing them off the scent and turned in a different direction?

Blakely decided to stick to the west until they reached the other end of the rocks and then have the native cast around until he found new tracks.

They reached the far side as it was becoming dusk, and once again Blakely decided to spend the night. Strangely, his anger was slowly changing from an early white-hot rage to something approaching pleasure; the pleasure of the long stalk after the best game in the world: a human being, with all the cunning of that species. The long anticipation would add a tremendous boost to the final moment of enjoyment when he killed his quarry.

Banjora was tied to a tree for the night. Blakely had no intention of losing him before Nash was sighted. Then he could bugger off to wherever they went to; that is if he decided to let him live! On second thoughts, no, he would kill the bastard as a bonus. They were only animals, after all, and he would be an unwanted witness.

CHAPTER NINETEEN

Thomas made good progress all that day, finding plenty of fruit to eat on the way, and by nightfall estimated that he had covered another fifteen miles. He was beginning to feel that he might just outrun his pursuers. He had no idea whatsoever how he would exist or where he would live but guessed there were more natives in the interior of the country, and if they could live there so could he.

He knew that henceforth and for the rest of his natural days he must stay far from civilisation. Knowing how other countries had been colonised he knew that the little penal colony and the new one at Rose Hill were only the beginning. In only a few short years the spot he was now standing on could very well be the main street of a new city. The further he went inland the more secure he would be. He had to keep moving.

He slept well again and rose refreshed to face another new day, feeling ready for anything, but he had gone not fifty yards when disaster struck. A lowlands copperhead snake was lying under a rock, its head sticking out onto his intended path, and he saw it at the last second as he was putting his right foot down.

He reacted by jerking his body sideways, so that the foot stayed in the air, but as he twisted away and crashed to the ground his left foot caught between two smaller rocks and sprained badly.

The snake slithered away, annoyed at being disturbed.

Winded, Thomas tried to pull himself upright but realised that he could not put any weight on his left foot. He sat down and felt around the ankle. It did not feel broken and would no doubt heal, but now he was a sitting duck.

He managed to stand and hopped on one leg a few paces. He needed a crutch, and with no tools it was going to be difficult to make one. The river was close by, and cold water might improve matters, but after the affair with the crocodile he had stayed well away from the water.

He hopped on, covering only a couple of hundred yards in an hour, but he was approaching a belt of small trees.

In it he found a young cabbage palm with a two inch diameter trunk and set to work to remove it from the earth, digging with his fingers.

It took him four hours of hard labour. Once he had dug it up there were many roots to remove, which he began to worry off with his teeth, but by nightfall he had a crutch with a little foliage at one end, which would wear off as he used it, and three upward-curling strong roots for his armpit to rest in.

He was despondent. The lead he had on Blakely and his men had diminished to practically nothing and at the speed he could now travel he had no doubt that they would catch up to him within the next twenty-four hours.

Travel at night in his present condition was out of the question, and he considered his alternatives. When he had woken that morning he had seen in the distance a range of mountains, and it had been towards them that he had intended to travel, for some obtuse reason believing that height would give him an advantage.

Now, even if he reached them he would not be able to climb them.

Darkness fell suddenly and he decided to sleep again and set off at dawn.

There was a small ridge half a mile ahead and he determined to go up it and look at his back trail to see if the pursuers were in sight. What his actions would be if they were he had no idea.

His dreams that night were full of nightmares, the pain in his ankle bringing him close to waking many times, and he woke listless and feeling ill and feverish. He realised that the wound in his arm had begun to hurt again and wondered if it had become infected.

With great difficulty, he set off, hobbling along at a snail's pace.

It was close to midday when he reached the top of the ridge and he sat down for a rest before looking backwards and fell instantly asleep.

Two hours later, with the sun in its daily decline, he woke

suddenly, angry with himself for his weakness.

He pulled himself erect, using a small tree for support, and turned his eyes to view his back trail.

For minutes long, he saw nothing and began to have hope, but then, about three miles distant, he saw movement.

With fingers crossed that it was a kangaroo, of which he had seen plenty since leaving Port Jackson, he kept his eyes glued on that area.

There it was again but it was no kangaroo, unless it was wearing a blue coat. They would be on him within the hour.

He turned to descend the other side of the ridge, and it was then that Blakely saw him. The movement on the distant ridge had him hauling the spyglass from his pocket.

Thomas was not able to hear Blakely's victorious shout, nor was he aware that he had been spotted, but he knew it was merely a matter of time.

The water had been his friend before and saved him; it would have to be his choice again now.

He was terrified that there might be more crocodiles, but even if there were and he was eaten it would deny Blakely his victory. It would be enough.

The slowly moving river was some seventy yards wide, and on the far bank, unlike the side he was on, which was covered in sparse scrub, a thick forest of eucalyptus and cabbage palm stretched to the horizon.

He considered swimming across. The current was sluggish and would be no trouble, but his pursuers were close, and he could well be shot, either while swimming or on the far bank, before he made the shelter of the trees. He decided to hide below the near bank.

The water was deep, even close in, the bottom not visible. He sat down and slid into the water, staying tight in to the bank. The crutch was useless now, and he let go of it and watched it glide slowly away on the light current. He began to swim, keeping close in to the bank. After a hundred yards or so, he found a place where two thick bushes overhung the water and pulled his body in below them, invisible from the bank unless someone leant well over and peered very closely. It was some five feet deep, but he could stand with his head just above water.

Blakely had urged the others on at a run. Through the glass, he had seen how awkwardly Thomas was moving and knew he was injured. He had him!

They reached the top of the ridge and Blakely used the spyglass to search the low scrub that reached almost to the horizon. Nothing!

''E's 'iding in the river. Must be. 'E's not in the bush.' He turned to Banjora, 'In river. You find!' He kicked the aborigine again for good measure. He was feeling great.

They descended to the bank, and Banjora pointed to where Thomas had gone in. Blakely was unsure, 'Which way did the bugger go, upstream or downstream? Amos, you come with me downstream. Charles, you take this black bugger upstream and don't miss anything!'

Banjora, looking ahead, judged where he would hide if he were in their quarry's situation and marked the two overhanging bushes as the most likely spot, although there were many other single bushes alongside the river, some quite thick.

He walked close to the bank, looking in all the time, while the soldier walked beside him. Blakely's henchman had lost interest in the pursuit even before they left Port Jackson, and now, with hunger his main concern, just wanted to get back to his hut for a meal and some well earned shut-eye.

When they reached the two bushes, Banjora stepped right up to the edge of the bank, leant over and peered down.

Just below the surface he saw a face; a face that he knew well. He almost fell into the river with surprise on seeing that it was his friend Thom-as they had been hunting and had to flail with his arms to hold his balance.

The soldier laughed and urged, 'Steady the Buffs!'

Banjora leant over again and gave Thomas a look that told him with a slow shake of the head that he was not about to be given away, then turned and continued his progress along the bank.

Blakely had found the crutch lodged against the roots of a tree sticking into the water and came running back with Amos.

Near the two overhanging bushes he shouted, 'Come back!'

When the four were standing together again Blakely said, 'I know 'e's been in this stretch of the river, and we know 'e can swim. 'E's swum across, but with a game leg 'e can't 'ave got far. I've got a better idea. 'E won't get out of this one. Come on.'

He led them half a mile upwind, then uprooted some dried grass and a bush.

Astonished, they watched him get his tinderbox out and kneel down to light the grass. The brush, dotted with hundreds of low trees and bushes, had been burnt brown with the drought and was bone dry.

The tinder caught and within seconds became a conflagration, the stiff breeze whipping the flames as they tore their way towards the river.

The three soldiers were so entranced at its progress that they did not notice Banjora creep away from them silently and then run towards the forest four hundred yards away.

Thomas had no idea what was coming. He was standing in water that came up to his shoulders and had pushed his head up to breathe after Banjora left when he smelt fire.

Within seconds, bits of burning vegetation were flying over him, and he plunged his head under the water again.

With his eyes open he could see a sky aflame above him and held his breath until he could hold it no more. He had to breathe. He decided to take one deep breath and then go below the surface again. The air immediately over the water should be breathable.

His misfortune was in the timing.

As his face broke the surface he took in a huge gulp of air, which was hot but not unbearably so, but at the exact moment when he closed his mouth and before he could move his head below the surface again the fire reached the two overhanging bushes. Bone dry from the drought and full of highly inflammable sap they literally exploded, turning the water on his face to boiling steam, which immediately dried, instantly burning off his eyebrows and the front of his hair and causing first degree burns over his whole face.

His scream was unheard in the roaring of the flames.

Almost fainting with the pain as he plunged his head below the surface he somehow managed to hold his breath long enough for the worst of the fire to pass his hiding place, and the next time he pushed his ruined face above the surface of the water he found he could breathe somewhat easier, though much of the oxygen had been taken from the heated air. His eyelids felt like cinders, and he seemed not to be able to control their movement. What caused him most distress was his inability to see, except for a faint light, like looking at daylight through thick opaque glass. He was blind!

Blakely stood looking at his handiwork, smirking with delight. The fire had leapt the river and set light to the sap-heavy eucalyptus trees on the far bank, after which the conflagration took on a new force. One by one the sap-laden trees exploded, and the flames reached up two hundred feet into the heavens. The breeze had picked up and spurred on the unstoppable inferno that was devouring forest instantaneously, like a dragon belching uncontrollably, having inadvertently drunk a bellyful of lighting oil.

Blakely whooped, ''E's a gonner for sure this time, boys. 'E wouldn't be able to breathe in that. We can go 'ome in a bit. Let's just wait a mo to see if we can see 'is body.'

Charles was looking at him in astonishment. 'Sarge, you are one mad bastard!'

Blakely regarded him almost with benevolence, 'I thought you always knew that, Charles. ' He suddenly realised that Banjora was missing and lashed out at both of the men, his momentary benevolence a forgotten weakness. 'You stupid, stupid bastards! You let that bloody abo escape. Now we've got a witness loose. 'E's a dead man if I ever see 'im again.'

Banjora had watched the fire and saw the two bushes explode. He had no hope that Thomas had survived but sat down on his haunches and waited with that same patience that his

179

ancestors had practised over thousands of years of waiting for a meal on legs to come out of hiding.

With the fire racing ever further away, the nearer forest was reduced in minutes to a landscape of smoking matchsticks.

An aged, arthritic male kangaroo had been sleeping just beyond the tree line only fifty yards from the river and had woken only when the first flames had singed his back. He leapt up and tried to hop away from the danger but managed only a dozen yards before being overtaken by the inferno and turned into a living, screaming torch.

When the flames had passed, Blakely thought he saw what he had been waiting for. He pulled out his spyglass again and adjusted the focus.

He yelled jubilantly, 'There 'e is! There 'e bloody is, boys! 'E's burnt to a bloody cinder! Look!'

He passed the glass to Charles.

Through the lens, he saw, as Blakely had, a charred body, lying between the still smoking tree stumps with blood and guts oozing out of it, its still smoking, skeletonised toes sticking up skywards.

Charles nodded, 'It's him.'

Amos refused the glass, 'I'll take your word for it. How far will that fire go?'

'Dunno', miles probably. If we're lucky it might kill off a few more abos.'

In fact, the fire devastated an area of over forty square miles, killing thousands of birds and animals and a group of five aborigines before finally being stopped by another, wider river.

Blakely felt great. One job well done. He was already savouring the thought that he was going to enjoy the other part of the job just as much or even more, with the added benefits. He was going to rape Nash's woman viciously and fill her with his seed before he killed her. That was a promise!

Charles asked, 'Do we look for the abo?'

Blakely considered for just a moment. 'Naw, 'e'll be bloody miles away by now. You know 'ow fast they can move and 'ide.'

In fact, Banjora had not moved and was less than half a mile from them, well concealed in an outcrop of rocks.

He watched the three men heading back the way they had come. After they went over the ridge he waited, thinking they might have set a trap for him and be watching, but eventually he followed in their footsteps and climbed to the top of the ridge for a look.

They were specks in the distance and still moving away.

He raced back to where the two bushes had been, fearful that his friend would be dead; overjoyed for a second when he saw the top of his head sticking out of the water but quickly realising the truth on seeing the burnt flesh of the face.

Thomas still could not see, although the daylight seemed stronger and he had regained some control of his badly burnt eyelids.

Terrified that he might lose his footing and drift away on the current, not knowing where he was going or how to save himself, he had grabbed hold of a root growing out of the bank and his body was half turned away from Banjora.

The aborigine dropped to his knees and called, 'Thom-as.'

Thomas was startled and lost his balance trying to turn too quickly. His feet slipped on the muddy bottom and he started to fall.

Banjora leant over and grabbed his arm, pulling him in towards the bank.

Thomas regained his foothold and felt for Banjora's other hand.

Though he tried with all his might, Thomas' body was too heavy for the slight aborigine to lift bodily.

He could plainly see that Thomas had no vision and guided his arm until he was sure that his friend had a good hold on the root again before standing up.

'I go, naa.'

Though Thomas' head was one huge ball of pounding pain his brain was still clear and he understood that Banjora was going to look for a shallower part of the river, where he would be able to leave the water.

He heard the native walk off and come back several minutes later.

'Good. Come.' He said, turning Thomas' shoulder in the right direction.

The shallows were where the river kinked and the current had deposited sand. When Thomas finally reached it he found that the bottom shelved rapidly upwards, until he was standing in water just up to his knees. He was able to turn and sit down on the bank before rolling his body over onto dry land.

He had been in the water for more than two hours and the skin on his finger tips and toes had shrivelled, though he could only feel and not see the digits.

The sun was hot and his body dried quickly. Banjora knew that Thomas' head must be kept in the shade and he stood like a sentinel so that his shadow fell over it while he watched his friend fall into a trance-like sleep.

Thomas slept for over two hours, during the last half hour twisting his body incessantly, the agony of his burns reaching into the far recesses of his brain. When he woke it was as if from another life and for a few moments he had no recollection of his recent past or even who or where he was.

He heard a voice call softly, 'Thom-as.'

Another voice he did not recognise as his own answered, 'Is that me?'

Banjora did not understand the badly slurred words but bent down and laid his hand on Thomas' breast.

'Thom-as no dead.'

As he came to full wakefulness Thomas also came to complete awareness, remembering the fire and the pain. He tried to look at Banjora but saw only a vague dark shape, and the fear of blindness overtook him again.

The burns on his face were drying, making the pain excruciating. He wanted to rub his hands over them to ease the hurt but knew he must not.

Banjora had waited with the aborigine's usual patient acceptance of fate but knew they needed to move from this desolate place to somewhere more conducive to sleeping and feeding in relative comfort.

He put his hand down, 'Come.'

Thomas took it and tried to stand, using his left leg. It buckled; a painful reminder of the sprain.

Banjora saw the problem and knelt down beside him. Thomas put his right hand on the aborigine's shoulder and stood using his right leg.

They moved off slowly, Banjora heading back towards the trees and rocks he had been hiding in while Blakely and his men remained in the area.

Once there, he settled his friend under the shade of a large cabbage palm at the edge of the wood and disappeared.

Thomas called out for him but received no reply. Within seconds, he was asleep again, suffering badly from the traumatic stress he had endured.

When he woke once more it was to feel a soft feather moving over his face, leaving a layer of animal fat on the damaged skin. Banjora had made a spear and killed a koala bear. He had skinned it, removed the fat and melted it in the hollow of a hot stone. As soon as he could leave Thomas he would search for witchetty grubs. Crushed into a paste and applied to the skin they were the aborigine cure for burns.

Thomas woke fully but did not move and kept his eyelids shut. The feather continued its work for several more minutes, and when he felt it leave his face he tried to open his lids.

Banjora's figure was still an indistinct grey shape, but Thomas fancied he could make out the eyes and mouth, and it gave him hope that the blindness was temporary.

His friend said, 'Eat', holding out a small strip of raw meat.

Thomas could not see it, but opened his lips, gasping with the pain as the skin ripped.

The meat tasted strange; he was not used to eating flesh raw but he was so hungry that he accepted several more portions gratefully.

He was asleep again almost before he swallowed the last morsel.

He slept for twelve more hours.

When he woke the sunlight was making a moving theatre of the shadows of the branches above, which were being blown back and forth by the breeze like ghostly actors rushing hither and thither looking for their places on the stage, though he was unable to appreciate it. All he could see was a vague mixture of blacks and greys.

He could hear the crackling of twigs burning in a fire and smell the smoke.

A voice murmured, 'Thom-as wake.'

He repeated, 'Thomas awake. Yes, Banjora. Thank you.'

The native laughed, 'You eat?'

'I eat.'

This time, the meat was roasted and more succulent. While he ate he became aware that his left ankle had a bulky vegetable poultice bound around it with a vine and realised that his face had been re-treated with some kind of fat or oil.

They stayed in that spot for nine days, and each day Thomas' sight improved, so that by the end of that time he could see the landscape, the trees, and Banjora's features, but blurred as if viewed through a badly incorrect spectacle lens. His ankle was completely healed, and he was walking without a limp. The skin on his face had been kept from hardening by the many applications of animal fat and fish oil from blue nosed trout-cod that Banjora had somehow coaxed from the river, and beneath the soft flakes on the surface new skin was beginning to form.

The pain had diminished to bearable limits, although even the touch of a falling leaf was enough to make Thomas gasp.

Banjora had been keeping a careful watch on progress and decided it was time to move off. There was game here but not enough, and he wanted somewhere more permanent if they were going to stay in the area. He was undergoing an internal struggle himself; his body, under the influence of generations of forefathers, was urging him to go for the 'dream time', while having to consider looking after this white stranger who had become his friend but was not of his family.

CHAPTER TWENTY

Sloane had friends keeping him informed of Blakely's movements and he knew when the sergeant and his two cohorts had left the settlement in pursuit of Thomas. News of the escape had spread through the colony as fast as the fire that had overtaken Thomas.

Sloane did not give the convict a hope in hell of escaping from the three men but kept the news from Martha.

While Blakely and his men were away from the colony he could relax a little from the tension he had been under, knowing that they would not stop at Thomas. Rainforde would have given them instructions to kill Martha and any children, and the lieutenant was under no illusion that he would have been excluded as a target.

Purely by chance, he saw Blakely and his men on the day that they returned, full of rum, swaggering and boasting to anyone who would listen that they had got their man.

Martha wanted to go to the communal washing place to do the laundry, but he asked her to leave it for that day, wanting to keep the news from her as long as possible. Watching her playing with Austin in the small garden in front of the hut he felt the pain he knew she would feel when she heard the news.

That evening, just before dark, he decided to visit the rude hut that the wags called the officers' mess, where good quality navy rum was served. He was not a drinking man but liked to chat with his fellow officers of an evening, and one flagon would help him sleep.

As he strolled along what passed for the street his ever-aware soldier's eye caught sight of a slight movement at the side of one of the rough dwellings. He stopped and bent as if to adjust his shoe, using his peripheral sight to catch a glimpse of the man watching his passage.

It was one of Blakely's two monkeys, and he knew immediately that something was afoot.

He stood upright again and strode out, whistling nonchalantly as he went.

The moment he was out of the man's sight he turned quickly down past the side of one of the huts, then ran along the back of the wooden buildings to the rear of his own.

Blakely, hiding behind the trees at the end of the row of houses, had watched the lieutenant leave his quarters, and at a wave from his cohort, who had waited until the officer disappeared from his sight before giving the agreed signal, sprinted across to Sloane's dwelling. He tiptoed into the front entrance and through to the back room, where he came upon Martha readying herself for sleep, wearing nothing but a nightgown. The child was asleep in the corner.

Blakely licked his lips. The woman had to be first. When he'd violated and finished her off, he would swing the brat by his ankles and bash his brains out on the floor. Beautiful!

He held out a dagger and ordered, 'Get that off you. Now!'

Terrified, Martha did so.

In the low, flickering light from the candle he took in her early pregnancy, her swollen breasts and the dark curly triangle on her lower belly. His erection was so hard it was hurting him, but first he wanted her to suffer mentally.

'Your man is dead. I burnt 'im to death and watched 'is flesh shrivel. Soon your other man'll follow 'im. But you're next. On the floor, bitch.'

Martha lay down, with her legs tightly closed.

'Open your bloody legs!' He undid his breeches and pulled them down, ready to drop to the floor to mount her, stunned when behind him he heard a bitter voice, 'Turn around, Blakely. I will not shoot even a dog like you in the back.'

Blakely spun, astonished and almost shitting himself with sudden fear. He had watched Sloane go to the mess. How could he be back here?

He tried to speak but took the ball in his forehead before he could do so.

Blood spattered Martha as Blakely fell beside her.

Sloane could not help his eyes taking in her naked body – the first time he had seen her thus, then quickly turned his back.

'Clothe yourself, Martha. I shall need to bring the Justice.'

Amos had heard the shot and was hiding when Charles found him.

'What has he done? He was going to strangle her. He did not have a pistol with him, did he?'

Charles, for all his size, felt mortally afraid. 'No, he left it with me. It wasn't he who shot. We need to clear out. Now.'

'In the dark? Don't be daft, man. I need a drink.'

'First thing tomorrow then, back where we just came from.'

'How will we live?'

'No idea, but if we stay here we shall be doing the hangman's hornpipe; that's a certainty. Come on. Let's get that rum.'

There were dozens of people in the street, come to see what had happened, when Sloane walked outside, and he asked one of the marines to fetch the constable. Two more he sent in search of Blakely's men. They found them in the canteen, swigging rum, and arrested them on the spot.

Held separately incommunicado overnight, they were brought before the magistrate the next morning, one at a time, Charles Strange first.

There was no English type preamble and no jury. Sloane and his fellow officers were the only people present, other than the magistrate Phillip had appointed and two court officials.

'You are charged with conspiring to murder. How do you plead?'

For a big man, Strange could cringe with the best.

'It wasn't me, your Honour. I had nothing to do with it. I was just keeping a watch out for Lieutenant Sloane's return. Blakely told me he was only going into the hut to steal some money. I did not know anything about a murder. Amos, Amos Breen, he told me after Blakely was shot that he'd gone in there to do murder. Honest, your Honour, I knew nothing about it.'

The magistrate had sat on the bench in England for fifteen years and recognised a lying story when he heard one.

'Take him outside and do not let him speak to Breen.' He told the court officials.

Breen was brought in next and gave an almost identical rendering, except to implicate Strange instead of himself. He insisted that he was completely innocent and had only been keeping watch while Blakely went into the hut, for what reason he could not for the life of him imagine, since Blakely had not given one.

Strange was brought back in and lined up next to Breen.

The magistrate wasted few words on the two miscreants: 'I find you both guilty of perjury and conspiring to murder. You will be taken from this court and hanged before sunset.'

Sloane returned to his hut, where Martha, still tearful, waited for news.

He merely nodded, and she understood the gesture.

She managed, 'I am glad we are now safe, Arthur.'

He agreed, 'We no longer need have fear of Lord Rainforde's long arm. I doubt he will try again.'

She saw the strange look in his eye and needed no woman's intuition to recognise it for what it was: love. She had known for some months how he felt, by little actions he tried to hide, but had forced herself to ignore it. She still loved Thomas with a fiercely protective love that would never lessen, but the harshness of the times forced a body to accept life the way it was. Thomas was dead, her babies needed a father, and Arthur would be a good one, she knew.

CHAPTER TWENTY-ONE

Three months had passed since the fire, and Thomas had learnt a great deal in that time. His eyesight had gradually returned after a fortnight and was now as good as before, and the skin had healed, leaving a man who wore a hideous mask instead of a face, with no eyebrows, a wrecked nose and a receded hairline. The wound in his shoulder troubled him from time to time but was now just two areas of puckered flesh. The old woman's poultice had saved him from infection.

Banjora had led him into foothills, where there was no river to look into, and he had no idea of his looks until, after a torrential rainstorm one morning, he had looked in a puddle of water that had collected in a dip in the rocks.

Banjora watched him, wondering how his friend Thom-as would react.

He was surprised. The white man looked for a long time without moving and then used a finger to lift first one then the other upper eyelid, followed by a repeat with the lower lids. Then Banjora heard a huge sigh.

The weeks of healing and then touching had given Thomas the worst kind of idea of his looks. What he had expected had been far worse than what he now saw.

Yes, it was true that he looked a fright and almost inhuman, but his imagination had envisaged something that could never have been shown in public again.

This, at least, was the semblance of a human face; the ears, though red and skinned their normal shape, two eyes still in the right places, a nose that was a much different shape, thinner than before, and burnt down to the bone, no longer the distinctive Nash 'conk', but with lips that had somehow almost repaired themselves, although much thinner than before. Human looking, at least.

He knew that if Martha could have him back he would still be loved, though he was fully aware that such pipe dreams would have to be eradicated from his mind. That part of his life was over, forever.

Only one feeling gave him a small modicum of comfort: the freedom of action that he had so mourned when he lost it was now restored to him. He was once more a free man, if not a freed man.

Banjora had been teaching him some of the skills of the aborigines. He now knew which spiders were dangerous and how to avoid their habitats; how not only to recognise an acacia bush but how to use a wooden tool to scoop out the roots and extract the witchetty grubs; how to recognise the edible fruits and berries; how to catch a snake with a forked stick, skin it and cook it, and how to eat ants. Their diet had been eclectic, with Thomas not knowing from one day to the next what would be on the menu. He had eaten eels, possums, wallabies, bandicoots, kangaroos, snakes, tortoises, wombats, koalas, frogs, the delicious freshwater crayfish called yabbies and insects of a dozen different kinds. Banjora had provided all the meat apart from snake up to that point in time but two days before had produced with a flair Thomas' own spear, made from the long stem of the grass tree, with the sharpened leg bone of a shearwater stuck onto the stem as a point He had used the orange resin from the same tree as glue and bound the leg bone on with the 'grass' from the tree, twisted into a kind of string.

For almost all of those two days he had made Thomas practise, using a target of eucalyptus bark, until his friend's right arm ached so much he could hardly hold the spear.

At first he missed by yards at even short distances and could only throw the spear a maximum of some forty feet. Banjora continually corrected his throwing stance, and by the end of the second day he was hitting the target more often than he was missing it.

Day after day the practice continued, and Thomas realised with a sad jolt one day that the aborigine was preparing to leave him, but not before he was sure that Thomas could provide for himself and survive in the Outback.

His shirt had disintegrated and his breeches were hanging in rags. His skin was burnt almost as black as that of his companion.

Banjora seemed quite happy naked, and Thomas knew that he would soon have to accustom himself to being in that state also.

The day he brought down his first emu was one of great celebration. Banjora kept repeating, 'Doo-gal bin-yang - big bird!'

He roasted the two legs, and it was all they could do to eat them for one meal.

Every few days they moved on building only the most basic of shelter at each place in the aborigine manner, heading always towards the Blue Mountains.

Towards the end of the year, Thomas' breeches finally fell to pieces, and he left the rags lying where they dropped. What was left of them was useless, even as strips of cloth.

With the passage of the months, he became almost as adept as Banjora with the spear. He kept a mental note of the days passing and knew almost to the day when the New Year of 1791 began.

Each morning he would catch Banjora looking into the distance with a vacant look in his eyes and knew the time was near when he would be alone.

On what he judged to be the third of February the aborigine suddenly pulled him down as they were walking through tall grass.

He whispered, 'What?' and Banjora held his finger to his lips.

Thomas could hear nothing other than the song of a bird close by, but several minutes later Banjora pulled him to his feet again and ploughed through the grass.

In a small clearing, they came across six aborigine women, three very old, two nubile young women with tight, round breasts, whom Thomas estimated to be in their early twenties or perhaps slightly younger, only one of whom wore the bar-rin over her pubic region, and a girl of perhaps twelve or thirteen, without pubic hair, but with perfectly formed small breasts.

Thomas' face might have been less than perfect, but the rest of his hardened body was in top class condition, and at sight of the naked young women his body reacted totally without his will.

The women had been surprised but did not take fright, seeing that the strange man was accompanied by Banjora, who had said something Thomas did not understand when they first came into view.

Their reaction at seeing the state Thomas was in was mixed. The oldest woman looked shocked and annoyed. The other two old ones were grinning lewdly, the two young women were gazing with great interest at his engorged member, and the girl was giggling so much that urine flowed down her legs and wet the ground around her feet.

He tried unsuccessfully to cover himself up and finally had to cup his member by putting one hand in front of the other and pulling it up to lie against his belly, the purple, tautly stretched head still peeking out between the thumb and index finger of the front hand and his scrotum hanging in full sight, making the whole exercise pointless.

Banjora began a long, involved conversation with the oldest woman, and Thomas, who had been learning more vocabulary each day, could follow perhaps a third of what they were saying.

Banjora asked why they were only females, and she told him that all the men and many of the other women had died very quickly of the 'spotted disease', which Thomas knew meant smallpox. The language was not the Kat-tang of Banjora's tribe, but there were enough similarities to make understanding possible

There followed another long harangue by his aboriginal friend, which involved many signed gestures obviously involving him, and he was intrigued to know what was being said but waited till the end.

At last, Banjora told him, 'They need man. Take you. I go; Mandu, Curriquinquin.'

Thomas was dumbfounded. He had been put on the block and sold, all cut and dried, without so much as a 'by your leave' from him.

The shock of his new situation cured his immediate lower body problem, and he took his hands away. These women were used to the nakedness of man and he owed them no deference.

What should he do? He knew that he could fend for himself and probably make a success of living on his own, always providing he did not fall ill or become injured, which would mean certain death. The options were clear: voluntary entry into a life of sterile hardship and self-enforced solipsism or accept a way of life that would have at least the vestiges of normal family life, however unusual, and the possibility of companionship.

The younger women were obviously keen to procreate and saw him as a means to that end. His own body had already made it plain to him that he was more than ready to accommodate them. He thought of Martha and of being unfaithful to her but knew he would never see her again and had already realised that once she had recovered from the shock and believed him dead she would consider marrying Sloane. He had recognised the look that came into the lieutenant's eyes when he mentioned her and was glad that Martha and his child, or children if their last joining was blessed, would be looked after.

That life was a closed book, and he had to forget it. The present was what mattered now, and his body had clearly told him, as well as these six females, that he needed a woman.

The answer was obvious: he had to join their band.

Banjora had watched him thinking and saw that he had reached a decision.

He said simply, 'Go-bye, Thom-as.'

Thomas knew it was useless asking him to stay for a while. He grabbed his arm and enunciated clearly. 'Tell Rog-er I live. Only Rog-er.'

Banjora nodded, 'I tell if see.'

He disappeared into the tall grass as only an aborigine could, and there was no sound of his passing.

Thomas felt an instant pang of loss. In the time they had been together, he had felt closer to Banjora than he had to any man before in his life, including his father. Now he looked at his new friends. Introductions seemed to be needed.

He went through the same routine as when he first met Apari's group, pointing at his chest and saying, 'Thom-as', which they all duly repeated, and he then asked their names.

The young girl said her name, 'Bibola'. He tried to remember a Kattang word that was similar, and when she lifted her hand and described part of a parabola in the sky he knew it meant 'Sunrise'.

The young woman wearing the bar-rin was called Kwaralia, which he recognised as 'Star', and the one without the pubic covering, who seemed unable to take her eyes off his crotch, causing him several times to feel a hardening and pulsing of his flesh with the imminent chance of a repeat performance down below, told him she was Harah, the sky.

He began to think that they were all named after the heavens, but the first of the old women he questioned was called Yahnee, which was very like the Kattang word for 'peace'. The second was Girrah, the magpie.

The oldest woman seemed to disdain him and was loath to answer. The young girl supplied the word, 'Ngorongal', which he knew meant 'old woman'. Had his face been as it once was he would have laughed. The woman's expression had not altered one bit.

They were no more than ten miles from the nearest of the mountains, and when they moved off it was in that direction.

Though he had been unable to follow the entire conversation between Banjora and the women he had come to understand that their home lay somewhere in the Blue Mountains.

He had not before seen mixed groups of aborigines, so was not surprised when he was not expected to go in front, as a native male would have done.

Ngorongal went first, and it was then indicated that he should follow. The other women followed in order of seniority, and he was surprised when every so often his buttocks were pinched hard enough to hurt. He wondered if it was because he was attractive to them or if they were just doing it to inflict pain.

They stopped several times to dig up roots with the wooden implements they carried, putting them into the bags that two of the older women wore on their backs, the string handles round their necks leaving their hands free to work. Now and then, one or another of them would move to one side to relieve herself, not making the slightest effort to hide. When it came to Thomas' turn and he could wait no longer he found that no matter where he went off the track they followed him. After several abortive attempts to avoid them, he merely turned his back to urinate. Before he could start the flow, however, he found that the two younger women had come up close on either side of him and were looking down to see how he handled matters, almost as if he were a god descended from the skies who used a different method to that used by their own men. Though his bladder was aching, he found it difficult to start with them watching, and was hesitant about the shaking when he finished. When he turned back, the eyes of the women were on his groin, obviously looking to see if there was any change.

He looked more carefully at the mountains as they approached. There was a deep valley cut between them, and at the extreme end of the left hand group there were three sharp, jagged peaks, close to one another. Harah saw him looking at them and said, 'Bulorra wuggool juroomin'. The accent and the words were slightly different from those of Banjora and his group, but he recognised it as 'Three sisters'. It was a good descriptive name.

As they marched, he hoped to come across some animal, so that he could show them his prowess with the spear, but for the moment at least he was to be denied.

The journey took up most of the day. The sun had gone behind the mountains and the long shadows of the peaks ran across the land like the fingers of a river delta filling after floods. The temperature near the mountains was distinctly chillier and Thomas felt cool for the first time in months.

At last they came to a clearing that they had obviously used before, since there was ash from a previous fire, some mile and a half from the cliffs. Here they stopped and the women set down their bags and began preparing the meal.

It consisted of roots he had not eaten before, roasted over an open fire and tasting remarkably like the toast Martha had produced on their hearth back home, bringing a bout of nostalgia that had his eyes filling with tears that had nowhere to go but down his scarred cheeks, the tops of his tear ducts having been destroyed by the fire.

Darkness fell much more quickly in the lee of the mountains, and one by one the women lay down to sleep, all except Harah, who continued to squat facing him, her legs wide open revealing everything she had, he imagined by design. He knew she was watching him as he sat near the fire trying to keep warm and he suddenly realised she was deliberately taunting him, trying to cause another reaction in his body.

She succeeded.

Of a sudden she rose, came to him and pulled his arm.

He had been expecting it and stood, struggling with his emotions, but he knew he needed this.

She took him just a few yards away from the others before lying down and opening her legs.

One thing surprised him: unlike Martha, Harah made not a sound during the intercourse, either of joy or pain. Despite himself, he found the act wonderful and almost like a rebirth for him. For the first time, he realised that he was ready to embrace this new life entirely and forget the old.

His climax was like an eruption that engulfed his whole body after the months of celibacy, and he allowed it to run its full course before he withdrew and pulled himself upright. Harrah rose too, moved off back to the fire and lay down. Throughout, not a word had been spoken.

He went back to his old position and soon drifted off into a dreamless sleep, from which he was awoken shortly before dawn by a hand fondling his crotch.

Kwaralia had come for her turn. He let her help him up and did his duty manfully, feeling somewhat like one of his breeding boars, hoping that twice in twenty-four hours would satisfy them.

The food for breakfast was the same as the previous evening meal and would become the staple dish throughout his time with them.

As soon as they had eaten they moved off again, straight towards the mountains.

196

When they reached the foothills they walked past a large gum tree and through several smaller bushes to a gap in fallen rocks, which led to the start of a well-worn path upwards, and after climbing hard they reached a series of caves, invisible from below, behind an outcrop of rock.

He realised that this was their permanent home, for just inside the largest cave he could see utensils made from the protuberances of the eucalyptus tree, a number of spears and stone axes, and other items he could not recognise. He guessed that the weapons must have belonged to their dead men folk.

As he had with Banjora, Thomas quickly became used to being part of his new family and adapted well. Every few days he was used by one or other of the two younger women, and one day saw Bibola looking with interest at his groin. In the short while he had been with them hair had begun to grow on her mons pubis, and he knew she had reached puberty. He had become so used to being totally naked that he gave it not a thought, but now every time he caught sight of Bibola's nubile young naked body his penis reacted and he felt he needed some covering.

He had learnt much of their language now and asked Harah if she could make him a riji.

She shook her head, laughed prettily and told him it was not necessary, they all knew what he had, but he said, 'Bibola looks', and Harah nodded.

'You mate with Bibola soon', she told him in her language. She held up four fingers and said, 'Four moons'.

In England, most girls were married young. The age of consent was twelve for girls and fourteen for boys, and many babies were born to girls of thirteen. Bibola looked to be at least thirteen, but then he imagined that aborigine girls matured much earlier than the English. He asked Harah, 'Bibola how old?'

She did not understand the concept. They did not count the years as he did. The aborigine words she used in reply meant, 'Old young', which he took to mean, 'Old enough'.

The last years of his life had taught him to philosophise much as the aborigines did: what happened happened, and there was nothing one could do about it. He would either lie with

Bibola or he would not. Looking at life that way avoided stress, and when he gave it thought he realised that, strange and unbelievable as it seemed, he was probably as contented with his present lot as he had ever been, living a life so simple that the only thing to worry about was the next meal.

When his knowledge of their language had improved enough he asked Harah what Banjora had talked about before he left, and she told him that 'Old Woman' had asked Banjora to stay and breed with them, because their tribe of almost fifty had been virtually wiped out by the smallpox, and their greatest need was to rebuild the tribe. Banjora had refused, not because he did not want to breed with them, but because he could not stay, and if he had children by them he would be pulled two ways. He had to leave; his forefathers were calling him to return to his brethren, and he could not resist. He told her to use the white man, because he was an outlaw, hunted by his own tribe, and could never leave them. Old Woman said she distrusted the stranger but realised she had no option but to accept or allow the tribe to die out.

When Thomas killed his first kangaroo for them she had smiled for the first time and told him her name was 'Gurrah', the wind. He was finally accepted.

Both Harah and Kwaralia grew large with child, and Harah gave birth first, to a baby boy so white that he looked like an English child, with almost blond hair and a straight nose. Thomas saw how the child became mothered by all the women and wondered once again at how close the aborigines in a tribe were one with another. There was much discussion as to what to call the baby, the older women preferring 'Giragira', the 'White Bird', Harah wanting 'Bundah', the 'Hawk', and Kwaralia and Bibola fancying 'Kurah', the 'Wind'. Thomas suggested several alternatives but soon realised he was to have nothing to do with the selection. In his mind, he had already named the boy 'Joshua', after his own father. In the end, Harah had her way, and 'Bundah' the boy became.

Kwaralia's daughter was a miniature of her mother, with coal black curly hair, a squat nose and the aborigine colouring. This time she was adamant, and the girl was named 'Gurrah' after her grandmother, who showed her pleasure by dancing a little jig and singing one of the ancient songs. Thomas' name for the child was 'Martha'.

Inside the cave, they were more or less immune to the vagaries of the weather, which in any case was equable during that spring with occasional light rain but no thunderstorms.

His farming instinct still strong, Thomas had considered planting some crops but shelved the idea, believing that at some point they might have to move on. Another consideration was that ranging hunters, seeing growing crops, would know people were living in the area, and that would bring danger. His new hunting prowess fed them well in any case, and the roaming life suited him.

One day, as he was returning with two snakes he had captured, he came across Bibola about a mile from the caves.

She greeted him and then, without further ado, lay down and spread her legs.

The time had arrived, and there was no denying his need. Harah and Kwaralia had shown no desire to be bedded again since the birth of their babies, and he imagined there must be some unwritten period between pregnancies.

Unlike her two older sisters, Bibola's sensuality quickly revealed itself. She bit his shoulder and drew blood as he did from her by tearing her hymen and she moaned with evident pleasure throughout. They were, for him, a few of the most memorable minutes of his life, and undeniably the most enjoyable. They were to be repeated regularly every few days.

Afterwards, she held his hand proprietarily all the way back to the cave, humming happily and turning to gaze into his eyes every few seconds. It gave him a wonderful glow to know that even with his mask of a face he could be so loved.

It was four months before she became pregnant, and during that time she had taken to accompanying Thomas on the hunt, taking one of the spears and becoming adept at its use. He allowed her most of the kills, unless it was a big animal or bird. Strangely, as the weeks passed, he found that he felt much closer to her and more in intimate commune with her than with anyone else ever. She had an inquiring mind, and her youth had an enduring appeal that he found irresistible. Her companionship came to mean far more to him than that of Banjora, or, in fact, Martha, although they had lived together much longer and worked together in the fields.

In her eighth month, he decided that she must stay behind when he hunted, pleasing the older women, but causing her to pout and hide her face from him. It was then that Harah and Kwaralia began to use him again.

Out hunting one day, as Bibola was reaching her term, a sudden heavy thunderstorm caught him out in the open in an area he had only visited once before, half a day's walk away from the caves.

He found what shelter he could among some huge rocks and when the storm had passed found that his way back was blocked by a new creek full of water from the flash flood.

He had not swum since the day his face was burnt but knew it would be no problem, even with the brush turkey he had speared.

He was about to enter the water when something caught his eye – something sparkling, reflecting the light of the sun, now shining from a cloudless sky.

He bent, pushed his hand under the sand around the sparkle and lifted it out. As his hand rose, water and sand with golden specks filtered out through his fingers, and he was left with a piece of bright golden metal the size of the nail on his little finger.

With a jolt, he realised that he was holding a nugget of pure gold, worth at least a year's wages for a labourer.

If there was one, he thought, there must be more. The flood had washed it down the gulley from the escarpment a quarter of a mile away.

In his present situation, with no access to white humanity, gold was of no value whatsoever, but hope, as he had read in Lord Rainforde's library, springs eternal in the human breast, and the desire to return to civilisation had long been with him, although repressed and hidden away in the farthest corners of his mind.

It could do no harm to have gold. One day, even if he could not, his children could use it for their benefit. He knew that this new land would eventually be filled with immigrants, spreading all over the country, and this tribe he lived with would be assimilated somehow into that society. There would be opportunities for investment.

Gold! The dream of every man.

He spent the whole of the rest of the day searching the bed of the creek and found eleven more nuggets before dark. He did not go home that night or the next. While the water was there, he had to get as much out as he could. He was not the only one to benefit from the flood. Every kind of animal and over fifteen species of birds came to drink. Having eaten much of the brush turkey and left the rest when it went off in the heat, he killed just one of the emus and cooked some of the meat.

By the evening of the third day he had forty-three small lumps of gold; a king's ransom! One of his small leather bags for carrying eggs held them.

The level of the water was dropping rapidly and it would soon be gone again, but as with everything else in his new life, time was of no real import. There was always tomorrow, and there would be more rain, if not this week then next, or the next.

He knew he had found all the easily located nuggets but also knew that there would be an inestimable number of smaller pieces and a great deal of gold dust mixed with the sand. He tried to remember the page of one of Lord Rainforde's books that described the panning for gold. As he remembered, it was simply a matter of using a shallow dish, into which the prospector put a sample of the river bottom sand and some water and agitated it, with the dish at a slight angle so that the lighter elements like sand slipped out over the side of the dish and left the heavier elements in the bottom. It sounded easy, but he did not have a dish with him or tools to make one. It would have to be fetched from home.

Instinctively he decided to hide the bag of gold instead of taking it back to the cave. His time as a convict had taught him to mistrust every other human, even those close to him. He knew the women would not want to steal the gold, but unbearable pressure could at some time be applied to them by unscrupulous men. If he were to amass a fortune in gold he would keep it hidden until the time to use it was upon him.

He faced a barrage of questions when he returned and answered them by describing a huge swathe of water that he could not swim. It was a reasonable excuse and easily accepted; the aborigines were not swimmers.

The next morning he was given strange looks and asked several questions as to why he was taking one of the wooden bowls with him. He told a garbled story about inspecting the stomach of birds he shot, which caused merriment. It was the kind of thing an aborigine might do to read the future, and he guessed they imagined he was becoming more like a native. They did not notice that he had also taken every leather pouch from the store at the back of the cave.

It was a long walk each day, but he returned every night to the cave after that, rising before dawn and not stopping work until he could no longer see.

He worked frantically, watching the level drop each day, the madness for gold almost as strong in him as in the men who would later take part in the gold rush.

By the end of two weeks, as the last of the water dried up, he had three bags of nuggets and eight bags of dust, all of which he buried under a rock that carried particular striations that he knew he could easily recognise again.

The creek filled with water three more times that year, and each time he panned it out, adding to his cache.

Life was peaceful, apart from the cries of children. Thomas had no idea of the conflict between whites and aborigines that was every day becoming more violent and extreme back in the areas that had been settled. There had been many incidents, in one of which Governor Arthur Phillip was wounded with a spear. At the time, he asked for no reprisals, but when his huntsman was killed by an aborigine he sent out parties to kill those responsible. Aborigines were being hunted and slaughtered with great regularity, and the killing was made legal when the new Governor, Philip Gidney King, issued an edict for white settlers to shoot aborigines on sight.

Bibola produced a bouncing baby boy with lighter, straighter hair than an aborigine but with mainly native features. He was born during a violent thunderstorm and had to be called 'Mongi', 'Lightning'. Thomas christened him after himself.

Kwaralia became pregnant again but lost the child in the third month. Harah gave birth to a daughter seven months later; a real aborigine, with no trace of white about her. They called her 'Garad', the 'Black Cockatiel'. To Thomas she was 'Elizabeth'.

Joshua was growing apace and was the exact image of Thomas as he remembered himself at the same age. He had no trace of his aboriginal parentage except for his more rounded eyes and a slightly darker skin than a purebred English child, no more than could be explained as from exposure to the sun, and he would be tall. With all the childrenThomas spoke only English, making them bilingual from birth.

Responding to urgent requests to accompany him on the hunt, Thomas began taking Joshua with him on the shorter expeditions, and on a bright afternoon, when high cirrus cloud was making the sun appear to be surrounded by a dozen silver rings, they had just returned to the cave when a distant gunshot made Thomas' hair stand on end with an almost spiritual fear, not for himself, but for his babies and his wives.

Harah, Bibola and Kwaralia were playing with their children outside one of the other caves and the old woman, Gurrah, was squatting near him, beating out a kangaroo skin. She had also heard the shot and had lifted her head enquiringly. It was a sound she had never heard before.

He asked urgently, 'Where are the others?'

'Out foraging.'

'Where?'

The old woman shook her head. She did not know.

203

He swore. Who had shot and at what he could not guess, but a shot meant white men, and white men almost certainly meant trouble.

'Stay here and take everyone into the cave. Do not come out until I come back.'

He had long ago found a path upwards and took it now, going up another thousand feet.

About five miles away, he could see two small clouds of disturbed sand in the air and below them what looked like two figures on horseback.

They were coming his way.

As he watched over the next half hour he could see that they seemed to be quartering, searching for something, and shortly afterwards he could just make out their quarry: three aborigine men, dodging from cover to cover and moving fast.

At just under two miles, he could clearly see from his high viewpoint the entire chase. The white men had divided up the search, one doing zigzags back and forth to the right, and the other to the left. The aborigines were attempting to make as much forward progress as possible, consistent with remaining in what little cover existed.

Thomas saw one of the horsemen lift his rifle and observed the telltale white puff of smoke at the muzzle a second before the sound reached him. One of the natives fell, and the horseman rode up and checked quickly that he was dead while re-loading.

A couple of minutes later the other horseman shot, and another aborigine fell. That rider too checked the body, and Thomas saw him jump down from the horse and use a knife to slit the throat of the man on the ground.

The last fugitive reached the edge of the scrub, where only a few bushes relieved a strip of sandy soil. He ran straight forward in the open and was overtaken in seconds by one of the horsemen, who turned in the saddle, aimed the gun at his prey and fired point-blank.

The two horsemen came to a halt and sat beside one another, and Thomas could see from their actions that they were laughing, waving their hands in the air, celebrating their victory.

One pulled a bottle of rum from his saddlebag and took a swig, before handing it over for the other to drink.

Thomas stayed at his vantage point, waiting to see what they would do next. Would they turn and go back to civilisation, or would they stay in the area?

After taking several drinks each, the larger of the two men replaced the bottle in the saddlebag and turned his horse as if to leave.

Just at that moment, Yahnee, who had been hiding with her sister well off to the left of the action, let her fright get the better of her and foolishly broke cover, making a dead run for the base of the mountain.

The movement caught the eye of the other horseman and with a whoop he set off after her. His companion had turned again, looking towards where she had broken from, and galloped in that direction to investigate.

Thomas left his spot and began to run downhill as fast as his legs would carry him.

Pausing only to pick up three spears from the cave he raced down the path, only slowing when he reached the last few yards, covered by the tree that grew near the bottom.

Yahnee was no more than two hundred yards away, being overtaken fast by the horseman, who had not reloaded his piece after having shot the last of the aborigine men.

He overtook Yahnee and slid his horse to a stop between her and the base of the mountain. He jumped off and held out his arms to stop her.

'Ay-up, my beauty!' He shouted, swinging the stock of the gun from side to side, 'See what the nice man has got for you.'

Yahnee was petrified with fear, and both urine and faeces escaped from her body, running down her legs.

The man laughed, 'Oh, that's lovely, that is. I like to see what fear does to you blacks.'

He was moving towards her when Thomas' spear slammed into his back, piercing the body and entering the heart.

He crashed to the ground. Thomas ran forward, grabbed Yahnee's arm and forced her towards the path, urging her, 'Run! Run!'

He turned to look at the dead man, astonished to find that it was Willy Crabb, older but still clearly recognisable.

Thomas knew instinctively that the other man would be Chatto Barnes. They had not changed their habits and were still the vicious pair of animals he remembered.

Girrah, he knew, was in dire trouble. He could hear her screams, but could not see either her or her attacker. Surely, he thought, Barnes would not rape an old woman like that, or would he?

Yes, he thought, that is exactly what he would do. He set off at a dead run towards the spot where Barnes' horse stood nibbling the sparse grass.

The pitiful screams continued, and Thomas reached the rim of a small basin in the earth where the struggle was taking place.

Barnes was on top of and inside the woman, who was trying to beat him with her fists. Every few seconds he stopped, drew back and hit her in the face with his bunched-up fist, then began humping again.

Thomas gritted out, 'Barnes!'

The word could not have caused more reaction if it had been a bullet.

The ex-convict leapt from the woman, scrabbling up and grabbing for the vicious knife that he wore in his belt. He stopped dead seeing the unrecognisable burnt face in front of him, put off for just a few seconds, 'Who the hell are you?'

'Don't you remember Thomas Nash?'

Barnes swore vilely, 'You're fucking dead!'

'Not quite.'

'What you doing here?'

'Stopping you from killing one of my friends.'

Barnes recovered some of his sang froid, 'You got to be joking, Nash. She's only some old abo bitch, an' she was bloody dry inside. Look at the state of my cock; she's made it bleed. We kill 'em all now, after them massacres what they done. You're a white man; well, sort of, looking at you, but you have to let us do our job. You stand back an' I'll finish her off.' He looked past Thomas, obviously expecting Crabb to arrive and help him, but still unworried.

Thomas saw the look and informed him, 'Crabb will not come to your aid, Barnes. He's dead.'

Now he saw real fear for the first time on the ex-convict's face.

The man had not noticed Girrah rise silently to her feet. She came up behind him and tried to grab the knife out of his hand.

He was too quick for her and too strong, and they fought for the weapon.

He twisted it from her grip and raised it ready to strike. Another second or two and the blade would enter her chest. Thomas hurled the spear.

It entered the back of Barnes' neck and went right through, to protrude six inches on the other side.

Barnes looked down at the barb, not believing what he saw, or the pain.

Blood gushed out of his mouth as his body collapsed onto the sandy ground like a jack-in-the-box with the child's finger pressure released. The legs kicked half a dozen times in the death throes and then the body lay still.

To his enquiry, Girrah assured him that she was all right and even made a joke that Barnes had not been as big or as good as her husband. He could see she was bleeding from between her legs and knew she was lying to hide her pain. It reminded him again just how resilient the aborigine women were.

He brought Barnes' horse down to where the body lay. Looking in the saddlebags, he found a rope, which he used to tie round the body and to the saddle. He took the bottle of rum from the bag, took a large swig from it; the first alcohol he had tasted since the last harvest on his farm, then tipped the rest of the contents out on the ground.

He had long ago found a deep, narrow crevasse higher up the mountain, which he had marked down as the perfect place to dispose of a body, and with the horses' help he dragged both bodies up to it and tipped them in, after removing all the clothes and a gold ring with a lapis lazuli stone from Barnes' finger.

The clothes he stored carefully at the back of the cave. He searched the pockets of both men and the saddlebags and found that between them they had eleven golden guineas, five moidores and a small number of crowns and smaller coins. The two men, he judged, must have been up to their earlier criminal activities again to amass that amount of money. He was pleased with his haul, since it meant he would not immediately have to use gold in order to live back in civilisation; the first time in years that such a thought had crossed his mind.

That evening as he ate his meal he suddenly realised just how much time had passed since he had joined forces with the women. He had kept a check of the years, of course, but had become inured to the passage of time and only now realised that it was the year of our Lord seventeen ninety-five. The convicts who had been sentenced to seven years' transportation had been released and were free men. There would be many more like Barnes and Crabb, some with murder in their heart, and his little tribe was in danger staying where they were. At some point, he knew, they would have to move further away from encroaching civilisation if they were to stay safe. Barnes had mentioned massacres done by aborigines and that they were being hunted to extinction. If that were true the women and his children were in terrible danger.

With two horses at his disposal, he could now ride back to see how things were progressing but on careful reflection he decided not to do so at that point.

An utterly mad, unthinkable idea was beginning to form at the back of his brain, and he wanted it to gel.

By the next morning, he had it clearly formed. He would need to wait a year, or maybe slightly more, but he could then present himself on Barnes' horse, wearing Barnes' clothes and ring, saying that he had been caught in a forest fire, only being saved from death, as he had been himself, by keeping his body immersed in the water. If Barnes had been burnt, the scars would need to heal as his own had done, and he remembered it had taken just over a year for them to finish healing.

When he left, he would make sure that the women and children headed off into the wide blue yonder, to keep them safe. He could always find them again. In the meantime, he had two good guns with plenty of powder and balls to fight off any intruders, which he could do with impunity from the height of the caves. They had fresh water enough from a small lake higher up in a fold in the mountain, and there were small animals and birds to be trapped on the heights. It was a good plan, and he began to get excited at the thought of seeing Martha and Austin again and possibly another Thomas.

The rest of the year passed without further incident and no more sightings of white men. With every rainfall, Thomas panned for gold and by the early spring of 1796 he had forty-seven bags hidden under the rock. Getting to and from the gold was much easier with the horse. It was but a scant hour's ride from the cave.

He began by talking seriously to Girrah, telling her that he was sure there would be many more white men looking to kill them and that the tribe needed to head well inland, away from the new settlements, in order to be safe. He saw many whispered conferences between her and the other older women, with Yahnee obviously very much in favour of what she was hearing.

Gurrah was resisting the plan, wanting to stay and die in the home she had known for so long and feeling too old and tired to undertake a long, hazardous journey, with no knowledge of what lay at the other end, but Thomas could see that they were gradually wearing down her resistance.

When he was sure that she agreed he called all of them together and outlined his plan.

They would leave when he did and take all their possessions with them. The children were big enough to walk part of the time and could take turns riding Crabb's grey when they became tired. If questioned Thomas intended to say that Crabb had gone off prospecting on his own, and the horse needed to disappear to back up his story. Thomas told them they should head due west into the interior.

The afternoon before the departure, he loaded sixteen bags of gold dust into his saddlebags; all that they would hold. He had realised when making his plans that if he presented himself to a banker in that country with gold nuggets it would provoke such a rush of men into the interior that the women might well be overtaken. Gold dust would not cause such a storm, and in any case he was not intending that much of it would see the light for a while. Only four of the bags he took would hold nuggets; the rest would remain hidden in his cache. He had worked out carefully how much he needed initially in order to further his intentions.

Something he was not looking forward to had to be done, and he went into the cave and pulled on Barnes' clothing. The rough cloth made his skin itch madly, almost as bad as the lice-infested clothing he had worn on the ship, and he had the urge to tear it off again but dare not give in to the desire. It was another necessary evil. He hid the coins in an inside pocket and slipped Barnes' ring on his third finger, the same one that Barnes used. A mistake with a small detail like that could give him away.

When he walked out of the cave he caused a wave of hilarity in which the children joined. Bibola caused the younger women to laugh even louder when she pouted and said, 'Thomas, you have hidden our toy.'

None of them had seen him fully clothed, and he realised he must look to them like something that had fallen from the sky. He grinned and shrugged nonchalantly but was infinitely glad when he was able to remove the garments to sleep.

The morning of their departure was a glorious one, with a gentle westerly breeze and a clear sky, save for a small patch of mile-high cirrus cloud in the far west, whose upward curling front tips seemed like the beckoning fingers of a welcoming god.

Thomas kissed each one of them and squeezed them to him. His eyes filled with tears, and the women's faces all showed their sorrow.

Joshua in his little man's voice asked, 'Can I not go with you, father?' It almost broke Thomas' heart as he answered, untruthfully he knew, 'Next time, Joshua. I promise.'

Martha and Elizabeth had happily accepted that being girls they should go with the women, and his youngest son was too young to understand.

Thomas waved them off, then turned and spurred the horse towards his future destiny, not looking back once. He had much planned, and only the fates could decide if those plans would come to fruition.

When he was still five miles from the place where he had almost met his end with the crocodile he stopped for the night, having seen signs of tree clearing a mile ahead. He made a meal of berries and dried snake meat that he had brought with him and settled down to sleep.

With his mind churning with ideas, he slept badly but woke with determination.

Just after waking, he heard a shot close by and stood up to look in the direction from which the sound had come.

He saw a horseman urging his horse forward and then stopping by the corpse of a large kangaroo, which he proceeded to butcher.

There was no time like the present, and Thomas knew he had to meet other men sometime. It might as well be now. He climbed onto the horse's back and walked it towards the man, who looked up when he heard the sound of hooves approaching but then bent again and got on with his work.

Thomas stopped five yards short and complimented him, 'Good shot.'

The man looked up and his head jerked back with astonishment, 'Man, what the hell happened to you?'

'Forest fire.'

'You poor sod.'

Thomas nodded. It was the first time he was asked a question that would be repeated so many times in the days to come that he heard it in his sleep.

'I am looking for a Lieutenant Arthur Sloane. Do you have any idea where I can find him?' Thomas had no idea if Sloane was in Rose Hill or Sydney Cove, but he had to start somewhere.

'Sloane. I've heard that name somewhere. Does he rear horses?'

Again, Thomas had no idea but was not about to admit it. 'I believe so.'

'Ah, then that will be the man you want. About six miles south of Parramatta.'

'Thank you. Enjoy the 'roo.'

'Can I give you a leg?'

'No, thank you, but I appreciate the offer.'

'Good luck with your search.'

The man went back to his work with the knife.

As he rode away Thomas heaved a huge sigh of relief. He had passed the first test.

The kangaroo killer had called the town Parramatta, so they must have changed the name from Rose Hill. He decided to ride through the town and then head south.

On a rise two miles away he stopped, amazed.

Before him, he saw a carefully planned town the size of Aylsham, with streets laid out in a perfect grid. Much later, he found out that Arthur Phillip, with his far-sightedness, had employed Baron Augustus Alt and the surveyor, Lieutenant William Dawes, to design the town; a design for the distant future. The main street was almost a mile in length and eighty feet in width and at its nearest end had an imposing building that could only be Government House. The side streets, running at right angles, were more than forty feet wide. Many buildings were two storeys high and all had large gardens. The largest building was near the centre and was a huge barracks with a redoubt. Other buildings to the right of it were probably barns and storehouses. There were wheeled vehicles of several kinds moving in the streets and many well-dressed pedestrians. Going out of the far end of the town was a wide road that led south towards Sydney Cove. What impressed him most was the sight of a ferry boat leaving the wharf and heading in that direction.

He was truly astonished at the transformation in the few short years he had been away and congratulated himself on his foresight in sending the women into the interior.

Wonder of wonder to the right of the town were more than a dozen fields of some kind of cereal ripening, looking from that distance like a golden patchwork quilt sewn by heavenly goddesses to bless the eyes of a weary farmer. He had not been informed that when he was selected to try to grow grain at Garden Cove, another ex-farmer convict, James Ruse, had been chosen to attempt the same thing at Rose Hill. There, with good, easily-worked, better quality soil, Ruse had managed to grow the first cereal crop to fruition, and each year had been better, removing at last the fear of starvation from the colony.

He rode the horse downhill and entered the outskirts of the town, letting the animal take its time, casting his eyes continually from side to side, taking in all the wonders.

This was no longer a frontier town but a real slice of civilisation. Arthur Phillip had worked wonders.

Thomas saw many people, including soldiers, look at him and turn away in horror, but no one accosted him or asked him his business, and he left the town and headed south.

He passed the fields of cereals and saw that they were of wheat and barley, both looking good, with full heads nodding in the light breeze coming off the low hill before him.

He spurred the horse into a canter and kept up that pace for two miles before slowing the animal to a walk again.

Over to his right he could see four low dwellings, each with a fenced area of around four acres in front of it, but could see no horses.

He estimated he had ridden some four miles from the town and probably needed to go on at least another two.

He passed several similar properties to those he had already seen, some with men and women working in the gardens, and began to think he must have missed the place he was looking for, but then he climbed a small rise and from the top saw a lush green valley with a small stream meandering through the middle of it, the entire area of about twenty acres fenced in with post and rail fencing. Eleven horses were browsing on the wonderfully green grass, five of them yearlings and all of them Arabians. A substantial wooden house, two storeys high, was set behind the fence at the far end, with its own garden, partially grassed, but with a vegetable patch to the side.

He had found the place, but was it owned by Sloane? If so, the lieutenant had become a farmer, no doubt aided in that enterprise by Martha.

Away to the right at the top of a rise, the forest of Red Gum and Eucalyptus had not been touched and would provide him with the cover he needed.

He spurred the horse on and climbed until he was among the trees. There he descended from the saddle and tied the animal to a tree trunk, after which he began his vigil, lying on a grassy bank to watch the area below.

During the afternoon, two young boys who looked to be some six or seven years of age came out of the house, playing with a large ball.

Thomas' heart turned over. Were they Austin and Thomas? He knew deep down that he should not entertain such hopes, but they were impossible to repress.

The boys played for almost an hour before going back indoors. What he could not know was that Martha had been sitting outside the front door, on the side of the building out of his sight, for two hours with the boys' new baby sister.

Half an hour before dark, with the little valley in deep shadow, a man came out of the door and made for the fence. Even in those light conditions Thomas could see the black eye patch and knew he had found his man.

He watched as Sloane used a pitchfork to pick up hay and push it over the rail to the horses, which had all cantered up to that spot as soon as they saw him exit the house.

Thomas was satisfied. He made sure that his own horse had plenty of grass around him, ate some of the dried meat he had brought with him and lay down to sleep.

Just before dawn next morning he unhitched the horse and rode him down to the fence, where he slid down from the saddle and waited.

It was barely light when Sloane exited the house and walked towards the rail to pitch more hay in.

At first he did not see Thomas, but when his horse neighed, wanting to join the others of his breed, Sloane looked over.

Thomas could not see his expression but could imagine it. What was a strange horse and rider doing so close to his property?

He ducked under the rail and strode across, and Thomas could see his angry expression change to one of mild horror as he observed the damaged face.

The anger returned, 'Who are you, and what do you want?'

Thomas tried to copy Barnes' voice, 'Do you remember Chatto Barnes?'

Sloane stepped back a pace, wondering if he was about to be shot, his hand going down to the pistol he no longer carried, 'I do.'

Thomas realised he had worried the man and changed to his own voice, 'And do you remember Thomas Nash, Arthur?'

He could see Sloane's immediate shock. His question had struck like a hammer blow. There was a long silence while the ex-lieutenant assimilated the knowledge.

'You are dead.' He sounded hopeful, the implications just too awful to contemplate.

'Officially, yes.'

'My God. What happened to you?'

'Blakely and his men happened to me.'

'They burnt you?'

'To death, they thought.'

'But now…do you…?' Sloane's mind was whirling. He had committed bigamy – that was in itself bad enough and made him a criminal, though with mitigating circumstances, but did this…man, this…horrific figure before him want to reclaim his wife and children?

Thomas put him out of his obvious misery, 'No, Arthur, no. Have no fear. I am not come back to cause you pain. I take it you and Martha are man and wife?'

Sloane nodded.

'And you have children?'

He nodded again, 'Two girls, Imelda and Eleanor. One year and four years.'

'And Martha, she is well?'

'She is in the very best of health.'

'And my sons? I take it I have two?'

'You do. Austin, as you know, and…'

'…Thomas. I also have four other children, two boys and two girls.'

Sloane frowned, bewildered, 'But how?'

Thomas gave him his history since leaving Sydney Cove, including the killing of Chatto Barnes and his sidekick.

Sloane absorbed the information that Thomas had lain with aborigines; not by any means the first man in the colony to do so but not something to spread abroad if one did not wish to be treated as a leper by neighbours. He pushed the thought aside and changed the subject.

'Blakely reported you dead. Positively witnessed. That is why we…married, Thomas.'

'Where is he? I have to avoid him at all costs. He would know immediately who I am.'

Sloane managed a weak laugh at last, the initial pounding in his heart from the shock of realising who his visitor was finally easing.

'That is something you need have no fear of. He is dead, and so are his men. I shot him in the act of molesting Martha. He had the intention of raping and then murdering her and Austin; the other two were hanged for their part in it.'

Thomas sighed, 'I feel as if a huge weight has been lifted from my shoulders. That I might run into them has caused me much heart searching when I considered coming back. Now, I believe, I can carry out my designs, providing I can find Roger Clarke. You have no idea of his whereabouts, I suppose? He would have finished his sentence at the same time as Barnes and Crabb.'

'I heard that he was making a good living playing cards with the members of the Corps but I have no idea where he is now.' Sloane was fighting an inner battle with himself, but his inherent decency won, 'Do you wish me to take you to Martha?'

Thomas had made his own decision, months before, 'No, Arthur, I do not want her to know. I wish her to remember me as I was. If she knew I was alive it would destroy your peaceful existence together and any tranquillity she has achieved. If she believes me to be dead she can have inner peace, and your lives will not be disrupted.' He saw the immense relief appear on Sloane's face.

'What of the three aborigines who lived near our workings at Garden Cove?'

'Two of them remained when I left, employed by the new guards as trackers.'

'That is good. I will meet with them.' He changed the subject, 'Do you make a profit with the horses, Arthur?'

Sloane looked suddenly downcast, 'When these eleven are thirty, perhaps. We are living on my rather poor pension.'

Thomas told him, 'I have had many long days and nights to think on this, Arthur: I am convinced that the future of this country lies not in horses, although they will play their part, of course, and an important one, but in sheep. Martha knows everything there is to know about them and could teach you.'

Sloane looked puzzled, 'But when I was discussing our future, she said nothing.'

Thomas tried not to show his pity, glad for once that his face was now bland, 'She is a woman who would never interfere in her husband's decisions, Arthur, no matter how wrong she imagined them to be. That is not her way.'

Sloane sighed, 'Then I am a mighty fool, Thomas. When speaking about breeding horses I noticed a strange look on her countenance and ignored it. Why, oh, why did I not ask?'

'Perhaps that wrong can be righted.'

Sloane shook his head sadly, 'We have so little money and would need far more land for sheep. I thank you for the idea, but it cannot happen. We shall just have to continue with the horses and hope for good fortune. But you, Thomas, what will you do and where will you go?'

'I intend to return to England to prove my innocence.'

'But if they find you out you will go back to prison. The rule, as you well know, is that any released convict can stay here, but not go back.'

'And as you well know, Arthur, I am not a released convict, but a felon on the run. If I am caught before I can carry out my designs I am lost anyway and will be hanged. However, money can open many doors.'

'But you have none.'

Thomas opened one of the saddlebags and pulled out a bag of gold dust. He passed it to Sloane. Then he passed another, and another, and another. He said, simply, 'Gold, Arthur.'

Sloane's face was a picture. Total disbelief tumbled through his brain with pleasure and astonishment mixed in equal proportions. He was speechless for several moments. When he did speak it was a monosyllable, 'Whew!'

'I am thinking now of when you and I are no longer on this earth and of our children. I wish them all to be secure, and to that end I would have you purchase as many acres of good grazing as you can as soon as possible and set up a sheep farm. Martha will need to be told that she is in charge, but she will need your help. I know you will be successful.'

'They call them 'stations' here.'

'Very well, a sheep station; the largest possible. There is another purchase I wish you to make, in the name of Thomas Nash. If there is a query on that, insist that it is for my son of the same name. I have drawn a map.' He pulled from the other saddlebag a large piece of Eucalyptus bark, on which he had drawn a map covering some thirty thousand acres, with the reference point the Three Sisters. The place where his cache of gold was hidden was well inside the boundary but nowhere near the middle, for safety, and the dry creek was four hundred yards to the south of it. The western boundary was the rising ground at the far end of the land he had recognised as highly fertile, where the trees had been burnt in the fire that had so nearly ended his life.

'These are the mountains the aborigines call the Blue Mountains, some fifty miles north west of here. You will need to visit the site with a surveyor. If they will let you purchase more than the area I have drawn, then please do so.'

'The 'Rum' Corps officers have been allocated all the best land for twenty miles around Parramatta, and the Major is trying to make them the rulers of the colony. They have the monopoly in liquor and they want and take the best of everything. No one can gainsay them. I have never seen anything so corrupt, but there is nothing anyone can do. He has cancelled all of Phillip's good plans for the place and introduced military rule. The land you want is much further away, so perhaps it will go through.'

'If it does not I shall have to go somewhere else, but do try.'

'How will I arrange for you to collect the title?'

'Is there a banker in the town?'

'There is one.'

'Is he trustworthy?'

'I am told so.'

'Then deposit it with him.'

'That I will do, but there is just one thing that worries me about this, Thomas. How can I explain away the gold?'

'I have thought of that. I had intended to tell you to say that you have been prospecting in the area, which would be dangerous, being likely to start a gold rush, but seeing the stream running through your property has given me a better idea. You simply say that you have, ever since you have been here, been panning the stream on your property and have now virtually exhausted it. Human nature being what it is the latter part of the statement will no doubt be disbelieved, and it should be most comical watching the horde of treasure seekers who will attempt to find more. You can also tell Martha the same story, explaining that you waited to tell her as a surprise when you had extracted all the gold that was there. I suggest you throw a couple of small handfuls of dust into the creek for them to find, 'seeding' I think is the term used, upstream and just beyond the boundary at the top of your property. It will be found to confirm your story and make them keener. You will naturally not let them onto your land and you will defend it fiercely, but when you put it up for sale you should have an avalanche of offers, at much above the price you paid.'

Sloane laughed out loud, shaking his head in wonder, 'Thomas, for a simple farmer, you have become a truly devious bastard.' He reddened suddenly, 'Oh, do excuse the last word, please. It was meant in jest.'

Thomas nodded, laughing with him, and answered truthfully, 'That I have, Arthur. That I have. And that last word I take as a high compliment. Believe me, there is much more to come. Lord Rainforde has no idea what a mighty storm his ship of life is about to enter if my plans go aright. I must take my leave now and hope when I return to see you king of all you survey.'

He extended his arm over the fence rail and Sloane took his hand and shook it mightily. His, 'Good luck, Thomas' was from the heart.

He stood watching until his ex-convict friend disappeared over the ridge leading back to Parramatta.

He found Martha washing the baby, and she looked up at him with tears in her eyes.

Imagining that she must have seen him speaking to Thomas left him speechless. He brushed an imaginary hair from her forehead and left his hand on the top of her head.

She sniffed, 'You will think me an emotional fool, Arthur, but I have just had the most remarkable idea enter my head. I had such a strong feeling that Thomas was very close and that he was no longer sad and wished us well.'

Sloane had to turn his head to hide a huge grin as he told her, 'Do you know, Martha, I had the self-same experience myself.'

CHAPTER TWENTY-TWO

Thomas rode through Parramatta again and took the road to Sydney Cove, arriving in time to buy a breakfast of fried eggs and toast at one of the newly built inns along the waterfront.

For the rest of the morning he walked his horse slowly through the area he had helped clear, now devoid of farming implements and convicts working to transform the intransigent land. Once Rose Hill had been found to be so much more fertile the poor land they had tried to use here was ignored for farming.

Buildings of all kinds were being erected everywhere between plots already occupied by structures, some of brick but most of timber.

The new, better quality tools that Phillip had insisted upon had made short work of the hardwoods, and no one lacked for a good supply of free building material.

He was surprised at the bustle and the number of people, both men and women. The population of the settlement, together with that of Parramatta, had grown from one thousand and thirty in 1788 to almost three thousand, with two thirds being free men and women; half of those released convicts.

He saw three small groups of aborigines, whose behaviour, even at that time in the morning, told him that they were falling-down drunk on rum, the semi-official 'new solution' to the native problem.

At the far end of the area, where he and Roger had built their hut, there were three houses being erected, and for the first time he saw chained convicts, bringing back sharply memories he would never completely lose, and he could feel again the iron shackles around his ankles, scraping against the old scars that would be with him until the day he died. A New South Wales corpsman was fast asleep under a tree nearby, his loaded flintlock musket lying beside him, seemingly unworried that one of his charges, two of whom included murder in their list of crimes, would use it on him.

There was no sign of Thomas' native friends and he slipped down from the saddle and walked his horse to where the convicts were working, digging the foundations of yet another house.

They turned as he approached, their faces showing every kind of expression from horror to interest.

One, taller and heavier than the rest, laughed, 'Bugger me, friend, you have been in the wars! Who did that to you?'

Thomas had a tale ready, 'The ship caught fire.'

'Did you have to swim for it?'

He nodded, 'This is bad, but I was the lucky one; I lived.'

'Poor sod. What you doin' here?'

'Looking for three natives, one who can speak English. Have you seen them?'

'You mean that banjo fellah?'

Thomas felt his heart give a sudden leap, 'That's the one.'

'They was here last week, but they comes and they goes.'

Thomas nodded, 'That is their way. Thank you.'

The convict was looking querulously at him, his head cocked to one side, 'Were you one of us?'

There was no point in prevaricating; it was part of his cover story. He nodded again.

'So there is an end to it?'

'There is. Do your work, try not to offend, and wait. This will be a great country one day, and you can be part of it.'

He could see that his words had brought cheer to them and remembered his own experience as a prisoner, when freedom was not even a pinprick of light at the end of a seemingly endless black tunnel.

He headed off, staying inland from the sea but in sight of it, and made camp three miles south of where the convicts were working.

Day by day he explored the area around his campsite, but it was over a week before he was re-united with his friends and he did not find them; they found him.

He was cooking two malleefowl he had trapped, unaware that he was being watched, until a voice close to his ear whispered, 'That bush grub will kill you, Thom-as'.

He smiled without turning and said, 'You may have learnt our language, Banjora, but you have not lost your native skills. I did not hear your approach. Where are the others?'

'Just behind me.' He gave the call of a kookaburra, answered immediately from just a few yards away.

Mandu and Curriquinquin appeared in seconds, both grinning madly and so obviously pleased to see him. They greeted him in Kat-tang, and he answered in the same dialect.

Banjora sniffed, 'That malleefowl smells bloody good, Thom-as.'

His meaning was obvious, and Thomas indicated with his hand that they should help themselves. Banjora pulled one of the skewered birds out of the fire and as one they set to, pulling it apart and stuffing it into their mouths.

Thomas allowed the other bird to cook more to his taste before he too began to eat.

Replete after the meal they squatted and chatted, bringing him up to date on what had been happening since he had been away.

Banjora told him, 'We keep away from the camp. The soldiers give the natives rum. These two were drunk all the time when I returned.'

Mandu and Curriquinquin looked sheepish.

'I had to drag them away from temptation.'

The information underlined Thomas' impressions of what he had himself seen. He wondered if the free issue of rum to natives was a deliberate edict.

He told them about the women and his children and how he had sent them into the interior, receiving nods of approval at his sexual prowess and foresight from all three of them. Then he asked them the enormous favour he had come there to ask.

'Will you, for me, go to find them and stay with them until I can come back? You have no women of your own and this is not your home. They need men with them to defend them, and I worry for my children. I must go across the water and I will be gone a long time. I shall return and we shall be together again but

223

I need to feel that they are safe. Banjora, you know the place I shall return to.'

He watched their faces as he spoke. Their expressions registered at first interest, then surprise, horror, indecision, defiance, and finally, in Banjora's case, what he believed to be acceptance.

A furious discussion began, so fast that he could not follow all of it, so used to the different language of the women.

At last, Banjora turned from the others and nodded, 'We will do it, Thom-as. They are not sure, but I am pleased that it will take them away from the temptation of the rum, and the soldiers have many times been out hunting the tribes and killing when they find them. Though they know us we could be killed if we stay here. We will find the women, and I will stay with them. These two may not stay, but I will try to keep them with me until you return. When will that be, Thom-as?'

That was a good question. Thomas himself could not be sure that he would ever return considering the task he had before him and the dangers of the oceans, but he offered, 'Four or five winters. In the sixth winter, I want you to lead them back to their old home, the caves near the Three Sisters. The women will tell you where. If all goes according to plan you will find me there.'

Banjora nodded in agreement. He stood and laid his arm on Thomas' shoulder, 'Go-bye, Thom-as.'

Almost before he knew it, Thomas was alone. As they always did, they melted away like wraiths, leaving those behind wondering if they had been there at all.

He packed up his camp and headed back to Sydney Cove, hoping that the next part of his plan would be as easy to execute.

He stopped halfway, allowing the horse to browse while he slumbered under the trees. It could be that he would need to be awake in the small hours, and a rest now would keep him fresh and with his full faculties, should they be needed.

As evening approached, and the usual clouds of mosquitoes began their pre-nocturnal raids, he remounted and quickly ate a little dried meat as he rode down to the water's edge. Finding a slowly shelving beach, he rode the horse into the shallows, dismounted and waited for the dark, free of the blood-seeking insects hunting hungrily near the water's edge.

He had noted half a dozen inns near the waterfront that morning, and when it was fully dark approached the first.

Inside, there were only four men at a table in the corner. His appearance caused some short-lived surprise, quickly suppressed. He ordered a tankard of rum, which he brought to his lips a dozen times without actually drinking during the next hour, observing the clientele, which steadily increased as the minutes ticked by.

More customers came in. A card game started in one corner and became boisterous as the rum flowed, but he saw no sign of Roger. He guessed, rightly, that the low stakes game in this drinking establishment would be of no interest to his friend.

He replaced the still full tankard on the table, stood up and wandered out into the night.

A couple of hundred yards further on, an open door was allowing the weak, flickering light of oil lamps to ingress the dark roadway, like groping, grasping fingers, reaching for the purses of the unwary passers-by, and he sauntered towards it, leaving his horse tied up to the rail outside the first establishment, knowing that it was safer there, with the death sentence in force for horse stealing in the colony, than it would have been in his fields back home.

The layout of the next drinking place was more like an English inn. A huge bald barman with a chest like a barrel and hands like hams stood dispensing drinks behind a wooden bar. There would be no trouble in that establishment, Thomas thought. Rough tables and benches, locally made, gave seating accommodation for over twenty, and half the seats were full, the rising crescendo of voices betraying the amount of liquor that had already been imbibed. As before, heads turned when he entered, faces registering the same expressions that he was becoming used to when they viewed his ruined face, only for the interest to wane quickly as they returned to their conversations.

He ordered the same drink and made pretence of sipping it, watching carefully through hooded lids, while not appearing to do so.

Two other men came in and joined him at the bar.

With a jolt, he recognised one of them as the convict supervisor of the group of which Barnes and Crabb had been members.

He turned away but felt a rough hand on his arm.

He turned and looked into the eyes of a man who knew him well.

The man looked unsure, 'Chatto?'

Thomas nodded.

'I thought so. I recognised the ring you won in that card game. What in hell happened to you?'

He had practised the voice he now used – a hoarse rasp, little louder than a whisper, 'Fire.'

'You buggered your vocal cords up?'

He nodded without speaking.

'Bloody hell! You poor sod. Never mind, you're still alive and a free man. Did you get any abos?'

Thomas nodded and held up two hands, showing seven fingers.

'Good for you. Did you get to…' He made the lewd movements of intercourse with his body.

Thomas nodded rapidly, as if still excited with the memory.

'Was it good?'

He rasped, 'Bloody good.'

'I fancy a bit of black velvet, but the only abos around here are males.'

Thomas whispered, 'Go out; look.'

The man grinned, 'I might just do that.'

Thomas put the tankard down and turned to go. He lifted a hand as a goodbye.

The men let him depart and he heard his interlocutor tell his neighbour, 'That bloody mask will slow him down with the white women. He'll have to keep going for the blacks. It's the only hole he's going to find open for him.'

Thomas visited every drinking establishment in Sydney Cove over the next five hours without success. If Roger was actively gambling it was not here.

He returned to where he had slept during the afternoon and spent the night. Tomorrow was another day, but he was suddenly impatient and could not understand it. The years when it had not mattered a jot whether a thing happened one day or the next, or even a week or a month later, had disappeared like a thick morning mist under a rising summer sun. Impatience was something that had rarely affected his life, the slow, natural pace of farming not giving much scope to that human frailty.

He dare not ask after Roger; he would have to persevere in his search until he found him.

A sudden thought struck him: was his friend still alive? So many deaths had occurred among the convicts. How could he find out? Were there records of those who had been released? Of deaths? He guessed there must be, probably at Government House in Parramatta. He should have asked Sloane to check for him, but it was too late for that now. He could not trouble the ex-lieutenant again.

He stayed in the forest the next day and rode into the town just after dark.

Once again, he tried the drinking establishments, with the by now expected reactions to his appearance, and again drew a blank.

At the last, before leaving, he asked the barman, 'Is there anywhere in the town where a man can get to play a serious game of cards?'

The man grinned, 'If you want to get skinned, try the hotel. They tell me the stakes are enough to make a hard man weep. I heard that one pot last night was over a hundred guineas.'

The hotel! Why hadn't he thought of that? Of course, there had to be a hotel, but where was it?

He asked.

'Near the barracks, where else? Those officers have more money than the ex-convicts and the settlers.'

Thomas thanked him and left, walking his horse down to where the barracks dominated the town.

The building which was the hotel was obvious once he was close to it; larger than most of the other structures in the town and with every room lit up.

He tied the horse to the rail in front, at the extreme left hand end, a dozen yards away from four others that already stood patiently waiting to be reclaimed by their owners, and entered by the main door.

There were three large ground floor rooms, and there was a game in progress in each of them.

One after the other, he stood in the doorway looking in, watching the faces and the play.

In the first, on the left, he counted eighteen golden guineas littering the surface of the table during the first hand he watched played. The players were so intent on their game that none had taken notice of him.

An officer in the uniform of a Captain of the New South Wales Corps, who had the largest amount of money on the table in front of him already, won a hand and scooped up the money with obvious glee.

Thomas crossed the corridor to look into the second room. A quick glance sufficed to show that all the players at the table were in the Corps uniform and of no interest to him.

The third room held a mixture of civilians and military. The head of the man sitting at the end of the table with his back to the door looked familiar, though the hair had turned to salt and pepper. Thomas was sure that it was Roger Clarke even before he heard him speak. His friend had always had a good appetite, and when they had been together could never get enough to eat. It seemed that problem no longer existed, for he had put on a considerable amount of weight.

The long-tailed coat he wore was new, and the ruffles of the shirt that protruded at the neck showed quality. He was obviously doing well.

On the table just to the left of his elbow he had a pile of golden coins, which Thomas estimated to be at least fifty guineas, and was playing with panache, alternating with losing and winning hands, holding his own during the half hour that Thomas watched. In that time, not one of the players had noticed him in the doorway. They were far too intent on the game, which seemed to be a serious one.

At last he crept out and waited in the dark by his horse.

It was, he judged, after two in the morning when the games broke up, and he watched the bleary-eyed players leaving.

Two officers, including the Captain, came to collect their mounts, causing the two others, which had stood stoically and quietly until then, to shuffle their hooves, suddenly impatient to go home themselves.

The crowd dispersed into the night, but Roger had not appeared.

Had he taken a room in the hotel? It was possible.

Thomas heard quiet conversation coming from inside and then the sound of footsteps on the wooden flooring.

Several lamps were extinguished, and two figures appeared in the doorway, one much thinner than the other.

The two men walked over to the horses, and Thomas hid behind his own mount as they approached.

He heard the sounds as they both mounted and a 'Goodnight' from each of them.

The thinner man went off to the left and the larger rider to the right.

Thomas mounted his own horse and followed.

At the first cross-junction, the rider in front suddenly spun his horse around. In the weak moonlight, Thomas found himself faced with a pistol directed at his chest.

He gasped, 'Don't shoot, Roger, for God's sake.'

He could not see, but imagined, the look of amazement on Clarke's face.

There followed a pregnant pause before an astonished voice asked, 'Thomas?'

'In the flesh, what's left of it.'

'Bloody hell! But, Christ, man, you're dead!'

Thomas laughed, 'You know, Roger, everyone keeps telling me that. Perhaps I should start to believe it.'

The pistol was lowered. 'You are bloody lucky I didn't shoot first, you stupid bastard. Fancy creeping up on a man. I thought you were after my winnings.'

'Did you win?'

Roger chuckled, 'I always win; never too much, just enough so they can tell themselves that it's luck and nothing else. I have not the slightest wish to become a convict again, but come, let us go to my house.'

Thomas was astonished in his turn, 'You have a property?'

'Oh, yes, Thomas; things have changed somewhat for me since you left. But do tell me, that bastard Blakely insisted he'd killed you and his two henchmen confirmed it; said they'd seen your corpse. How did you escape?'

'Wait until we are inside, Roger, and then I shall tell you everything.'

In the dark, Clarke had not been able to see his face, but after they had stabled the horses, removed their tack and entered the one-storey building his friend lit an oil lamp. Turning from it to speak he took a step backwards and gasped. 'Christ, man! Look at you! What the hell…?'

Thomas shrugged, 'Blakely did his level best.'

He spent the next two hours telling his friend everything except about the gold.

Roger asked incredulously, 'You lived with the abos and fathered four kids?'

Thomas nodded.

'You disgusting old bugger!' Roger grinned lasciviously, 'What are they like? You know, do they go like rabbits?'

'They are normal human beings, Roger, and can teach us so-called cultivated people a great deal about relationships.'

Roger shrugged, surprised at having been put down, 'I'll take your word for it, Thomas. So what are you going to do now?'

It was the point where Thomas' future would be decided, and he was unsure if this was the right time. He hesitated, and Roger read his mind.

'You've cooked up some weird scheme where you need my help, am I right?'

Thomas nodded, 'If you are game.'

'Will it be dangerous? I mean, could I wind up back here as a convict again?'

'No.' Thomas fetched from his inside pocket the heavy bag of dust he had taken from his saddlebag while waiting outside the hotel.

He pushed it across the table. 'This is a gift, Roger, from me to you. No strings attached; none at all. With it you can stay and build your own hotel if you have such a mind.'

Roger lifted the bag and hefted it in his hand, 'Are you telling me this is gold?'

'You can look if you like.'

'Bloody hell, and bloody hell again. What have you been up to? Where did you get it?'

'All in good time, Roger. I will tell you my idea, and if you decide you want no part of it I shall walk away and leave you in peace with your bag of gold.'

He laid out his plan in minute detail, and Roger listened in silence until he had finished. Then, after giving it some consideration, he nodded his head thoughtfully, 'I agree with you that it could just possibly work, but if it does, how do you know I will not cheat you once I have my hands on the loot? I am a crook after all, Thomas.' He said it with inordinate pride.

Thomas laughed, 'Oh, Roger, I am only too well aware of that, but I have two forms of insurance: in the first place you are no farmer, but much more importantly, if you carry the plan out to the end and we return here, I promise to make you the second richest man in Australia.'

His friend looked astonished, 'You mean there is more of this?' He hefted the bag of gold.

Thomas laughed much louder, 'Oh, yes, Roger. Much more. Much, much more.'

Roger's face was a picture as he said again, 'Bloody hell!'

Dawn had broken as they were speaking, and a golden ray of sunshine spread itself like a fast incoming tide over the surface of the table, with the bag of gold in the centre of the glow; an island of infinite comfort.

They grinned at each other and Roger said, 'You beauty! That convinces me! Now our first move has to be arranging our passage. That is where we take our greatest chance, for if we are found out we shall be prisoners once more.'

'What's the situation with the returning ships?'

'They go empty from here and try to load a cargo in Batavia or Africa.'

'So there are cabins free?'

Roger nodded.

'How do we get on board?'

Roger tapped the side of his nose. 'There are two ships in the bay at this moment: the '*Scarborough*' and the '*Reliant*', and the master of the last named likes to play cards on the waterfront. He could lose heavily one night and thus have desperate need to take two paying passengers, without a lot of questions asked.'

'You rogue.'

'Aye, Thomas, that I am and mighty proud of it. But come now, we have talked all night, and if I am to be at my best tonight I need to sleep. There is a spare palliasse in that room.'

Thomas determined to use his saddlebags as a pillow. Until they were at sea, he was not about to trust Roger that far. By his own admission he was a crook.

~~~oOo~~~

Thomas had never been interested in cards, or, in fact, in games of any sort. Farmers had no time for such diversions, their whole lives being spent working, not playing, and it was an education watching Roger control an entire table without any other player being aware of it.

Losing steadily for almost an hour, then winning most of his losses back, then losing again, and always to the master of the

'*Reliant*', Roger had the man thinking he was on a winning streak. The more rum he swigged the more confident he became, and the greater amount he bet. He was one of the world's worst gamblers, his hand gestures and his expression clearly giving away the possession of a good or a bad hand.

Thomas watched his face glow triumphantly after Roger had turned over another card and knew that the man believed he had a winning hand.

Thomas had no idea what game they were playing, nor the rules. Roger had told him the game was called 'faro', but with a variation. Normally, all cards were dealt face up, but with this new version, each player held three cards face down, which the other players could not see until they were turned over to determine the winner.

The ship's master bet recklessly, pushing the bets up with each round. All the other players backed out as the bets increased, leaving only the master and Roger betting against one another.

The seaman was becoming angry that Roger would not give in and pushed everything he had on the table into the pot.

Roger raised him again, and the master had nothing more to bid with.

If he failed to bid the pot would be lost.

Roger smiled sweetly at him and offered, 'I will take your IOU, Amos.'

The ship's master showed his disbelief, 'But I sail tomorrow.'

'Then if you lose I shall have to wait until you come again to these shores, shall I not?'

The master eased his hole cards up to have another look.

Thomas was sure he felt that he could not lose.

'Then you have my IOU for forty guineas, sir.'

He laid down his cards. He held four queens.

Roger turned his hole cards. Three kings. With the one showing on the table, he had four.

The master looked devastated and pushed his stool back.

'You win.'

He began to walk out unsteadily, and Roger followed him.

Outside, he took the man's arm and whispered urgently in his ear, 'Would you like your money back, Amos?'

The ship's master pulled his head back, 'What trickery is this?'

Roger spoke quietly, 'No trickery at all, Amos. I wish to help you. A friend and I need to go to England, with no one here the wiser. Do you understand?'

He understood only too well, 'Two ex-convicts want to go home.'

'That is correct, Amos. All your losses back, and fifty guineas in your pocket to boot.'

It was no contest. The money totalled more than a year's earnings. The master's good sense won.

'Do I get my money now?'

Roger guffawed, 'So that you can lose it all again? Oh, no, Amos. You stay on board tomorrow. What time do you sail?'

'On the tide, at six in the evening.'

'Send a boat for us at five.'

'Do you know where?'

'On the wharf, at the far end.'

'The boat will be there.'

CHAPTER TWENTY-THREE

Thomas had Roger sell his horse for him in Parramatta and bought himself three large portmanteaux, into which he had the saddle maker sew false bottoms, beneath which he stashed the bags of gold. Two sets of new clothing and two topcoats completed his purchases, paid for with the money he had found in Barnes' pockets.

The two men travelled by ferry to Sydney Cove, arriving an hour before the time for their pick up.

Thomas was on tenterhooks the whole time they waited and he could see that his fear had affected Roger too. If they were questioned now all would be lost.

When they saw the longboat lowered from the ship they both heaved huge sighs of relief, but their hearts still pounded louder and faster until they climbed the rope ladder to the deck.

As they came over the gunwale they found the master waiting for them, his hands out. They both knew that they would have gone overboard in an instant if he were not paid and saw his relief when Roger handed him a pouch, saying, 'It is all there, Amos, with an additional ten-guinea bonus.'

Now they stood on the deck, watching the seamen dashing around them, letting fly sails and adjusting sheets. The anchor was winched up, and the ship began to heel to the wind.

Watching the land recede and finally disappear over the horizon, swallowed up by the mists of distance, brought them both mixed feelings. What they were leaving was a place where they had spent the hardest years of their lives, and for that reason they were heartily glad to see the back of it, but it was also an intriguing new country, which they had, to some extent, helped to build and make their home. For Thomas it was particularly poignant, for he was leaving behind the only woman he would ever truly love and six children it was possible he would never see again.

The difficulties and terrors of the fifteen thousand mile trip were not to be underestimated.

The first seventeen days were balmy; a good, strong, steady wind from the west filled the sails and pushed them through the water at more than seven knots under bright sunshine every day. On every one of those days, Amos Swales suggested a game of cards and was refused.

The ship's master might not be a wizard at the card table, but he more than made up for it by his masterly knowledge of the sea. They observed how he constantly watched the sails, ordering dozens of minute alterations to the sheets to obtain the fastest speed through the water. He was a disciplinarian but a fair one and the morale on board could not have been better. Every evening, they were entertained to singing and dancing by the sailors and even joined in, learning to dance for the very first time and enjoying the delights of harmless exertion. Though the fresh meat and vegetables had been eaten, the food produced from salted meat and fish, with boiled dried cereals, was perfectly edible and nourishing. Thomas relaxed for the very first time in his life, enjoying the sheer luxury of carefree freedom and lack of immediate worry.

On the morning of the eighteenth day, the dawn sky was the strangest Thomas had ever seen. It was as if the sun had been fitted with a dark lens that turned the heavens around it into a heavy blue-black blanket, and the sea had a strange, eerie luminosity that heightened the sense of unreality.

Though the wind still blew the air had become stifling, even at that time in the early morning, the humidity close to maximum.

Swales came down to where they were seated on one of the forward hatch covers.

'The glass is falling fast. We are in for a mighty blow by midday. You should tie down your possessions and stay inside.'

He began shouting orders to shorten sail.

The sky, though still clear of clouds, became even darker, threatening, like a stage whose lights are dimmed to instil in the audience a sense of impending doom, and by eleven of the forenoon it seemed like night, although the sun still stood in the eastern sky like a silent, lonely sentinel, fearful that the power of his position is in imminent danger.

The wind slowly diminished and died, until the ship rode with no forward motion on a sea whose long rollers lifted and lowered it like a large leaf at the end of a branch in a continually changing breeze; an unusual motion that induced a feeling of sickness even in seasoned mariners who would never normally experience that unease in the worst of gales.

Amos Swales knew exactly what was coming; he had experienced it twice before, and was holding tight onto the rail on the upper deck, to which he was also tied by rope, as was every seaman on deck, to one rail or another, but even he was surprised by the utter, unbelievable ferocity of the first gust.

With only the bare minimum sail to which he had reduced the ship, she heeled until the tips of the masts were no more than three yards from the water, with the ends of the spars dragging through the waves, and he felt she must founder on the instant, but a moment's pause in the gust saw her lift just enough to save her, and as he turned her to take the wind on her stern she came upright.

In their cabin, Roger and Thomas had been thrown off the bunks onto the floor, body slamming into body, and Roger's nose hammered into the wooden bunk base, blood from it spurting like a gusher over Thomas' breeches.

They hauled themselves upright and held on for dear life to the support rails built into the side of the bunks, waiting for the next blow.

The sea, which had been smooth apart from the long swell, was in seconds changed to a maelstrom, with eight-foot waves growing taller by the minute and spume flying constantly, stinging those seamen on duty watch on deck like salty whips, wielded by vengeful gods.

Swales was used to crossing the Roaring Forties and had endured similar conditions more times than he cared to remember. He was unworried – the 'Reliant' was a well-found ship from a good yard. It had always lived up to its name, and he had no reason to doubt that it would ride out this storm as it had so many others. The nearest land was the Polynesian group of islands over fifty miles to the north, and the ship was now on an east-north-easterly heading. They had good seaway, he had put out a sea anchor, and the storm should not last that long.

But it did.

After forty hours of sleepless, foodless, non-stop battering, the crew were in bad shape. The topsail on the forward mast had split and when it whipped round the tip of the mast had snapped.

Swales sent two seamen aloft to stop its damaging traverse, and one had received a broken arm when it smashed into him. He was lucky to reach the deck alive but would lose the arm.

Swales had not been able to fix his position once in those two days. Knowing that the wind had shifted more to the south, he feared that they were nearing the islands.

After another night when the only sleep was wakeful dozing, the dawn came sunless, with roiling heavy cloud down almost to sea level. The wind was still near storm force in the heavier gusts. During the night, the mainsail on the main mast had split along its whole width. Swales had let it fly. Though he hid it well he was now more worried than he had ever been in his life before.

He scanned the horizon constantly, though for the most part it was obscured by high-flying spray, filling the air above nine and ten foot waves.

In mid-morning he saw what he had feared: cliffs reaching scores of feet high, with boiling water below, signifying shoaling bottom with large rocks, less than three miles away. They were being blown inexorably onto a lee shore.

He turned the ship to attempt to bring it into wind, only managing to make their situation much worse as the vessel came side on to the huge waves, which began to throw it from side to side like a cork agitated in a bowl by a child trying to force it over the edge, the mast tips continually touching those of the waves, one side then the other.

He sent a seaman, tied, as all on deck still were, to fetch Thomas and Roger.

When they had fought their way to him he yelled, 'She is going to founder. I believe we are going to die. Look at those rocks!'

Both the ex-convicts were thinking the same thing: all the trials and tribulations they had endured, the pain they had suffered, and now that they were free at last they were about to lose their lives. The irony was palpable.

As the coast loomed nearer they could see what awaited them: jagged rocks up to twenty feet high along a coastline which stretched away to east and west as far as the eye could see.

Suddenly Thomas shouted, 'Look there! A gap!'

Swales directed his eyes to where Thomas was pointing, his hopes rising, only to be immediately dashed when he saw the width of the opening; less than twenty yards, barely wider than the ship, and behind it further spray, indicating more rocks.

He shook his head and shouted, 'No chance! Much too narrow, and it's not clear. There are more rocks inside it.'

Thomas took Swales' arm, clutching hard, 'She'll hit, I know, but if we run aground there we might just have a chance of swimming for it. We will not have that chance out here or if we hit those rocks.'

It was clutching at the most minute straw, but Swales could see the sense in it. The problem was that with such minimal sail he had no control over the ship.

He could not possibly send the men aloft in this, or could he?

He shouted urgent instructions, met with disbelief by the men, who made no move to obey, until he shouted, 'Do you want to die?'

One seaman moved to do his bidding, starting an avalanche of stumbling figures, attempting to climb the rigging, being thrown about like rag dolls, feet and arms flying, but somehow they climbed and miraculously loosened the sails and pulled in the sheets.

The rocks were only three hundred yards away now, the roaring of the wind and the waves smashing into them clearly audible.

Swales shouted, 'For God's sake, help me!' and he, Thomas and Roger exerted their full strength to turn the ship's wheel. The moment that she came around it was like a racehorse leaving the stalls, the hull leaping forward as if the ship itself knew there was but one minute chance of survival.

Swales, with the help of the two men, hauled and swung, hauled and swung, trying to beat the vagaries of the ever changing, storm force wind.

The rocks loomed, one hundred yards, fifty yards…

All on board braced themselves for the crash as the ship stormed headlong into the seemingly tiny space between the huge rocks.

They felt three hard bumps as the bucking vessel hit and scraped the bottom, watching huge ship-killing rocks pass less than five feet to port and starboard, fearing that the next second would be their last, but suddenly the vessel slowed infinitesimally and they saw in front of them a wind-whipped but much calmer lagoon, with tall cliffs behind; cliffs they would be smashing into in another minute.

Swales swung the wheel as hard as he could and the ship responded swiftly, coming up into wind, with the cliffs not a hundred yards from them.

He had issued no orders, but as the ship came into wind the rigging became alive with men, like maddened flies in a damaged spider's web, frantically bundling the sails together and tying them. Three others were at the anchor capstan, one knocking out the retaining pin.

Swales stood at the wheel, a ghost of a man, dropping with fatigue and relief. Had it not been for Thomas, he would have lost his ship and the lives of all on board on the rocks outside.

The gap they had come through was the only one they could see in the barrier of rocks. It had been the tightest squeeze of Swales' life, bringing back memories of his early training with small yachts, his tutor making him take them through ever-smaller gaps and into berths which from fifty yards away appeared virtually non-existent.

He looked at Thomas who was in little better state than himself and offered, 'I owe the ship and the crew to you, Thomas. I would have wrecked her and killed us all.'

Coming from a hardened seaman, it was a speech Thomas would remember his whole life long.

The anchor was down, and the vessel at rest. Though the wind still howled with a sound like Furies denied their pray the ship and its crew were safe.

Swales heaved a huge sigh, 'Sleep, then food, then more sleep. Tomorrow can take care of itself.'

They stayed for three days, repairing the ship and renewing their energies, while the storm raged to a close. Swales had worried that they could have sprung a leak from the bumping on the rocks as they entered the lagoon but was able to rejoice that the hull was still sound. There was no possibility of landing on the shore; the cliffs rose straight out of the sea, but they were able to vary their diet with the useful addition of the many fish that the men caught with hand lines while they lay at anchor, after the work of repairing the sheets, spars and sails had been completed.

Swales held a council of war on the deck and laid out the problems, 'We bumped the bottom coming in, and from the tides yesterday and today I reckon it was near the top at that time. We may be stuck in here like the cork in a bottle, never to get out, but we have to try. At the top of the tide tomorrow morning, we'll have the two longboats out with tow lines if the wind is favourable, and see if we can pull her out. With the weight of the two boats and their crews off the ship, she will ride a little higher. We can only hope.'

Just before ten the next day the anchor was raised and the longboats launched. Lines were attached to the bow of '*Reliant*'. The men set to, pulling hard, and slowly the ship began to move forward, the speed gradually increasing to almost half a knot.

The wind had dropped to a light westerly, and the sea surface in the gap was smooth.

Progress went well until they were at the narrowest point of the channel, where the rocks seemed to reach out for them, almost near enough to touch.

They were all holding their breath when the ship touched bottom the first time.

The scraping sound seemed to go on forever before it ended, and huge sighs were heaved all round. Twenty yards more the vessel moved forward with no problem, then suddenly they felt a heavy jolt and she stopped dead.

The longboat rowers tried valiantly but in vain to move her, and Swales swore vehemently.

Thomas, Roger and the remaining crew on board watched him as he pondered the situation.

Finally, he made up his mind and passed orders for the longboats to row to the stern and try to pull her off.

For almost half an hour they struggled, rowing furiously without success, and Swales was becoming desperate, when a rogue wave washed in through the gap and lifted the vessel for just a few seconds, as the rowers were giving it their best.

She moved and once moving continued to do so.

Swales shouted orders to row back to the bow and to take the ship to the extreme right hand side of the channel instead of the middle. There was little time left before the ebb began, and he knew they had only one more chance on that tide.

The 'Reliant' moved slowly forward, inch-by-inch, until the right-hand rocks were scraping along the side of the ship. They felt a lurch and then another as she touched bottom, expecting to come to a stop again at any second, but she kept moving and with another couple of small bumps she was through.

A concerted 'Hurrah!' went up from twenty-eight relieved voices.

After offering up a silent prayer of thanks, Swales ordered the boats brought back on board and full sail set.

They stayed in sight of the long island all that day, hoping to see a place where they might land, but found nowhere suitable, and just before nightfall Swales changed their heading.

Thomas and Roger stood near him on the upper deck, watching a baleful sun set the distant horizon ablaze, the apparent flames dying to a purple glow that slowly disappeared into the never satisfied, all-enveloping ocean.

Thomas asked, 'Where next, Amos?'

'The place they call Tierra del Fuego, at the southern tip of South America. The winds can be furious there too.'

'What island was that?'

'I am not sure exactly what that one is called, or if it even has a name, but it was part of the Kermadec group. They were discovered only four or five years ago by a Breton ship's master, Jean-Michel Huon de Kermadec, who reported there to be a dozen or more in the group.'

Thomas regarded the man with respect. He had remained cool under the most hazardous conditions; an utter fool when it came to parting with his money, but a genius when it was a matter of life and death. He would be a good man to have on one's side. Another idea was forming in his brain.

'Supposing we do arrive safely in England, when will you leave again?'

'That will depend on when the next lot of convicts are ready for transport.'

'You will take convicts again?'

'I have to. The payment is better than the amount I could make in trade, unless I ran the ship as a slaver and I could not do that. It goes against all my principles. Taking convicts is bad enough, but at least they are being punished for misdeeds. Slaves have done no wrong. I am pleased to see there are moves afoot to ban slavery completely.'

'I could not agree more. Incidentally, Amos, not all convicts have committed crimes.'

He found Swales regarding him quizzically and added, 'Of that I can assure you.'

The master nodded, 'I see.'

Thomas continued the discussion, 'How much were you paid for the last shipment, if I might be so bold?'

Swales hesitated before answering, 'A gentleman does not normally venture such questions. I take it you have a reason for asking it?'

'I have; a good one.'

'Eighteen pounds, eleven shillings and six pence per male convict. Slightly less for the females.'

'And how many convicts?'

'Sixty-three men and five women.'

Thomas did a quick calculation, 'So, a scant eight hundred pounds.'

'Seven hundred and eighty-eight and a few shillings, if I remember aright.'

'I shall have money when we reach England. How much would you need for a charter, should we wish it?'

'To return to Australia?'

Thomas nodded.

'For just the two of you?'

'Possibly up to twenty more.'

Swales considered. It would be a far more pleasant trip with none of the problems associated with the convicts. He liked these two men, although he still smarted at his card losses to Roger.

He gulped deeply before offering, 'Seven hundred and fifty guineas.'

Thomas ploughed even deeper, 'And to buy the ship?'

Swales guffawed with laughter, tears running from his eyes, 'Now you jest, Thomas!'

He saw Thomas' jaw harden, 'No, Amos, I do not, I assure you.'

Swales' laughter suddenly ended, and the next silence lasted much longer, before he gave his considered answer, 'She is eight years old and is more than one third of the way through her expected life. Her cost when new was eight thousand, three hundred pounds. Just one question: would I remain master, should you purchase her?'

'Absolutely. That I guarantee you.'

'Then, two thousand seven hundred guineas.'

Roger joined in the conversation, 'That sounds reasonable, Amos.'

The two ex-convicts exchanged glances. Thomas had discussed the proposition with Roger during their sojourns together and Roger knew precisely what Thomas had in mind.

They chatted on about nothing in particular until almost midnight, with a panoply of stars filling the entire void above them, and a friendly westerly breeze taking them onward to their future destiny.

Despite Swales' predictions, rounding Cape Horn was child's play, the westerly wind increasing to a low gale but with no rain squalls and no surprises.

Food and fresh water were both becoming short, and Swales called in at Rio de Janeiro to re-stock. They stayed for three days, and though some of the seamen went ashore, Thomas and Roger stayed on board. They trusted Swales but did not want to leave the gold unattended with so many of the men left on board.

Spirits were high and morale renewed when they sailed on the tide from Rio, watching the cake-shaped mount called El Corcovado recede over the stern until it disappeared in the enveloping evening mist.

Using the trade winds and the ocean current they made the five thousand mile crossing in thirty-seven days, arriving in Portsmouth harbour on the third of February 1797.

There they stayed for just one day for re-victualling before sailing out again, bound for Great Yarmouth, having promised to pay Swales another thirty guineas for the extra trip.

A big cause of concern had been the fear that the French might be blockading the east coast, but a Royal Navy officer had assured Swales that the French were staying safe in port, having suffered huge losses to the English, whose fleet of over six hundred ships made their two hundred and twenty seem puny.

Though Swales kept a good lookout no French sail was seen on the voyage up the coast.

It was in a far different mood that Thomas and Roger greeted the town of Great Yarmouth for the second time in their lives. The port was heaving with activity, at that time of the year so full of drifters near the harbour mouth, over two hundred of them, that one would have been able to walk from the deck of one to the other and cross the river dry foot, were it not for the narrow channel left for shipping in passage. On the quays both sides of the river, scores of women and girls, many from Scotland, gutted the herrings; the 'silver darlings' for which Yarmouth had for centuries been famous, the special knives called 'cutags' flashing, and fish guts flying as they each handled forty to fifty fish a minute for up to twelve hours a day, three in a team, two gutting and one packing the barrels with fish and salt, and all for the princely pay of ten pence per barrel, split between them. For a whole season's work, if they were very lucky and worked each day till they dropped from fatigue, they might return home with as much as ten pounds apiece.

Beyond the drifters, there were many more ships than before, and Thomas and Roger were wryly amused to see the '*Fly*' and the '*Pride of Hull*' berthed in exactly the same places alongside the wharf as they had been when they first saw them.

'Waiting for the next lot of poor sods, I fear.' Roger commented.

Before disembarking, Thomas removed one of the bags of gold dust from its hiding place and handed it to an astonished ship's master.

'This is a down payment on the '*Reliant*'. We shall have need of a twelvemonth here. Can you trade from here for that length of time?'

Amos nodded, 'I have used this port before, bringing timber from the Baltic ports. It will be no trouble.'

'Be here a year from this day.'

Swales expression still showed his amazement. Hefting the bag, he asked, 'You trust me with this, knowing how I like to gamble?'

Thomas leant his head to one side as he assessed the man anew. 'You are an inveterate gambler, Amos, and a terribly bad one, as you well know, but you are an honest man. I know you would not gamble with another man's gold.'

The master grinned wryly, 'Methinks you know me too well, Thomas. Your gold will be safe, and the ship will be here when you need it.'

Thomas had another fish to fry, 'Do they build ships here?'

'They most certainly do. The town comes second in the production of shipping in the whole of England.'

'Ascertain the cost of building a new ship similar to the *'Reliant'*.'

Now he had Swales full attention. The master was like a hunting hound on point as he answered, 'The *'Reliant'* is four hundred and eighteen tons, and the building cost for such ships has been twenty pounds per ton for many years. You wish to purchase one?'

Thomas shook his head, 'No, Amos.'

Swales face showed his deep disappointment, 'Ah, I thought not.'

'No,' Thomas told him, 'I do not wish to purchase one.' He paused, playing the ship's master like a fish, 'I had in mind four – to begin with, at least.'

The ship's master's face was a picture: total shock, disbelief, amazement and joy mixed and struggling for supremacy.

Thomas assured him gently, 'If I am to be a man of commerce I shall need vehicles to ensure my lines of communication. That is a simple, irrefutable fact.'

He was aware of Roger's astonishment also but saw that worthy's expression change to one of agreement and congratulation. He was nodding firmly and offered, 'For a simple man of the soil you have grandiose ideas, Thomas.'

Thomas shrugged, 'I am beginning to amaze myself, Roger.'

CHAPTER TWENTY-FOUR

The hired closed carriage took them to Norwich in great style, the four-horse team making short work of the badly rutted road. They had discussed plans for when they arrived and had agreed that in order to make a statement there was only one place fitting to stay: that fine hostelry renowned for its cock fights, the Blue Bell, at the bottom of Timber Hill; the inn they had passed as they left the Castle as prisoners.

Thomas was satisfied that even an old neighbour would not recognise him but worried for Roger, who had lived long in the City, although with a completely changed hairstyle and the thick beard and moustache he had nurtured especially for that purpose his anonymity should be assured. He had even changed his way of speaking. Roger laughed off his concerns but made himself a promise that he would be ultra careful. At the inn, they introduced themselves as Thomas Barnes and Roger Crabb.

They dined well on prime Norfolk beef, swilled down with ale that the innkeeper assured them was the best in the county, brewed by Tomson, Stackhouse and Co in King Street and supplied only to the best hostelries in the City.

'And there are a-plenty, are there not?' Thomas asked. They had made a point of stating that it was their first time in Norwich.

'Reputedly the most of any city in the country; many more than one for every day of the year.' There were, in fact, at that time well over five hundred.

'A good business to be in.'

The innkeeper agreed modestly, 'We do well, and the cockfights bring in a goodly number of customers.'

'I may have need of legal advice while in the City. Is there such to be had here?'

'Most assuredly. Those gentlemen are grouped like a greedy gaggle of geese around Dalbeys Bank in Redwell Street.' He nodded in farewell and drifted off to see to others of his customers.

That night, lying in a four-poster bed on dry land for the first time in months, Thomas felt his body swaying with the waves when he closed his eyes. It was a sensation that would be with him for more than two days; a facet of every seaman's return to land from a long voyage.

Next morning, after a massive breakfast of ham and eggs, Thomas left Roger and went in search of his first quarry.

The portmanteau was heavy, and he hired a boy with a handcart to take it with him the four hundred yards to Redwell Street, surprising the lad with a sixpence for his trouble; more than three days' pay for such a small amount of work.

Hefting the portmanteau in through the imposing main doors of the three-storey brick building, he requested to see Mr Dalbey himself.

The clerk, attempting but failing to cover up his initial horror at the sight of Thomas' face, dealt with most of the business himself and was offended enough to want to refuse, but he took in the cut of the smart new grey morning coat with silver buttons and the expensive waistcoat, shirt and pantaloons that the prospective client wore and realised that his relatively well paid employment could be put in jeopardy should he refuse.

He coughed politely to cover his embarrassment and said, 'If your Lordship would care to take a seat.'

Thomas chortled to himself, wishing it were still possible for him to grin. It was the first time in his life he had been awarded that particular title, though it would not be the last.

The minion had knocked at and disappeared through a side door in the elegantly clad mahogany wall, and out of the corner of his eye Thomas saw him reappear, followed by a florid gentleman, who stood for a moment in the doorway observing the upstart who had dared to request his personal presence.

Patently satisfied with the visitor's outward appearance, despite the horrific damage to his face, he came forward, holding out his hand.

'Roger Dalbey, how may I help you, Sir?'

'Thomas. I wish to deposit a large sum with your bank.'

Dalbey was surprised at the omission of the surname but ignored it for the moment. A Quaker, scion of a family whose history in England began with his ancestor, Hugh de Daulbay, arriving on these shores with William the Conqueror, as had Thomas' own, he was renowned, as had been every member of his family down the ages, for his honesty, reliability and fair-trading.

'Do come into my office.'

Once seated, Thomas began, 'I wish to set up a banking facility with you which may involve international trade. Would that be possible?'

'Of course. The world as we know it is becoming much more accessible with each year that passes. We already have much trade with the Continent, and have successfully carried out trades in the Americas. My brother John and I have great plans for expansion.'

Thomas bent and opened the portmanteau, bringing up one bag after another and placing them on the top of the magnificent mahogany partners' desk.

Roger Dalbey had long since learnt to maintain a gamblers' bland expression, but could not help an amused smile appearing on his lips.

'Do I take it that the contents of those bags is gold?'

Thomas nodded. 'Four of nuggets, the rest dust.'

'Not found in Norfolk, I'll be bound.'

'No.'

'And there is more?'

'A great deal more.'

'You gave only your given name. I take it there was a reason?'

Thomas nodded, 'There was. I wish to remain incognito for the time being.'

The banker had dealt with that particular problem more than once, as had his ancestors. The changing politics and religious mores of the country had often required gentlemen to hide their identities.

'We would, of course, need a name for transaction purposes.'

'I had considered that. Shall we say James Nash?'

'James Nash will suit admirably.'

'I believe you issue your own banknotes?'

'We do, with guaranteed value.'

'Could I take a mixture of notes and gold coins when I leave?'

'Certainly. I shall have these weighed and valued and then we can complete the rest of your business. Do you wish to be present at the weighing?'

Thomas knew he was being tested, 'No. Your reputation for fairness is well known.'

It was the right thing to say and was perfectly true. Dalbey beamed.

A half hour later Thomas shook the banker's hand and left the building to go just fifty yards to another office, to which Dalbey had directed him.

It was a much more modest affair, on the third floor of a partly wooden building in rather poor condition, and again Thomas had to negotiate with a clerk, but this time one who was far more difficult to persuade of the necessity to bother his master.

'I deal with all enquiries, sir. Attorney Pomeroy is an extremely busy gentleman, and we have dozens of potential clients urgently needing his services. You must tell me exactly what your needs are, and *I* shall then decide if we are able to be of service or no.'

Thomas tried the financial incentive approach, 'It is to deal with the requirement for legal representation that will reimburse your master considerably.'

It was not enough, 'I would need to know the amount involved.'

Thomas tried not to show his increasing anger, but his voice rose, 'Is considerable not enough?'

He heard movement in the inner office, and the door opened.

Pomeroy put his head round the doorjamb and gasped, trying to resist the 'My God!' that came unbidden to his lips.

'What is all the commotion, Collins?' He demanded.

The clerk shrugged resignedly and indicated Thomas with his hand, 'This gentleman insists on seeing you, sir.'

To the obvious annoyance of the clerk, Pomeroy nodded his acceptance, 'Come in, sir.

The office was sparsely furnished: a cabinet with drawers on the far wall, a small desk, bare but for the book the attorney had been reading, and two hard chairs. It seemed the clerk's story of many clients might well have been stretching the truth somewhat.

Pomeroy remained standing but waved Thomas to a seat and asked, 'What could be so important, sir?'

Thomas spoke with one of the accents he had acquired in his time away, 'I have been informed that an attorney may not disclose to anyone details his clients may have told him. Am I correct in that supposition?'

Pomeroy interest was aroused, 'You are. Client confidentiality is our watchword.'

Thomas leant forward and whispered, 'Could you send out your clerk?'

The attorney frowned, his anxiety showing clearly in his countenance.

'If you are thinking of robbing me, sir, I should inform you that I have no money about my person or in the office.'

Thomas laughed, 'Have no fear on that account.' One had merely to look at the threadbare state of the attorney's clothes to realise the truth of that statement.

'Very well.' Pomeroy got up and opened the door, 'Go down to the street for half an hour, Collins. Knock before you come back in.'

He waited impatiently until the outer office door closed then turned back and asked urgently, 'Now, sir, what is this matter that is so important? You have just two minutes to tell me or I shall ask you to leave.'

Thomas began, in his own voice, 'Do you still have the boots and buskins, Pomeroy? You are not wearing them today.'

The man's reaction was a delight to watch. He stepped back a yard, his face showing total disbelief, 'Thomas Nash?'

Thomas nodded, 'The very same.'

'But...but...'

'Quite so.'

Pomeroy, stunned, dropped into his chair, 'Tell me.'

The half hour was almost up when Thomas completed the story and stated his requirements.

Pomeroy had listened enraptured. Now he said, 'We shall need the help of a top barrister, preferably one from Lincoln's Inn in London. I know the very man, and you can leave that part to me. When you are about to conclude the business, give me two days' warning and I shall arrange for him to be here. He will not come cheap.'

Thomas drew out a packet from his pocket, 'These are notes on Dalbey's Bank for one hundred pounds. Will that suffice for the moment?'

To Pomeroy, whose very future depended on new clients, seemingly in the last year to be a dying breed, the sight of so much money had him almost overcome.

He gulped, 'It certainly will, Thomas.'

It was all going according to plan, and at mid-morning Thomas hired a horse and rode the twelve miles out to the Rainforde estate. He was appalled at the state of the fields, many lying fallow, with a two or three-year growth of weeds, quickly going back to nature. Where there were crops the foliage was sparse and yellow through lack of sustenance. The hedges had not been layered and were a dozen feet high, with irregular branches growing wild. There were no workers anywhere. He rode across half a dozen fields to come within sight of the Manor from a distance of a couple of hundred yards. It appeared dilapidated and unoccupied, and there were windows broken on the top floor. Worried what he might find on the land that was rightfully his, he rode out along the track to Danfield Hall. Here also the fields had not been tended, and trailing blackberry tendrils grew all over the way; an invading army with no defenders to resist them. There was not an animal to be seen until he spotted a mangy old dog fox stalking an unwary rabbit in what had been the vegetable garden. The building itself looked shabby. The door stood open, and when he jumped off the horse and went inside he was appalled.

The table and chairs his grandfather had made were gone; the posts of the bed had been sawn off, and the entire building had been ransacked. Rubbish lay in mouldering heaps on every floor. All he remembered had been wantonly destroyed.

More angry than ever with Silas Rainforde he mounted again and rode on to his destination, hope at the forefront of his mind, with fear close behind it at what he might find.

Martha's youngest sister Jane had married Jacob Breen, the blacksmith in Oxton, a mile the other side of Buxton, and Thomas rode up to the smithy, where that big, bulky man, in shirtsleeves and with a leather apron over his breeches, stood at his anvil, shaping a shoe for the piebald pony standing patiently in the yard. A much younger man, standing with his back to the road, was using a punch to cut holes in a piece of leather strap, a liver and white spaniel lying at his feet.

Thomas dismounted, his heart pounding furiously, ignoring the reaction of the blacksmith to his looks, not this time of horror but of sorrow and pity, understandable when one considered the many accidents that befell men in his trade, where fire was a large part of their daily existence, and accidents were rife.

'What can I do for you, sir?' He asked.

Thomas had long rehearsed this part, 'Thomas Nash, you know of him?'

He noticed in his peripheral vision the way the young man pricked up his ears and then moved quickly away from his previous position, keeping his head averted, and carefully moved around the side of the building and out of sight through a gap in the wall. The spaniel went with him.

The blacksmith pulled himself up to his full height, the hammer held like a weapon, his chest expanded, his anger palpable but controlled. 'Who wants to know?'

'A good friend of his, Jacob.'

Now the anger became open, 'I would need proof of that!'

'Proof, Jacob? Very well. At your wedding to Jane, Martha and I came in a cart pulled by Blaze. You made a new shoe for his left front hoof before we left, and I am sure that the spaniel I just saw with James answers to the name of Rascal.'

Thomas watched the changes of expression on the man's face: angry distrust changing through doubtful disbelief to hopeful acceptance.

'Thomas? Is it really you?'

'It is, Jacob.'

The blacksmith dropped his hammer and rushed forward to take Thomas in a huge bear hug, almost crushing the wind from him.

When he pulled back he said, 'They came three times trying to find James, then the years passed. When you asked that question I thought Rainforde was trying again. Come, we must tell Jane and James. They will be over the moon.'

Jane stood defensively, her arms akimbo, outside the kitchen door. She had aged well and looked scarcely older than when he had last seen her all those years before.

Thomas read her expression: fear and anger in equal parts.

Jacob raised both hands as they approached, 'All is well, Jane. Come inside.'

She objected, 'But what about...?'

Jacob laughed, 'James?'

She looked horrified at the use of the name.

'You will not believe it, but this here is your brother-in-law, Thomas.'

'Thomas? Thomas Nash? Martha's Thomas? No!' Tears sprang to her eyes.

'Yes. Come, sit down. No doubt he has a long tale to tell. I will fetch James. The usual place?'

She nodded, and he disappeared outside again, to return two minutes later with the young man, whose expression betrayed his utter disbelief, mixed with unalloyed pleasure.

Though Jacob had prepared him, his shock at the close sight of Thomas' face stopped the lad dead in his tracks for a second, but he immediately overcame it and rushed forward to take his father in a hug only slightly less breath restricting than Jacob's.

He hugged and hugged, not wanting to let go, until Thomas eased him gently away to take a good look at him.

Jane said it for him, 'He is the spitting image of you at that age, Thomas, is he not?'

He was: Thomas could see himself at a much younger age standing in front of him. The same build, eyes, hair, Nash nose, expression even.

'It is well Rainforde has never set eyes upon him.'

'Yes, indeed.'

Jane said, 'Now sit down and tell us everything.'

Jacob grinned, 'Make him a drink, woman, while I go and finish shoeing that nag. You just hold the story until I come back, Thomas. Promise?'

'I promise.'

While Jane busied herself at the stove, Thomas made enquiries of James, 'How much do you know of farming?'

'Not as much as I would like, but for five years, until Jacob needed me, I worked for the Sancerre family at the Hall. I worked with the animals: pigs, sheep, goats and cattle for three years, and then learnt to plough and hedge.'

Thomas was more pleased than he could say with the answer, but would say no more about it for the moment.

Jacob came back, and Thomas asked the question burning in his mind, 'What of the estate, Jacob? It lies apparently derelict. Why?'

A grim smile accompanied the answer, 'There was not a man who would remain there. Months passed with no pay, save for an unasked-for beating if the lord and master passed by, and every man had to hide his wife, for Rainforde was demanding droit de seigneur, and not just on the wedding day. Girls old enough to be serving wenches hid with them in fear rather than taking employment in a house in which no female stays a virgin for even one day. The families left to try to find work; they were starving here and preferred to starve elsewhere in less danger.'

'Can you find those men?'

Jacob shrugged, 'Some for certain; others have moved on to seek employment.'

'Find those you can. I shall have need of them. They will be employed.'

They talked the whole day through, ceasing only for repasts.

Thomas gave Jacob an order to fill that was to take up most of his future time: the very finest quality tools he could forge: saws, axes, spades, forks, hammers, rakes, cutters, pliers and all manner of other implements. Jacob saw clearly that he would be working into the evening for a long time to come. Jane finally insisted that they stop conversing and made up a bed on the floor for Thomas, it being too late for him to return to Norwich.

CHAPTER TWENTY-FIVE

The daytime had been for Thomas, but the night was when Roger went abroad stalking.

This was the time when he was most vulnerable to detection, visiting his old haunts where the games of chance were played.

At each one he searched the faces carefully, looking for old acquaintances in the same line of business and for his prey. He had only Thomas' description to go on, but Rainforde's appearance was different from that of most men, and Roger guessed he would recognise him if he saw him.

There were dozens of establishments in the city where a man could lose his money, and he ignored those where the stakes were minimal and the clientele lower class, but even so it was only at the eleventh place he visited that he came across the man he sought, in a gaming house in Pottergate.

He almost disregarded him. Thomas' description had not included the facial disfigurements that this man now had. His hands and face were covered with angry spots and some of those on his face were raw. Occasionally his body would twitch. Roger had seen such symptoms before. The man had the French pox.

He watched the play for some time.

Though in the latter stages of the pox the hands lost much of their dexterity, Rainforde still had enough control to manipulate the cards, and Roger, past master with a deck, saw easily how the man was cheating. He was cunning, not betting for much of the time when others dealt, and only dealing from the bottom irregularly when he dealt himself, keeping the pile of coins in front of him more or less constant, so that when he won a pot his fellow players accepted the win as luck.

The stakes varied but towards the end of the night's game became considerably higher, with Rainforde taking two large pots near the end, apparently recklessly, but Roger could see how he worked the trickery. He was not in the same class as Roger but had learnt his trade well. It would not be easy to get the better of him.

Roger left just before the game concluded and watched from a doorway as the players exited from the building.

Rainforde came out alone and looked carefully around him before walking off towards the Maddermarket. Roger saw him stop outside a house only a hundred yards further down the street and check his surroundings again before entering.

It had been a rewarding night and Roger returned to the hostelry to sleep until midday.

Next morning he found Thomas seated in the bar room with a flagon of ale and a beef pie in front of him and asked, 'Did all go well?'

'Well indeed. My son is healthy and in good spirits, and with you?'

'I found our man. He stays at a house in Pottergate and gambles in that same street. He plays carefully and well but he plays a sole hand without accomplices, and that bodes well for us.'

'When shall you begin?'

'This very night. 'Twill take a sennight, I wager, to bring the matter to a satisfactory conclusion. I shall need to whet his appetite for my money to such a pitch that he cannot resist.'

'I would like to watch.'

'Perhaps on the last night.'

'Agreed.'

Thomas returned to Oxton and passed three idyllic days with his son and the family who had taken him to their breast for so many years, telling them something of what he had in mind, should everything go to plan.

Jane confided, 'Since we lost Simon to the cot death I have not been able to conceive again. James filled that gap in our lives and has been a wonderful son to us. I shall be mightily sad when he goes.'

Thomas laughed, 'But Jane, he will be but a stone's throw from you when he goes. You shall visit each other regularly. You visit Elizabeth, do you not?'

'Of course.'

'Then you need go only a couple of miles beyond.'

James, he found, could hardly contain himself; such wonderful thoughts of what lay in the future had been going through his mind. Thomas also told him of his plans for the lad's brothers and sisters on the other side of the world.

'Shall I ever see them, father?'

Thomas nodded, 'I shall make every endeavour to make such a thing possible, James. We are a family, after all, and with our own ships it would be quite feasable, once you have everything here back as it once was and running smoothly.'

'And mother?'

Thomas sighed, 'I believe she is happy in her new life. She cannot be told that I still live, but to see you again would give her infinite joy. If you write a letter to her I may be able to have it delivered. You can write?'

'Yes, father. Mother…er…Jane has taught me my letters.'

'Good, then that is what we shall do. Now, tell me again exactly what you know about animal husbandry.'

When he left again for Norwich, Thomas was content that James had knowledge enough to become successful as a farmer. What he had not known, Thomas had told him.

He accompanied Roger to the gambling house in Pottergate that night and watched from the doorway as the pile of coins in front of him slowly made their way across the table to Rainforde. He was astounded that the other players were unaware that they won nothing from Roger and assumed they were merely pleased that he was losing. Near the end, when there were but a couple of shillings left in front of him, and only three players left in the game, Roger took from his inner pocket a bulging wad of banknotes and pulled two five-pound notes from the wad before replacing it in his pocket.

'Now, Lord Rainforde,' He asserted, 'I want some of my money back! Deal the cards!'

Rainforde's eyes flashed when he saw the roll of notes and dealt himself a losing hand.

Roger grabbed the winnings eagerly, 'Aha! See, you begin to lose!'

Rainforde worked it so that Roger won the next six hands, and Thomas was amused to see how his friend assumed open expressions showing gleeful avarice and triumph, completely different to his usual dead-pan face when playing. Knowing what was afoot added spice to the whole experience.

On the next hand, Rainforde pretended again to have losing cards and increased the bets only gradually. Roger, on the other hand, bet rashly and foolishly pushed the amounts up, his eyes glittering with mock avarice.

Suddenly, Rainforde trebled the bet, taking the stakes to double the amount that Roger had before him.

Roger took the bet, pulling out more notes to cover it, and Rainforde displayed his cards.

Roger put on such a magnificent display of enraged disappointment at losing the hand that Thomas was convinced he could have made a successful career on the stage.

Rainforde's false condolences fell on deaf ears as Roger rushed from the room, apparently in desperation.

Outside, he and Thomas ran to the end of the street, where, after they had turned the corner, they fell about, laughing hilariously.

Roger wept tears of sheer amusement, 'He took it, Thomas, he swallowed it; hook, line and sinker!'

'You think he is ripe?'

'Ripe for the plucking!'

'Tomorrow night it is then.'

Both men slept soundly and woke with the cock's cry the next morning.

The sun shone out of a cloudless sky, and Thomas had the feeling that Martha would have called it a good omen.

Shortly after finishing their meal that evening Roger excused himself, saying that he had another small piece of business to conduct.

Thomas was curious but had come to trust his friend's judgement and asked nothing further.

At the gambling house that night there was no sign of Rainforde, and by ten o'clock they both feared he had taken the money and run, but at just before half past the hour he came in and took a place at the table. Noticing Thomas seated at the edge of the room with another stranger beside him he sneered at the sight of the scarred face and made a rude comment to one of the other players as he sat down.

Roger had won steadily from each of the others before Rainforde joined them, but now he began to lose regularly, and almost every time to the unlikely lord.

Rainforde, Thomas could see, was becoming more and more confident as the night progressed, and he watched with interest when Roger had to take more notes from the wad in his pocket.

Another toff came in, well in his cups, and loudly demanded a seat at the table. He lost his money quickly and staggered out again.

Roger had taken most of the new money and began to lose again to Rainforde, who started to increase the stakes. There were two large pots, Roger losing both, looking like a desperate man who is determinedly attempting to get his money back.

Another hand began, and Rainforde pushed the bets up mercilessly, way beyond the money on the table. Roger took out the wad and counted out the bills as the hand progressed, until all were on the table. The other players had thrown in their hands, the bets far beyond their means.

Rainforde looked triumphant and re-doubled the bet, sure that Roger had reached his limit and would have to fold and lose, not being able to match the bet.

To his astonishment, Roger pulled two large leather pouches from the small portmanteau beside him on the floor and placed them in front of him on the table.

'Gold! I re-double your bet, and re-double again; the bet is eight thousand pounds.'

Rainforde's confident smile disappeared like a scared rabbit down its hole, rabid fear spreading across his scarred countenance.

'I have not the funds to match that bet.' He had to admit. 'Would you, as a gentleman, accept my IOU?'

Roger gritted, 'Were you a gentleman, Rainforde, I might so do, but we both know that you are not. If you have not the funds you must fold, and I win the bet.'

Rainforde's face betrayed his fear. He had played with every last penny he possessed, thinking to take this man's money from him, and now he was faced with ruin. He looked angrily at the gleeful faces watching him, most of them men from whom he had take their all, but one annoyed him most.

'Who is that bloody freak over there, looking at me like that? Get him out of here!'

Thomas made no move to get up and Rainforde looked away.

Roger waited his moment, until he knew his prey was squirming with indecision. At last he said, 'Have you no property you can put up as surety?'

Rainforde's relief was palpable, 'You would accept that? I have an estate, worth much more than your eight thousand. You would need to reimburse me somewhat should I lose the hand.'

Roger laughed grimly, 'How do I know what your so-called estate is worth? I believe I should not take it, but just your money. If you want to bet the land, then to me it is worth exactly the amount I have staked, not a penny more.'

Rainforde looked desperate, afraid that his opponent would take the pot by default and still sure he had the winning hand and that Roger was bluffing. He had no option.

'Very well, then.' He acceded, 'the estate against your money.'

It was the moment Roger had been waiting for. He drew a sheet of paper, a travelling inkwell and a quill from his portmanteau and nodded to the man sitting next to Thomas.

Pomeroy rose from his seat, from which he had witnessed one of the most enjoyable scenes in his life, remembering the rigged court case he had lost, and strolled around to where Rainforde sat.

Roger had been drilled in the precise wording to be used on the document and Pomeroy remained silent while Rainforde wrote what was dictated. He looked up when Roger added, 'And all other such land, buildings, furniture and possessions that I own.'

Rainforde protested angrily, 'You would leave me with nothing but the clothes I stand up in, destitute?'

Roger grinned, 'As you would have me, were the boot on the other foot, Rainforde. Sign the paper. Then if you lose the hand I shall give you one ten-pound note.'

He heard the unrestrained irony in Rainforde's gritted, 'Bloody generous.'

Pomeroy checked the document carefully and then added his own signature and qualifications.

Roger gave one of the other players a guinea to add his signature also, making the document foolproof.

'Now let us turn our cards together. Ready…now!'

Rainforde had four kings and thought his hand unbeatable. He could not believe his eyes when he saw Roger's four aces. He had deliberately stacked one ace in the centre of the pack just before passing the cards to be dealt and knew that it could not have come to the top to be dealt.

He leapt to his feet and cried, 'You have cheated! The aces were not…' He suddenly realised that in order to make the charge he would have to admit cheating himself. He knew he would be lynched by the other players he had defrauded. He had to content himself with a gritted, 'You conniving bastard!'

He spat on the floor in front of Roger and almost screamed, 'Bloody good luck with it! It's only good for pulling down.' He snatched the banknote Roger was holding out for him before staggering to the door in distress and disappearing out into the street.

Thomas moved as if to leave the room, but Roger stopped him, 'Wait a while.'

It puzzled him, but perceiving the look on his friend's face he knew there was more to come from the evening.

Roger had taken no drink while the cards were being played, but now ordered three glasses of gin. When they came he clinked glasses with Pomeroy and Thomas and toasted, 'To continued success.'

They finished their drinks and left the house. Outside in the street, they could see a small crowd made up of the erstwhile card players, looking at something on the ground.

Thomas began, 'Did you…?' but changed his mind. He had no wish to know but guessed it was the 'other small piece of business' Roger had attended to earlier.

Roger remarked calmly, 'Now I wonder what that commotion might be.'

Pushing through the men, they looked down.

Rainforde lay groaning on the wet cobblestones in his underwear, his coat, waistcoat, breeches and boots gone. Also, of course, the ten pound note. Blood was running from his nose and lips. He had been badly beaten but left alive.

Roger shrugged and smiled grimly, 'Oh, dear. Well, looking on the bright side of things, it could not have happened to a nicer fellow. It is the poorhouse for him, no doubt.'

Pomeroy took his leave of them near their lodgings, a broad smile on his face, and promised that he would attend to the other matter the next day.

CHAPTER TWENTY-SIX

On the Thursday, two days later, the attorney sent word that the barrister had arrived and was awaiting their instructions.

They had ascertained that Rainforde had been found by the night watch and taken first to the Guildhall as a vagrant and from thence to the poorhouse in Hellesdon.

Thomas ordered a coach and met Pomeroy and the other legal man outside the attorney's office in Redwell Street.

The barrister, an impressive looking, tall individual of some fifty years, with prematurely grey hair and an aristocratic face that reminded Thomas of a picture of King George he had once seen, was introduced as Sir Walter Daltrey.

They shook hands, and Thomas mentioned the likeness.

Daltrey smiled enigmatically, refraining from mentioning that the monarch happened to be his second cousin.

The four men travelled the three miles to the Hellesdon poorhouse, with Daltrey checking that the facts he had been given of Thomas' indictment, sentence and innocence were accurate. By the time they turned into the gateway, he seemed convinced.

At Roger's meaningful insistence, the two ex-convicts took the coach to the nearest inn while Pomeroy and Daltrey entered the gaunt redbrick building, the bars on the windows making it appear more like a prison than a place where free men and women passed their days.

Roger jumped down outside the inn, expecting Thomas to follow, and surprised when he did not.

'You are coming in, are you not, Thomas?'

During the five minutes it had taken to drive there from the poorhouse, Thomas had been remonstrating with himself and had made a decision.

'No, Roger. I am sorry. I know what you intend and cannot participate in it. I am no murderer.'

'You will not be committing murder, Thomas, you will merely be taking a flagon of ale with a friend.'

'And instigating murder.'

Roger looked at his friend sadly, 'That man paid not once but twice to have you, Martha and James killed. He is no better than a rabid animal, needing to be put down.'

'I heartily concur, but I cannot be a part of it, Roger.'

His friend looked up at him, 'And I respect you all the more for it, Thomas. I, however, am desperately thirsty.' He turned and entered the inn, grinning widely as he ordered a drink.

The innkeeper regarded his amused client, 'Why, sir, you seem in remarkably good spirits.'

Roger nodded and said in a loud voice, 'I have, landlord, just seen one of the funniest things ever. I was visiting two of my father's parishioners in the poorhouse and saw an attorney give one of the inmates a large bag of gold. Just imagine: a bag of gold in a poorhouse! The man receiving it insisted on calling himself Lord Rainforde. A likely story for a pauper, do you not think?' He laughed aloud and took a long drink from the flagon, looking straight to his front, but keenly aware that two large, rough-looking characters at a table near him had quickly pushed their chairs back, stood up, and exited the inn.

He finished his drink, thanked the innkeeper and went out himself.

Back at the carriage he told Thomas, 'One of the most enjoyable and rewarding tipples of my life. Most excellent!'

~~~oOo~~~

The two attorneys had found Rainforde lying on a bed, wearing cheap linen trousers and a jacket that might have been white once upon a time, but which had been washed so many times that they were now a dirty grey.

His countenance was pallid and he looked ill. The bruises on his face had turned purple and he had a black eye. Two front teeth were missing.

He glared at Pomeroy, 'You again! What do you want this time, you leech?'

Pomeroy smiled sweetly, 'And a good day to you, Lord Rainforde.'

'Get on with it. Can you not see how infernally busy I am?'

Pomeroy waved his hand around at the other beds and inmates, 'It seems you do not appreciate your surroundings.'

He was rewarded with a vicious growl.

Daltrey introduced himself and asked equably, 'What would you be prepared to do for a bag of gold, Lord Rainforde?'

Rainforde sat bolt upright and looked at him as if he believed the barrister quite mad. 'You would make fun of a ruined man, sir?'

'No, Lord Rainforde. I would never do such a thing. My question was quite genuine. A bag of gold worth five hundred pounds.' He drew a leather pouch from the briefcase he carried, opened the drawstring and held it out for Rainforde to see.

Rainforde tried to laugh but ended up coughing badly.

When he could again draw breath he asked, 'Who is the unlucky man I have to murder?'

Daltrey, not renowned for his sense of humour, managed a wry smile, 'Nothing quite so drastic, my Lord.'

The use of the title got to Rainforde. 'Then what?'

'You falsely accused a farmer by the name of Thomas Nash and perjured yourself in order to acquire his land. We merely wish you to sign a paper stating that you did so.'

Rainforde's eyes suddenly became hooded, and his expression dangerous, 'I know not of what you speak.'

Daltrey shrugged nonchalantly and lifted both hands in the air, 'As you will. I have obviously been misinformed. We will bid you good day then, my Lord, and wish you a pleasant stay in these wonderful surroundings.' He pulled the drawstring tight, replaced the pouch in his briefcase and turned away.

Pomeroy had already turned his back and taken two steps towards the door.

'Stop!'

The worried shout came from the man on the bed.

They turned back.

Rainforde's expression was desperate once more, 'What do you intend, that I should be imprisoned for what you see as my crime? Is that it? Justice from the grave? The man is dead. What can he possibly want from me?'

'There is not the slightest chance that you will be charged with any crime; that I can assure you, my Lord. Thomas Nash's family merely wish to have his name cleared, so that they may claim back the land for his offspring.'

'They will need luck.' Rainforde muttered under his breath.

'I beg your pardon, my Lord, I did not catch the remark?'

'This man beside you knows well enough that I no longer own that land.'

'Then merely to clear the name.'

'And you will not use my signature against me?'

'My solemn promise, my Lord.'

'Where is the document?'

Daltrey placed his bag on the end of the bed and withdrew an official looking sheet of parchment, which he handed to Rainforde to read.

It was a clear statement of confession to the crime.

Rainforde knew well that he would be placing himself in a situation where he could suffer the same punishment as that inflicted on Thomas Nash, were they to renege on their promise, but the mere thought of the remainder of his life spent in that place convinced him. He needed the gold. With it he could gamble, more carefully this time, and regain his old place in society.

'Where is the quill?'

Daltrey produced the inkwell and feather, and Rainforde signed for the second time that week.

He grabbed the pouch held out to him and greedily opened it, checking its contents by taking a pinch of gold out and rubbing it between his fingers, watching as the dust fell back into the bag, while Daltrey examined the signature and powdered the ink before replacing it and the rest of the bagatelle in his receptacle.

Without a word of farewell, the two legal men turned and walked away from the bed.

Silas Rainforde sat gazing starry eyed at his unexpected treasure. He wanted to leave, but not in the clothes he was wearing. Where was the Warden? They had a store of clothes taken from the inmates. There would be something there he could use until he bought more elegant attire. He pulled the drawstring tight on the bag.

The two legal eagles were surprised to see Thomas waiting at the door as they exited the building.

'You have been successful, gentlemen?' He asked.

Pomeroy nodded, 'Exactly as you planned, Thomas.'

'Good. I would have a word with the ignoble lord, if you could wait upon my return?'

Pomeroy nodded, 'Of course.'

Thomas found Rainforde impatiently waiting for the warden, looking away from him down the aisle between the beds.

'Good day to you, my Lord.' He began.

Rainforde's head turned quickly.

'My God! 'Tis the freak. What in Lucifer's name do you here, Sirrah?'

Thomas would have smiled had it been possible, 'You recognise me not, my Lord?'

'Recognise you? No, but for your presence at the game of chance.'

'And do you not recall my voice?'

'How should I?'

'You took my land and tried your level best to take my life. The first I now have back and yours to boot; the second I also still have, as you see. Do you not recognise me now, *my Lord*?' He made the last two words sound like a vile curse.

Rainforde stared hard at the mask of Thomas' face, his speeding memories clear on his countenance, then uttered disbelievingly, 'Nash?'

'The very same, my Lord.'

'But you are dead.'

'So many say, and every last one of them mistaken. You have, I grant you, tried your very damnedest and done this to me,' He pointed to his face, 'but that is all that your paid minions could achieve, and with their deaths they paid for it. As you see, I live, and I have bested you, Rainforde, bested you, and the pleasure of you knowing that fact will live with me forever. You have, with your last signature, made me a free man; a landed gentleman once more, and, Rainforde, what will hurt the most, your better.'

Rainforde looked stunned, 'But…they have cheated me! You have cheated me! They said you were dead!'

'Oh, no, my Lord. Oh, but pardon me, that was ever incorrect, was it not? As the born bastard that you are you were at no time entitled to that grand appellation but usurped it, having murdered a man ten thousand times your worth to gain it. No, Silas, I may call you Silas, may I not? They did not hold me dead. You wished merely to believe it so, and as to cheating, have you not your entire life followed that path? You should know that when you tried to take the money of my friend it was he who so easily cheated you. I tell you now; it was at no time a fair played game. At cheating with the cards you are but an amateur, a bungling fool, so easily deluded, as, indeed, you are in life.'

Rainforde's brain surged with anger and hatred, but above all else humiliation. This 'thing' before him, this freakish horror, a pig-ignorant son of the soil with no learning, had played him like a fish and made a blatant fool of him. Tears of impotent rage came to his eyes, observed by Thomas, who was at long last satisfied. The mere sight of the being before him, poxed, ruined, disgraced, made up in some part for the years of his own suffering, but now the man must die. One thing would ensure that outcome, for Rainforde would react in typical fashion, and it would not be colluding in a murder, Thomas told himself, but a determined effort to prevent it.

'Methinks you should consider your position, Silas. Here in this house you are safe. Stay here, I pray you, for your own safety. Outside there is a big bad world in which, as we have so easily demonstrated, you are nothing but an untutored child, whose sweetmeats can be taken from him at will by beings he believes are inferior to him. You will not survive if you leave this place. That is a plain fact. You have not the necessary acumen.'

Rainforde snarled, 'I have gold and with it I shall hire men to destroy you, Nash. With looks such as yours you cannot hide and will be easily found. This time you shall not escape and live to enjoy your spoils. You think to have won? Hah! You will be dead within the day.'

Thomas smiled with his voice, 'We shall see, Silas, we shall see.'

CHAPTER TWENTY-SEVEN

Thomas and Roger took their leave of Daltrey at the coaching station at the Haymarket in Norwich, after being assured that he would do his utmost to obtain the King's pardon. He would inform them of the outcome, he said.

Thomas was surprised next morning to find that he was, unusually, at breakfast before Roger, whose desire for food stemmed not only from their years of starvation.

A large plate of ham and eggs had been dispatched before his friend's cheeky grinning face appeared in the doorway, under his arm a copy of that day's Norwich Mercury.

Thomas smiled, 'I took you not for a reader of scurrilous gossip, Roger.'

His friend shrugged, 'There are certain occurrences in which I take a deep, morbid interest, Thomas. This one, for instance.'

He had folded the paper to show a column with the heading, *"YET ANOTHER POORHOUSE MURDER."*

Thomas read the article through. It appeared that one of the inmates had proven himself to have pecuniary advantage and been allowed to leave, only to be set upon and robbed beyond the gate. He had received a cut to the throat, which had proved fatal.

'Now I wonder who that might have been.' Thomas murmured.

'No one we know, I wager.'

'I just hate to think of all that gold wasted.'

Roger winked knowingly.

Thomas sat back, puzzled, 'Was that supposed to mean something, Roger?'

His friend shrugged, his eyebrows raised, his head held to one side and his lips pursed, before he told Thomas, 'I fear we cheated Rainforde once more. Gold there was on top, 'tis true, the rest was golden sand. Had he searched deeply we would have been found out, but having come to know the way the man's mind worked I took the chance. Of course, I told not the barrister. He is an upright man and could not have been so persuasive had he known.'

Thomas could do nothing but shake his head in wonder at his friend's insight.

The world suddenly seemed a much brighter place. His plans had come to wonderful fruition and his nemesis utterly degraded and destroyed.

He left Roger at the inn and returned to Oxton, leaving the titles to the Manor and his own land secured in the vault at Dalbey's bank.

He had also arranged loans for the shipbuilding, a proposition in which the banker had expressed a keen interest, proposing a possible partnership.

He was welcomed with open arms, and when he told them the news there was jubilation. Jacob Breen spread the news around the small village, and soon the smithy was overwhelmed with well-wishers.

Thomas began speaking to men Jacob had recommended as good workers who had no employment and those he had found who had worked the Rainforde estate before. Since the war with France had begun in 1793, there were thousands more paupers, and though life was desperately hard, few countrymen were willing to go as part of William Pitt's infamous 'quotas', introduced in 1795: the Government's attempt to fill the numbers required for the Navy fighting the French, having not found enough volunteers and pressed men.

Thomas had on his last visit asked Jacob to attempt to find Rainforde's tenant farmers, all of whom Silas Rainforde had thrown off the land their families had farmed for generations. He had located four of them and had queries out for the other two.

The four were sent for, and they came one by one during the next four days, all astonished when told to go back to their farms to try to pick up the pieces. Thomas promised free seed and animals for them to start again and assured them there would be no annual rent to pay for the first five years, after which it would begin again, but only at the old figure, with no increase.

He hired labourers for the estate and the Hall, twice as many as would be needed in the long term, and gave them the option of travelling with him to Australia, promising to provide each of them with at least a hundred acres of land and fifty sheep providing they worked for him for ten years, at double the English rate. To men expecting to end their lives as they started, with nothing to show for a lifetime of toil, and only the poorhouse if they became ill, it was akin to being presented with a genie's lamp. Fifteen agreed, one more than the number he had in mind. It was another mile covered on the road to his intended destination. Carpenters and maids were also hired for the Manor, and he and James moved there, along with Jane, as a temporary measure, to supervise the female staff and reorganise the workings of the house. Having watched them work and been satisfied he offered two of the carpenters the same terms as the labourers, and both accepted, work for their trade being scarce indeed in England at that time. He needed a wheelwright too, and Jacob found one for him.

The days passed in a blur, all of them working from dawn to dusk.

At the end of five weeks, the Manor was restored to its former glory, and work on the Hall was begun.

Thomas and James went to the livestock market in Aylsham and purchased everything on offer: cattle, sheep, pigs, goats, chickens, geese and ducks.

The fields were ploughed and the hedges layered.

One morning in August, Thomas stood with James at the window of the Manor library, looking out over the moat to the clean fields beyond, stretching away to the horizon.

'Look at it, James. It is all yours.'

'Can you not stay and farm it with me, father?'

Thomas sighed, 'Would that I could, but your brothers and sisters on the other side of the world now need me more than you do. I am happy that we have back our land. That was my main reason for returning to England. I have heard nothing from London, so I fear that the other aim has not been achieved. Ah, well, it would have made things easier for me in Australia, but was obviously not meant to be.'

James was wistful, 'I wish that I could meet them one day, those brothers and sisters.'

Thomas put his arm round his son's shoulders, 'The world is a much smaller place now, and we shall have our own ships. One day you shall meet at least some of them, of that I am sure. But James, to speak of yourself; you need a wife.'

'I know, father, and once everything is running smoothly I shall begin looking.'

Thomas nodded, 'I know you will pick wisely.'

'A woman like mother. I remember her, you know.'

'They are not so easily come by.'

'But they are to be found.'

'Yes, they are.'

There were but five weeks of the twelvemonth left when Thomas took his tearful departure and returned to Norwich.

He found Roger in great form. He played cards nightly in the barroom below his quarters and assured Thomas that he had not cheated once but had won a princely sum during the period they had been apart. Thomas lifted one eyebrow in disbelief.

Roger grinned his wicked grin, 'Well, perhaps once or twice, just to keep my hand in you know. Old dogs, Thomas, old dogs.'

'You have heard nothing from Pomeroy?'

'Who?' Roger feigned loss of memory, 'Oh, that attorney fellow. Yes, he did come around one day…now what was it he wanted? Let me see…there was something. Very unimportant, you understand…something quite trivial really. Oh, I remember now, he said you had received the Royal Pardon.'

As the last syllable left his lips he leapt up, threw his chair back and began running, out of the door and down the street, chased furiously by Thomas, who had the urgent desire to knock his block off. Everyone in sight believed a thief was being pursued.

They ran and ran until both were completely out of breath, Roger collapsing at last onto the ground beside the wall of a draper's shop, and Thomas piling on top of him, his hands playfully around Roger's throat. Both dissolved into howls of laughter that lasted minutes long, passers-by eyeing them with wonderment.

276

At last Thomas managed to gasp, 'You are a lucky man I had no musket in my hand when you spoke!'

Roger was still chuckling when he told him, 'You should have seen your face, Thomas, and all this time I thought you could no longer show expression.' He suddenly pretended seriousness, 'Did you know you are sitting in a pile of dog shit.'

Thomas' hands went round Roger's throat once more and the laughter renewed.

They both went to visit Pomeroy, who was jubilant as he handed the parchment with the Royal Seal to Thomas.

'You are now officially a free man, Thomas Nash. It has given me the greatest joy of my life to serve you in this respect, and has, at last, restored my flagging faith in the English justice system. It has many faults, and I fear some may never be corrected, but this is one small crack repaired in that faulty brickwork.' He held out his hand, 'May your life be a good and successful one.'

Outside, Roger looked wistful, 'Would that I could obtain such a document.'

'You are a freed man, Roger.'

'Aye, but not an innocent one with parchment to prove it.' He began to laugh and Thomas joined in again. The very thought of Roger as innocent was hilarious.

Three days before the date they were due to meet Amos again Thomas and Roger rode hired horses to Yarmouth to make arrangements for enough victuals for the men voyaging with them.

The *'Reliant'* was in port, having arrived the day before with a cargo of Norwegian pine for the sawmills in the port. Amos had unloaded and had been preparing for the coming voyage, expecting only two passengers.

Roger stayed on board, helping with the changes, while Thomas rode back to Norwich and then to Oxton, to arrange transport for the men. Most had families with them to see them off, and five had sweethearts, all in tears. Thomas had already told the men that if their womenfolk wished to join them later it could be arranged free of charge, which had softened the blow somewhat.

It took an entire day at the plodding speed of the horses, but at last they arrived and boarded the ship, some of the men fearful, as only landsmen can be who have never been on the water before.

They sailed on the twenty-eight of February in the year of our Lord seventeen ninety-eight, and Thomas looked back at the land of his birth from a mile out to sea, thinking that he might never set eyes on it again.

They had discussed their route with Amos and he had suggested attempting the run to Rio without stopping off at Tenerife.

'We have ample stocks of salt meat and fish, and I acquired many sacks of onions, carrots and turnips. I believe it is possible.'

Thomas shrugged, 'You are the master, Amos.'

In the event, Amos came to believe himself the master of a possibly disastrous fate.

After a tremendously successful run down the coast of Africa, with good weather and steady winds all the way, taking them past Tenerife and later the Cape Verdes, the seamen subjected the landlubbers to the ordeal of 'Crossing the Line', with Amos as King Neptune, to merriment all round.

The next day, they turned away from the West African shoreline for the crossing to Rio, accompanied by a huge pod of dolphins, to the delight of Thomas' new men.

Again, they enjoyed almost perfect sailing conditions, and Amos was pleased with his decision until they became suddenly becalmed two hundred miles short of land.

The heat was relentless, with not the slightest breath of wind, the sails hanging like drawers on a washing line. Below decks, it was almost impossible to breathe and on deck the planking burnt the men's feet, even through the soles of their shoes.

Skin that had become hardened by outdoor toil became burnt in minutes if out of the shade. Even the nights were unbearable, though everyone on board slept on deck.

Twenty-six days passed with no relief, and their meals were reduced to the last of the dried vegetables and cereals, all the salt meat and fish having gone bad in the heat and been thrown overboard.

Things looked bleak indeed until Thomas came up with another brilliant idea. The whole time they had been becalmed the seamen had tried fishing with their usual hand lines, rarely hooking anything in the mile-deep water beneath the ship. He was watching them again as dusk fell, six of them, trying desperately to catch their dinner. What made it infinitely worse were the shoals of flying fish that suddenly appeared several times a day, shooting past the ship two and three feet over the waves at almost forty miles per hour, like flights of silver arrows discharged by serried ranks of invisible bowmen. So much food in sight and not available to them.

All attempts at catching them had failed.

As dusk fell one day, Thomas took the master's elbow, 'Lower the longboat, Amos, and fetch me a lantern or two. I'll need four men and a large piece of sail.'

Amos thought Thomas had gone mad and intended trying to tow the '*Reliant*' to port, not that he had not considered the selfsame thing himself in desperation.

Intrigued, he watched the goings-on.

Once on the water, Thomas had two of the men remain on the oars while the other two stood upright at the stern, straining the sailcloth taut between them and standing on the bottom of it. He stood by the centre thwarts, holding the lanterns aloft.

An hour went by, then two. His arms ached, as did those of the two seamen with the sailcloth.

Suddenly it was as if a battery of artillery had found their position and begun bombarding them. They were struck all over, and the sailcloth almost ripped out of the two seamen's hands as scores of fish, attracted by the lights, hurtled through the air over the boat. With the fish weighing anything up to half a pound and travelling faster than the fastest galloping horse they hurt human flesh, and Thomas and the men could stand it for only a few minutes.

He was the worst affected, holding the lights as he was, lights that themselves had taken even more hits than his flesh, almost torn from his hands with the blows.

He sank into the bottom of the boat amongst a mass of squirming fish, and still they rained in, as he tried vainly to turn his back on them.

It ceased as quickly as it began, like a lamp turned off with the wheel.

One of the seaman started it, a giggle, then a guffaw. Within seconds they were helpless with laughter, rolling in the bottom of the boat, their attire smeared with scales and fishy juice, watched silently by the crowd on the deck of the ship with amazement, then, like an uncontrollable wild fire, the laughter spread, until all were tumbling on the deck in uncontrollable glee, the removal of the nightmare of starvation feeding their merriment.

The experiment was repeated with the same measure of success, but with a difference. Thomas having shown the way Amos had the ship's carpenter make up a frame to hold the canvas and another to hold the lanterns, both fixed onto the longboat with clamps, saving the seamen from the pain they would otherwise have suffered. Thomas was black and blue all over. Once was enough, but he consoled himself that they all now had plenty of sustenance to see them through.

Five days later one of the lookouts noticed a small fluffy white cloud on the far eastern horizon, like a tiny ball of dust gathered on a long-unswept blue marble floor.

Three dozen eyes eagerly watched its slow, spreading development into a thin line of white, changing oh so gradually through light grey into dark, expanding upwards and outwards, its top growing taller and more uneven, changing again into towering turrets that joined and towered more, until its leading edge seemed to lean over them like a giant ogre, ready to devour them, a mass of whirling cumulus, with the wind they had so long awaited inside it, but still they lay becalmed.

Amos had set minimum sail, knowing that the first gusts could dismast the ship if he overloaded the spars.

Though they expected the blow, when it came they were still unprepared for its force, grabbing hold of anything fixed as the ship suddenly leapt forward, as if a giant whale moving at top speed had taken her in its mouth.

The landlubbers who had never voyaged before wore scared expressions, but Amos calmed them, laughing hilariously at the exhilarating speed the ship was making, knowing how safe she was, his laughter chorused by the others of the crew on deck.

The fierce, gusting blows lasted only twenty minutes, after which the wind became a steady half-gale, and Amos crowded on sail, until they were making more than eight knots through the water.

Rio came in sight twenty-three hours later, with sighs of relief from everyone on board.

The ship's master made a promise to himself that in future, no matter what, he would call at Tenerife and also the Cape Verde Islands before crossing the Atlantic.

After that one almost disastrous episode, the rest of the voyage was an anticlimax. Good winds took them from Rio across to the Cape of Good Hope, where Thomas bought horses and forage, while Amos re-stocked with victuals and water.

The Southern Ocean was also kind to them, with no violent storms, and the entire compliment spent most of the time on deck, enjoying the playful antics of more shoals of flying fish, pods of dolphins and whales, and now and again the triangular fins of marauding sharks.

They made the fastest run to date of any ship from the Cape to their final destination and dropped anchor just as the last light of the day made the treetops on the western shore appear like the dark turrets of a dozen adjacent, unlit castles.

They disembarked the next day, taking the horses Thomas had bought in Cape Town, one for each man with four spares.

Thomas told Amos to wait in harbour until he returned with more gold before sailing back to England to complete the purchase of the new ships.

'You will be the Commodore of the Fleet, Amos, and I shall leave it entirely to you what cargoes to carry, what personnel to engage and what destinations to visit, but I expect to see you here on Christmas Day at least once in every two years, with the reckoning. You will call the ships the '*Martha Nash*', the '*Thomas Nash*', the '*James Nash*' and the '*Austin Nash*' and you will register the shipping line as the Nash-Swales Line. Are you content with that?'

Amos had no need to tell him he was over the moon; his expression said it all. He managed a simple, 'That I am, Thomas.'

Roger gripped the master's arm tightly, 'And do not gamble, Amos. I reiterate, you are the world's worst player, and your face gives your hand away every time. Even Thomas, who plays not at all, can read the value of your cards from your expression. Taking your money is as effortless as falling off a stool. It is that simple. If you need to be free of your money, throw it overboard into the wind; it would go less quickly.'

Amos nodded. 'Thank you for your advice, Roger. I have learnt my lesson I assure you.'

Knowing well the compulsion that drove gamblers Roger was not convinced. He was worried for Thomas' investment but shrugged his shoulders philosophically. Time alone would tell.

Amos watched them until they disappeared in a distant dust cloud under the far trees.

In Parramatta, Thomas wheeled his horse round onto the wooden bar in front of the single storey building that had the simple title 'BANK' inscribed on a plain board over the door and dismounted.

Inside he found just one man behind a grill in a timber wall.

He introduced himself and asked if the man was an employee or the banker himself and was told the latter, James Carter.

Thomas stated his business, and Carter nodded and told him yes, Sloane had negotiated the purchase of the land and left the deeds with him, but that the major in charge of the New South Wales Corps had issued an instruction that any land not given to Corps members had to be vetted personally by him and had taken the deed.

'Where can I find him and what is his name?'

'Johnston, at the Grand Hotel. Certainly not at the barracks. He is not renowned for his attention to duty, unless there is money at the back of it.'

'I take it he is not your favourite person?'

'Nor anyone's, except for his men, to whom he gives away favours like sweetmeats, as did Grose before him, though the Governor tries to restrict him.'

'Does he still hold the deed?'

'He does.'

'Arthur Sloane, who brought the deed to you, do you know where his new land is?'

Carter laughed, 'You mean the man who emptied his creek of gold and left only the tailings for the rest of them?'

'That's the one.'

'He could not find decent land near town and has purchased fourteen thousand acres roughly forty miles to the west of here. He told me he was going to call it 'Dreamtime Station', whatever that might mean.'

Thomas left, told the men he would be back shortly and rode the short distance to the hotel, which was still under construction.

On entering, he found five officers playing faro in the first room to the right, and recognised the major's emblems on the shoulders of the man at the far end, a robust character with a round, pig-like face that held a permanent sneer; a sneer that became much deeper at the sight of Thomas.

'You, what business have you here? This is a private game.'

'I would speak with you, sir, if you could spare me a moment or two of your valuable time.' Thomas was polite but had no intention of being obsequious with this self-important popinjay.

'Concerning?'

'Land that I have purchased.'

A cunning gleam came into the officer's eyes, 'Land, is it? And who are you?'

'Thomas Nash, sir.'

'You are an ex-convict?'

'I was falsely accused and now hold the King's Pardon.'

'Do you indeed? And how comes it you are acquainted with our monarch?'

'By right of birth.'

'How so? You class yourself a gentleman?'

'I do.'

'Mm.' What had seemed like a simple transaction, the forced purchase of what might in any case be a worthless piece of land, had suddenly become a much trickier business. If this freak before him really had the right to be called a gentleman he would be able to get the Governor's ear, and although that worthy was a weak man, he could, if he felt so inclined, overrule any decision Johnston might make.

'And what, pray, do you intend to do with this land?'

'A small portion of it is fertile, where I intend to make my home and breed horses, but the much larger part is infertile scrub, and that I shall fence and raise emus, intending to sell the meat to the people of the town.'

'Emus? You must be as mad as you look!'

Thomas was pleased to see the intended hilarity his ridiculous stated intention had produced in the group of officers.

Johnston sat thinking. He had carefully checked every application for land, ensuring that nothing worth farming went to anyone outside the Corps, despite ongoing efforts by the succession of Governors to stop him, like his predecessor, Groves, and he remembered clearly reading the surveyor's report on this particular piece of land. There was, as he recalled, what the surveyor called "potentially farmable land" to the other side of a river, amounting to approximately one quarter of the land requested. The rest was arid scrub, and in his words, "totally worthless". Johnston chuckled. Emus indeed, what a joke.

'Peter, fetch my briefcase, will you?'

The officer to his right rose and left the room, coming back a few moments later with a leather satchel, which he handed to Johnston.

The major pulled out an official looking document with the Governor's seal on the bottom and handed it to the officer who had fetched the case.

'Give it to him. He's welcome to it.'

He shouted across at Thomas, 'We'll expect a wagon load of emu meat when you bring it to town!'

His officers knew that they were expected to laugh loudly when their major made a joke and duly obliged.

As Thomas left, with what passed with him for a smile, he heard behind him, 'He needs to go and live in the bloody outback. If he stayed here he'd be the town bogeyman.' Yes, he thought, you may well laugh, but he who laughs last...

His men were relaxing on their feet but mounted again when they saw him coming back with what they knew was intended as a grin. They had had plenty of time on the voyage to get to know him, and all of them liked him well enough to want to work for him.

A short distance along the road, they found a general store, and Thomas had them load up enough supplies for a week, knowing that he would be able to feed them after that time, though they would have to get used to bush grub. He grinned wryly to himself as he thought of trying to get them to eat witchetty grubs. That one he would leave for a couple of years, he decided.

There was a new inn at the north end of the town, and they stopped for a meal before heading off towards their new home.

All the forest had been cleared for the first twenty miles beyond the town, and Thomas was amazed to see the number of cabins and the efforts to grow vegetables. Two men waved to them, interested to see such a large party of men travelling out into the wide blue yonder.

When they reached his land it at first appeared the same, but then Thomas started to notice the differences. Where the fire had been there were now isolated new eucalyptus trees, the fastest growing tree in Australia, with immature cabbage trees dotted between them. Low bushes covered the rest of the ground.

He pulled to a halt, pointed across the river and told the men, 'There is your home for the next few years, lads. I want two buildings built sixty yards below the top of that far slope, facing this way. That will be your first job. You will fetch the timber from that forested area we have just passed through and build the house and your bunkhouse next to one another.' He had pointed out the various types of tree on the way, telling them that the Red Gum was useless for building. 'Your accommodation comes first, then mine. There is a ford just two miles up river; we'll cross there.'

The men, only two of whom had travelled as far as Norwich from their home village, were still inspired with the wonders of the voyage they had made and were in holiday mood, enthused by what they were seeing: kangaroos, wallabies, emus, wombats and koalas, and the colourful birds, with parrots everywhere. They would see many more strange and wonderful creatures in the years to come.

They crossed the river safely, with Thomas watchful for crocs without mentioning them to the men, and he spurred his mount forward gleefully, with a deep, warm feeling of finally coming home, a feeling that he had strangely not felt when he saw the Hall again. He imagined that he had, for years, thought of it as James' home now and not his. He had loved his land in England but he loved this land more. If only Martha could have shared it with him.

He had spent countless hours on the voyage talking with the men he had picked to go with him and now knew their strengths and weaknesses: which of them could read and write and which had potentially greater talent than they themselves knew. He had ever been a good judge of men and had honed that ability during his incarceration and subsequently. He had firmly decided on his future Tee-man whilst still on the ship. Andrew Coulson, a big built man with a permanent smile on his round face and a shock of sandy hair, had been a tenant farmer near North Walsham and had fallen foul of a new landlord when the previous landlord died, in very similar circumstances to Thomas himself, though without the accompanying arrest. He had since worked sporadically for one or two farmers at harvest but otherwise had found no permanent employment. He had had a minimal education but could read and write, and Thomas found that it was impossible to best him with arithmetical questions. He was a natural genius with figures. Even better, he was popular with the other men.

Thomas called him over and told him, 'I must go back to the ship for two days after I have rested for a few hours. You are in charge until I return.'

He called the men together and told them of his decision, then walked over into the shade of a eucalyptus and was asleep in minutes.

He woke shortly after dusk, said his goodbyes and rode off, with his own and a spare horse, both with large saddlebags. He trusted his men but was glad he was safe from their eyes once he crossed the river, more worried about crocs when he could not see them.

He found the way to his cache easily in the dark, as he had so many times before, removed eighteen bags of gold and filled the saddlebags. He then walked the horses over two hundred yards, ground hobbled them and returned to the cache site with a large bush he had torn from the ground, using it to erase all traces of his footsteps, before mounting and heading off towards Sydney once more.

He rode wide of Parramatta, joining the road a quarter of a mile beyond the town, and completed the journey towards noon.

Using the agreed signal, a repeated flash with a small mirror, he drew the attention of the lookout on board, who in turn alerted Amos.

The longboat was lowered almost immediately and Thomas saw Roger's bulk descending the rope ladder.

The men pulled hard and were at the quayside in less than ten minutes.

Thomas had taken the saddlebags from one horse, leaving the others on the one that would be Roger's.

His friend bounded up the steps and gave him a bear hug, as if they had not seen each other for years, and Thomas quipped,

'You will have the local populace believing I am a shirt lifter if you are not careful, Roger.'

'Let them think what they like. You can buy them all now.'

Thomas indicated the saddlebags on the horse. 'There are nine bags of gold there, Roger, as was my promise to you. You are now officially the second richest man in Australia, but you must be very, very wary. There is a Major Johnston of the New South Wales Corps running things, and he is a most avaricious man. What have you in mind? You do not intend to gamble, I hope?'

'No, Thomas. I willingly call myself a crook but deep down I know that appellation was forced upon me and I would that I could live an honest life, if such is allowed me. I see myself as an hotelier, perhaps with many hotels, built over the whole of this continent. You mention gambling. That also I have in mind, but for my clients, not for me. I shall build a horseracing track, as good as or better than that at Newmarket, and reap great rewards from it. Next to it I shall build a training stable, and I alone will know the capabilities of every horse. The racing will be perfectly straight; no cheating, but I cannot fail to win with every bet I make. You must admit that will not be gambling, but taking the food from the mouths of infants.'

Thomas looked at his friend with respect, 'Roger, that is a most tremendous idea, one that I wish I had thought of myself. This new country, with almost every man a horseman, will embrace such a scheme with open arms. Do you fancy a partner?'

Roger placed his hand on Thomas' shoulder, 'You *are* my partner, Thomas, in everything I shall do. All shall be under the two names, 'Clarke and Nash', with equal shares in the profits.'

Thomas protested, 'But Roger, the gold I have given you was a free gift, with no obligation.'

'Then our partnership is my equally free gift to you, Thomas.' He held out his hand, and the two men shook solemnly.

Roger suddenly grinned, like a schoolboy who has been told he can have the day off, 'May we have many years to enjoy the spoils.'

As the longboat pulled for the '*Reliant*' Thomas watched his friend and now partner ride off towards his own destiny.

On board, Amos met him at the gunwale and accompanied Thomas into the master's cabin, where the gold was removed from the saddlebags Thomas had brought on board and stowed in a strongbox, brought from England for that very purpose.

'Whatever moneys are left after the purchase of the ships and the hiring of the crews I would like you to take in person to Dalbey's Bank in Norwich and deposit it in the name of James Nash.' He held out his hand, 'Until Christmas in two years, Commodore.'

Amos swelled with pride, 'You will not be sorry, Thomas.'

Thomas nodded, 'Of that I am sure, Amos. May good weather accompany you always.'

It was a buoyant ex-English farmer who spurred his horse northwestward towards the place he had come to love.

CHAPTER TWENTY-EIGHT

The difference was obvious, even from two miles distant. In the two days he had been away, the entire top of the slope had been cleared of saplings and scrub, and the men's bunkhouse was already up to three feet, with the corner posts rising like flagpoles waiting for a salute to be raised. Thomas had the urge to put the horse into a gallop but resisted the impulse. His mount was weary, and Thomas was ever aware of his animals' health, be it horse, dog, sheep or swine. He let the horse walk on at its own pace.

All of the men, stripped to the waist, had sweat on their faces and bodies but were in holiday spirit, enjoying their new life. The weather was equable; they had full bellies and hard but pleasantly rewarding work to do. The fact that their master had insisted on their accommodation being built first had made them realise that they had made the right choice in coming here.

Thomas was as weary as Blaze but jumped off the horse with an exuberance that was only partly false, grabbed a spade and joined them at their work.

Thirty-four days later they all stood watching as the last plank was nailed onto the two-storey house. The two buildings, substantially built with wood from the She Oak, shone like two huge rubies on the hillside, reflecting the dying embers of the evening sun.

Andrew Coulson, like Thomas, was watching the faces of the men. Suddenly he whooped, 'Three cheers for Thomas Nash; hip, hip hooray!'

The cheers tore their way into Thomas' heart. He had come home.

By spring, with careful work, the entire area he had bought had been cleared to ground level, after which grass and ground cover were allowed to grow. It was time for the animals.

A livestock market had been set up in Parramatta, and he had visited half a dozen times, appraising the stock. Now it was time to buy.

He took six of the men and two of their new wagons and drove into town.

There were horses in abundance, a few scraggy cattle, fifty or so pigs, chickens, ducks and geese, and he purchased a few of each as breeding stock, but he was really only interested in the sheep.

There were over a dozen pens, seven containing Leicesters, which he knew well. The remainder were a breed called Merinos, of which he had heard, but had no personal knowledge. They had come originally from Spain centuries before and had been introduced into some parts of England, he knew. The Leicesters were heavy boned and slow to grow. The Merinos were attractive looking animals, with white faces and legs. He ran his fingers through a fleece and found that the long wool fibres were finely crimped.

As he was bending over a voice he knew murmured behind him, 'Has it come that far, Thomas?'

He whirled, overjoyed.

'Arthur! How are you?'

'I am well, Thomas. I see you are admiring my sheep.'

'They are yours? They do you credit.'

Sloane shook his head, 'Most of that credit goes to Martha, but I am learning fast.'

'Tell me of her.'

'She has changed not one iota since the day I first saw her. She wears the years well, far better than I. She speaks of you often, as if you live, thinking of what you might be doing were you working with the animals alongside her.'

'And does that not wound you, Arthur?'

Sloane hesitated just a second or so before replying, 'No, Thomas. At least not deeply. I know how she loved you. We have a good relationship, but she has never loved me, nor ever will.'

Thomas had so many questions that needed answers but had scarcely begun again when Sloane stopped him.

'I would like you to come with me, Thomas.'

Intrigued, Thomas followed him down the covered passageway and out into the sunshine. Before him, looking into a pen containing six highly coloured ducks of an unusual breed, were two lads, one about ten years old and the other two years younger.

Sloane pulled his sleeve and they stopped a dozen yards away.

'Your sons, Austin and Thomas. Would you wish them to know you?'

His heart hammering in his chest Thomas gasped, 'Will they tell Martha?'

'Not if you do not wish it. We have never hidden from them the fact that I am not their father, but they know not that you live. If you wish I shall introduce you as a friend but if you wish them to know you are their father I would honour that wish.'

'But my face. They will think me a horror.'

'I think not. I know the boys. They will be shocked, no doubt, but they have grown up seeing the vagaries of nature, and what she can do to bodies.'

'As a friend then.'

'Come on.'

The two boys turned as they heard the steps behind them, and Thomas watched the expressions on their faces as they caught sight of him. He had seen so many hundreds of different reactions to his disfigurement that he was prepared for anything but hoped so much that they would not cry out in disgust. The taller of the two, so like James that he was sure for a moment that it was a younger he, merely cocked his head to one side at the sight of his father, frowning in concentration and seemingly only interested in how a face could become disfigured in that manner. A fleeting moment of horror passed over the younger lad's face, good breeding replacing it quickly with a forced smile.

Sloane said, 'Boys, I want you to meet a very good friend of mine. This is Thomas…' He stopped himself just in time, almost having said the surname.

Austin held out his hand, 'I am pleased to meet you, sir.'

Thomas took it and then the hand of his younger namesake, who had recovered his poise and was inspecting his father's face with closer interest.

'Thomas was burnt in a bad forest fire.' Sloane told them.

Austin asked, 'Does it hurt?'

Thomas produced what passed for a grin; a strange grimace that did nothing to show humour, 'Only when I laugh, Austin.'

The lad drew back a pace, frowning, 'You know my name, sir?'

Thomas recovered quickly, 'Your father informed me of it as we approached.'

The younger lad was looking at him strangely, 'And you carry my name, sir.'

'That I do, Thomas.'

'Few people do.'

'So I believe.'

'Have you come to buy stock?'

Thomas nodded, 'I believe I have just bought all of yours.' He looked at Sloane for confirmation.

'He has.' Sloane told the boys.

'You can help me load them, if you will.'

'Certainly, sir.'

They ran off towards the pens.

'That went well, Thomas.' Sloane opined.

'Very well. Now tell me about your daughters.'

'They grow apace and resemble their mother. They are fine girls, ready to help whenever we need them.'

'I am pleased to hear it and would love to meet them one day.'

'We must arrange it.'

'Now, about these Merinos. Are they more productive than the Leicesters?'

'They grow much faster, and their wool is finer. At Martha's instigation, I have begun to cross them, but it is too soon to tell the results.'

They chatted on, and Thomas watched proudly as his sons helped the men load the animals onto the wagons, sorry when he had to take his leave of them and Sloane.

Back at their home, with Sloane working outside, and the girls playing in the sun, the boys chatted on excitedly about their day and told their mother of the friend with the ruined face their father had presented them to.

Martha turned her back to hide the fierce love pain that pierced her heart, tears springing to her eyes with the knowledge that Thomas was safe. How long had Arthur known, she wondered, and why had Thomas not wanted to see her? Could he not know that she would love him no matter how disfigured he might be? Did he no longer love her?

'Go and help your father, boys!' She urged desperately, wanting to be alone with the hurt and knowing that she must help preserve the lie. She wondered how she could possibly hide from Arthur the knowledge and the joy that the only man she could ever truly love was alive. Not only alive, but nearby.

CHAPTER TWENTY-NINE

The year passed, the sheep bred, and with all under control and the men exercised in their daily tasks, Thomas took to crossing to the other side of the river and riding up to the caves each day, standing in his old lookout spot and gazing to the west, hoping for a sight of the returning tribe.

His patience was rewarded on the seventh of June 1802, when he saw through the spyglass he had bought in Norwich several brown bodies and one much paler in colour moving in their usual careful way through the brush five miles away.

As they came closer, he could recognise Banjora, Curriquinquin and Mandu, accompanied by an easily recognisable but older Bibola, followed closely by Harah, Kwaralia, Yahnee and nine younger aborigines, one no more than three years old. With them was a young white man, a foot taller than the others, but moving with the same natural grace. Through the lens, Thomas imagined he was looking at James. The similarity was striking. There was no sign of 'Old Woman' or of Kirrah, and he guessed they had passed on.

He descended to the base of the mountain and waited for them, staying out of sight behind a tree.

At a quarter of a mile, with the tribe out in the open between low scrub bushes, he saw Banjora suddenly hold up his hand. They all stopped and dropped to the ground, trying to hide their bodies.

Thomas was puzzled until he saw Banjora begin flitting forward, dodging from bush to bush, his spear ready to hurl, listening intently and sniffing the air. As he neared Thomas' hiding place, he reduced his pace to almost nothing, still sniffing curiously but appearing to be less worried from the attitude of his spear, which was pointing upwards.

At fifty yards, he suddenly stopped and made his kookaburra call. Thomas had tried unsuccessfully many times to copy it but had never really mastered it. He called back and was rewarded by a hearty chuckle, followed by, 'You will never learn that call, Thomas. You would not fool a chicken.'

Thomas walked out, 'You old bugger. How did you know I was here from that distance?'

'You smell rotten, Thomas. The air is full of that stink of white man's soap.'

It was not the first time Banjora had surprised him with his animal's sense of smell.

The aborigine waved to the tribe and they came on, not with the exuberance of white men and women, but at the same steady pace as before.

The greetings and the talk went on throughout the rest of the day. Thomas could hardly keep his eyes off Joshua, who had greeted him politely with, 'Hello, father, it is good to see you again'.

The lad had the natural grace of the aborigines. Close up, he could almost pass for James, but his skin was slightly darker and his eyes gave away his ancestry if one looked carefully enough and with suspicion. He had the Nash nose, rather than the flattened nostrils of the aborigine, and Thomas loved him. Kwaralia's two daughters, Gurrah, 'the Wind', and Garad, 'the Black Cockatiel' had made up into fine young women. All the youngsters spoke acceptable English, and Joshua told him they habitually used that language when at rest and their native tongue when working or hunting. Thomas looked at them with pride. His blood.

He told them that he now owned all the land they could see and that it was theirs forever, or for as long as they wanted to use it. He had enough men to protect them should there ever be any trouble and would like them to feel free to come and go as they pleased and roam over the rest of his land as they wished.

At that point, Joshua asked apparently solemnly, 'Can we steal some of your sheep?'

Puzzled, he was about to say they could when Banjora began laughing. He was joined by Joshua, and then all the others, until they were rolling about in the dust, howling with glee.

Joshua at last recovered his breath and said, 'You can keep them, father. They do not taste as good as bush grub. Here, I have been saving these especially for you.' He got up and brought over a handful of witchetty grubs.

Thomas took them, grinning, as they watched to see if living as a white man again had changed him, and popped one in his mouth, chewing with gusto, making all and sundry laugh again.

At last Yahnee yawned and told him they should take the children to their sleeping place.

He rose and said he would come back the next day and that they should visit his home.

Over the months that followed, his children became favourites of his workers and regular visitors. Joshua spent more and more time with him, learning sheep husbandry and the ways of the white man. By the beginning of the next winter, he was sleeping in the house. The rest of the tribe remained in the caves, using the land for hunting, as Thomas had suggested. He did no more extraction of gold and did not mention it to anyone but transferred the rest of his bags to the house, hidden behind a false panel. The metal still in the ground was there for the future and was not going to go away.

One year passed into another, and another. Every second Christmas Thomas rode to Sydney Cove to meet with Amos, taking Joshua with him.

The third time they went, Joshua took his father's arm as they waited for the longboat and asked urgently, 'Could I be a sailor, father?'

Thomas drew back, astonished, 'A sailor? Is that what you wish, Joshua? Really?'

'Yes, father. I have given it a great deal of thought. I know I appear at first sight to be white, and on our own property I am accepted as such, but look at my eyes and the colour of my skin. The aborigines are still not accepted as full citizens of Australia, and I truly believe they never will be. Certainly not in my lifetime, at any rate. If I stay I can never be looked up to as you are. I shall forever be second-class. At sea, if Amos' crew is anything to go by, I would be accepted for what skills I have, not for the colour of my skin or eyes. I can find my place by hard work.'

'But I own the line with Amos.' Thomas insisted, 'You can go as my representative. You have no need to learn sailoring.'

Joshua smiled knowingly, 'As a figurehead, father? Were you I, would you be content with such a life? No, you would not. I have watched you at work; you ask no man to do what you cannot do better, faster, and with more aplomb. I shall start at the bottom and I shall become a master.'

Thomas shrugged resignedly, 'So be it, Joshua. I well understand your motives, and you have my full blessing. Have you told your mother?'

Joshua smiled enigmatically, 'Oh, father! Come now. Think.'

Of course. The aborigine way. When it was time to go, they went. There was never regret, only the knowledge that one day they might possibly come back, but that wherever they were, it was where they wanted to be.

'You will be able to meet your brother, James.' Thomas had long before described the estate in England. 'You shall deliver my letter personally.' They had begun exchanging letters with the ships regularly once every two years, and Amos had brought two with him this time; one of them for Martha, the second one she would receive from her son in England. James had extended his land holdings yet again and reported good harvests and profits. He mentioned a girl, Eleanor, twice in the letter to Thomas, and it was obvious reading through the lines that a wedding could well be in the offing. It seemed that on both sides of the world things were in fine order.

Amos was agreeable to Joshua's suggestion and it was arranged.

'I want no favours.' Joshua assured the ship's master, but Thomas noticed the look in Amos' face and knew the lad would get them.

Amos showed Thomas the company's books, audited by Dalbey's employees.

'The fleet now numbers twelve, Thomas, and two more ships are being built at this moment. We trade with America, Australia, Africa and Europe; everything imaginable except slaves, and with some items the rewards are five and six-fold. There is no war at present, though of course there are always rumblings in Europe. Your far-sightedness has made me very wealthy.'

'Wealthy enough to gamble, Amos?'

The master grinned widely, 'That was a lesson never to be repeated, Thomas, thanks to Roger.'

'He has a racetrack now and many Arabians.'

'So I hear. Another very rich man.'

Thomas smiled wryly, 'Would one have thought it possible, all that time ago?'

Amos shook his head vehemently, 'No, Thomas, never in a million years.'

As the longboat pulled for the shore Thomas resisted looking back at his son, the pain of parting still with him, but he nodded to himself; it was a good decision on Joshua's part. He was intelligent and would make a fine ship's master in the fullness of time.

Passing through Parramatta Thomas sighed, wishing it were market day, when he might meet the boys again as he had on a half dozen occasions, having made excuses to go to the market when he needed nothing. He still thought of Martha every day, and she of him.

On an evening in October of that year, 1807, he was sitting outside on the veranda with Coulson, eating roast mutton chops, when he noticed a cloud of dust in the far distance, gradually being able to make out a closed gig drawn by two black horses, following the course of the river towards the bridge his men had built over it.

He fetched his spyglass and focussed on it. The carriage was bouncing heavily on the rutted path, but for a brief second he imagined he could recognise Austin at the reins. The other figure beside him could be Thomas.

He threw his plate down and jumped up without a word, startling Coulson, and rushed to grab a horse and jump on it bareback.

The astonished tee-man watched his pell-mell descent of the slope to meet the gig as it came over the bridge.

The gig was pulled to a halt, and Thomas, worried sick that Martha was ill, demanded to know what was wrong.

Austin waved his hand, 'Mother.'

The gig door was opening, and Martha stood on the step, looking at his face.

Martha, his beloved Martha, looking as lovely as she had on the day he married her, the only changes a few lines around the eyes and hair that had more than a hint of grey, as had his own.

Time stood still, and the little scene, watched by Coulson from the veranda, seemed for almost a minute to be a fixed set in a stage play, without motion from any player. Then suddenly it was hurried activity as Thomas leapt from his horse, Martha jumped from the step, and the two lads climbed down from the box.

Thomas took Martha in his arms and buried his face in her hair, while their sons came close to them and watched, enchanted.

At last Thomas drew back and held her at arms length, suddenly worried.

'You have left Arthur?'

'He is dead, Thomas, two days since. His heart.'

Thomas could not get over his puzzlement, 'But how did you know? Did he tell you?'

'No, he did not. You kept the secret well, both of you, but the first time you met the boys I knew: a friend of my husband, a man named Thomas and with a badly burnt face? I knew at once. How I stayed away from you is something I shall never understand, knowing you were close, but both you and I owed Arthur so very much. I could not hurt him.'

'But now you have come home?'

She nodded vehemently, 'That I have, Thomas.' She looked up at the house, 'and what a magnificent home.'

'What of your sheep station, and the girls?'

'I have two stockmen looking after the place, and the girls…'

Two other female figures jumped down to join them, two pretty girls, one almost an adult, with already a woman's figure, and the other a young teenager, just as tall as her sister but still with a boyish figure and no obvious breasts.

'Imelda and Eleanor, I'll be bound.' Thomas greeted them. 'Welcome to Danfield Station.' He gave each of them a hug and a kiss on the forehead.

He was trying to think of a way to tell Martha that some of the brown bodies seen around the station were also his children, thinking himself cowardly as he was unable to do so, but he need not have worried.

One morning, a week after her arrival, looking out through the kitchen window as she served breakfast, Martha remarked casually, 'You know, if Mongi and Gurrah were white, they could be your son and daughter, Thomas. Just look at the way they hold themselves, not like aborigines at all.'

She heard a splutter behind her as Thomas tried unsuccessfully to swallow the liquid in his mouth and turned, smiling widely.

'When were you going to tell me?' She asked.

He gulped and she told him, 'Though you may not believe it, your expression is a sight to behold, husband mine.'

When he managed to get his breath he said, 'How long have you known?'

'Since the moment I first set eyes on them.'

He sighed and began the long story of his exile.

She listened carefully without a word until he had finished, then said, 'I shall love them as my own. They are quite beautiful.'

She and her girls quickly became fast favourites with the men, starved for female company as they were, and Thomas noticed Coulson's proprietary interest in Eleanor and her coquettish behaviour around him. It also made him realise that his men needed more female company and he went into Parramatta with Martha to hire female staff. They brought seven young women back with them as maids, although none were strictly necessary, and life at Danfield Station took on a new lease of life.

Eleanor and Coulson married when she reached sixteen, and a house was built for them on the spot they picked, down near the river. Other marriages took place, and soon the station was dotted with new buildings. The tribe wandered over now and again, well integrated with the men and women working there.

Three Christmases later, after another visit to Amos, Thomas brought Joshua home to stay for a week while the ship's master re-victualled the five ships he had brought with him, full of new immigrants. Joshua proudly told Thomas that he had become Second Mate on Amos' ship.

He was introduced to Martha and to his white brothers and sisters, who marvelled at his physique and resemblance to Thomas. He brought two letters from James, and Martha cried tears of joy as she read them, sitting down immediately to write replies.

Though storms and other problems came and went, life went on almost idyllically, with marriages, the birth of grandchildren, and the replacement of the original wooden dwelling with another built of brick, with huge colonial style stone pillars. Thomas had bought and studied books on mining methods and had purchased equipment for pulverising rock. He built a sluice by diverting part of the river and had six of the men begin working the mine. He had been right in assuming that the rocks at the head of the gully were gold bearing, and though it was not a massive strike, as some of the others in Australia would turn out to be, it made him one of the three richest men on the continent, where he had once held the number one spot.

Though she was unaware of it, Thomas was planning a huge celebration for Martha's sixtieth birthday on the twenty-eighth of December 1821.

Joshua had left the ship to stay with them for the holiday and would return in time to sail.

Thomas had been to town on many occasions in the months leading up to her birthday, arranging all kinds of special surprises, and on the morning of that day he slipped out of bed quietly, went out into the garden and cut just one superb yellow rose, which he placed in his mouth, then visited the kitchen and fetched the bottle of vintage champagne and two glasses and returned to the bedroom.

He placed the bottle and glasses on the bedside table, sat on the bed and tickled her ear playfully.

She came awake instantly and looked up at him, shaking her head in amusement at the sight of the rose held across his mouth.

He removed it and handed it to her. 'A rose for a rose. Happy birthday, my darling.'

She looked at him lovingly, 'You are an old fool, Thomas Nash, and I love you dearly.'

'Those feelings are mine exactly for you.'

At nine o'clock, four wagons arrived from Parramatta, one with a six-piece orchestra, the other three with jugglers, fire-eaters, conjurers and performing animals. Behind them, another wagon carried Roger, now an opulent figure, with his young wife, Amelia, and two children.

The aborigines had come from the caves and were spread out over the lawns in front of the house, where tables groaned under the weight of every kind of delicacy.

The orchestra played, the conjurers conjured, the fire-eaters ate fire until it seemed they would explode, the jugglers juggled, and the performing animals performed. The day went with a swing, and as the sun began its daily dip towards the distant horizon, Thomas nodded to a man who had come with the last wagon and had set up a strange-looking stand lower down the field.

Suddenly, the darkening sky became lit with the most wonderful coloured stars, flashing lights like miniature flashes of lightning, and all manner of wonderful illuminations, with additional minor explosions, which made the children gasp. Cries of wonder arose everywhere.

Thomas had learned that such things could be obtained from China, and Amos had sent a ship there specially to obtain them for this day.

As the last spark died out and the applause rippled to its conclusion, Martha, standing beside him on the veranda took his arm and whispered, 'That was the most magnificent day of my life, my darling. Thank you.'

Thomas looked at her enquiringly, 'Is there any one thing that could make it more complete for you, Martha?'

She smiled, 'It was perfect. The only thing that could is impossible even for my wizard of a husband.'

'And that is?'

'For a sight of my firstborn.'

'But he is in England.'

She sighed heavily, 'Yes, indeed.'

He turned and held his hand over his eyes, looking down the hill into the descending dusk. 'Perhaps if your wizard should wave his magic wand?' He waved both arms as if signalling with semaphore.

She followed his gaze.

Approaching fast was a lone horseman, spurring his mount urgently up the hill towards the house…

~~~The End~~~

Printed in Great Britain
by Amazon